THE LEGACY

BOOK 1: THE PREPARATIONS

BOOK 2: THE TRIALS

BOOK 3: THE RETURN

BOOK 4: THE BROKEN

OTHER BOOKS BY
DANIELLE N. MCDONOUGH

The Cursed Half Moon – Book 1

The Cursed Half Moon – Book 2

WWW.THELEGACYBOOKSERIES.COM

THE
BROKEN

DANIELLE N. MCDONOUGH

ILLUSTRATED BY
ANNA CASTRO

EDITED BY
REBECCA MARTINEZ & TERRY MCDONOUGH

The Broken
by Danielle N. McDonough

Printed in the United States of America
ISBN (Paperback): 978-1-950296-06-4
ISBN (Hardcover): 978-1-950296-11-8
ISBN (eBook): 978-1-950296-07-1

Illustrated by Anna Castro
Edited by Rebecca Martinez & Terry McDonough

The Legacy series books are available online at
www.thelegacybookseries.com.

Dedicated to my Mom and Dad
for all their wisdom and guidance.

To my brother, Steven, for his
unending support.

And to my sister, Becky, who has
walked this path with me.

THE LAND
OF THE CLAN

THE VILLAGES

THE PARAMOUNT

THE MAKING

THE BARRACKS

THE GOLDEN FIELDS

RIVERSIDE

THE FARM

THE QUARRY

TREESCAPE

THE NORTH WIND

CHAPTER 1
DRIFTING

"How deep was my soul? How far down could I push the recollection of what I had done? As far as you need to in order to survive, a voice whispered in my head. You're a survivor; you'll make it through this. It doesn't matter what you have to do; you can and will endure."

When I heard him calling my name, it seemed to be very far away, through deep water.

No, I thought wearily. *Leave me alone. I'm finally at peace.*

But he wouldn't leave me alone. He kept repeating my name over and over again.

It was Cole. It had to be Cole. He'd found me.

The knowledge did not move me.

Cole didn't have the strength to tether me to this place. I drifted further away, teetering on the edge of this world and whatever came next.

"Astra! Astra!" His voice was louder, closer, but still a million miles away. A hand fell on my shoulder, feeling like fire compared to the frigidness of my body.

As soon as he touched me, I knew it wasn't Cole.

It was Todd.

My mind reacted slowly to this new thought.

I tried to look forward to the other side but sensed nothing except darkness. This was a choice I would have to make blind.

"Astra, wake up," Todd ordered.

His voice touched me. He was gripping my hand, and I could feel heat seeping back into my arm. I pushed out toward him, trying to find my way back. Everything was dark. Everything was

1

cold. However, the fiery grasp on my hand gave me a point of contact with the world of light and life.

Finally, I surfaced. My eyes blinked open. I was lying on my side, right cheek resting on the ground. Todd was crouching over me, his face was streaked with sweat and dirt.

"Todd?" The word came from my lips softer than a whisper.

"I'm here," he said quietly, his dark brown eyes intent on my face. "Why were you following me?"

"To stop you," I gasped.

"Why?" he demanded.

"You- you know too much," I managed to say. "Too much about The Clan."

Todd furrowed his brow. "So you came to kill me?" he asked.

"We had to," I whimpered. "But I- I couldn't."

My gaze shifted past him, but I was unable to focus on anything farther away than the nearest trees. The forest seemed dark, or it might have simply been my own eyes that were weak and dim.

Even with blurry sight, I could tell that we were alone. In a rush, regret broke over me. Cole should have been here too, and Rollan and Kisa and Joss and...

If only things had worked out differently. But it was too late now. Todd was here alone, which meant Cole must be dead, just like the rest of my team.

Tears filled my eyes, overflowing in salty drops of liquid. The last time I had cried this hard in front of Todd was the day Joss died. Wasn't it right that I mourn the same way for Cole?

My whole team was gone. I was alone—the last surviving member of the winning team of the eleventh trials.

Todd's face was obscured as the tears blinded me. He slowly placed a hand on my forehead. I shuddered, knowing that the same hand touching me now had ended the lives of my friends.

He said something, but I couldn't understand him. His words were meaningless anyway.

It didn't take long for darkness to close over me again. However, this was not the darkness of death; it was merely the senselessness of sleep.

When I awoke again, I was lying on my back in an unfamiliar grove of young birch trees. I sensed more than saw Todd sitting to my right. My head hurt, but the dull ache was nothing compared to the burning in my leg.

Shakily, I tried to sit up. Todd pressed one hand against my shoulder, easily pinning me to the ground. Even without his interference, I wasn't sure I could have managed. Part of my mind feared that while I was so helpless, Todd might kill me. However, if he had wanted to, he could have already done so.

The small exertion of trying to rise had taken all my energy. I could feel my arms and legs trembling as a cold sweat broke out on my forehead.

"You're in no condition to move," Todd told me. He vanished from my sight only to reappear a moment later with a water canteen.

"Careful," he instructed, slowly slipping an arm under my shoulders and raising my head a few inches. The canteen he pressed to my lips was my own and still about half full. Slowly, water flowed into my parched mouth. It tasted sweet, and I felt some life return to my body. After several swallows, Todd put the canteen down and lowered me back to the ground.

There wasn't any reason for Todd to be doing this, unless…

I took a minute to sort through the tangled mess of thoughts plaguing my mind. There was only one explanation: I was needed as bait. I should have chosen death when I had the chance.

"Cole?" I whispered. Much as I dreaded the answer, I needed to know.

Todd didn't speak for a minute. Instead, he studied my face intently.

"I didn't find Cole," he admitted finally. My eyes scrutinized him. He was an adept liar, and I knew better than to trust his words. Most of his actions had turned out to be nothing

3

but an elaborate farce. He'd played along with us, pretending to be our friend so he could learn about The Clan and gain glory and honor among his people when he betrayed us to them.

As I looked into his dark eyes, I did not know what to think. I'd trusted him once, but never again.

Even if Cole was alive, Todd had already murdered the other two remaining members of our team. That was why Cole and I had left The Land of the Clan and tracked him here. However, when the moment came, I could not make myself take his life. This was what he had done to me in return.

I licked my lips. Speaking was painful, but I wanted to know what he was planning next.

"Todd," my voice was barely audible. "Are you going to look for Cole again?"

Todd nodded.

"Just let him go," I pleaded.

Todd glanced at me sharply. "I'm going to find him," he told me.

All I could manage was a single whispered word, "Please."

He shook his head. "I must find him. My people are coming. It's time for me to pass the rite of manhood."

"Then kill me now!" I gasped as loudly as I could. "What are you waiting for?"

I was quickly growing exhausted from so much talking. These last two sentences were the end of my strength.

"No," Todd shook his head quickly. "I have a better way."

I wanted so badly to stand up and beg him to leave Cole alone. I opened my lips, but not one word would come out. The air in my lungs seemed too heavy to exhale, and my heart felt weak and fluttery. Blackness rose behind my eyes. Unsuccessfully, I tried to fight it and remain alert, but in less than a minute, the sky grew dark, as though night had fallen.

It felt like many years had passed when I came to my senses once more. This time I was alone. Slowly, I sat up, fighting off the sudden dizziness brought on by the movement.

My leg was throbbing. I lifted the piece of fabric binding Todd must have put there and was finally able to get a good look at the cut. It was a little above my right knee and about three inches long. Todd had also cleaned it and applied some of the herbs from my pack. There was still pain, but it was bearable, at least for now.

I glanced around the grove and realized with a small stab of panic that I had absolutely no idea where I was.

In vain, I tried to figure out if it was still the same day or if I'd been unconscious all night. The sky was blanketed in gray clouds, completely obscuring the sun.

My canteen and backpack were close beside me. The vessel had been refilled, and I was barely able to lift it. My arms felt wobbly after the minuscule task of giving myself a drink.

Inside the pack, I still had a bit of food. Even though I wasn't hungry in the least, I forced myself to eat some deer meat. There were also a few crusts of bread. These had been completely flattened during the fight with Todd, but I choked them down as well.

Before I was done chewing, exhaustion set in. I fought my heavy eyelids, not ready to sleep again. I needed to plan, but my mind was fuzzy and unfocused, taking minutes to comprehend what I could usually process in seconds.

I wondered if I should start yelling. Cole might be close enough to hear me. However, that could bring Todd too, and I dreaded what would happen if the pair ever faced each other.

I considered leaving, but if lifting a water canteen had wearied me, I'd never be able to walk, much less carry my pack or my…

I glanced around quickly. My bow was missing. Vaguely, I remembered throwing it down during the fight with Todd.

My hand went to my hip. The knife, which I hadn't pulled, was gone too. Todd must have taken the weapons with him.

Maybe he's using them to hunt, I thought.

To hunt who? The darker part of my mind asked as I realized I'd supplied Todd with a fresh way of killing Cole.

5

I couldn't remain upright anymore and settled back down. I listened but heard no footsteps. I watched, but there was no movement save that caused by the wind. The glade was utterly silent.

No one's coming for you, a voice whispered. *You will die here alone.*

That's stupid, I told myself, pushing down the terrifying idea. *Todd wouldn't have left the supplies if he wasn't coming back.*

Then maybe...

Maybe what?

He's using you to draw Cole into a trap.

I had no answer for that thought. Todd could be watching right now, waiting for me to call out. Concealed from sight, he would be ready when Cole made an appearance.

The thought horrified me. I couldn't imagine anything worse than watching my last friend die. *It will be just like the day you met Todd,* the voice whispered. *Only this time, you won't be able to save Cole.*

No, I thought desperately. *I won't let that happen. I'll stay quiet; that way, Cole won't come. I'll keep him safe. No matter what Todd does to me, I won't make a sound.*

The other voice was silent for a moment. *Then I guess your teeth are his other option,* it hissed. *He needs to prove he's killed someone to complete his rite.*

I tightened my jaw and stopped responding. Instead, I watched the forest. Much as I wanted to remain vigilant, it didn't take long for my head to start spinning.

The focus I had held onto for the last ten minutes slipped away, and I found my thoughts wandering somewhere between the sleeping and waking worlds.

It would be best if Cole gave up and decided to leave me behind. I was sure Core and Myna would be beyond furious, but maybe they would let Cole off easy since I had been the one to bring Todd to The Land of the Clan.

Myna would probably figure I'd gotten exactly what I deserved. At first, I'd thought I was only imagining her malice. However, she seemed to have associated me with the tragedies of her past and the death of her daughter. I was guilty on one count.

I'd never known my own mother, but I couldn't imagine she would have been anything like Myna.

I understood now why, even though she was lonely, Myra never opened up to anyone, why she despised showing any weakness and felt that she had to do everything on her own. I had many of the same tendencies, but I had always thought growing up without parents or siblings produced those qualities. As it turned out, Myra was nearly as much of an orphan as I was.

What I still could not comprehend was why she had felt the need to win Myna's approval. I'd seen her continually strive to be the best at everything she did. Sadly, her efforts always seemed to go unnoticed.

Life could be so unjust.

The trials had destroyed them both in completely different ways.

It's destroyed you too.

I blinked. Would I be the next Myna? Could I grow that cold? Had I already?

No, I thought, *not yet. If I'd killed Todd, then maybe, but I didn't- couldn't. That means something, doesn't it?*

I had no answers. In the past year and a half, I seemed to have lost myself. I used to be so sure that I understood exactly how the world worked. Not anymore. I didn't know anything anymore. The world was a hundred times bigger than I had ever imagined. It contained far too many secrets for any one person to ever discover.

A branch snapped close by. My eyes opened to find that there was still light in the sky. I wasn't certain how much of the day was left. Everything was as gray as before, but there was some gold mixed into the muted light, signaling that sunset wasn't far off.

The sound of footsteps to my right made me sit up quickly. I was met with a wave of blackness. When it passed, I was no longer alone in the clearing.

A young man stood there. He was probably in his early twenties, thickly built, with tan skin and huge arms. The brown hair growing from his head was coarse and oily. His face was round and had an unpleasant, sneering look to it.

He wore no shirt, and the material of his pants was strange to me. Threads of many different shades had been woven together seemingly at random to form the cloth. For all that, the color wasn't particularly bright.

Moments later, another man joined the first. The second man was at least three decades older. His black hair was streaked with gray and hung in tangles halfway down his muscular chest. The face was thin and long, like the rest of the older man's body. He stood at least three inches taller than his companion, and his very pronounced jaw was topped with a narrow nose and dark eyes.

Scars, too numerous to count, were visible on his skin. The most prominent one ran from the eyebrow to the corner of the mouth on the left side of his face. The mark was faded, leaving the skin a shade paler than the rest of his flesh.

His clothes were made of the same fabric as his younger companion's. He didn't wear a shirt either, and both men had necklaces strung with four small, white stones.

As their eyes fell on me, I felt my heart accelerate. My hand groped around, instinctively looking for a weapon, but found nothing save a rock. I clenched it tightly, ready to put what little strength I had left into defending myself from these men.

CHAPTER 2
BLEEDING

I fought a private battle with fear and won, but not by much. I held my head high, though I hadn't risen from the ground. All three of us remained frozen for a long moment.

Movement behind the two men caught my attention. My eyes flittered to the forest where Todd emerged from among the trees behind the men. A feeling of relief spread through me. I knew it was foolish, but in this unknown place, faced with two strangers, there was something comforting about his familiar presence.

The older man glanced back at Todd, then advanced several steps toward me. Todd silently shadowed his every move, watching intently. The older man appeared not to care. Instead, his eyes traveled up and down my body, examining me from head to toe.

Finally, his gaze came to rest on my wounded leg. His feet brought him to a halt about two yards from where I sat in the grass. Slowly, he turned and addressed Todd, who stood motionless behind him.

"For once, you have done well, my son," the older man said in a low, solemn voice.

Todd dipped his head respectfully at the praise. "Thank you, Father."

"When Shovato, the leader of the hunting party you ran into, reported that you wanted us to meet you here, I wasn't sure it could really be you," the older man continued. "After such a long absence, I thought you had failed."

"Shovato said it was important that I come to you immediately. Tell me, what was so urgent that you couldn't have simply returned and completed your rite in the normal fashion?"

My heart skipped a beat as a cold sweat broke out on my forehead. He was going to tell them about The Clan.

"I wish to present my sacrifice and pass the rite of manhood publicly," Todd explained.

The man, who he had addressed as "father", narrowed his eyes. "Is that so? Do you think yourself worthy of such attention?"

"Yes. I have much to tell regarding my exploits and hoped that you would help me make the necessary arrangements," Todd said, confirming my worst fears.

A sudden laugh echoed through the trees. I'd forgotten about the other man, but he chose this moment to join the conversation. "Always needing help with everything, little brother," he sneered.

Both men had the same strange accent as Todd. However, Todd's was slighter, and I'd grown so accustomed to hearing it that I hadn't noticed its existence for a long time.

"Need help?" Todd chuckled. "No. I am simply seeking our father's advice on how best to bring honor to *our* house."

Todd's father snorted. "It's not complicated, and she will do excellently. I'll alert the proper persons tonight. On the morrow, you shall complete the rite of manhood."

Todd nodded, a slight smile on his face. My blood ran cold at the older man's sinister words.

"We should head back," the younger man said. "I, for one, would like to reach home before nightfall."

"Afraid of the dark, brother?" Todd asked, with a malicious look at the speaker.

"No, but I don't fancy falling from my horse because it steps in a hole," his brother shot back.

"Todicmadaya, Arkensallay, enough," Todd's father commanded. It took me a moment to realize that he was saying their names. I had been calling him Todd for so long I'd nearly forgotten it wasn't his real name.

"Yes, Father," Arkensallay, Todd's brother, answered.

"Let's go," Todd's father ordered.

"I'm not sure she can walk," Todd admitted.

10

"You'll have to find a way to get her to the city, or you can kill her right here and forget the triumphant return you have planned," the older man announced.

Todd's father turned to look at me once more. This time, he met and held my gaze, waiting to see how I would react.

Slowly, I rose to my feet. It was agony, and darkness swirled at the corners of my vision. I wasn't sure I'd be able to walk anywhere, but for now, I was standing.

"I don't know how he managed to capture that one," Todd's brother muttered to their father.

"I was so certain he wouldn't survive," Todd's father mused. "However, he seems different now."

Todd gave no sign that he had heard their words, though it was impossible for him to have missed them. Instead, he approached me slowly, as I would approach a frightened horse. I remained stock-still until the other men had started walking away; only then did I turn to face him.

"Cole?" I whispered.

Todd shook his head.

"Are you going to tell them about The Clan?" I pressed.

"No," Todd answered. "I have a better way."

By killing you, a voice hissed.

If that's the price I have to pay, then so be it, I vowed internally.

It was surprising just how calm I was. I supposed a large part of me was beyond caring.

"I wish it didn't have to be this way," Todd told me. "But I don't have any other choices. I tried to find Cole, but he's gone."

I'd thought I was too exhausted and drained to feel such things, but a small bubble of joy welled up inside of me at his words. Cole was beyond Todd's reach now. I was going to take his place, and he could go home.

Have you forgotten? someone whispered. *Going home is the harder road.*

"Any day now," Arkensallay called.

11

Todd quickly seized my pack and slung it over his shoulders.

"Can you walk?" he demanded.

I shrugged. Did it really matter if he killed me now instead of tomorrow? What was the difference?

"Here." Todd placed my right arm over his shoulder so he could help support me. I was repulsed by his touch and didn't feel particularly inclined to accept his assistance.

The first step was impossible. I bit down on the inside of my cheek until my mouth filled with blood. The second step was easier as adrenaline began rushing through my body. The pain diminished slightly, and my muscles loosened up. Before we had gotten across the glade, my leg was bleeding again. Todd halted and used a shirt from the pack to stanch the flow of blood. He wound it tightly around my leg and tied the arms together to hold it in place.

Todd's father had vanished from the clearing, but the path he had taken was easy to see. It was the same way they had come. The trail was narrow and filled with brambles.

Todd's brother was waiting at the edge of the clearing. As we approached, he fell into step behind us.

"I've never seen eyes that color," Arkensallay said. "Her hair is unusual as well."

Todd was too busy keeping both of us from tripping in the dense undergrowth to respond.

"She's so strange looking that I can't really tell if she's beautiful or not." The words sounded as if he were speaking of a plant or an animal.

"How come you didn't freeze to death during the winter?" Arkensallay went on, completely changing the subject. "What have you been doing all this time?"

Todd didn't bother to provide answers to any of his brother's questions.

It interested me that while Todd seemed to have a deep reverence for his father, he had no such respect for his brother. Arkensallay was the larger of the siblings. Especially when they had been children, his age and size would have given him a serious advantage. However, if anything, Todd treated his brother as a mild annoyance. There must be something that gave Todd an edge, which, in childhood, had made the two equals. Unlike Rollan and any of his older brothers, Todd had found a way to level the playing field.

After walking for about five minutes in the forest, the pain in my leg began to increase. Every step was harder than the last. I nearly fell several times and would have if Todd hadn't put a hand around my waist to hold me up.

I vaguely wondered if Todd would really gain so much more honor by completing his rite publicly that it was worth keeping me alive another day.

At one point, I nearly brought both of us down. Our eyes met as I pulled on his shoulder to regain my feet. He didn't think I could make it, but I refused to lie down and die.

I knew of someone who would have continued to press on regardless of the pain. I thought of her and tried to forget all else. My leg hurt more than anything I had ever experienced, but I would not give up because she never had.

I don't believe we traveled more than a quarter of a mile, but it felt longer than our entire journey to and from the mountain during the trials. A thin trickle of blood was steadily running down my leg, soaking my boot.

Thinking took forever because my head felt clouded. Each thought needed at least a minute to come to fruition. My body seemed to be shaking. The woods all around us grew dim and blurry.

Finally, we came to a halt. It took me a full minute to realize why. We'd reached the edge of the forest. The land sloped down before us into a vast, grassy plain.

Behind us, in the west, the sun was setting, still masked by clouds, but with a few escaping streaks of red and gold light.

Ahead, I could make out a small ridge of hills. I knew that beyond them lay the ocean.

Tired, hopeless, and bled out as I was, a sudden desire to see the rolling waves one last time seized me. From everything I'd learned about Todd's people, my wish might be granted before death found me.

The sound of something heavy hitting the ground caused me to turn. Three horses were standing tethered to trees at the edge of the woods. My mind had been too weary to perceive them earlier.

Todd's father untied the tallest of the three. None of them were particularly large, and their coloring was strange to me. Instead of the normal coat colors I was accustomed to, their fur was a silvery gray, speckled with tiny black flecks.

Todd guided me to the second horse. While he adjusted the saddle, I raised my hand to its neck. The fur was soft and silky, like a rabbit's. The horse, I was pretty sure it was a mare, turned to look at me. Her head had a more angular shape than I'd seen in any horse before, and the eyes were darker than the night sky.

After finishing with the saddle, Todd moved back to me. I did not fight him as he took both my hands in one of his and bound them together at the wrists with rope he'd taken from my pack. He watched what he was doing without looking up.

Todd had to help me onto the animal's back. Had I not been accustomed to mounting, I'm sure I would have fallen to the ground, but I managed to thrust my wounded leg over the saddle far enough to maintain my balance. Spasms of pain coursed through my entire body. I could focus on nothing except drawing my next breath until the agony became more bearable. My eyes watered, but no tears fell.

Getting up behind me, a little clumsily, Todd gathered the reins. He guided the mare after his father's horse, content to follow as the animals headed into the expanse of open space.

I hoped my wound would stop bleeding now that I wasn't moving as much. Pulsating pain split my head with each beat of my unsteady heart. Riding was easier than walking, simply because I didn't have to do anything save endure it.

14

A few tears wetted my cheeks, but they were safely concealed from sight by the dusk. I tried to brace myself against the anguish, but my will was quickly crumbling now that I had nothing to focus on except the pain.

Todd shifted behind me. Taking the reins in one hand, he wrapped the other arm securely around my waist. Without noticing, I had started leaning heavily to the left.

He pulled me upright in the saddle and back against him.

"If you try anything, I'll take you to the ground with me," he warned.

His fears were unfounded. I was struggling just to stay awake. It didn't take long for me to give in to the darkness surrounding the edges of my vision. Unconsciousness was a relief from reality, but not from the fire in my right leg. No matter how far I was from my body, the pain was a constant tether between us.

I never remembered much of that night. The few times I regained any sort of consciousness, the horse beneath me was trotting or cantering along in a smooth rhythm. The sun had left the sky, and my mind was far too muddled to distinguish anything in the moonlight.

When Todd's horse finally came to a halt, I revived just enough to hear the sound of the waves on the beach. It was muffled, emanating from at least a quarter-mile away, but it comforted me all the same. It was something familiar, reminding me of good times and better days. The pause was brief, and then we were riding again, leaving the waves behind.

When Todd dismounted, I barely had the strength to remain in the saddle and nearly toppled from my seat. Instead, I slumped forward over the mare's neck. She smelt of sunlight and straw and wide-open fields of green grass, all the things that made me think of my childhood in the stables.

The next thing I knew, I was being half-carried, half-dragged into a lighted room. I don't know whose hands pulled me along, but I could tell they weren't Todd's.

There was the sound of soft voices. I didn't even try to make out the words. I just waited to be released so that I might crumple to the floor and rest.

I was laid on my back and saw the unfamiliar face of an older woman leaning over me. After a moment, she moved to my leg and started unwrapping the saturated bandage tied over the gaping wound. I tried to keep from crying out as the bloody cloth was pulled away from my skin.

I heard a gasp, not from the woman, but from someone else in the room. The older woman studied the wound gravely, then seemed to be conferring with another, softer voice. A moment later, she poured some kind of liquid on my leg, which burned like fire.

This time, I didn't have to struggle to keep from screaming. My entire body went rigid as the horrible, fiery sensation paralyzed me. I'd treated enough injured horses to know that sometimes healing salves stung. I hoped that whatever the older woman was doing would make my cut better and not worse.

It took an excruciating amount of time for the fire to die from my leg. I wished unconsciousness would claim me again, but that was too much to hope for.

Finally, little by little, the pain began to abate. My muscles relaxed, leaving me limp and quivering but still unable to move. My half-opened eyes could make out very little in the dim firelight that flickered across the ceiling above.

A second woman, younger than the first and very beautiful, knelt beside me. She put a wooden bowl to my lips. The contents tasted like milk. I nearly choked as a small amount of the liquid hit the back of my throat. At last, fatigue overwhelmed me, and I fell into a deep sleep, which neither pain nor dreams disturbed.

CHAPTER 3
SACRIFICE

When I opened my eyes, my head was clearer than it had been in a long time. Morning light slanted into the room through the open door.

I took in everything quickly. The walls were made of light-colored plaster. Stone was visible beneath it in a few places where it had started to crumble. Woven grass mats covered the hard-packed dirt floor.

I was resting on a makeshift bed along a wall opposite an open fireplace. Just to my left was a hallway, which appeared to proceed further into the dwelling. Beyond that was a wall with large, airy windows set on either side of a doorway leading outside. There was a fire burning on the hearth across from me, a stack of wood close beside it. Dried spices and other types of food hung from the ceiling on strings.

The two women I remembered from the night before were there, both working busily. The younger of the pair had her back turned, so all I could see was her dark hair, which flowed in glossy waves halfway down her back. She was kneading bread on a tall table in the center of the room.

The older woman was seated on a low stool, turning the handle of some sort of device made of stone. Every so often, she would add a handful of grain kernels to the hole in the top.

After watching her for a moment, she looked up, and our eyes met. Her face was lined with wrinkles, and her brown hair, which was long and frizzy, had a strong tinge of white.

Neither of us spoke. We simply watched each other.

Before five seconds had passed, a man, Todd's father, came through the door. Upon his arrival, the older woman instantly dropped her gaze back to her work.

"It's time," he announced, striding across the room toward me. He seized my left arm just above the elbow and, without any warning, drug me suddenly from the makeshift bed.

I staggered, unable to find my feet, and ended up on the floor. I gasped as the impact jarred my injured leg.

"No, Lord Arshenn! You'll reopen the wound," the older woman protested, rising to her feet.

My arm was released as Todd's father turned on her. To my great horror, he struck the woman full across the face. She dropped back to the floor and covered her head with her hands. A swift kick instantly followed the initial blow.

The younger woman cautiously approached the man, Arshenn. She gently placed a hand on his shoulder.

"Please, my master," she said in a sweet, coaxing tone. "Yetta didn't mean it. She simply didn't want the girl's leg to start bleeding again and hinder you."

Todd's father swung his head toward the second woman, who flinched from him. I worried that he would hit her too. Instead, he relented and turned back to me. I rose carefully, putting as little weight on my leg as possible. Whatever care these women had given me during the night, my wound seemed far better.

A moment later, Arshenn had latched onto my arm again and was shoving me out the door. The last thing I saw was the younger woman kneeling beside the older woman. I hoped she was all right.

Outside, the sunlight was blinding. Before my sight could adjust, a blindfold was placed over my eyes and knotted behind my head.

There must have been someone with Todd's father, because before the blindfold was completely secure, another set of hands was working to bind my wrists.

I didn't fight them. There was no point.

I knew what was going to happen. What had to happen. After it was over, The Clan would be safe, which was all that mattered to me.

Even without being able to see, I could tell Todd was not present. I was confident that I would feel it if he were close by, just as I had known it was him when I nearly bled out in the woods. All I sensed now was the presence of strangers.

Once my eyes and wrists were secure, a hand gripped my arm with dreaded familiarity. Walking on my injured leg had been hard enough; now I was forced to do it without the aid of sight.

I stumbled a few times and stubbed my bare feet more than once. Someone had removed my boots last night, along with the maroon cloak I had been wearing. I didn't mind too much since the morning was warm. I could feel the sun through my light jacket, which had not been taken from me.

Todd's father set a hard pace, and I was forced to almost run to keep up. At first, the ground was grassy and wet with dew, but it soon changed to a dirt path, then to a hard, flat surface, which could only be stone.

It didn't take long for my limbs to grow weary and my head to start aching again. I was glad I hadn't been given any breakfast. My stomach felt uneasy and was churning as each beat of my heart sent a fresh wave of pain through my body.

The second man was walking behind us, his footsteps echoing dully on the ground. There were no sounds of other people until we reached the stone part of the road. It was then that I heard the great murmuring of many voices.

The noise grew louder until it was coming from all around us. Todd's father did not falter as we moved among the voices. I was fearful of running into someone, but when we came to a stop, somewhere near the middle I judged, I hadn't come into contact with anyone.

The grip on my arm didn't relax for even a moment, but the reprieve from walking was welcome. Gradually, a silence fell over the assembly.

About five minutes elapsed, then a cheer rose from what must have been a vast crowd. It started on the outer edge of the group and was gradually taken up by others until it grew into a deafening roar. If my hands hadn't been bound, I would have covered my ears. The noise made the throbbing in my head a thousand times worse.

Without warning, the cheering cut off abruptly, and silence reigned as completely as chaos had the moment before.

"Welcome!" called an unfamiliar, masculine voice. The speaker sounded young, maybe a few years older than I was. I also had the distinct impression that he was standing somewhere above me.

"Today, we will witness a boy becoming a man," the same voice went on. "Though, as you can see, it appears that much of the transformation has already taken place. Only one thing now remains to be done.

"I, Tohoshin, Lord of the Brimming Lake and all those who dwell here, do not usually attend ceremonies such as these. However, when I heard that it was Todicmadaya, son of Lord Arshenn, one whom we had all but given up for dead, who was returning to pass the rite of manhood, I could not stay away.

"Never have I heard of anyone returning after the half-year mark, but Todicmadaya remained in The Western Woods more than nine moons!"

There were deafening cheers, forcing the speaker to pause momentarily.

"This feat has already accorded him great honor, though he is but a child. However, his sojourn has not ended since he is yet to return to his home. Last night, he remained in The Temple of the King, thanking the gods for their deliverance and provision.

"His family is among the most prominent members of The House of the King, and today, through the shedding of blood, he will join them as a noble brother."

More cheers.

"I, like you, am eager to hear the tale of his exploits, but first…" The Lord of the Brimming Lake, Tohoshin, trailed off suggestively. Those close at hand began to applaud.

"Bring forth the sacrifice!" Tohoshin called over the cheering voices.

With a jolt, I was yanked toward the speaker. I struggled to remain balanced as my foot connected with something hard, stone probably. I paused, but was instantly pulled forward again by the hand encircling my arm.

I stepped onto the stone, still unable to see where I was putting my feet. Carefully, I raised my foot and explored the area with my toes. The first stone led to more; it seemed there was an entire staircase before me.

After about twenty-five steps, we came to a halt. I was gasping for breath by the time we'd reached the top. To my great relief, Arshenn released his hold on me. The feeling in my fingertips had started to vanish from the vise-like grip constricting my arm.

The climb had left me feeling weak and dizzy. I remained perfectly still, not wanting to move in the wrong direction and fall to the ground below. I didn't know exactly how high up we were, but from the sound of the crowd beneath us, it was at least fifteen feet.

A hand was suddenly placed on my head, and the blindfold was torn away. Instantly, I shut my eyes against the brilliant light of the sun. After a second or two, I blinked them open to take in the scene.

It was amazing how, in such a chaotic place, filled with rancorous noise, I was able to perceive so many details at a glance. I was positioned on top of a stone platform. Three of the sides were composed of rock steps, each tier smaller than the last. The final side of the platform was a solid wall, towering twenty feet above my head.

There were four of us atop the structure. Todd, his father, myself, and a stranger, who I reasoned must be The Lord of the Brimming Lake. He was garbed in a flowing, purple robe, trimmed with gold. There was a band of metal around his head. It was gold too and had small, colorful stones fixed to it.

I had been off when guessing his age. The man was probably in his late thirties. Unpronounced wrinkles were beginning to form in the corners of his face.

21

On the ground below were at least a thousand men and boys, Todd's brother among them. I could see a handful of girls as well, but none over the age of ten.

We were in the middle of some sort of village. Its streets were stone, and its buildings were stone and plaster. It went on as far as I could see to the left and to the right. Facing forward, with the rock wall behind me, was a river. It ran toward the east, not even a hundred feet from me.

Across the water were more buildings, similar in style to the ones on this side. A few people had gathered and were looking over the river at us curiously.

Todd stood on the far side of the rock platform, slightly behind The Lord of the Brimming Lake.

He had exchanged the gray pants from The North Wind for a pair similar to those he'd worn when we first met. They were dark brown and long enough to just cover his knees. He wore his bear claw necklace but was without a shirt, as was nearly every man present.

The crowd had finally settled enough for Tohoshin to begin speaking again. "My friends, the men of my house, and the subjects to whom I have dedicated my life, witness the making of a man."

The Lord of the Brimming Lake raised a long, silver knife above his head. This time, the cries and calls of the assembly below were doubled.

Looking at the curved blade, I shuddered internally, but forced myself to remain completely still. The Lord of the Brimming Lake turned to Todd and presented him with the knife.

"A gift to one who will win much honor for himself, his house, and his people," Tohoshin said. He was not addressing anyone but Todd, and the words were almost drowned out by the dying cheers.

Todd bowed stiffly, from the waist up, and reached out to receive the shiny blade. His movements were slow and precise. The silver weapon glinted in the sunlight as it changed hands.

Todd raised the knife above his head and faced the crowd. They roared with exuberance. He remained in that position a full thirty seconds, then turned toward me.

His eyes didn't quite focus as they met mine.

With calculated slowness, Todd approached me. I remained where I was as his hand fell on my arm. His grasp was far lighter than his father's.

I did not resist as he guided me to the back of the platform, where the rock wall rose far above my head. My back was to the icy stone.

"Do you want us to hold her?" Todd's father asked.

"No," Todd answered, without taking his eyes from my face. "That won't be necessary."

He was right. I wasn't going anywhere. I would die here, and Todd would never need to tell anyone about The Clan. They would be safe.

Maybe, a voice whispered. *They're still in the hands of Myna and the council.*

Not for much longer, I reminded myself. *Cole got away. He'll be in charge soon. There is no one I trust more with the future of The Clan.*

If he's still alive.

Of course he is.

The rest of them are gone. If Cole doesn't make it back, even the memory of you and your team will be forgotten.

I was tired of it. Tired of the voices. Tired of thinking and worrying about things I couldn't control. I didn't care anymore.

If we are all meant to die, then so be it.

Todd's hand traveled from my arm to my shoulder, firmly pinning me against the rock.

Then his eyes did focus on mine. In the dark brown depths, I saw something surprising: fear. It was the same terror I had seen there long ago when our positions were reversed.

"I'm sorry," he whispered, so softly only I could hear.

The words did not affect me.

23

He raised the knife and put it against the left side of my throat. Instinct told me to close my eyes, but I didn't. Couldn't. It was as if I were made of stone, just like the crumbling statue I'd seen in Axella.

I felt the razor-sharp tip of the knife against my skin. One swift motion, and it would be over. Todd's hand moved, and blood began to run down my neck.

CHAPTER 4
GIRL FROM THE STARS

Three drops of blood were all that fell from the wound. Slowly, Todd lowered the knife.

I didn't understand.

I was supposed to be dead. He should be crouching over my body, cutting the teeth from my mouth right now.

Instead, his hand went to my wrists and, with the same blade he'd used on my neck, he cut the bindings from my hands.

I was still staring at him in surprise when he took me by the shoulder and guided me forward until we stood at the very front of the platform.

"I have completed the rite of manhood," Todd announced in a loud voice. "I claim this girl's life. She will be to me as Trisna was to Dezydery. Instead of death, I will grant her life, so long as she serves me."

There was cheering again from below us. Was I the only one who didn't fully comprehend the situation?

I lifted my hand to the cut on the side of my neck. My fingers came away wet with blood. The wound wasn't bad at all, but my legs didn't feel stable. I feared that if I passed out, I would fall headfirst down the steps.

The clamor of the crowd might have gone on for a while longer, but The Lord of the Brimming Lake stepped up beside Todd and raised a hand. The noise died almost instantaneously.

"Todicmadaya has completed the rite of manhood. Now we will hear the story of his exploits."

Someone hastened to bring a chair to the top of the platform for Tohoshin. Another was brought for Arshenn, but not quite as quickly.

25

Todd pushed me down into a sitting position on the top step.

Clasping his hands behind his back, he began to speak. As he did, he paced back and forth, addressing the entire assembly. Most were silent, ready to hear what he said. I noticed a few of those on the outskirts of the group began to disperse.

"Listen well," Todd started, speaking in the same grand voice he had always used when telling stories to my team during the trials.

"For I have been to a sacred place: The Undying Garden. Only the blessed are granted dreams of that mysterious land, and no other living soul has visited the lair of Todkala in more than a century."

Stunned silence settled over the assembly. Those who had intended to slip away hurried back, suddenly eager to hear what Todd would say.

"I set out on my journey heading north, along the coast. Each night, I beseeched the gods to allow me to prove myself worthy of manhood, but no situation presented itself. Yet, I refused to turn back until I had completed my rite. I continued traveling for more days than I can remember.

"One night, the gods sent a mighty storm, which drove me from the coast. The waves were taller than two men, the thunder shook the very mountains to their roots, and in the lightning, I saw the monstrous creatures of the depths rearing up out of the water.

"To escape, I hurried from the seaside into The Western Woods. The storm continued for five days and five nights. All the time, I pressed forward through the raging wind and blinding rain.

"On the sixth day, at sunset, the rain ceased. As the sky cleared, I saw a single star in the heavens, shining down brightly through a gap in the clouds. That star gave me hope, hope that I might live and succeed in my quest. I took it as a good omen from the gods and passed that night peacefully.

"In the morning, I found the place I'd come to was lush and beautiful, a welcome sight after so many days of rain. A deer was feeding close by in a meadow. I slew the creature with a throw of my knife and spent the rest of the day cooking the meat.

"I made a sacrifice of the right shoulder to Arsh, the fat of the tail I burned for Jiya, the feet for Sur, and the heart I offered to Todkala, my namesake. I begged him to guide me and not leave me abandoned. When I rose in the morning, even the ashes of the offering had vanished, showing the gods' acceptance of my sacrifices.

"Nearby ran a small stream of clear water, which I followed west. The land there was very strange. Trees I did not know grew in abundance. Flowers I had never before beheld sprouted from the ground. I did not need to turn to the right or to the left, for game was plentiful.

"I carried on in this fashion until, one night, I had a dream. In this vision, I was swiftly borne through the air as a hawk flies, traveling north and east, over mountains and under trees. A long way I went, covering a great number of miles. Then I was swept into a tunnel, and all was blackness. A moment later, I found myself in the midst of the most beautiful garden in the world. It was midnight, and a full moon hung overhead. I knew in my heart it was not a place of men but of the gods.

"When I woke in the morning, I could not shake the dream from my mind. So I turned from the river and began to seek the land.

"For many days, I traveled northeast, searching the horizon for signs of the garden. I climbed mountains and journeyed through forests. After almost four moons of searching, I came to the mountainside where the tunnel had been. I knew the sea lay close at hand. Though I could not hear the sound of the waves, the air had a salty smell. White seagulls often passed through the sky overhead. Their mournful cries carried to my ears by the wind.

"But alas, the mountainside was solid stone. I checked the rocks carefully, searching for an entrance, but it was as if the tunnel I had seen never existed.

"There, before the great mountain, I lay down for the night, determined to begin climbing the peak in the morning, though its summit was ten times higher than all the others.

"It was then that I had my second dream. A cloaked figure appeared before me, shrouded in darkness. 'Long have you searched,' he said. 'How much longer are you willing to go on seeking?'

"'As long as it takes,' I vowed.

"The figure smiled. I could see nothing of his face save his mouth. The teeth were sharp and slightly pointed.

"'Then seek,' he whispered. Twin pools of purple light suddenly sparked out of the darkness under his hood, and I knew I was looking into the eyes of no mere mortal.

"I awoke under the light of a full moon. It illuminated the frost-covered clearing and the base of the great mountain.

"Something stirred in the forest beside me. A red, furry tail vanished into the undergrowth. Instantly, I ran after it. The creature never let me get a good look at him but was never quite out of my sight.

"I do not know which way I ran or how long I followed the beast. It seemed to be a great many days, though the moon never set and the sun never rose. I ran until every part of my body was numb from exhaustion. Just when I felt that I could run no further, the mountain reared up before me once more. This time, there was a dark tunnel precisely as I had seen in my first dream. The fox plunged inside. I followed him without hesitation.

"Running in the dark was more challenging than running through the moonlit forest, but I dared not stop. After an eternity, I emerged into the cold light of dawn. The fox was gone, but the first rays of the sun revealed a vast expanse of golden grass.

"At the very center was The Undying Garden, which grows green all year round. A hooded figure awaited me among the golden grass. I approached with caution, confident that this was the great god Todkala, he who is the fox in the night.

"I drew near and knelt, presenting him my knife.

"'What would I want with your little blade?' the god laughed.

"'It does not matter to me,' I told him. 'You have but to name it and I will do it.'

"He smiled, showing his long, sharp teeth. 'I am pleased. When you began this journey, you were a weakling, but no more. You have begun to find your strength.'

"'I am more blessed than I have any right to be,' I replied. 'I can depart this place and live the rest of my days in contentment, for I have seen that which few men have ever beheld.'

"'True,' Todkala answered me. 'However, if you leave now, those days will be very few, for winter is upon the land. I will allow you to spend the cold moons here, in my garden, which knows no season save summer. Expect my return once the outside land has come back to life again. At that time, I will give you a great test to see if you are wise as well as strong.'

"Having spoken those words, he left me.

The Undying Garden was not large, but nearly every kind of fruit tree grew there. A stream flowed in a perfect circle on the borders. After crossing the water, I dared not go back, for I could soon see snow piling up on the far side of the stream. However, inside the garden, all was warm and comfortable. The sun never set, and I feasted on the sweetest fruits ever grown.

"In the garden, days passed without indication. The time slipped away as smoothly as the water in the brook. I slept on the soft grass, climbed the trees' highest boughs, and bathed in the river. Indeed, there is only one thing in this world that rivals the beauty of The Undying Garden.

"I offered prayers of thanks to Todkala for his provision nearly as often as I drew breath.

"In this way, I watched the winter pass, and the grass begin to grow again. Still, I remained, waiting for the god to return as he'd promised.

"After the snow had vanished from the ground, and the land was in full flower, the powerful Todkala did appear once more.

29

"'My lord,' I said when I found him in the garden with me. I dropped to one knee, again presenting my knife to him.

"'I am glad to see you chose to remain rather than perish in the cold,' he replied. 'It is time now for your test.'

"I feared this test, for Todkala is the trickster. When he is near, you cannot always trust your eyes and ears.

"With a snap of his fingers, the garden vanished. For an instant, we were in darkness, and then the stars began to come out, one by one, until the heavens above us were filled with brilliant lights. They were of many different colors, some gold, some blue, some red, and some silver.

"Todkala threw back his hood to reveal his face, boyish and slightly pointed, like that of a fox. His purple eyes glowed brightly in the dim light.

"'Welcome to the treasure house of the gods! All that you see fell from the sky and were brought here,' he told me.

"A hooded figure appeared, bearing a torch. In the firelight, I was able to see that each of the lights above was not a star but a jewel. There were thousands of them, each as large as a man's head. They were embedded in glossy black rock, which I had taken for the night sky.

"'These are true treasures,' Todkala said, raising his hands to encompass the entire chamber. The flame from the hooded figure's torch blazed brighter as he spoke, disclosing an opening in the rock to my left. It also revealed for an instant the face of the torchbearer. It was not the face of one of the gods, but the face of a mortal girl.

"'You may choose one, whichever you would like. Decide, and it is yours, only, you must take it with you through the tunnel.' He gestured to the passage I had noticed in the rock.

"'The tunnel will lead you back to your world. There will be great peril, so make your selection with care.'

"His voice had been soft, but, suddenly, it came out of him like a clap of thunder. 'Choose now!' he cried.

"I looked at all the gems, so beautiful as they sparkled in the firelight. How could I decide between them? And how would I ever manage to free one from the rock and carry it between realms? These were the thoughts that plagued me.

"I turned in circles, trying to get a good look at each of the stones. Todkala was rubbing his hands together in pleasure, enjoying the test far more than I was.

"Looking toward the god once more, I realized the answer to the riddle.

"'I chose this prize,' I announced, pulling the hooded girl to my side.

"'Truly?' Todkala asked. 'With so much wealth offered to you, you would choose a mere girl?'

"'What good would any of these jewels be to me if I were dead?' I countered. 'I do not imagine I would make it back alive with any of them. I have chosen the girl with the light, so that I may keep the greatest treasure of all, my own life.'

"'Wise words,' Todkala praised me. 'You are the first to ever choose the girl from the stars as your prize. So be it, take her and welcome. If you can reach your realm, she is yours, and I will grant you other boons as well.'

"He smiled then, and it was truly terrible to behold. 'But you must both survive first.'

"With the girl from the stars following, I entered the tunnel. Its walls glittered with specks of gold, and the floor beneath my feet was sandy and dry.

"By the light of the torch, I was able to see many pits and chasms along the path. Some had no bottom. Others were filled with the bones of those who had tried to pass this way in the dark. I hoped that with the torch, our passage would be easy, but I knew better than to expect it.

"Indeed, the trickster had laid a trap for us. Just when I was sure we were almost to the other side, the girl from the stars screamed and dropped the torch.

"I spun around and saw the shape of a great brown bear emerge from a side passage. It raked its claws across the girl's shoulder, flinging her back the way we had come. I rushed forward, drawing my knife. The girl was forgotten by the animal as

I struck at its face. The beast turned and advanced on me. I had little hope of killing it with my knife, but could not flee because it was between the girl from the stars and myself.

"If I departed the tunnel without the treasure Todkala had granted me, I was sure I would face a fate worse than death. So I chose battle.

"Many times I struck at the bear, ducking its massive paws all the while. The animal would have mauled me quickly, but it was unable to maneuver in the restricted space.

"With a great burst of speed and agility, I ducked under the bear's paws and wriggled beneath its belly. On the far side, I sprang up and seized the torch from the ground. The bear was trying to turn around in the narrow passage. While it was trapped, I pressed the torch to the creature's shaggy fur.

"The animal bellowed in terror and surged forward, away from us. We could hear its cries for a long time as it crashed through the tunnel, blinded by fear and pain.

"The girl from the stars and I carefully navigated the rest of the passage. There were no more traps, and soon we emerged into the evening air. The body of the bear lay beside the mouth of the cave, dead, its fur still smoldering.

"Todkala stood beside it, his eyes blazing with violet light, from anger or joy I did not know.

"'Well done,' he told me. 'You are the first mortal ever to find your way out of the treasure house of the gods. Well, the first two. The girl from the stars is yours now.'

"I thanked the god profusely, but he motioned for silence. With a blinding flash, he vanished. In my hands were left jewels. None so large as the ones within the cave, but each just as beautiful. The girl's wounds were healed to nothing but scars, and a pack of supplies was left at my feet.

"The girl from the stars and I rested there that night. I cut the claws from the bear and salvaged what I could of the meat.

"When morning came, we started the journey home. I will not tell you of the adventures and challenges we faced on our return, for they would seem droll and commonplace after the tale I have already related."

As Todd finished speaking, a hush lay over the crowd for a long moment. It was broken all at once by a hundred voices. Many called questions to Todd, but I was unable to make them out. My mind had wandered during the story. I felt as if I'd actually seen all the things Todd described.

"There is no way that *boy* killed a bear!" bellowed a man from somewhere in the crowd.

"No one is smart enough to escape a trap of the trickster," another person put in.

"Todkala would never allow a mortal into The Undying Garden."

"He's a liar!"

Todd waited respectfully as The Lord of the Brimming Lake rose and approached the front of the platform. The crowd quieted as he raised his hand.

He was smiling, but I had a feeling the story he'd heard was not what he was expecting.

"Your account was well given," Tohoshin announced. "However, you are not the first who claims to have seen the gods. Sometimes it is true and sometimes not. I do not think I am the only one who would like to see some evidence of the tale you tell."

"Of course, my lord," Todd dipped his head respectfully.

"Here is proof that I have slain a bear." Todd removed his necklace and held it aloft. The large, black claws were quite visible.

"He probably found it dead." It was the first voice again.

Todd did not respond to any of their comments. Instead, he crouched down and seized my arm, then pulled me to my feet. I gasped as the movement sent fresh waves of pain up and down my leg. The sound was lost in the clamor.

"It was very much alive. I will show you." Todd let go of my arm and pulled the light jacket from my shoulders. Underneath, I was wearing a maroon tank top.

33

"Here," Todd gestured to the scar that ran from my shoulder to my elbow.

Tohoshin drew near, scrutinizing my arm.

"It is as he says," The Lord of the Brimming Lake reported.

"I have one more piece of evidence, and then you may all make your own decision on whether what I have said is true or not. Here is the other prize the trickster bestowed upon me."

Todd pulled a pouch from his side. It could easily have held three or four apples. The top was closed with a drawstring. Carefully, he opened it and took out several items ranging in size from peas to walnuts.

A hush fell over the crowd. Todd's father leapt to his feet, mouth hanging open in surprise.

For the first time, I felt truly betrayed. Despair started leaking into my soul. They were such little things, but seeing them in Todd's grip broke my heart.

CHAPTER 5
FAMILY

The tears I had felt too exhausted to cry earlier flooded my eyes.

In Todd's hand were several colorful stones from the cave in The Valley of The North Wind. He must have taken them before fleeing The Land of the Clan.

It wasn't like they actually belonged to me, but I'd always felt that they belonged to that place. They were a small piece of home that had been snatched away and would never return.

There were thousands of stones in the cave. Todd couldn't have fit more than thirty or forty into that bag, I tried to reason with myself. But it was no good.

A few tears escaped and ran unchecked down my cheeks. Thankfully, no one was looking at me anymore. The entire crowd was staring at what Todd held.

The Lord of the Brimming Lake gazed at the stones in awed silence. A moment later, he straightened. "I- I didn't even really believe myself, but now there can be no doubt," he announced to the crowd.

At his words, cheers rose from those gathered below— great cheers of acceptance and praise. Todd was grinning ear to ear as he basked in their applause. He glanced at me, and the smile froze in place. Instantly, he turned away and faced forward again.

Things happened very quickly after that. Tohoshin congratulated Todd once more before departing. Much of the crowd dispersed along with their lord, although a few of the more curious ones lingered to stare at Todd and me. Todd's brother, Arkensallay, joined us at the top of the platform.

"Does this 'girl from the stars' have a name?" he asked Todd, with a side glance at me.

"Her name is Astra," Todd answered.

"I'm more interested in where you found the jewels," Todd's father put in.

"I told you," Todd replied. "I–"

Todd's father waved his hand dismissively. "Yes, yes, I heard what you said, but unlike that fool, *Lord* Tohoshin, I am wise enough to know a lie when I hear it."

Todd furrowed his brow. "You have heard my story. It is your choice whether or not you believe it." Todd turned away and put his hand on my shoulder once more, guiding me toward the steps. As we reached the edge, I saw Arshenn narrow his eyes. Neither he nor Arkensallay followed us.

Going down was more painful than climbing up had been. After only three steps, I drew up short with a gasp. Black clouds pressed on the edges of my vision.

Todd looked back at me from the step below. His hand had slipped from my shoulder when I'd stopped.

I took a moment to brace myself; there was still a long way to go before I reached level ground. Todd rejoined me on the third step. Without speaking, he put his arm around my waist and drew mine over his shoulders, as he had done the previous day.

My body froze at the unexpected action. I didn't want him to touch me or help me. I didn't want anything but to be left alone. However, if I struggled to escape his grasp, I would probably fall. Instead, I used him for balance and hopped more than walked down the remaining steps.

He let me rest for a moment at the bottom. When we started moving again, the direction he led took us south, away from the river. It was difficult to tell, since I had been wearing a blindfold, but it seemed we were retracing the same path Todd's father had brought me along that morning.

Once, I would have been excited and interested to see how different this place was from the villages I knew so well. But now, I kept my eyes on the road ahead. We passed dozens of buildings, and I did not give even one thought to what they were used for or who might live in them.

It wasn't until we reached the edge of the village that I started paying attention to the landscape. The dwellings and stone road gave way to a dirt path, which wound through green fields dotted with clumps of trees.

There were structures here as well, but not nearly so many. Up until that point, we had passed an abundance of people, all of whom stared openly. Now there was no one save the two of us.

"You have to stay here. Forever," Todd told me, breaking the silence between us. "If you do, I won't tell anyone about The Clan."

I nodded, too weary to reply.

"Are you angry with me?" he asked.

Was I angry with him?! He'd pretended to be my friend, murdered Kisa and Rollan, tried to do the same to Cole, and almost killed me. It would make sense for me to be furious. However, when I thought of Todd, anger wasn't what came to mind, pain was. I couldn't be angry. I had been too badly hurt to feel anything else.

"No," I answered.

"Really?" Todd sounded skeptical.

I didn't make any response.

The buildings in the village had been close together, one almost on top of the next. Here, they were set in small groups. Todd chose a path leading to one of these. Where the trail ended, there were several buildings arranged in a semicircle.

A pair of large, gray dogs bounded over to meet us. They greeted Todd with wagging tails and lolling tongues. Neither was quite sure what to make of me. The larger of the two, whose shoulders almost reached my waist and Todd called Boulder, raised his lip in a snarl. The other dog was named River. He gave me a curious sniff before quickly darting away.

On the left, I could make out a stable. Beyond it were fenced paddocks and fields where several horses grazed.

The largest building was only one story tall but seemed to sprawl out in many directions. The rest appeared to be small, one-room structures that were fairly identical. Only one had a unique feature, which caught my attention. It was on the far right as we approached. Two enormous chimneys sprouted out of the back corner.

About ten men were milling around the different buildings. None of them spoke to us, but a few of the closer ones gave Todd deep nods of respect.

Only once we'd set foot inside the largest building did I realize it was the same place where I had woken up that morning.

The first room we entered was devoid of people. Todd quickly turned down the hall on the right. The ceiling was domed and covered entirely by pale plaster.

The second chamber was three times the size of the first. A large, wooden table took up much of the room, with ten uncomfortable-looking chairs arranged around it.

A stone fireplace was set in the nearby wall. It was unlit, but four huge windows let an abundance of light and air into the room.

The two women I had seen that morning were sitting on low stools beside a small, circular table close to the empty hearth. They appeared to be making a blanket.

At our entrance, the younger woman, the beautiful one, glanced up. At first, her face was stunned, then she burst into tears.

"Todicmadaya!" she gasped, rising to her feet and rushing forward to embrace him. "My son, you have come home at last!"

Her words were only the second thing to make any sort of impression on me all day. For a moment, I was back in The Paramount, watching as everyone else was greeted by their families.

It was so unfair that I seemed to be the only person in the world without someone who cared for them.

The other woman had risen too but did not approach. If the beautiful woman was Todd's mother, I couldn't imagine who the second woman might be. She looked at least ten years older than the first, but surely she wasn't old enough to be his grandmother.

"Have you passed the rite?" Todd's mother asked him, pulling back to look at his face. She raised a hand to touch his cheek.

Todd nodded solemnly. "Yes, Mother. I am a man now."

A delighted smile passed over the woman's lovely face.

Todd turned to me. "This is Astra," he said by way of introduction. "She's going to be staying with us. I've claimed her as part of my rite." His words were proud, as though he had achieved something remarkable.

"Astra," he said, turning to me. "This is my mother, Jiyata."

I nodded to her, unsure of what to say. Jiyata gave me a shy smile. Her brown eyes were friendly but a touch reserved.

"Will you teach her the ways of the house?" Todd entreated his mother. "She knows almost nothing about our people and our customs."

"Of course," Jiyata answered softly. Deep emotion engulfed her face as she embraced her son once more. "I'm just so glad you're safe." Her voice dropped to a whisper. "I thought I'd lost you."

It was at that moment that Todd's brother entered.

"Still a mama's boy," Arkensallay sneered at Todd, who slowly released his mother.

"There is nothing dishonorable about respecting one's mother," Todd announced.

"I suppose, but you won't catch me doing it. How about we try something manly instead?" he suggested.

"Like what?" Todd asked.

"You've grown some since you left. Want to see if you're finally a match for me with our swords?"

Arkensallay gave Jiyata a stern look, as a small gasp escaped her lips. She would not meet his gaze, but the suggestion clearly disturbed her.

"I'm really not in the mood," Todd told Arkensallay.

"That's a step in the wrong direction." Todd's father materialized from the hallway behind Arkensallay. "You always used to be so eager to practice. Has all that time in *The Undying Garden* made you soft?"

"No," Todd growled.

"Prove it then," Arkensallay challenged.

Todd glanced at Arshenn's stern countenance. "All right," he yielded.

Both men smiled. Although Arkensallay's grin was larger, there was something far more sinister in the twist of Arshenn's lips.

He turned to the rest of us. "Jiyata, do come and watch. You too, *girl from the stars*."

Arkensallay was already hurrying Todd back down the hall, toward the entrance to the dwelling. Arshenn followed them.

"Come," Jiyata said to me in a low voice. "The most important rule while living in this house is that Lord Arshenn's word is law. You must never refuse him anything."

I nodded to show I understood.

As we followed the three men out of the dwelling, I wondered why the older woman's presence wasn't requested as well. Not a single person had even taken notice of her existence.

Outside, in the center of the semicircle formed by the buildings, Todd and Arkensallay were choosing their weapons. Jiyata seemed distraught, but I had witnessed many sparring matches and even been in a few real conflicts.

The men, who had watched Todd and me enter the dwelling a few minutes earlier, gathered around to create a ring around the pair. I observed that some of them wore metal bands on their ankles.

Two of the men were dressed differently from the rest. Their clothing resembled that of Arkensallay.

The others wore a wide array of garments, most of which were tattered and filthy. The tallest one, who had a shaven head, was the only man among this group whose clothes weren't held together by patches.

I stood beside Jiyata for a moment, but my legs were too wobbly. Without intending to, I dropped to the ground. There didn't seem to be any point in rising, so I stayed where I had fallen. Arshenn turned to glare at me, but he didn't approach us, so I pretended not to notice.

The grass was soft, and its refreshing scent made me think of the pastures of The North Wind. I found my mind wandering through the rolling fields until the sharp sound of metal on metal pulled me back to the present.

The duel between Todd and his brother started out friendly, but before long, it took a more serious turn. The men cheered loudly whenever one of them seemed to be gaining an advantage.

Arkensallay used the sword skillfully. He was tall and powerfully built. There would have been very little competition if Todd hadn't been able to dodge quickly and strike again a moment later.

After about half an hour, both boys' bare chests were bathed in sweat. Arshenn had watched them impassively, opposite from where I was sitting beside Jiyata. She had her hands clasped, and every time the blades connected, she drew in a sharp breath.

Todd managed to land a glancing blow with the flat of his sword on Arkensallay's shoulder. In response, Arkensallay planted both feet and wheeled around, swinging at his brother with all his might. His sword was moving so fast I could hardly see it. If the blade connected with Todd at that speed, it would surely kill him.

Todd dodged neatly and managed to get inside Arkensallay's defense. With a precise flick of his blade, Todd sent Arkensallay's sword clattering to the ground.

Arkensallay froze, the edge of Todd's weapon pressed to his throat. His skill was met with cheers and applause from the gathered men.

"So, you actually did learn a few new tricks while you were gone," Arshenn observed, showing signs of life for the first time since the match began. He approached his two sons, glancing between the pair.

Todd lowered his sword and turned toward his father. Arkensallay sprang forward to retrieve his blade. He would have started the fight up again, but Arshenn's words cut him short.

"That's enough for now. Really, Arkensallay, I'm not sure how you would bear being beaten by your little brother twice in one day."

Arkensallay narrowed his eyes. His face, which had already been red from exertion, turned crimson with fury.

"He just got lucky," Arkensallay protested.

Arshenn raised an eyebrow. "Now you have excuses? Tomorrow you will duel again, and we shall see if that really is the case."

Neither of the boys appeared pleased by this announcement.

"Everyone, back to work," Arshenn commanded.

"You should come inside and rest," Jiyata told me as the group dispersed.

I nodded. My injured leg had grown stiff from being still for so long. Now it shrieked with pain as I limped to the door.

"This is the kitchen," Jiyata told me, as we passed into the dwelling.

The older woman was still in the second room.

"Is all well?" she asked, glancing up. Her voice was husky.

"It is. For now, at least," Jiyata answered, then looked at me. "It's Astra, yes?"

I nodded.

"Astra, this is Yetta, Lord Arshenn's first wife. Yetta, this is Astra."

Yetta nodded deeply to me but did not rise from where she sat, still working on the blanket. I returned her nod.

"Wife?" Todd had used that word before. "Like a life mate?" I asked.

"I suppose," Jiyata seemed unsure. "I am Lord Arshenn's second wife."

My people only took one life mate, but Todd had mentioned that having more than one life mate—or wife—wasn't uncommon for The People of the Brimming Lake. If I recalled correctly, one of the gods had taken a second wife, but that had been a great grievance to both her and the god she truly loved.

42

"Come this way," Jiyata directed me.

At the far end of the room were two hallways leading in different directions. Jiyata pointed to the one on the right. "You must never enter this part of the house without permission from one of the men."

"Why? What's down there?" I wondered.

"It's the men's quarters. There are six rooms, but only half are being used at the moment," Jiyata told me.

"What are the other rooms for?" I asked.

Flashing a quick look at Yetta, who didn't appear to have heard us, Jiyata just shook her head. She led me down the other hall. We passed two side rooms, which I was told were for storage. The hall ended in a room about as large as the kitchen.

"This is where Yetta and I usually sleep," Jiyata told me.

Three beds lined the back wall, and there were several rows of boxes, which appeared to contain clothing. The room had only two windows, neither more than a foot tall and set close to the ceiling.

Jiyata took me to the bed in the far right corner. "You can rest here. This was where Suriken slept before she ran away."

I didn't bother undressing, even though my clothes were filthy.

"If you need anything, I'll be in the main room with Yetta," Jiyata told me softly as she slipped out.

The small windows cast the room in shadow, even though the sun was still high overhead. I didn't think any amount of light would have mattered. Sleep took me before my head hit the pillow.

The day had been so surreal to me that when I woke up in a hayloft in The North Wind, it took me a moment to realize I was dreaming.

Myra was sitting there, perched on one of the bales of hay which formed a circle. Unlike the time she had actually visited the loft, she seemed to be completely at ease. I rose slowly, relieved that the pain in my leg had not entered the dream with me. I sank down on the hay bale beside hers.

43

"You've really messed everything up," she told me. Her voice was gentle, but bore a mild reproach that made me sure she thought I was an idiot.

"Yes," I agreed with both her spoken and unspoken words.

"Are you going to stay forever?" she asked.

"It is my duty to sacrifice myself to protect those I love, just like you did in the mount–" I broke off and had to swallow before continuing. "You would be doing the same thing in my place."

"No," Myra shook her head slowly from side to side, gray eyes serious. "I would have killed him."

I considered that for a moment.

"He was my- friend," I reminded her. "I can't- couldn't just bury that."

Myra's eyes met mine. "You misunderstand. I would have killed him the first time, before I ever knew him."

"I don't believe that," I told her. "Not if you had been where I was and seen what I saw."

"And what did you see?" she asked.

I hesitated before answering, recalling the moment in my mind. It had been filled with rage and adrenaline and fear, fear for myself and my friends, but also fear of what I might do.

"I saw a boy," I whispered. "A boy who was afraid to die."

"He's not a boy anymore," Myra pointed out. "But I think he is still very afraid."

CHAPTER 6
AWAKENING

After my dream of Myra, darkness filled my head. I was engulfed by a feverish wave of heat, only to find the sweat suddenly frozen into frost.

The sensations were repeated over and over again. One moment, I was burning as if there was a fire in my bones, then a sudden chill, colder than the air in The Valley of The North Wind, would wash over me. I shivered and sweated in turn for what seemed like hours.

I woke a handful of times into the pitch-blackness of night. My mind wasn't working right. I couldn't remember where I was or how I had come there.

The next time I opened my eyes, it was day, but the gloomy room gave no indication of a time. It seemed that I blinked, and the light suddenly became brighter and more golden. The woman, Yetta, was leaning over me. She had a bowl of something in her hand.

It smelled like food, but the last thing I wanted to do was eat. However, I was not conscious enough to resist her, nor could I taste the liquid substance she poured down my throat.

Heat swallowed me again. I wished I could shed my skin as easily as horses lose their thick coats in the spring. This period of burning lasted longer than the ones before it. Fire spread from the cut on my leg. It filled my limbs with a hot pulsation and caused my head to ache a little more with each beat of my racing heart. If only it would break open and relieve the pressure.

Waking and dreaming were a blur. I had no way of knowing whether I was seeing the real world or the darkness of a nightmare. It felt not like hours and days, but like months and years that I lay, paralyzed by the fire of the vicious fever.

Slowly, it began to ebb, like the tide of the ocean. It receded, then came back with a vengeance, then receded again. The cycle seemed never-ending, until I was certain I would spend the rest of my life trapped in the same pattern of suffering and relief.

It was early morning when, at last, I woke with no trace of the fever left. Dawn was creeping through the windows. In the twilight, I could see that only one of the other beds was occupied. From the tuft of hair, I guessed it was Yetta.

Vaguely, I wondered how long I had been lying in that bed. Surely more than just one night, but not nearly so long as it had felt.

I rose slowly, testing my leg as I carefully placed it on the floor. There was some stiffness but almost no pain. The wound was covered in a fresh bandage. Slowly, I stood and walked out of the room. One thing I was sure of, I did not want to sleep anymore.

I expected to find someone in the main room, but it was vacant, as was the kitchen. Outside, I heard a horse whinny, and a longing to see the animal came over me suddenly.

I was out of the dwelling in a moment. The stable was close by, but the horses had been left out to graze during the night. I walked over to the nearby fence and leaned against it for support, feeling weak after my long slumber.

Ten horses were scattered about the pasture, feeding on the dew gilt grass. All but two of them were a silver-white, and their pale coats almost glimmered in the first rays of sunlight.

"Running away after only four days?" a voice asked.

I turned my head and saw Arkensallay standing a few feet behind me. There was a bucket in his hand.

"I don't think I'd get too far," I pointed out.

He squinted at me, and I realized my dry humor was wasted on him.

"You're not supposed to leave the house without permission," he told me.

I blinked at him, taken aback. "Why?"

Now it was his turn to be surprised. "Because that's where you belong."

I almost laughed; the thought of me belonging anywhere was so foreign.

As I began making my way back to the dwelling, Arkensallay's voice stopped me. "Girl from the stars, did everything happen as my brother told it?"

Pausing, I looked back over my shoulder. "We had a great adventure," I told him. "There was a bear and a cave of treasures."

Arkensallay didn't seem to know whether I was speaking the truth or not.

"And before that?" he asked, closing the distance between us until he was less than a foot away. "When you were with the gods, what was that like?"

"I have no memory of that time," I answered honestly.

"So, you don't remember anything before meeting Todicmadaya?" Arkensallay challenged.

My answer came quickly, my words inspired by Todd's way of weaving together half-truths. Everyone must believe Todd's story. Otherwise, the real account would be demanded.

"I remember the sun and the moon, the grass and the trees, the sound of the wind in the mountains, and the coolness of the night air."

Arkensallay raised his fist. His hand impacted my left cheekbone. It did not knock me off my feet but was hard enough to turn my head.

"Stop speaking in riddles," he hissed as I turned back to face him. "Tell me, what do you remember?"

I didn't answer. He raised his hand again. I didn't flinch, but this time I was driven back a few steps. I could taste blood in my mouth. The left side of my face felt hot and bruised.

My first response was to fight back, but instinct told me not to. I knew I didn't have a chance. The fever had taken my strength, and I hadn't had a decent meal in days, not to mention the fact that this man was nearly twice as large as I was.

Instead of doing something foolish, I stood, waiting to see what he would do next. Our eyes were locked; his were brown like Todd's, but a lighter shade.

"Well?" he asked.

"Every word I have spoken to you is the truth. What more would you have me say?"

He curled his lip in frustration. I turned away from him and walked back to the dwelling. I could sense his eyes on me the whole way.

Jiyata and Todd were in the kitchen when I entered. Jiyata was cooking some eggs in a metal pan over the fire. She glanced up at me only for a moment before turning back to her work.

Todd's eyes went straight to my swollen cheek. He seemed about to ask a question, but just at that moment, Arkensallay barged in behind me. Todd's mouth snapped shut, and his jaw clenched.

"Better keep a closer eye on your girl, brother," Arkensallay announced. "I found her wandering around by the pastures."

Todd's words were stiff as he replied. "I don't mind if she wants to see the horses."

Arkensallay shook his head. "You're too soft. You need to teach her discipline and break her spirit. If you don't, then I certainly will." The threat in his voice was clear, and the evidence of his words was plain to see on my face.

"Perhaps I can learn from your wisdom," Todd answered sarcastically. "Let's take a walk, and you can tell me your ways."

Jiyata glanced nervously at the boys as they left the dwelling together.

"You should not anger Arkensallay," Jiyata told me softly once they had departed. "My eldest son is very much like his father."

I took a step closer to Jiyata. "Why did you choose him for–" I was going to say your life mate, but remembered that she didn't know that phrase.

Jiyata seemed to understand. "My father arranged the marriage when I was fifteen. Lord Arshenn's family has always been wealthy, and he was- displeased with his first wife, Yetta."

"Why was he displeased?"

Jiyata pursed her lips. "Yetta was unable to bear a son."

"So?" I asked.

"Sons are very important. They are the ones who make the house strong. They are the providers and protectors. If any from The House of the Warrior attacked, we would be helpless without them."

Well, with that attitude, certainly, I thought.

Jiyata turned back to her work and removed the eggs from the flames.

"Can I assist you?" I asked.

She nodded and directed me to clean and cut some fruit from a large basket on one of the many shelves lining the walls. I'd never spent much time cooking, but the breakfast we prepared seemed to be fairly simple. Yetta joined us a short time later. Out of Yetta's hearing, Jiyata explained to me that Yetta had watched over me the past four nights and gotten little rest herself.

I felt slightly guilty that a woman I had hardly spoken to would dedicate so much time to caring for me. Out of the corner of my eye, I observed her, resolving to find a way to repay her efforts. She came across as a serious, no-nonsense person. Not once all morning did I see her smile. Her voice was calm, but not soothing like Jiyata's. The slightly wrinkled face showed little emotion, but the hazel eyes were sharp and missed nothing.

Once the food was ready, we took a portion of it to the main room and set the table for three. I was pleased to learn that we would be eating separately. Arshenn watched silently as Jiyata and I prepared the table. As we were adding the finishing touches to the breakfast, Arkensallay and Todd returned.

Arkensallay was grinning from ear to ear. In contrast, Todd's brow was furrowed, and he wore a serious expression.

Jiyata nodded toward the kitchen, and I followed her out of the main room. There was still a large amount of food remaining, the majority of which was given to a man waiting by the kitchen door. He was the tall man with the shaven head I'd seen before. He accepted the food from Yetta before heading off toward a narrow, rectangular building beside the stable.

As the three of us settled down to eat what was left of the eggs, bread, and fruit, I tried to recall the last time I'd eaten a decent meal sitting at a real table. It had been the night I dined with the family Kisa lived with after the trials.

Kisa.

An image of the golden-haired child filled my mind. Sorrow at a life cut short stole my appetite. I only managed to swallow a few mouthfuls of the delicious breakfast.

Yetta seemed to notice and gave me a sympathetic glance, even though she had no idea of my grief. It was a relief that she didn't press me with any uncomfortable questions.

After the others finished eating, we cleaned the kitchen and started prepping lunch and dinner. I'd never realized how much work was involved in keeping a family fed.

I started cutting up several different kinds of vegetables. Yetta had to intervene a few times to show me a better way to hold the knife.

"Did you not work in the kitchen where you lived before?" Jiyata asked. Clearly, she had not yet heard Todd's story.

I shook my head.

"Are you from across the river?" she continued.

"I–" The meaning of her words was not clear to me.

"From The House of the Warrior," Yetta specified.

"No," I shook my head.

"Oh," Jiyata said wonderingly. "We assumed that was where you came from."

When I did not reply, she let the conversation drop, even though there was an edge of curiosity in her words.

"Am I doing this right?" I asked fifteen minutes later. Yetta and Jiyata worked in almost complete silence, and, though I spoke softly, my voice seemed too loud for the quiet kitchen.

Yetta came to look at the vegetables I was chopping. "The potatoes are good," she told me. "The carrots and leeks need to be smaller."

I nodded as she walked away. Once the vegetables were the proper size, I put them in a bubbling pot of water, which hung over the fire. The stew we were making was for dinner and would have to simmer for many hours.

I turned from the pot and almost ran into Todd. I staggered backward a step.

"Careful," he said, catching my elbow.

After regaining my balance, I firmly pulled my arm from his grasp and walked around him, back to my work.

"Mother," Todd said, addressing Jiyata. "Do you mind if I borrow Astra for a little while? I want to show her the grounds."

"Of course not," Jiyata answered brightly.

He turned to me. "Will you come with me, Astra?" he asked.

I considered refusing but didn't. There was little enough to do here now that the stew was cooking. Lunch would be four fat chickens, which were already roasting on a spit beside the stew pot.

"Fine," I agreed, wiping clean the knife and wooden board I'd been using.

We left the kitchen and stepped into the sunshine. It was surprisingly hot considering how early in the year it was.

River, the smaller of the two enormous hounds, appeared and followed after us as we paused in the middle of the yard.

"You've seen the house, but I wanted to show you the rest of the place," Todd explained. "When your leg is better, I will take you to see the whole city."

Todd didn't seem to notice my lack of enthusiasm.

"We'll start with the forge," he decided.

I followed as he walked toward the building on our left. It was the one with the large chimneys sprouting from the roof. Todd lifted the latch and held it open while I entered.

Inside, all was dark since the shutters were closed. The enormous fire pit, which took up nearly the entire far end of the room, was unlit.

"My father doesn't really like working as a smith," Todd told me. "We don't need the money, so he only uses the forge on the days the apprentices, Artin and Reeshon, come. They are only here every three to four days, so it's empty most of the time. My grandfather was different. He loved making things and forged hundreds of swords and spears.

"I'd like to learn the craft of blacksmithing. I've asked my father to teach me. Now that I'm a man, he's considering taking me on as an apprentice too."

Instead of answering, I slowly walked through the little forge. It was filthy. Clearly, no one ever cleaned the place. Layers of grime covered most of the tools, which appeared to have been discarded in no particular order.

After the forge, I saw the smokehouse, the washhouse, several storage sheds, and the slave quarters.

Todd told me that his family owned nineteen male slaves who worked in the fields just beyond the horse pasture.

"We're lucky," he boasted. "We grow most of our own food, so we don't have to buy much from the city. Plus, my father makes enough money from teaching apprentices to pay for the rest of our needs. Anything we sell, livestock or produce, is extra."

I looked at the small shack of a dwelling and felt a swell of sympathy for the men who inhabited it. Even though I was in the same situation, I hadn't grown up that way. I had seen what lay beyond the borders of this land and the next. Did the slaves here really spend their entire lives under the heel of people like Arshenn?

Todd observed my prolonged gaze. "Stay away from the slaves," he ordered. I glanced at him. "They're a vile lot. Husanil is all right, he's the head slave, but I don't really trust the others."

He turned away from the hovel and headed toward the largest of the buildings.

"I've saved the best for last," Todd announced, changing the subject. "This is the stable."

As we entered, familiar scents washed over me. I wished I were allowed to sleep in the hayloft since it was the closest thing to home I was ever likely to see again.

Inside, there was only one horse, a white mare, heavy with foal.

"She belongs to Arkensallay," Todd mentioned. "He was reluctant to breed her, since she'll be out of commission for at least a year, but his friend offered him a good deal with one of his studs."

I approached the mare, slowly raising my hand to pet her glossy neck. Her nostrils flared, and she laid her ears back when I was still half a dozen feet away.

My feet came to a halt as the mare eyed me savagely. Was everything in this land hostile? Aside from Jiyata and Yetta, I was yet to meet a single creature who wasn't malicious and ill-tempered.

"What do you think?" Todd asked.

"The horses here are very different from any I've seen before," I observed.

"I meant about the whole place," he replied.

I shrugged without glancing in his direction.

"So much for not being angry with me," he muttered.

"I'm not."

"You're certainly acting like you are," Todd countered swiftly.

"I'm not angry at you." I turned on him. "But whatever friendship there was between us is gone now. You are a stranger to me."

"I guess that's why it was okay for you to try to kill me," he snapped.

"I could have if I'd wanted to," I told him.

Todd clenched his jaw. His dark eyes, full of rage, were glaring at me.

From somewhere outside, Arshenn began shouting for both of his sons.

Todd turned on his heel and marched out of the stable. I followed, intending to return to the dwelling.

"Wait, girl from the stars," Arshenn called to me as I headed back to the kitchen. "Don't you want to see today's match?"

I had a feeling this wasn't really a question but a command. I stopped in my tracks and turned back to the yard where Arkensallay and Todd were choosing weapons. A group of men, I assumed the slaves Todd had told me about, came out of the woodwork to watch.

Indifferently, I observed the two brothers stalk around each other. They weren't using swords today, but each had a pair of long knives.

If anything, Todd seemed even more skilled with these than with a long sword.

At first, Todd appeared to be winning. He landed a few glancing blows on his brother and even knocked him to the ground once. As Arkensallay struggled to regain his feet, Todd glanced in my direction.

When the combat started back up, Todd's movements were slower. He didn't land any more hits on Arkensallay. The match lasted nearly half an hour, as Arkensallay began to drive Todd back. I saw a few openings where Todd could have changed the momentum and begun attacking himself, but Todd wasn't quick enough to capitalize on them.

In the end, Arkensallay used his foot to kick one of Todd's knives out of his grip. After that, there was little Todd could do. Arkensallay ended the match with a swift thrust toward Todd's head. The blade must have nicked him because I saw a thin trail of blood running down Todd's right temple.

"Enough," Arshenn called as Todd was thrust to the ground.

The two boys both stood as their father approached them. "Well done, Arkensallay. Have you finally learned your brother's tricks? After four days of defeat, I was starting to worry."

Arkensallay swelled with pride at his father's words. "I won't lose anymore," he vowed.

"As for you," Arshenn turned on Todd. "I thought you'd finally become a man, but I suppose we'll see if that really is true, just like your tale."

Todd grimaced. "I will do better, Father."

"I've expected great things of you in the past, and you have always failed me. Make certain it does not happen this time," Arshenn warned.

I turned away and entered the dwelling. It was no concern of mine what passed between Arshenn and Todd. He didn't matter anymore.

CHAPTER 7
THE BRIMMING LAKE

The next day was much the same. I spent the early hours helping Jiyata and Yetta prepare the morning meal. My leg was healing quickly. Last night, Yetta had changed the bandage. There was no sign of infection anymore, and the cut was all but closed.

This morning, it was my cheek that felt swollen from where Arkensallay had struck me. I was certain there would be a spectacular bruise.

Todd, along with his father and brother, was gone much of the day. According to Yetta, they were overseeing the slaves in the fields.

Several afternoons later, Yetta and I took a wooden spinning wheel from one of the storage rooms. I'd seen a few while training at The Making, but had never really thought about their purpose. Since they rarely required horses for anything more than picking up and dropping off supplies, The Making was one of the villages where I'd spent the least amount of time.

Over the next couple of hours, Yetta taught me to pump the pedal and twist the wool into a fine thread. While I practiced on the spinning wheel, Yetta returned to helping Jiyata with the same blanket they had been working on since I arrived.

They were almost finished. All that was left was to sew the hem into place. I was fascinated by the way the two women's needles worked together in perfect unison. Just before it was time to serve the evening meal, the blanket was completed. I had only wrapped a few spools of coarse thread, but Yetta said they were well done, so I was pleased.

"Tomorrow is market day," Jiyata told me while the three of us prepared a dozen cow ribs for dinner.

"I- don't know what that means," I replied. "What is a market?"

"In the name of the gods, where do you come from that they don't have markets?" Yetta exclaimed incredulously.

I shrugged.

"A market is where merchants sell their wares. People go into the city and buy the supplies they need for the next six days," Jiyata informed me.

"Why six days?" I wondered.

"Because on the seventh, it's market day again," Yetta answered.

"Todicmadaya asked me earlier if your leg would be healed enough for you to join us," Jiyata said.

I considered for a moment.

"No," I decided. "It's probably better that I stay here."

Jiyata and Yetta exchanged a quick glance.

"Astra," Jiyata started, "you aren't thinking of running away, are you?"

"No," I answered earnestly. "It had not even crossed my mind."

"Good," Yetta told me. "The punishment is death in the most hideous way your master can come up with or, sometimes, they sell runaways to the fighting pits."

"I'm not planning to run away," I affirmed.

Jiyata nodded, but Yetta didn't seem convinced. "We didn't think Suriken would run away either, but she did."

"Who was Suriken?" I asked curiously. The name had been mentioned several times with no explanation offered.

"She was a slave girl Lord Arshenn won in a bet last year. He may have intended her for Arkensallay's first wife, but she vanished without a trace about four moons ago," Jiyata clarified.

I blinked. "Four moons ago would have been the middle of winter."

Jiyata nodded. "No one could figure out how she managed it, but she was here one day and gone the next."

If Suriken had been able to escape in the dead of winter without getting caught, then it meant there was a way. I had been honest when I said that I wasn't thinking of running away, but it was good to keep my options open.

"I'll tell Todicmadaya that you aren't well enough to go to market," Jiyata said, returning to the original subject.

"Thank you," I replied.

The next day, Yetta and I rose early, even though we wouldn't have nearly as much work as usual. Most of the slaves had the day off. Yetta informed me that those who were trusted were allowed to go into the city and enjoy the market unaccompanied.

"What will they do there?" I asked.

Yetta shrugged. "Be unruly. Sometimes they get a little work and earn a few coins. Then they can bet on the fights."

"I see," I replied, although her words were mystifying to me. "What are the fights like?"

Yetta shrugged as though the topic didn't interest her. "Two men fight to the death while those watching bet on who will be standing at the end."

"And they can find men willing to risk their lives?" I asked.

"Most don't have a choice," she responded. "They'll be killed if they don't fight."

"But some do choose it?"

Yetta nodded. "Just before Todicmadaya was born, there was a slave here who was a beast of a man. On his days off, he'd enter the fighting pits as a combatant."

"What happened to him?" I asked.

"He won," she answered. "He won a lot. Eventually, he managed to earn enough money to buy his freedom."

"Was that hard to do?" I wondered.

"Yes," Yetta nodded. "He had to kill nearly thirty men, most of them seasoned fighters. He became so well known that they wouldn't let him fight one-on-one duels anymore. They had to set him against at least two other men, or no one would bet against him."

"What did he do after he won his freedom?"

Yetta sighed. "There was a woman he loved, but she cost twice as much to free as he did, so he went back to the pits."

"He didn't win enough to free her," I guessed, taking in Yetta's expression.

"No," Yetta answered. "He died in a match less than four moons later."

"That's too bad," I said.

She shrugged. "That's life."

We spent the rest of the morning weaving new rush mats to cover the dirt floor in the main room. We took a break to prepare lunch for the slaves who had been left behind. The one with the shaven head came to the kitchen door to retrieve it. He was the same one who always collected food for the slaves. I had learned his name was Husanil and recalled Todd telling me that he was the head slave.

I guessed him to be in his late twenties, but the hardship of his life seemed to have aged him prematurely. His face was gaunt and his muscles stringy. There were scars across his back and legs.

When I asked, Yetta explained to me what was meant by "head slave".

"He's the most trusted of the slaves," she began.

"So, he doesn't get to have a day off because he has to watch the others?" I guessed.

"He and one of the others take turns," she told me. "Although Husanil does it more often than not. He gets certain privileges, but that means extra responsibilities."

I nodded. More privileges and responsibilities were something I understood very well.

We were working on dinner, and I found the task of cutting repetitive, so I continued the conversation.

"If his name is Husanil, does that mean he's from The House of the Warrior?" I asked.

"He is," Yetta replied. "But not everyone is as traditional as Lord Arshenn. Some born to one of the houses are named for gods

59

from the other. The Lord of the Brimming Lake himself is named for the wild one, though he is from The House of the King.

"Husanil was born into one of the greatest families of The House of the Warrior. However, his father did a very dishonorable deed and was disowned. As a result, his entire family was sold into slavery.

"Lord Arshenn paid a good deal more than he would usually spend on a slave to buy Husanil, who was only fourteen at the time."

"Why?" I wondered.

"He enjoys owning a member of such a prominent family, especially since they belong to The House of the Warrior. Twice in the years since, his relatives have tried to buy him back, but each time the sum Lord Arshenn named was exorbitant."

"Do the houses truly hate each other so much?"

Yetta shrugged. "Yes and no," she answered. "Some people do. Lord Arshenn is one of them, but that is more common among the powerful families. Those who dwell in the city don't think too much about it, since they work and live with those from the other house on a daily basis.

"Under the current Lord of the Brimming Lake, there has been a time of peace. It's one of the reasons Lord Arshenn dislikes him so much."

"What are the other reasons?" I wondered.

"When the last Lord of the Brimming Lake died, Lord Arshenn and Lord Tohoshin were the final two combatants in the tournament to determine who would represent The House of the King in the death duel," Yetta told me. "If Lord Arshenn had won, he would have only needed to triumph over the champion from The House of the Warrior to become Lord of the Brimming Lake himself. The defeat is something Lord Arshenn has never forgotten."

I nodded but didn't ask any more questions. Yetta had given me much to think about.

Jiyata, Arshenn, and their sons returned in the late afternoon. A pair of slaves were with them, guiding a horse and cart. They unloaded the supplies, and I helped put away the ones that went in the dwelling.

Male slaves were almost never permitted inside unless it was to deposit a load of firewood by the kitchen hearth or bring a bucket of water from the well.

As we cooked dinner, Jiyata told us about the market. Yetta didn't seem to care, but I listened with interest as she described the assortment of foods she'd seen and chosen for the household.

"Do they have other things at the market?" I asked.

"Of course. Everything you'd ever need is for sale on market day, from horses to knitting needles."

I couldn't imagine such a place, where items could be obtained by the exchange of small pieces of metal. In The Land of the Clan, if you needed something, it was requested, then, once approved, delivered to you. Of course, you didn't always get exactly what you wanted, since someone else made the choice for you. How many times had I hoped there would be fish for dinner and we'd had chicken instead?

A few mornings later, Jiyata roused me earlier than usual.

"Today is wash day," she announced.

Even though I didn't know what she meant, I nodded, climbed from the bed, and dressed quickly in some of Suriken's old clothes. She'd left nearly all of her few belongings behind when she'd fled. The clothes were about the right size, except I think she was quite a bit shorter than I was. The brown pants ended mid-calf, and only a few of the shirts were long enough. At least they covered the scar on my arm. I didn't want anyone to stare.

As I emerged into the main room, Yetta handed me a great bundle of clothing, then picked up one of her own. A moment later, Jiyata joined us from the men's rooms, carrying a third bundle.

No one else in the dwelling seemed to be awake, so we slipped quietly out into the early morning light.

I was surprised to see Husanil waiting for us just beyond the door. He had a large sack flung over his shoulder and a long staff, tipped with a metal point, in his hand. At first, I assumed he was going about his own work, but as we headed along the dirt road, I saw him fall into step behind us.

As the sun started to rise and the twilight gave way to dawn, I saw that we were not heading for the city, but to the west. I hadn't the faintest notion where Jiyata and Yetta could be leading me.

Home is in this direction, I thought.

I heard the river before I saw it. Soon, we were walking along its banks on a well-traveled path. It sloped up, and the ground beneath our feet turned into a hill. Yetta set a slow but steady pace as the trail grew steep. Just as the sun broke the horizon, we reached the crest of the hill.

I finally understood why these people called themselves The People of the Brimming Lake. At the top of the slope was a vast expanse of water, twice the size of the lake next to Riverside. It rested atop the rise, allowing only a small stream to escape down the hill we had just climbed.

I followed the water with my eyes. It flowed east, back the way we had come. For a moment, the low-hanging sun blinded me to all else, then I gasped. The river cut a path down through the distant city, dividing it in half. The brilliant morning light turned the streets of stone to gold. A haze was rising from the waters of the river, casting a sheen of glittering mist across all that lay below.

The course of the stream was so straight that I, standing beside the source, could see where it met the ocean several miles away. Or at least, I would have been able to if a massive building wasn't erected directly above the river at the far end of the city.

From one of Todd's stories, I recalled that it was the palace of The Lord of the Brimming Lake. Two other huge buildings rose on either side. They weren't as large as the palace itself but had great spires reaching into the sky. I suspected these were the temples for the king and the warrior.

Looking down on the vast structures from above changed my perspective. The day I'd been taken to the center of the city, I'd been fighting a fever and in too much pain to notice much of anything. Now, I could see the entire place at a glance. It was far larger than any one of our villages. There were also many dwellings set apart in clusters similar to the one where Todd's family lived.

"She's not listening," Yetta chuckled.

I turned to look at the two women. So enraptured was I by what lay before me that I'd forgotten where I was.

"I'm sorry," I apologized.

"It's all right," Jiyata told me lightly. "The awakening city is a beautiful sight."

We moved to the shores of the lake. Together, Jiyata and Yetta demonstrated how to wash the clothing we had brought. The cool lake water felt nice on my feet as the sun grew warm.

Although we were among the first to arrive, soon many other women, some with small children in tow, joined us on the banks of the lake. Jiyata and Yetta knew several of them.

I was introduced to a few, but none of the names stuck with me. Each group of women had an escort; most were slaves. Husanil joined a group of these. It seemed strange to me that so many men had come, but not a single one did any washing.

Just as we were finishing with our last few articles, a group of children and their mothers emerged from the same trail we'd climbed.

Without hesitation, the children leapt into the water and started chasing each other around the shallows. The scene reminded me of how the children used to play at Riverside. Images of Kisa, Rollan, and Joss sprang to my mind unbidden. Three friends I was never going to see again. I felt my chest tighten.

After we'd washed the last shirt, all the clothing had to be laid out in the sun. It was a good thing we had prepared breakfast and lunch for today the night before. Even though the sun was bright, I couldn't imagine the clothes would be dry in less than an hour. It seemed likely to be close to midday by the time we made it back to the dwelling.

While we waited, Jiyata chatted gaily with several of the other women washing nearby. Yetta listened but didn't speak much. I had little interest in gossiping, so I sat on the grass and enjoyed a few moments of peace.

I'm not sure how I heard it, but a sound, like that of hooves crushing leaves, reached my ears. I glanced around sharply; there were no horses at the lake.

Out of the corner of my eye, I saw something move. I looked toward the forest, which grew right up to the edge of the lake, about a hundred yards from where the women were washing.

I don't know why, but I sensed something was in the woods. Without realizing I had stood, I found myself on my feet. My eyes searched the spot, wondering if there was really something there or if I was just imagining it.

A few trees rustled even though the breeze was gentle. I glimpsed a dark form moving between a gap in the trunks. I only saw it for an instant, but I knew something was there.

I started forward, curious to see what it could be. I'd made it about a quarter of the way to the woods when a sudden cry from Jiyata brought me to a halt. She was hurrying toward me, Yetta following as fast as she could.

"What are you doing?" Jiyata asked.

I pointed to the spot where the movement had been. "Something's in there," I told her.

"That's very bad." Jiyata clutched my arm and started pulling me back toward the other women.

"Why?" I asked.

"Because it could be a mountain lion or some sort of monster," she answered with a frightened glance over her shoulder.

"Or," her voice dropped to a whisper. "It could be some boy trying to complete his rite of manhood.

"Here, by the lake, we are protected," Jiyata nodded toward where the men were standing. Almost all of them had a weapon of some sort in their hands or placed nearby.

"I think it's a horse," I murmured. Jiyata looked at me like I was crazy. I allowed her to guide me to where the laundry was spread on the grass and only glanced back at the dark trees once.

64

Soon the clothes were dry. We bundled them up and returned to the dwelling just in time to set out lunch and start cooking dinner.

CHAPTER 8
TORTURE

"Jiyata, Astra!" It was Arshenn calling us from outside.

I put down the chicken carcass from which I had been plucking feathers. Quickly, I rinsed my hands in the nearby bucket of water, then dried them. Jiyata had stepped out of the kitchen to answer Arshenn's call. Before I could follow her, she hurried back in, and we almost collided.

"They're going to spar," she told me quietly in response to my inquisitive glance.

I sighed. It was such a waste of time. Every day it was the same. Arkensallay and Todd would choose their weapons, spend about half an hour working each other down, then Arkensallay would defeat his brother.

While I'm certain it was good physical activity for the two combatants, I didn't understand why Jiyata and I were required to be present. Not that Arshenn called us every day, but at least every other.

Yetta watched us leave the dwelling without comment. I felt guilty that she was left to work alone in our absence.

Today, the boys were fighting with swords. I looked on indifferently as the long pieces of metal struck each other again and again. In contrast, Jiyata had both hands clasped over her heart and sometimes averted her eyes from her sons.

The slaves and apprentices had formed their customary circle around Arkensallay and Todd. Arshenn was close to them but stood back a few feet. It seemed that he preferred to watch Jiyata and me as opposed to the combatants. I had to admit, the fights were rather impressive. Arkensallay was powerful and rained down blows as fast as Todd could deflect them.

He always finished with the same series of thrusts that Todd was completely unable to defend against. I hadn't seen Todd win a single duel since the first day. I think he'd won others when I was struggling with the fever, but none since. If anything, Todd's abilities were steadily growing worse. Arkensallay, however, only seemed to get better.

Today was no different. Arkensallay used the same attack as usual, and Todd's sword dropped to the ground. Without hesitation, Arkensallay plowed straight into the disarmed Todd, shoulder first.

Arkensallay stood two inches taller and had at least fifty pounds on his brother. Todd hit the ground hard, and Arkensallay pressed his blade to his brother's throat. Jiyata let out an unconscious cry of concern. Arshenn glanced at her and smiled.

"Enough for today," he announced. The group began to disperse back to their work.

Usually, this was the end, but it seemed that Arshenn had more to say to his sons. I would have gone back inside, but Jiyata took an unconscious step forward. I was loath to leave her alone.

"I have carefully considered your request," Arshenn told Todd as he struggled to rise from the ground. Arkensallay's impact seemed to have knocked the breath right out of him. "I have decided that I do not wish to take on another apprentice at this time. You'll have to find a different mentor to teach you the art of blacksmithing."

Todd's face, which had been stoic and determined up to that point, fell slightly in disappointment. He didn't bother arguing but turned away and collected his sword from the ground.

"As if anyone would want someone as useless as him," Arkensallay said to his father.

Arshenn laughed. "Todicmadaya is welcome to seek, but he might have to go to The House of the Warrior–" Arshenn spat on the ground "–to find anyone willing to take him as an apprentice. I have certainly been telling all of my smith acquaintances how very worthless he is."

Todd pretended not to have heard them. He placed his sword inside the weapons cabinet, which was mounted on the outside wall of the forge. Arshenn locked it each night with a metal key before coming to dinner.

Jiyata appeared as though she would have liked to go to her younger son, but I could see Arshenn looking our way with his piercing gaze. Reaching out a hand, I touched Jiyata lightly on the arm. She remembered herself then, and we rejoined Yetta in the kitchen.

The next day, there was no duel. Todd left early in the morning and didn't return until after dinner. I heard Arshenn asking him where he'd been.

"Around," was Todd's only response.

In the morning, Todd was gone again before breakfast. Jiyata was relieved that a loaf of the bread we'd baked the night before was missing too. She reasoned that at least he was eating something.

I'd started to get into the rhythm of waking up early, cooking meals, mending clothing, and doing whatever else needed to be done. Nearly all of it was new to me, who had literally lived half my life in a stable and the rest on the back of a horse. Jiyata and Yetta taught me a great deal. I tried to return the favor by working hard and taking some of the burden off of them.

One day, I heard the sharp whinny of an agitated horse. I peered out one of the windows in the main room and caught sight of an enormous, white stallion being led by two of the slaves. One of them was Husanil. I'd never been told the names of the others, nor had I seen enough of them to tell them apart at a glance. From a distance, they all had the same rugged clothing, sunburnt skin, and dirty faces.

Each of the two men held one end of a long lead rope connected to the stallion's halter. It appeared that the pair were taking the horse to the forge.

"What's going on?" I asked no one in particular.

Neither Jiyata nor Yetta could give me an answer. The riddle was solved a moment later when Arshenn opened the door of the forge. One of his apprentices, Reeshon, I think, came out with a red-hot horseshoe clutched between a pair of iron tongs.

The stallion reared at their appearance, nearly dragging the men from the ground. Two more slaves rushed over to help get the beast under control.

The men managed to lead the startled animal into a tiny square enclosure. The fence-like sides were so close that the horse could not even turn around.

Arshenn lifted one of the stallion's hind legs with great care. Reeshon placed the hot metal against it and shook his head.

The glowing piece of metal was removed. Arshenn and Reeshon returned to the forge, while Husanil and the other men remained to keep an eye on the animal.

I turned away from the window.

Jiyata gave me a questioning glance.

"They're shoeing a horse," I reported. "A huge, white stallion."

Yetta merely nodded, but Jiyata said, "He's the finest of Lord Arshenn's herd."

"I bet he'd be a dream to ride," I commented, recalling his flowing muscles and powerful legs.

"No one, save Lord Arshenn, is permitted to ride him," Yetta told me.

Too bad, I thought wistfully, before returning to my work. The stallion lingered in my thoughts the rest of the afternoon.

When I opened my eyes, I was in a stable. It took me a moment to realize it was the eastern stable of The North Wind. But it was all wrong. The once familiar halls were empty. The air, which was usually sweet, had an acrid edge.

Wake up, I told myself uselessly.

I didn't know what this dream was going to entail, but I doubted it would be very good. The last time I'd stood here had been one of the worst days of my life.

There wasn't another living creature in sight, but I heard the soft buzzing of insects somewhere close at hand. I didn't move, refusing to try and find what horrors this dream held for me.

69

"Astra?" The voice belonged to Kisa.

My breath stopped.

No! I thought, closing my eyes. *No, please.*

I wanted no more dreams. I wanted to wake up. I wanted anything but to face this.

"Astra?" Kisa's voice was faint and full of panic. "Astra, help me! I need you!"

My eyes flew open, but everything was the same.

"Astra!" Pain and fear filled Kisa's voice. It was a dream, and I knew it was a dream, but I had to find her. The voice seemed to have come from a nearby stall. I darted to the door and threw it open, then gasped in shock.

Rollan's corpse was resting on a bed of hay, body torn apart and flies feasting on his flesh. His eyes were milky white, and the expression on his face was one of twisted horror.

I staggered back, trying not to be sick.

"Astra, save me!" Kisa's voice caused me to spin around. There were so many stalls, how would I find her?

I opened the first door I reached. Even though I was prepared for what I might find, I cried out in horror as I saw Cole's body in much the same state as Rollan's. His face had been sliced open, and only one of his blue eyes was visible. The other had been ripped away.

I sank to my knees. Why couldn't I wake up?

"Astra." My name was a whimper directly to my left. I rushed to the stall from which the sound had emanated. Another sickening sight awaited me, but this one wasn't human.

A goat was lying on the hay. Half its body was rotten and maggot-eaten, but the eyes were still open, and there was fresh blood on the straw.

The sudden impression that I'd seen something similar before swept over me. Then a strangled screech shattered the quiet of the stable. There were no words, only the horrible sound of someone I loved in pain.

"Kisa!" I called, rushing from door to door, desperately searching. At least now the stalls were empty.

70

Finally, I found her. She was lying on her back inside the last stall I entered. Todd was there too, crouching over her lifeless body. As I rushed forward, he looked up at me with wide, brown eyes.

"What have you done?" I screamed at him. My blood boiled as I saw the cold, pale face of my precious friend.

I'd come too late. I always came too late. In life and in dreams, I never managed to make it in time.

I sat up, gasping for air. The room was still dark. Only a tiny beam of moonlight made its way through the narrow window. It took me a moment to catch my breath.

Jiyata was sleeping in Arshenn's room that night, but Yetta sat up and looked over at me sharply.

I couldn't see much more than the ruffled outline of her hair in the dim light.

"I'm sorry," I whispered. "It was just a dream."

I assumed she'd lie back down, but instead, she got up and drew near to my bed.

"You have nightmares quite often," she observed.

I nodded. Due to the lack of light, I'm not certain she saw.

"I'm sorry–" I started again, but she cut me off before I could apologize.

"You are so young," Yetta began, in her deep, steady voice. "What evil have you witnessed for such ill dreams to haunt you?"

In the safety of the darkness, it would have been easy to pour out everything to this kind woman.

But I could not.

I guarded my secrets more closely than my life. So I only allowed a little bit of truth to come out of my mouth.

"I've lost my- friends," I whispered. "Five of them. They're all dead now, except for maybe one. And he's alone, just like me."

"I'm so sorry," Yetta replied. Slowly, she reached out and laid a hand on my shoulder. We remained that way for a time, then Yetta returned to her bed.

I felt better, but only a little. Sleep was the last thing I wanted, but there wasn't much choice since dawn was still hours away. Reluctantly, I settled back down.

In the morning, the first person I saw was Todd. The terrible dream hit me once more, and I felt the blood leave my face as our eyes met. I quickly dropped my gaze to the ground.

"Astra? What's wrong?" he demanded.

I shook my head and hurried away. It took half an hour for my stomach to stop churning and my breathing to return to its normal rhythm.

Even though I didn't see Todd for the rest of the day, every time I closed my eyes, his face appeared in my mind. The face I'd seen in my nightmare wasn't as he was now. It had been the way I'd seen him when we'd first met, innocent and frightened. The face I'd trusted.

The following day, Todd departed before the sun rose and was gone until it was nearly time for dinner. I heard him and Arkensallay sparing in the yard as I assisted in putting the finishing touches on the evening meal.

It wasn't long before the three men came in. A jagged cut on Todd's right arm, which was still oozing blood, clearly indicated who the victor had been. He passed through the kitchen wordlessly and headed down the hall to the main room, his father and brother close behind.

When Jiyata and I brought the food a moment later, I saw him sitting at the table, studying his plate, while Arshenn heaped praise on his older son for winning the combat.

As I set a tray of roast lamb on the table, Arshenn turned to Todd. "Any luck finding a blacksmithing master to teach you?" he asked.

"Yes," Todd answered, almost brightly.

"How many of your jewels did you have to trade him to take you on?" Arkensallay laughed. "Half of them?"

A twinge of resentment rose in my stomach. They weren't *his jewels.*

Todd shook his head. "I've only sold two. The apprenticeship didn't cost the price of even one."

"Must not be much of a blacksmith then," Arshenn commented coldly.

Todd didn't answer but merely sank further down in his chair.

Once we'd left the main room, I noticed a furrow in Jiyata's brow. She was also biting her lip distractedly. I took my seat beside Yetta, and we waited while Jiyata got a cup of water for herself.

Our meal was eaten in silence, as was the norm. We all kept a keen ear out in case the men should call.

After the main room had been abandoned, I helped Yetta clear the table. Gathering a stack of dishes, I headed for the kitchen. To my surprise, I found Todd there, speaking with Jiyata. As soon as he noticed me, he stopped talking.

Jiyata glanced up, eyes wide, but I hadn't overheard what they were saying. I set my load down and, when I turned back around, Todd had vanished.

"How is your leg?" Jiyata asked while I started drying the plates she was washing.

"Nearly perfect," I answered. She knew as well as I did that my leg was fully healed.

Jiyata nodded without looking at me. "It doesn't pain you?"

"No," I replied, her questions making me wary.

"Do you think you would be able to accompany us to market tomorrow?" she quietly asked.

I paused, the soaked plate I'd been handed dripping on the ground. A moment later, I resumed drying with twice as much vigor as before.

"Probably not," I answered smoothly. I'd turned down the invitation several times and had hoped she would stop asking me. Supposedly, market day was enjoyable, but I didn't care.

I glanced at Jiyata, knowing I was putting her in a hard position. She still wouldn't look at me. It felt wrong to cause this gentle, caring woman any form of distress. However, if Todd was

73

determined to use his mother to manipulate me, then what choice did I have?

CHAPTER 9
STRUGGLE

In the morning, I watched from the doorway of the kitchen as Arshenn, Jiyata, and the rest left for the market. I turned to where Yetta was grinding wheat for bread.

"Why does Jiyata always go to the market, and you always stay here?" I asked.

Yetta didn't look up. "The master of the house decides who goes, and he chooses Jiyata."

"I see," I answered.

We spent the morning and early afternoon working. There were plenty of tasks to be completed. It was peaceful and less oppressive with everyone gone. I started in the kitchen and didn't call it quits until every surface had been polished.

When I finished, I found Yetta focused on reordering one of the storerooms. I started trying to help her, but she directed me to work in the main room. I removed all the woven mats from the floor and swept up the loose dirt.

The mats I carried outside and shook until they were free of dust. After I replaced them, Yetta and I took a break to eat a late lunch. It was a simple meal, just the leftovers from the supper of the night before.

Husanil had taken all the slaves to watch the combats at the fighting pits, so we didn't have to feed anyone other than ourselves.

Yetta and I spoke very little during our repast. She didn't have the same shy, quiet air as Jiyata, but rarely voiced any opinion without being asked. Today, I was content to leave the silence unbroken.

Perhaps it was because of this silence, or maybe it was because many years of living in a stable had made me more attuned to such sounds, but as I set down my water cup, I heard something that made my heart skip a beat. It was the cry of a horse in pain.

In an instant, I'd abandoned my lunch and was out the door.

"Astra?" I heard Yetta call behind me.

I sprinted toward the noise. It emanated from across the semicircle of buildings, where the stable stood. The door was closed, latch down. I fumbled with it for a moment.

"Astra, you aren't supposed to go in there," Yetta called as she followed me across the yard.

The door wasn't locked, just stuck. With a tremendous thrust, I pushed it open, heedless of Yetta's warning.

Inside, I saw Arkensallay's mare lying on the ground. Her bulging sides were heaving as a low moan came from her throat.

Yetta, who had reached my side, froze in shock at the sight, but I leapt forward. It wasn't normal for horses to deliver their foals on the ground. I was by the mare's side in a moment. She laid back her ears, but I ignored the hostile gesture. The poor creature was hardly in any position to resist my assistance. I placed a hand gently on her neck and ran it all the way down the length of her body.

"Easy, pretty girl," I breathed, checking her all over for signs of what was causing her distress.

"How long has she been pregnant? Ten months? Eleven?" I asked, glancing over my shoulder. Yetta just shook her head helplessly.

I turned back to the mare and laid my palm on her flank, hoping to feel the baby move. If it were dead, my method of treatment would change significantly.

"You should leave it," Yetta told me, drawing a step nearer.

"She might die," I replied. "No one else is here. If they were, they would have heard her cries."

Yetta shook her head. "It's no business of yours," she tried again.

76

I looked up at her sharply. "Well, it is now. You can go back to the dwelling and pretend not to have seen anything, or you can assist me. Your choice." My voice was confident, but I desperately needed someone's help.

Yetta glanced between me and the mare a few times, then slowly nodded, which I took for assent.

"Excellent, please boil a pot of water. Bring that and some soap to me as soon as it's ready." Yetta hurried back toward the kitchen without a word.

I stood and made a quick inventory of the stable. All I managed to find was a knife with a decent blade, which I hoped I wouldn't need to use for anything but the umbilical cord.

When Yetta returned, I scrubbed my hands with the soap and washed them in the water. I hadn't birthed a lot of foals. Most of the time, the mares delivered during the night, and the baby wasn't found until morning.

Only during two of the births I'd witnessed had there been any serious complications. In the first, the head had appeared before the second leg. We'd had to force the mare to walk until the foal shifted enough for both front legs to find their way out.

The other case hadn't gone as well. The placenta separated too early. We did everything we could but were too late, and by the time the foal was born, it was already dead.

With that in mind, I carefully reached into the mare, feeling for the baby. I'd never done this part, but I'd observed it on occasion. Often, whoever was assisting with the birth would describe in detail the exact steps they were taking. I tried to recall everything I'd heard.

My hand found something hard, a hoof. The foal didn't respond to my touch for a moment, and then it gave a tremendous kick. The mare whinnied shrilly in response.

As I felt above the hoof, I determined that it was a hind leg. That wasn't good. It meant the foal was breech.

Another hoof brushed against my hand. I furrowed my brow in confusion. This one was a front foot. The poor foal was completely twisted up in the womb. If I couldn't get it straightened out, the little thing would get caught on the mare's pelvis due to the contractions' constant pushing. Then half the foal would come out, while the other half would remain firmly wedged in the birth canal. The baby would die of asphyxiation, and the mare wouldn't have much of a chance for survival either.

I attempted to secure both the front legs, but I couldn't find the second one. The mare cried out in pain as a long spasm shook her body. I felt the foal move a few inches. Time was running out for the hapless pair. One leg would have to do. I latched onto the front hoof and started pulling. At first, nothing happened, then I felt the foal begin to shift.

The mare kicked with both hind legs, connecting with the side of her stall. The sudden noise made Yetta jump; I'd nearly forgotten she was beside me.

I tried to go more slowly, but I worried that we were already past the point of saving the mother and baby. As another contraction occurred, I attempted to move with it, pulling the front leg forward and hoping the foal would straighten out.

It didn't help. With every breath the mare drew, she was pushing her child into a tighter and tighter space. In an almost panic, I yanked as hard as I could. The foal struck out in response. Its hind legs seemed to move back a bit.

"That's it, little one," I whispered, pulling again. The foal didn't kick, but I was able to turn it slightly.

Sweat was running down my forehead, and I was panting from the exertion of my efforts. The foal flailed its legs, and I lost my grip.

"No," I hissed, feeling blindly for something to hold onto. My hand touched a leg. It wasn't the same one I'd had, but it was a front leg, so I held on.

The foal struggled, and I pulled, shifting it closer to the birth canal. I wasn't sure exactly how its body was positioned, but I hoped we were making some progress.

Something brushed my hand, so soft and delicate it had to be the head. The foal was straightening out, but there was still a long way to go.

The mare sucked in a great breath as the largest spasm yet ran down her body. I heaved while the foal fought wildly. In anguish, the mare struck her feet against the wooden stall once more.

A moment of stillness followed, broken by a sudden gasp from Yetta. I looked to see what had alarmed her and realized we weren't alone. Arshenn, Arkensallay, Todd, and Jiyata were visible at the stable entrance.

Arkensallay was in front. His eyes met mine.

"What do you think you're doing?" He sprang forward with a cry.

His tone and charging form startled the mare. She struggled for a moment, as if to regain her feet, but gave up and fell back just as quickly.

Arkensallay didn't notice the alarm he'd caused. Instead, he seized me and attempted to drag me away from the mare.

I lost my grip on the foal, who had started thrashing when the mare began to rise. Just as I was pulled away, I felt something rip, accompanied by a gush of blood. The mare's shrill screech was terrifying.

I think Arkensallay was yelling something, but I didn't have time to pay any attention to him.

With the placenta torn, the foal would die in minutes. I'd put too much work into saving the pair for it to end like this. With all my strength, I twisted away from Arkensallay. The movement took him by surprise, and I managed to escape his clutches.

I threw myself back at the mare, reaching for the foal once more. Arkensallay was right behind me. I felt his hand fall on my shoulder. He was going to pull me away again.

"It's suffocating!" I screamed at him. Something in my tone made him falter, and he released me.

I found a front foot and pulled. There was no more time. If the foal didn't come now, it would be too late. My hand was slick with blood, and the baby was fighting me with everything it had.

Keep fighting, I thought. *Don't give up; don't stop struggling.*

The mare contracted, the foal lashed out with all four legs, and I pulled. My hand and a hoof emerged. A moment later, the second hoof followed, and right behind it was the head.

I heaved a sigh of relief. The foal could breathe. Even now, I saw its delicate nostrils flare as it took its first breath.

I kept a hold of the hoof and pulled whenever a spasm took the mare, but the hard part was done. Less than five minutes later, the foal was resting on the straw-covered floor.

In wonder, I watched as the small creature lifted its head and looked around at its new world.

The mare rose, careful not to step on the foal. Her white flanks glistened with sweat and blood. There was foam around her mouth and on her chest. Gently, she began cleaning the afterbirth from her baby.

I smiled at the sight and glanced at the others. Yetta and Jiyata were nowhere to be seen. Arkensallay was scowling down at me from where he stood, looking over my shoulder.

Arshenn's expression was more passive, but I wouldn't go so far as pleased. He was looking at the horses, not me. Todd was standing beside him, wearing his now-customary perturbed expression.

Arshenn was the first to speak. "Is it male or female?" he asked Arkensallay.

Arkensallay leaned forward to look. "It's a colt," he announced.

"Excellent," Arshenn said to his son, before turning on me. "Now, girl from the stars, tell me where exactly you learned to assist in the birthing of a foal."

"I–" The question took me completely by surprise. "Is it not natural for a female to be educated in such things?" I countered.

"Horses are very different from women," he returned.

"True. However, the process of giving birth is fundamentally the same." I hoped he would come to the conclusion that I had acted out of instinct rather than experience.

80

"Funda- what?" Arkensallay asked as Arshenn gave me a hard look. He suspected something. I didn't know exactly what. However, I had a bad feeling his mind might eventually light upon the truth, and the secret existence of my people would be discovered.

CHAPTER 10
DINNER PARTY

Yetta and Jiyata both sprang to their feet as I entered the kitchen, their eyes wide with horror.

"What did they do to you?" Yetta gasped.

I blinked. "Nothing."

"Then what's all that blood?" Jiyata wondered.

I glanced down and realized for the first time that both arms were red past the elbows, and my maroon shirt was stained nearly black.

"It's not mine," I told them. "It's from the mare."

"And is she—" Jiyata trailed off suggestively.

"She'll be fine," I answered the unspoken question. "Her and the colt."

"Colt?" Yetta asked.

"The foal, it was a male," I explained.

"Of course," muttered Yetta sourly.

I paused, uncertain of her meaning.

"Let's get you cleaned up," Jiyata suggested, breaking the uncomfortable silence.

It wasn't hard to get the blood off my skin. The only place it lingered was beneath my fingernails. However, my shirt and pants were beyond hope, so I put on more of Suriken's old things.

One of the slaves who had gone to market with the family returned about half an hour later with their purchases. I helped unload the supplies into the kitchen.

"This seems like more than usual," Yetta commented, eyeing the pile of food.

"Oh, in all the excitement, I forgot to tell you that we met Lord Rettrin by the king's temple. Lord Arshenn invited him to dine with us tomorrow night. He will be bringing his whole family."

Yetta nodded. "Doesn't he have a daughter the right age to marry off?"

"He does. Her name is Jiycess."

"Is she lovely?" Yetta asked.

"Very," answered Jiyata.

"What does that have to do with dinner tomorrow?" I wondered.

Both women paused, as if unsure how to answer my question.

"Well, you see," Jiyata started. "If Lord Rettrin brings his daughter here tomorrow and she is pleasing, there is a chance he may want to sell her as a wife."

I opened my mouth to say something, then decided against it. Perhaps Jiyata's way of explaining things had come off sounding harsher than it was, or maybe I needed to start realizing what a broken place I had come to. Either way, I would find out tomorrow night.

As it turned out, the dinner was considered a *family* affair, and I was expected to attend. This was the first time I'd eaten in the main room instead of the kitchen.

Arshenn and Rettrin each sat at one end of the long table. On Arshenn's left was Jiyata, next to her was Yetta and then me. Arkensallay sat on his father's right, with Todd beside him.

It was the opposite for Rettrin. He had his two life mates, I'd heard there was a third at home with an infant, on his right and his children on the left.

Of the children, the oldest was the girl, Jiycess. The way Jiyata and Yetta had talked about her, I'd assumed she would be a little older than I was, but she couldn't have been more than fourteen. She was slender, with fine, blonde hair falling halfway down her back. Her eyes were hazel and set perfectly in her round face.

She was seated the farthest from her father, next to Todd and directly across from me. On her other side were two boys, between eight and eleven, and another girl of perhaps five.

One of the boys was blond, like his older sister. The other had curly, brown hair, as did the five-year-old.

Looking at the two wives, it was easy to see which of the children belonged to each. Jiycess spoke only when asked a direct question and spent the entire meal looking at her lap.

The other three children were much more animated, particularly the boys. Sitting still was a great hardship for them. More than once, a stern glance from their father caused them to freeze, only to start wiggling again the moment his eyes had turned away.

I didn't speak once. In fact, not a single one of the women did, unless directly addressed by one of the men. Even when the blond little boy loudly demanded his mother tell him when they were going home, she only smiled and nodded at him.

Jiyata, Yetta, and I had spent all day preparing the meal. It turned out quite grand. An entire roast piglet was the centerpiece, surrounded by plates of steamed vegetables in delicious sauces.

I hadn't had much of an appetite for days. Even though the food smelled and looked delicious, I hardly tasted any of it.

Most of my attention was focused on the men's discussion. Arshenn and Rettrin conversed loudly from either end of the table. Occasionally, Arkensallay would interject. Todd remained almost entirely silent, but I did notice him make a few comments to Jiycess from time to time.

She smiled politely but gave little reply. Only once did she go so far as to look him full in the face.

When the meal was concluded, I rose to help Yetta and Jiyata clear the table. The other two women assisted us as well. Soon we'd gotten everything into the kitchen.

"What do you think, Jiyata?" the blonde woman asked. "Is Lord Arshenn of a mind to buy my daughter as a wife?"

"I'm not certain," Jiyata answered softly, glancing toward the other room. "Arkensallay hasn't taken much interest in her."

The mother of Jiycess shook her golden locks. "I was hoping that would be the case," she admitted. "He seems far too much of a brute for little Jiycess. However, Lord Rettrin is excited by the prospect of joining our house with yours. Might you be able to persuade Lord Arshenn to take her for your other son, Todicmadaya?"

Jiyata shook her head. "I'm sorry, Zertil, but Lord Arshenn has not been pleased with Todicmadaya of late. I doubt he would make any sort of motion on his behalf."

"Really?" asked the other woman, who had curly, brown hair. "I thought he had won much renown during his rite of manhood."

"He did," Jiyata told them proudly. "But Lord Arshenn makes him and Arkensallay battle each day. To me, it only makes sense that the older and larger would win, but my master does not see it that way. He seems only able to love his sons one at a time. Whoever has been victorious that day, he praises, and the other he scorns. Todicmadaya loses every day."

A sigh escaped Zertil. "Jiycess is such a tender young child; I worry for her. Todicmadaya seemed the gentler of the two, and I had hope–" The woman cut off. "Well, I suppose it was silly. He is a second son and has not yet established himself."

"It's a pity Jiycess is so beautiful," the brown-haired woman commented.

For a moment, I wondered if she was being facetious, but the other three women all nodded their agreement.

"Lord Rettrin really does have affection for the child," Zertil told us. "But even that won't stop him from trying to use her to his advantage."

Just then, we heard a burst of rancorous laughter from the other room. Jiyata sighed. "I believe they have brought out the wine.

I was the last one to re-enter the main room.

"What's wine?" I whispered to Yetta, who was just in front of me.

"Alcohol," she spoke the word by way of definition, but I still didn't comprehend.

"It's a drink made from grapes," she added, taking in my blank expression. "It has the power to make men lose their senses."

I wanted to ask more, but we were in the main room by then. Each of the men had a large, wooden cup in front of him.

Whatever they were drinking seemed to have made them all happier than usual. I glanced at Todd. His cheeks were flushed and his eyes bloodshot. He was laughing and joking with his brother, who was in much the same state.

"And so–" Rettrin appeared to be finishing an account of something foolish he'd done in his youth.

"I grabbed one goat under each arm and took off running. The man from The House of the Warrior came chasing after me, waving his pitchfork, but I didn't stop. The two goats were struggling and bleating as I reached the river. I leapt straight in–"

"Tried to jump over and fell in, you mean," Arshenn interrupted.

Both men bellowed with laughter. It was chorused by all the children, except Jiycess.

"Fine, fell in, then. The goats went stock still from terror. The man who the goats belonged to didn't follow me. I doubt he could swim, but he stood on the bank and yelled such obscenities that I almost turned around and offered to duel him to the death.

"However, that would have meant giving up the goats. I finally reached the other shore and pulled myself and the goats from the river. Their fur was sodden, so they weighed twice as much as they had dry. I carried them home and placed them in the little field I'd prepared.

"They were to be the start of my fortune. From them, I hoped to grow a huge herd. But–" The man cut off with a dry chuckle. "It wasn't until that moment that I realized they were both males!"

Howls of laughter emanated from all around the table. Only the women remained passive.

Rettrin laughed until he was out of breath, then took a long swig from the cup in front of him. It left a red stain on his lips as if he were drinking blood. A moment later, he wiped it away with his forearm.

To my surprise, his eyes turned to me. "So, this is the girl from the stars everyone is talking about?"

"Indeed," Arshenn answered. "So it has been told."

Rettrin nodded. "I wasn't in the square when Todicmadaya completed his rite. The account of his adventures has been passed from mouth to mouth, but I should very much like to hear it from his own lips."

Arshenn glanced at Todd. "It appears that will have to wait until another time," he commented.

It was only then that I noticed Todd was having trouble remaining upright. One of his elbows rested on the table as he tried to balance his head on the adjoining hand. His eyes were glazed, and there was no spark in them.

I glanced at Jiyata. She wore a slightly troubled expression, but since she didn't spring to her feet, I doubted anything could be too much the matter with him.

"Well, perhaps we can hear the story from the girl then," Rettrin suggested, turning to me.

I hesitated, waiting until it was clear I was supposed to answer for myself.

"I am not much of a storyteller," I replied. "I would never be able to do the tale justice."

A moment of silence followed my declaration. I fervently hoped they wouldn't insist I repeat the story. I wasn't confident I would be able to recall all the particulars, thus giving away its untruthful nature.

As I awaited their decision, Todd attempted to rise from his seat. He was unsuccessful and ended up toppling to the ground. Everyone turned to look, myself included. Todd was many things, but never clumsy. I watched in shock as he tried to regain his feet, only to fall again.

Arshenn, Arkensallay, and Rettrin burst into laughter. "He's had more than is good for him!" Rettrin bellowed.

"It is his first time. He appears to have outdone himself," Arshenn agreed. "Take him to bed, Arkensallay."

Grudgingly, Arkensallay rose, none too steadily himself. He half-carried the reeling Todd from the room.

With the distraction gone, Rettrin turned back to me almost at once. "If you, girl from the stars, will not tell me your story, then perhaps I shall tell you some of our history. Would it interest you to hear how our people came to The Brimming Lake?"

CHAPTER 11
FOUNDERS

I nodded, eager to shift the focus of the conversation from myself even though I'd heard this story before. Todd had told me once about the woman, Perdita, and how she traded her life to save her people.

As Rettrin began speaking, I expected to hear a similar, if not identical, account, but his story began much further back than Todd's.

"When the world was young, mankind dwelt in peace, but they were scattered and without direction. The gods watched over them as they grew more powerful and learned the art of war.

"More kingdoms were forged and forgotten than there are stars in the sky. Through it all, the humans of the earth remembered the gods and sacrificed to worship them.

"Arsh was the unchallenged king in those days. He ruled supreme with his best friend, Husam, and his queen, Jiya, at his side.

"As the centuries passed, mankind spread out across the face of the earth. Their armies grew larger and their weapons more deadly. They began to believe themselves all-powerful. The memory of the gods slipped from their minds as water flowing out of The Brimming Lake passes to the sea.

"Enraged, the eight gods descended to the earth and ravaged the greatest city of man. Even after its destruction, they were not satisfied and began to hunt the remaining humans, determined to eradicate our entire race.

"The father of our people, Peter, was among these, but he was old and could not flee far. He alone had the courage to meet the gods and speak to them on behalf of the people. His humility and faithfulness convinced Arsh to relent and grant the human race a second chance.

"Arsh and the other gods realized their actions had been rash. They constructed a new home for mankind, The Untouchable Land, also called Edden, the place that the gods swore never to destroy.

"Generous as Arsh had been, his mercy did not change the hearts of those who entered into the land he created. There was a corrupt one, a betrayer, in Edden who corrupted many others as one sickly goat infects the entire flock.

"Those who listened to the betrayer fell prey to jealousy. They saw the beautiful land created by the gods and wanted it for themselves. The portion they had been given was not enough to satisfy their greed.

"These corrupted inhabitants of Edden, led by the betrayer, thought themselves better than all the others. They were very learned, although most of their knowledge had been lost when the great city was destroyed.

"Together, they conspired to take control of Edden, knowing the weak-willed would follow them like sheep. The gods were infuriated by their arrogance. Even still, they had given their word not to interfere.

"However, our ancestors, led by Peter, were still loyal to the gods. He refused to yield, but there were far too few of them to resist. Peter attempted to reason with those who had been corrupted. He begged them not to taint the god's blessings.

"The betrayer found him and stabbed him in the back.

"His two sons and their followers were exiled, driven away from the only home they had left.

"The anger of Arsh burned against mankind because of what those in The Untouchable Land had done. He had offered them a second chance, and they had scorned it.

"Arsh no longer believed that humankind deserved to live. So he attacked our ancestors since he could not eliminate those in Edden. Many perished, for Arsh made the sun grow hot and angry, killing plants and tainting the water. The two sons and those following them were forced to hide beneath stone. They could only venture out for a few hours at dawn and dusk to search for food. Sickness and disease were rampant, and many perished.

"Peter's sons were strong and clever. They were the ones who began worshipping the warrior.

"Arsh could not bear to see them praise Husam instead of himself. He would have smote the people out of existence, but Husam intervened on their behalf. He found that he liked receiving the praises of men.

"This is how the feud between the gods began. It has continued ever since. The war of the gods was terrible. The sons and those loyal to them made a run for it, following a map they had brought with them from Edden.

"Eventually, they reached The Brimming Lake and led our people to its shores. They discovered a forgotten haven to use for shelter where they could hide from the wrath of the gods. Within this haven, they found food and water.

"The people newly come to The Brimming Lake resumed worship of the gods. However, they were now divided. Half continued to praise Husam, for it was he who saved them from Arsh. The other half reverted to worshiping the king, recognizing him as the true ruler of the gods, only turned against them by the betrayer.

"After many generations, Arsh's heart was turned toward our ancestors again because of their faithfulness. At least, it was turned toward those who called him king. For their sake, he made the sun gentle and the land fertile so that our people could venture out of the haven and begin to live in the world again.

"They built our great city, the temples, the palace, and everything else. Though we continue to strive one house against the other, the conflict has made us strong, as conflict always does, and we are a great people once more.

"However, we must be careful never to turn away from the gods again."

Rettrin drew to the end of his story. I sat in silence with the others, contemplating. The little, curly-haired girl had fallen asleep with her head resting on the table. The boys beside her were paying strict attention to their father.

Out of the corner of my eye, I could see Arkensallay slumped in his chair with a glazed look on his face.

Rettrin took a drink of his wine, then turned to me once more. "That is how The People of the Brimming Lake lost Edden. Many have set out in quest of it; few have ever returned. It is said that one day our people will return and conquer the land that should have belonged to our ancestors."

I blinked slowly and wondered what Rettrin would do if he found out about The Land of the Clan. I decided it would be better never to find out.

"Look how deeply she ponders your words," Arshenn commented to his friend before turning to me. "Have you heard the facts differently?"

"Slightly," I admitted.

Arshenn and Rettrin exchanged a quick glance. Even though the two had consumed more wine than either Arkensallay or Todd, they didn't seem dazed in the least.

"Tell us," Rettrin ordered.

I licked my lips and began slowly. "I heard that it was a woman named Perdita who had a vision showing her a place of safety. She drew the map, which her brothers followed after she disappeared."

Arshenn's stiff posture relaxed.

"Is that all?" Rettrin asked, more to himself than to me.

I nodded.

"No one really knows where the map the brothers followed came from, but they had no sister. Those are lies spread by women to make themselves feel important. Do not dwell on such tales," Arshenn told me. He gave Yetta and Jiyata a scathing glance. I wondered if I should admit that Todd was the one who had told me the story.

I didn't get a chance because the next moment, Arshenn and Rettrin had struck up a lively conversation. Arkensallay was roused from his stupor by the volume of their voices and joined in, as did the two younger boys, all talking over each other.

Even as I sat quietly amidst the jubilant conversation, I could feel the keen eyes of Arshenn watching me.

The rest of the dinner passed uneventfully. Arkensallay fell into a deep sleep shortly thereafter. Arshenn and Rettrin continued drinking and laughing long into the night.

Finally, the other family departed, allowing Jiyata, Yetta, and me to get some sleep. It was much later than usual, so we left the cleanup for the morning.

Several days later, I accompanied Jiyata and Yetta to The Brimming Lake. We weren't washing clothes this time, only blankets and bedding. Husanil had, once again, come along as escort.

The sun was bright and surprisingly hot for such an early hour. I could not remember it having rained even once since I'd arrived here, but the lake was still full of water. Maybe it did not rain in this land, but no, that couldn't be correct.

Every day when the slaves returned for lunch, burnt by the sun and dripping with sweat, they grumbled about the weather because they had to haul water to the fields for the crops.

I was having trouble being bound to the dwelling. Now that my wound was closed, I'd started feeling cooped up. I would have liked to see the fields or spend some time in the stable, but I was certain those activities would be frowned upon.

Wash day was my one chance to be outside and feel the sun on my face. From the banks of the lake, I could look down on the city below and see all the way to the ocean, where hundreds of boats cast their nets for fish.

We did not remain long once the sheets and blankets had dried. I rued returning to the dwelling, the sight of the city and the waters beyond still fresh in my head.

The ocean. What I wouldn't have given to walk on the hot sands and hear the rhythmic lapping of the waves. Sometimes, when the wind was blowing just right, I could close my eyes and smell just a hint of salt on the breeze.

Two days later, I entered the sleeping room and found Jiyata and Yetta talking quietly. They cut off abruptly when I entered.

Jiyata didn't waste any time in coming to the point.

"Will you go to market with us the day after next?" she asked directly. Before I even had a chance to answer, she rushed on, "It would be very wise to agree. For now, it is only a request. You can gain favor by responding in the proper manner."

It took me several seconds to process what she had said and consider.

"I'll go," I assented softly.

Jiyata looked overjoyed. "You'll love the market," she promised me. "There's so much to see! You might even be able to make a few friends."

Not likely, I thought. Friends had been hard enough to come by in my own land. I couldn't imagine finding one here. Besides, they were just another thing that could be taken away.

I glanced swiftly at Yetta. She had turned and was settling down in her bed. I wondered what she thought of my response. Did she long to join us as well? Or was she just as happy to be left in peace?

I stood on the beach, my bare feet just inches above the swell of each wave. Unmoving, I stared out toward the east, where the endless expanse of both water and sky stretched on as far as could be seen.

The sun and the wind were to my back. Several strands of my hair flitted around my face, but I ignored them. I was so happy to be here once again. Above my head, a pair of silver birds wheeled. Every so often, one would let out a shrill cry.

Someone approached me from behind.

"Is it time to go?" I asked, turning toward the person.

I froze. I'd been expecting Todd or Jiyata, but the eyes looking back at me were gray.

"Myra," I whispered.

She didn't answer but stood beside me.

"Do you think they actually touch?" she asked, looking across the sapphire waves.

"I–"

"The heavens and the sea," she clarified. "Or do they both go on forever?"

"I don't know," I answered. "But I don't think anything goes on forever."

Myra didn't respond.

"Except," I started again. "Except greed and hatred. Those things have always been and always will be. In all of Todd's stories and even the history of The Clan, there is nothing but the misery they cause."

"And in your life?" Myra asked.

"My life?"

She nodded.

"I have had two constant companions throughout my life, loneliness and sorrow. They are all I know, and I will never escape them."

CHAPTER 12
MARKET

I opened my eyes and, for a moment, I could still hear the waves and feel the sand under my feet while the sun warmed my skin.

My desire to see the city had vanished. I didn't want to get up, didn't want to move; all I wanted was to be left alone with the only two companions I had ever known. But I'd said I'd go, and there was sure to be a fuss if I didn't.

Slowly, I swung my feet around and put them on the dirt floor. Yetta and Jiyata were just beginning to stir as well. I dressed quickly, pulling on a dark pair of pants. I wasn't sure of the exact color in the half-light of dawn. The shirt was dark too, probably close to black.

The three of us headed to the kitchen, where we packed a lunch for those going to the market. I cringed internally as Jiyata and I left the dwelling to join the group assembling outside.

Arshenn was giving instructions to one of the slaves who was staying behind. Arkensallay had yet to appear, but Todd was watching the door as if waiting for our appearance.

Jiyata took the bag of food and gave it to Husanil. He and another slave were to accompany us. Husanil took the bundle and set it in the back of a small cart. The second slave was holding the bridle of the rugged-looking horse harnessed to it. The gelding was old, with a dull coat, but there was still a proud arch in his neck.

We departed a few moments later, as the first ray of sunlight broke upon the horizon. Arkensallay hurried from the dwelling just in time to take the lead with his father. To my surprise, Jiyata walked close beside them, nearly brushing shoulders with Arshenn. I followed, and Todd fell into step on my right.

The path to the city wasn't as long as I remembered. During our walk, Arshenn and Arkensallay conversed freely. Even Jiyata was brought into the conversation. Maybe Arshenn was in a better humor than usual, or perhaps the family dynamics changed on market day.

I had my answer not ten minutes later. We were walking along the river, approaching one of the bridges, when Arshenn stopped to speak with a man. I got the impression that the two were new acquaintances. Arshenn introduced the whole family, starting with Jiyata.

When he turned to Todd, he said, "This is my fine son, Todicmadaya. He has only just completed the rite of manhood, but the way in which he did leaves no doubt of the honor he will achieve for his family. Truly, he is one who is worthy of being part of The House of the King."

Arshenn had never said anything of the kind regarding Todd before in my presence. His voice sounded sincere, but I knew the true feelings he was repressing.

As soon as the man had taken his leave of us, Todd turned to his father. "With your permission, I would like to show Astra some of the city."

Arshenn thought for a moment, rubbing his chin with one hand. "There have been reports of men from The House of the Warrior making attacks on those they consider easy prey," he remarked.

"I am certain I can look after myself and Astra," Todd announced.

Arshenn feigned concern. "I'd like to believe so, but when I think of how many combats you have lost to your brother, who is but one person, I cannot trust your words."

Todd's face fell.

"I have a brilliant idea," Arshenn went on. "Why doesn't Arkensallay go with you? That way, I know you will be safe."

Arkensallay looked about as pleased with that suggestion as Todd was. However, neither argued, since it was clear to see how pointless that would be.

"Fine," Arkensallay grumbled. "But we're going to make this quick."

The three of us surged ahead, leaving the rest of the party to follow in our wake. The streets were getting more and more crowded as the city woke up. I could see people setting up little tables full of fruits and vegetables. It was still strange for me to think that the people here traded bits of metal for food.

Arkensallay fell behind as Todd led us swiftly to the outskirts of the city.

"Look, Astra," he said, pointing to a small building. It was a one-story structure with two chimneys, neither of which were releasing so much as a trickle of smoke.

"That's where I'm apprenticed," Todd announced.

Arkensallay burst out laughing. "There?" he asked. "Really? Well, that just figures."

I did not understand his mirth and glanced at Todd for an explanation. Todd was too busy scowling at his brother to notice. Arkensallay gave him a petulant grin. Todd turned on his heel and continued down the street.

"I see there's a tavern across the way," Arkensallay called after him. "Been stopping there after you finish your work?"

Todd ignored him.

"Come on," he called to me over his shoulder.

I followed Todd and was more than a little pleased to see Arkensallay heading into the building he had called a tavern. It appeared he wasn't going to be bothered with us anymore.

I didn't try to catch up to Todd, but he slackened his pace until we were next to each other. The street with the forge on it had been nearly vacant. After taking several different turns, we were soon surrounded by a throng of people.

Todd and I hadn't really spoken all morning. Now that we were finally alone, minus the crowd bustling about on all sides, he turned to me.

"Do you want to see the temples?" he asked. "They're next to the palace, so I can show you that as well."

I vaguely remembered that both locations had come into several of Todd's stories from the history of The People of the Brimming Lake.

"All right," I agreed. The part of me that had wondered about Todd's people and their culture was curious to see what the palace and temples would be like.

We found our way back to the river. The city's main road seemed to run straight along it, with many other pathways sprouting off toward the south. The entire stretch of the river was probably between two and three miles. This city was far more vast than any of my people's. It was nearly all made of stone.

One of the tables we passed was covered with unusual items. They were small rectangles, of what I wasn't sure, but each looked like images of the real world.

"What are those?" I asked Todd, pointing.

"Those are paintings," he answered. "Remember that drawing of the horse, Rykis? It's just like that, but with more color, so it looks more realistic."

It had been an image of Rysa, Rykis's brother, actually, and I did remember his drawing. On one side had been the image of the horse, and on the other was the map Todd made of our land. In all the confusion, he'd left without it. I hoped he never tried to make another. That kind of information was dangerous.

As we continued along, following the river toward the ocean, Todd began pointing things out to me. I'd already noticed a few statues. I found it unnerving the way they seemed to watch me with lifeless eyes. Some were of people, some were of animals, and there were a few I couldn't place.

The entire city was built on a slope. In the distance, I could see what Todd called the palace for half an hour before we reached it. Even when I had first looked upon the structure from the banks of The Brimming Lake, I'd been able to tell it was massive. The stones from which it was constructed were nearly as tall as I was, creating walls that rose at least fifty feet high. The building easily spanned the width of the river. Ten steps led up to a large, open platform, which also bridged the river. Pillars rose like great oaks from the stone beneath our feet. These supported the second floor of the palace, which overhung the platform.

I had counted dozens of bridges along the length of the river. Each was a few yards wide, arching above the water with rails on the sides.

The open space before us had no railing. If you fell off into the river, you would be carried directly under the palace.

"The first floor is smaller than the others," Todd told me, pointing. This much was evident since the expanse and pillars took up half the footprint of the structure.

Todd started walking across the platform, only stopping when he was standing over the very center of the river. I followed, and we stood facing the palace. At such close quarters, it was impossible to take in the entire structure.

Gesturing to a staircase leading to a pair of giant, wooden doors, Todd said, "That's where the meeting room is. When The Lord of the Brimming Lake needs advice, he calls together some of the lords from both houses.

"They gather in that room and give him their advice, not that he often takes it. In fact, sometimes the meeting ends worse than it began," Todd laughed.

"Why?" I asked.

"Because the houses hate each other," he explained. "You'd be surprised how many men have died during such discussions." Todd seemed to find the subject humorous, while I just found it revolting. As far as I knew, no one had ever died in the council building of The Clan.

"The Lord of the Brimming Lake and his family live on the second floor," Todd went on. "The third floor is where the priests of both houses live."

"Do they kill each other too?" I asked sarcastically.

Todd shook his head. "Since their lives are devoted to the gods, no one dares kill them, even those of the opposite house.

"There are only three stories?" I asked, looking up to take in the grandeur that seemed frivolous to me.

Todd shook his head. "There are four. The top floor is for the slaves and servants who look after the palace."

Of course, I thought. *What would the world be without slaves? You might actually have to do things for yourself.*

"Come on," Todd said. "The temple of the king is over here."

Todd turned to the right, leading us back to the same side of the river we'd been on all day. The temple was easy to distinguish from the surrounding buildings. It was even taller than the palace, although nowhere near as large. Its stone walls were a deep gold that made me think of The Barracks.

Just as we were about to descend from the platform over the river, something caught my eye. It was a tiny hovel made of dark stones. In one wall was set a doorless entryway covered by long, tattered curtains. The fabric was opaque and could have been almost any color once. Now, it was too weather-stained for me to even hazard a guess.

I slowed. "What is that?" I asked softly, a strange feeling creeping over me.

Todd turned back. It took him a moment to realize what I was referring to.

"Oh, that," he said. "That's the shrine for the unknown god, the one who remained in the heavens. Since he doesn't have any followers, it's not very big."

That was an understatement. The entire thing was smaller than a horse stall.

As I turned and walked away, it felt as though someone was watching me. I glanced back but could make out nothing inside the dark interior of the shrine. The only movement was the ragged ends of the curtain fluttering in the breeze.

I didn't hear half of what Todd said as we neared the temple of the king.

Just outside, he stopped and gave me a serious look. His voice dropped to a whisper.

"You must not speak while we are inside," he instructed. "There will be people praying and worshipping, but no matter what happens, say nothing."

I nodded.

A foreign scent hit my nose the moment we entered. It was sweet and musky, almost like pollen but more potent. At first, I could see nothing. Outside, the sun was shining brightly, but there wasn't a single window in the temple.

The only light came from a handful of candles scattered around the single room.

We paused to allow our eyes to adjust to the gloom. When I could finally make out what I was seeing, I was stunned. Whatever I had been expecting, this was not it.

The walls were of a deep, midnight blue. Every piece of stone in the place had been polished until it glinted in the firelight. White lines twisted around, creating strange symbols. The domed ceiling rose high over our heads, vanishing into darkness where the candlelight ended.

In the center of the room were several steps leading down to a lowered section. The space was about twenty yards long and the same in width. A mass of pillows and mats was placed there. Some of these were occupied, mostly by men, but there were also a few women and children who knelt, sat, or lay flat out on the assortment of cushions.

The majority appeared to be silently lost in thought, but a few were making strange noises. One man, far to my left, was screaming with his face buried in a pillow. Most of the sound was muffled, but what did escape was blood-curdling.

There was also a pair of men sitting together, weeping and crying out in a pitiful manner.

A few men in long, golden robes walked around, occasionally touching people on the shoulder or speaking to them softly. I saw one replacing several of the candles that had begun to burn low.

I advanced, sensing that Todd was following me. At the farthest end of the room, I could make out several strange objects, which I was curious to take a closer look at. The largest item was an enormous rock slab of the same blue color as the walls, floor, and ceiling.

Its surface glistened too, but not in the same way. When I was about ten feet from it, Todd put his hand on my shoulder, and I stopped.

The scent of freshly spilled blood hit my nose the next moment, and I understood. The huge square of rock was covered in crimson liquid.

Beyond the slab was the likeness of a man carved in stone, only twice as large as any living man. The face was long, with a hooked nose and stern mouth. In his hand was a spear, and from his head grew long hair, which fell to his shoulders. Resting upon the stone man's head was a crown, just like The Lord of the Brimming Lake had worn, only this one was far more exquisite.

Mounted on the back wall behind the statue were hundreds of items. I saw swords and other weapons, blankets with strange patterns on them, and items such as cups and plates, all made of a golden metal.

Todd gently pulled on my arm. Slowly, I turned away and followed him. We went back to the center of the room. Todd seated himself on one of the pillows and closed his eyes. I knew he was praying. I'd seen him do it before, not that it had ever done much good. As far as I could tell, Arsh was about as alive as his carven likeness at the end of the room.

After a quarter of an hour, Todd rose, and we left the temple. On the way out, Todd dropped several pieces of metal in a wooden box mounted near the door. Midday had just passed. The sunlight was so blinding that we had to wait twice as long for our eyes to adjust this time.

"What did you think?" Todd asked.

"It's not what I expected," I admitted. "What did you pray for?"

"The usual things," Todd told me.

We began to meander along the river, back the way we had come. "Health for my family and good fortune as well."

I nodded. "Is that all?"

"I prayed for my mother, that she would be happy. The rest of it, well–" he hesitated. "Let's get something to eat."

Honestly, I hadn't thought about food in a long time, but there was a hollow feeling in the pit of my stomach. The morning was gone, and breakfast seemed very long ago.

I assumed we would rejoin Arshenn and the others now that Todd had shown me what we'd set out to see, but Todd didn't appear to be in a hurry to find them.

He traded a silver piece of metal for something called pies. They were like a loaf of bread stuffed with stewed meat and vegetables. We had no utensils, and they were messy to eat but tasted delicious. However, I burnt my fingers a few times on the hot interior.

Todd turned to me when we'd finished eating. "Is there anything else you want to see?" he asked. "We could watch some of the artists work or go hear some stories or music."

My dream from the night before came back to me, accompanied by the desire to visit the ocean and stand on the shore with the sand beneath my feet. I pushed the feeling away. I'd been far too free with myself today. The last thing I wanted was for Todd to think we were going to be friends again. I'd come with him to satisfy my own curiosity, but several times, I'd let it get the better of me, asking questions and answering his. Things could never go back to the way they were.

"I have no desire to see anything," I told him flatly.

"Okay, let's find the others then." There was a twinge of disappointment in his voice, and I knew I'd made the right decision.

CHAPTER 13
THE WILD SPIRIT

I could have searched the city from top to bottom and found neither hide nor hair of Arshenn and Jiyata, but Todd knew exactly where they would be.

The afternoon sun beat down mercilessly as we trekked back up the path beside the river. The crowd and the heat only got worse the further we went. I was jostled on every side as the items displayed on the long tables turned from leather saddles to fabric and clothing.

"Mother," Todd called suddenly.

I didn't see Jiyata at first, but as we approached a table covered with purple pieces of cloth, I spotted her slender form. Arshenn was a few feet away, talking to one of the other merchants.

"Todicmadaya!" Jiyata welcomed her son with a joyful smile. "Astra!" Her greeting for me was almost as warm. "Where have you been? Arkensallay returned long since."

"We went to the temple of the king to pray," Todd answered.

"That is very good," Jiyata praised her son.

"Are you almost done here?" Todd inquired.

Jiyata nodded. "We have made almost all of our purchases. Lord Arshenn said something about picking up a weapon. As soon as he finishes his conversation, I believe we will head in that direction."

"We shall join you," Todd told her.

"Did you get anything to eat?" Jiyata asked us.

"We had pies from the man on the corner by the temple," Todd said. "His are the best in the market, but not nearly as good as yours."

Jiyata beamed at him before turning to me. "What did you think of the palace and the temple?" she asked.

"They were quite impressive," I told her honestly. "I've never seen–"

Arshenn joined us then, and I ceased speaking mid-sentence.

"I see you have found us again," Arshenn addressed Todd. "Just in time to take a look at the new spear I've commissioned for Arkensallay."

Without waiting for an answer, Arshenn took Jiyata's hand firmly in his and led us to a less crowded section of the market.

Along the way, I saw dozens of tables displaying hundreds of swords, clubs, and every other type of weaponry imaginable. I expected Arshenn would stop at the one covered by long-shafted spears, but he didn't even appear interested. The man standing beside the table was calling out that "he made the best spears this side of the river".

"*Worst* spears is what he means," I heard Arkensallay mutter. "The last one I bought from him shattered after only two thrusts."

"That is what happens when you try to spear rock," Todd pointed out cheekily. Arkensallay shot a glare at him, but there didn't seem to be as much malice in it as usual.

Arshenn led us down one of the winding roads that branched off from the main one. We turned several times until I wasn't sure in which direction the river lay. The streets here were almost entirely vacant. Before long, I figured out why. This part of the city reeked.

The dwellings along the poorly maintained path were small and unkempt. Putrid scents of rotting food and unwashed bodies filled the air. I saw a gang of filthy, rag-clad children roaming the streets. A nearby man struck one with a stick, sending the others scrambling over each other in an attempt to get away. The poor, stricken child, a boy of maybe ten, lay in the street crying and clutching his bloodied ear.

To my surprise, the man bent down and picked up a small sack from the ground. It jingled like it was full of metal.

"Dirty, little thief," I heard the man spit as he stalked away.

No one else paid any attention to what had just taken place, but I could hear the child wailing for a long time after he was out of sight.

Finally, Arshenn came to the place he was seeking. It was a run-down dwelling with a crooked door. Like the other buildings in the city, it shared a wall with the neighbor on either side and didn't have a yard. A bit of foliage would have done wonders for this place. Although, I had a feeling that any grass planted here would be left to grow wild with thistles.

Arshenn walked straight to the door, knocked four times, then went in immediately. The rest of us followed. Inside, the front room of the dwelling was almost entirely barren. Just as the door closed behind me, an old man emerged from a long, dark hall across from us.

"Hello, Master Tiylious," Arshenn greeted the ancient man with a deep nod of respect. I'd never before heard such a tone in his voice.

"Brother Arshenn," Tiylious politely greeted Todd's father. "You're here about the spear, correct?"

Arshenn nodded, and the two fell into conversation. Arkensallay stood by them but did not speak.

In contrast to the exterior of the dwelling, the interior was spick and span. Not a speck of dirt was to be seen in the empty corners. The ceiling, where bare beams of wood were visible, much like a hayloft, held not a single cobweb.

Tiylious stepped back down the hall for a moment. He returned bearing a long-shafted spear.

"I know you like to do the sharpening yourself," Tiylious said, handing the shaft to Arkensallay but speaking to Arshenn. "So it's a tad dull. Would still cut somebody, but not as cleanly."

Arshenn nodded and started counting out pieces of metal. He counted out quite a lot. Arkensallay began skillfully swinging the weapon.

107

Todd was watching him intently. I could easily imagine that he would be feeling the sharp end of the spear before too long.

Finally, we headed back outside, a process that took a surprisingly long amount of time. Arshenn and Tiylious seemed to be on intimate terms, and their conversation lasted nearly half an hour.

"We will meet you at home," Todd announced. "I want to show Astra one more thing."

Arshenn raised an eyebrow but watched us go without comment.

As soon as the others were out of sight, Todd stopped walking and turned to me.

"I don't really have anything in mind," he admitted. "I just didn't want to walk home watching Arkensallay play with his new toy." There was a note of bitterness in Todd's voice.

"Unless you've changed your mind about wanting to see more of the city?" he added hopefully.

"No," I replied. The way his face fell made me regret my answer slightly, but I would not change my mind.

He nodded. "Okay, I guess we'll just take the long way back."

Todd wasn't exaggerating. We really did take the long way. There was little of interest to be seen on our journey. Most of what we passed were more of the small, dilapidated dwellings.

I found them hard to look at. Todd walked forward confidently, neither turning his head to the right or the left. Several times, I saw full-grown men staggering about the street. They reeked of the same bitter scent I remembered from the night Rettrin's family had come to dinner.

Dozens of children, barefoot and wearing nothing but patched scraps of fabric, sat on the side of the road and watched us with large eyes. Every single one of them was thin and didn't appear to have bathed in weeks.

The palace could just be seen in the distance, over the nearby rooftops. Its size and luxury seemed like nothing now but a

108

cruel joke when, not two miles away, people were living as if they had been thrown out with the trash.

Todd even had the audacity to stop beside one particularly young child and give her a small bit of metal.

He turned to me with a wink. "We are blessed when we give to the poor," he announced, even as twenty other children crowded around hoping to receive the same.

It felt like ages before we left that squalid and miserable part of the city behind. We were on the outskirts now. There were still some buildings on our right, but to the left was nothing except fields and clumps of trees.

I had my head turned away from the stone structures and was watching the antics of a couple of squirrels as they chased each other around a giant oak tree. Suddenly, the shrill scream of a horse rent the air.

Instantly, I saw the animal ahead of us and froze. I knew this horse; I had seen it before, years ago. I blinked, and the illusion dissipated somewhat. The animal's head was the same shape, and the thick legs were identical, but the horse I was thinking of was bay, and the animal in front of me was silver.

Slowly, Todd and I approached. Two men were struggling with the beast. Not that she was much of a beast. She was young, between two and three years old, and still had the look of a filly.

Despite her age and size, she fought savagely against the bridle held by her two captors. Each grasped a long rope attached to the bit. I wasn't certain what the men wanted the horse to do. They seemed to be yanking her head around without giving her any clear direction.

The one on the left suddenly gave a terrific pull. The horse froze, then, with unbelievable speed, lunged toward the man. She would have proceeded to sink her teeth into his flesh, but the other man wrenched her in the opposite direction with all his might.

"Evil creature," the one who had just escaped her teeth snarled. There was a stick in his other hand, which he used on the filly's head. She tried to aim a kick at him, but was held fast by the pair.

"I got it. Keep her still now," a third man said. He emerged from a nearby stable carrying a saddle.

"This should be good," Todd whispered to me. "Let's see what happens." We had already come to a halt, the path blocked by the horse and the men.

I had no desire to witness the outcome of this disastrous situation.

The filly showed the whites of her large, dark eyes as the third man approached. She'd grown still, save for the great, blowing breaths she let out. The man threw the saddle on her and skillfully secured the girth all in the same swift movement. As he pulled the synch tight, the filly reacted. She reared, trying to turn and kick the man, but he leapt away.

This time, the battle lasted nearly five minutes as the animal struggled desperately to free herself from the saddle on her back. I'd never seen anyone treat a horse in such a way.

After the filly ceased moving, the third man walked up to her. Instead of easing the girth tighter, as I would have done, he gave it a yank, which set the wretched creature off again. Her silver fur was darkened with sweat, and the foam dripping from her mouth covered her broad chest.

The man seemed to grow impatient and again approached the horse even though she was still snorting and kicking up her feet. He was either very stupid or very brave because as soon as he saw an opening, he made a mad leap for the horse's back. Somehow, he managed to get in the saddle.

That was when it became apparent to everyone that the filly had been holding back. The breath in her lungs came out in a screech of fury. She rose on her hind legs, partially lifting the men holding her off the ground.

With only two feet on the earth, she turned her body and leapt forward. She charged away from the city, into the open meadow on our left.

Todd and I watched in surprise as she raced through the grass, dragging the two men with nothing but her mouth. There was a stone fence cutting off her escape, but she refused to accept defeat. Instead, she attempted to jump over it.

Her front legs cleared the fence, but when the men holding the ropes impacted the wall, she was pulled to the ground headfirst. The man on her back was thrown a good twenty yards.

I hurried forward, not even sure how to help. The men had finally released their hold on the reins. I could see terrible rope burns on their arms and hands. One of the pair also had a cut on his head. The third man was groaning. He sat up, but made no attempt to rise.

Since none of the men seemed in danger of dying, I turned to the downed horse. Both of the long ropes were caught in the fence. One was stretched across her side, forcing her head up, but not allowing her to rise.

A wild cry broke from her as she tried to get to her feet. I could see the bit cutting into her mouth as her own body pulled the rope tight.

I placed my hands on top of the fence and vaulted over.

"Stay away from her! She's dangerous," one of the men bellowed.

I ignored him; right now, it was just me and the silver filly.

Slowly, I circled the animal until I was in her line of sight. She kicked out wildly as I started to approach.

"Easy," I breathed. "Easy."

Calmly, I extended a hand toward her.

There was blood coming from the filly's mouth where the bit had scored her soft gums. She grew impossibly still, but I wasn't fooled; I'd seen how quickly she could explode into action.

She almost did when I touched her. However, just as she started to react, I froze in my turn. The filly quieted, uncertainly. My hand went to the bridle and froze again. In this manner, I gently undid the knot holding the rope to the bit.

The moment it came loose, the filly surged to her feet, and I retreated. The horse probably would have run off if the second rope hadn't been caught in the wall as well. The filly fought it for a minute, but not with much will, then gave up. Now that she had her feet, she grew still, not the fake calm she had portrayed earlier, but actually calm.

I looked her over again. Something about her was definitely familiar. She didn't resemble the horses I had seen here. The long, graceful neck was there, but her head was too large and her legs too thick. She had the pale coat that seemed most common among the horses of this place; however, hers was flecked with deep red in some places instead of gray. The filly's knees, hocks, and face were tarnished a similar color. A silver blaze cut straight down her face. The foreign features reminded me of the horses in The North Wind.

Without a moment's hesitation, I reached forward and put my hand against the filly's nose. She balked a little, but that was it.

"Get away from that evil spawn!" someone yelled.

The horse reared, only to be pulled earthward again as the least injured of the men yanked the second rope free of the wall. The other two men were supporting each other back toward the stable.

I stepped away, more in response to the horse than to the order.

"You crazy?" the man snarled. "This horse is the most dangerous animal in my master's stable. It nearly killed five men last week alone!"

He spat blood onto the ground.

"Why does he keep it then?" Todd asked.

I'd completely forgotten about him. He'd come to stand on the far side of the fence. He seemed happy to be on the opposite side of the short wall from the filly.

Swinging his head around, the man noticed Todd for the first time.

"She's bred of the master's finest mare," the man answered

"It doesn't show," Todd laughed.

The man's face began to redden. "It's because of the monster that sired her," he snapped.

"What do you mean?" asked Todd.

"It was the phantom stallion."

A laugh escaped Todd's lips. "Right, of course it was. Everyone has a foal sired by that myth."

An angry twist appeared in the man's lips. "It's true. I saw him! It was nigh on four years ago, in the late fall. At dawn, I was sleeping in the hayloft, and I saw him come walking down the road like he belonged here. Didn't seem nervous at all to be in the city."

"What did he look like?" Todd wondered. I could tell he didn't believe this "phantom stallion" story one bit, but Todd was always up for a good tale.

"Huge," the man answered. "Biggest horse I've ever seen, his legs were so long he could have stepped over this fence. He was dark brown with a black mane and tail and had no markings on his face.

"My master's horses were out in the pasture." The man gestured to the field the filly and I were standing in. "There was a stallion with the herd, and the two fought, even as I roused the other men.

"We ran out with torches and sticks to chase the brute off, but he'd already gotten to the master's prized mare.

"Eleven months later, that spawn of evil was born." The filly had been standing quietly throughout the story of her lineage, but when the man turned a malicious look her way, she tossed her head and tried to pull the rope away from him. There wasn't much fight left in her. I could see more blood oozing out of the corners of her mouth.

"She probably would have been sold as a weanling, except that her dam died during the birth. My master can't afford to take a loss on her. He thinks if he can train her and slap her mother's name on her, he'll be able to get a pretty penny, but that horse is a nightmare. In my opinion, there's nothing for her but to be slaughtered for her meat and skin."

I looked at the animal sadly. She had such wild beauty. I did not claim to know if anyone would be able to tame her, but if they did, she would serve them well.

CHAPTER 14
DESPAIR

It was wash day again, and the sun was blazing down as hot as ever. I turned away from the water of the lake. The shadowy patch of woods, where I had once seen something move, was to my left.

The great, sweeping branches of the oaks and elms promised cool shade. Almost without intending to, I started walking in that direction. A voice behind me called out, but the words were indistinct, and I paid no heed.

I needed to reach the woods. There was something I must find.

I had been to the lake just under a dozen times, but only once had I seen movement in the forest. However, on each visit, the urge to walk beneath the trees had grown stronger. Now it was irrepressible. I had to find what was there, had to know what was waiting for me.

As I neared the spot, I once again saw movement. Briefly, the words of warning I'd received regarding possible dangers entered my mind. They vanished just as swiftly, without leaving any lingering impression of their passing.

As I stepped into the woods, a cool breeze touched my face. The harsh light of the sun no longer burned down upon my head.

I felt instantly refreshed. I closed my eyes and smiled, enjoying the moment.

When my eyes opened, someone was in front of me. Not standing, but sitting on a fallen log.

It was a girl with gray eyes.

"Myra?" I asked in wonder. My dreams had started feeling so real lately.

She gave me a questioning look.

"Aren't you supposed to be there?" Myra pointed back the way I had come, through the gap in the tree trunks.

I glanced over my shoulder at the lake. The entire scene looked far too bright. The land around the water's edge was completely abandoned. As far as I could tell, Myra and I were the only two in existence.

"Well?" she pressed. "Why have you come here?"

I shrugged. "I thought I was supposed to," I answered.

"Why?"

I sighed, tired of her riddles. "I don't know anymore."

"But you did once?"

"No." I shook my head. "I've never known. I've always let my life flow by and merely followed the current, never caring or worrying about what it was that I was supposed to be doing or what I really wanted."

Myra was silent for a moment, allowing my own words to sink in.

"What do you want?" she asked.

Sharp emotions filled my chest. It was amazing how such a simple question could elicit such a reaction.

"I want to go home," I whispered in defeat. "I want to see the Mountains of The North Wind again, ride among the harvesters in The Golden Fields, spend a day hauling wood at Treescape. I wouldn't even mind visiting The Paramount, if only it meant I might get to look north to where The North Wind lies."

Myra blinked and shook her head softly. "As I told you long ago," she began, "you don't have a home anymore."

I did remember her words. They had pained me at the time, but that was nothing compared to the agony of emotion I was gripped with now.

"But I did go home the last time!" I argued. "I made it back. We all did, except Joss and–" I cut off, unable to finish.

"No, you didn't," Myra murmured. "In your heart, you never left the mountain."

Tears filled my eyes. I hadn't done much crying since arriving at The Brimming Lake. I'd felt too empty. Now, in my dream, droplets fell from my eyes like rain.

"You went to that place looking for something that's been missing your whole life," Myra whispered. "Until you find it, you will never have the kind of home you are looking for."

With her parting words, she faded from my sight, as did the rest of the dream. The last thing to vanish was the glaring image of the lake, utterly void of life.

My cheeks were wet when I opened my eyes. I couldn't tell the time, but I didn't care. I rolled over, turning my back on the others slumbering in the room. Instead of falling asleep again, I gave in to weakness and had a private cry. I don't remember when sleep finally found me, but it was long after.

The days passed meaninglessly after that. I didn't care what I did or how I did it. I just waited for each day to end so I could climb into bed and sleep. I had no more dreams, only darkness, and that was what I craved.

I don't think anyone noticed. Arshenn and Arkensallay didn't have much contact with me. Even Todd rarely glanced in my direction. He was gone at his apprenticeship more often than not. When he came home before dinner, he and Arkensallay dueled. Todd continued to be defeated every time. Before long, he ceased returning to the dwelling until after sunset, smelling sourly of wine.

Jiyata would hurry to him and ask if he was hungry. I would turn my back, refusing to even so much as look at him.

Jiyata was always too preoccupied with her favorite son to see my reaction. If Yetta noticed, she said nothing.

One night, as I worked with Yetta to set the table, my foot caught in a small divot of the floor. I nearly dropped the plates I was carrying in my attempt to stay upright.

"Your mind is far from here," Yetta observed.

I didn't have time to respond because Arshenn and Arkensallay entered the room.

"What smith did you say it was?" Arshenn asked.

"The little one, on the southern fringe of the city. It's run by Koslon."

Arshenn let out a bark-like laugh. "A jewelry maker? Is that what Todicmadaya's going to become?"

"Not much of a surprise," Arkensallay replied.

I ignored their conversation but did ask Yetta what a jewelry maker was when we were back in the kitchen. She raised an eyebrow at my ignorance as she explained that it was someone who made necklaces, bracelets, rings, and other such articles from metal and precious stones.

She let the comment she had made earlier drop, possibly from forgetfulness or, more likely, kindness.

The days grew hotter and hotter, with still no rain to quench the thirsty earth. It was impossible to keep the dwelling clear of dust. We took the woven mats out day after day and shook them clean, but it did no good.

One of the slaves died in the fields of heatstroke. When they brought his body back to the house, and I looked at his face, sorrow filled me. I hardly knew the man, there had never been a word spoken between us, and I did not even know his name, but his passing still felt tragic.

Jiyata and Yetta barely glanced out at the yard to see what the commotion was. Arshenn's only care was that slaves were costly. The other men treated their comrade's death like it was all a big joke.

I was fairly certain that when they threw his corpse into a shallow grave, I was the only one who felt the need to grieve.

Late one night, when I was too hot to sleep, I slipped outside under the light of the moon and stood vigil for a few hours, until a gentle breeze started blowing from the north. It wouldn't help cool the dwelling, but it did refresh me. As I headed back to bed, I wiped away the last of the tears I'd shed for the man who hadn't had a single friend in the whole world.

The next day, Jiyata, Yetta, and I were in the kitchen, making breakfast, when a voice bellowed, "Arkensallay!"

Jiyata was so startled she dropped an egg on the floor. It cracked, and both of us bent to retrieve it at the same moment.

"Todicmadaya!" the voice cried again. It was Arshenn, and he sounded furious.

Yetta glanced up sharply. Jiyata's face turned pale, and her fingers trembled as she tried to pick up the egg. I snatched it from the floor and managed to fling it into the waste bucket a moment before Arshenn entered the kitchen.

"Where are those boys?" he demanded.

Jiyata had straightened. "I do not know, my lord," she answered, head bowed.

Arshenn's gaze shifted from her to me.

I did not bow my head. "I don't know either," I told him.

He narrowed his eyes.

"Since they are nowhere to be found, perhaps you can assist me, girl from the stars."

"What is it that you require of me?" I asked.

"My lord, you can't expect–" Yetta started.

"Silence!" he snarled at her. Yetta grew still, and Jiyata cringed as though he'd struck her.

"What do you want me to do?" I wondered.

"There is something for you to see in the stable. Come with me," Arshenn ordered.

I shrugged. There was no place I'd rather be. Jiyata and Yetta watched us leave but didn't dare interfere.

"Now that you have been here several moons, what do you think of The Land of the Brimming Lake?" Arshenn asked in an almost friendly voice.

The tone in which he spoke was so different from what it had been a moment earlier that I was instantly put on my guard.

"It's very hot," I answered, using the first thing that came to mind.

Arshenn narrowed his eyes. "So it is cooler where you are from?"

I nearly stumbled as I realized I'd given something away.

"It is very cold among the stars," I said, trying to smooth over my mistake.

In one violent movement, Arshenn seized me by the forearm with a grip that could have crushed stone. I was pulled to a halt and forced to look up at him, our faces inches apart.

"I have the distinct ability to know when I'm being lied to," he warned me. "So don't try it again."

As suddenly as he had grabbed me, he released me and continued walking.

Inside the stable was Arshenn's stallion; I'd heard his name was Pride. It certainly fit him. From his arched neck and long, flowing legs to the tips of his slender ears and silky tail, the horse was the image of grace and perfection.

Today, however, the stallion showed the whites of his eyes as he turned toward me. Something had happened to him. Crimson stained the silver coat, and almost a dozen deep cuts covered the animal's neck and chest.

The beast half reared in its stall as I took several steps forward.

"What do you make of this?" Arshenn asked sourly.

At first glance, it was hard to tell what could have caused the injuries.

Even as I was studying the horse's wounds, Arshenn was studying me.

"Well?" he asked.

I just shook my head. I'd already given enough away by opening my mouth. It was going to stay shut from now on.

"No ideas on how this happened?" Arshenn pressed.

If I'd been in The North Wind, my best guess would have been that Pride had gotten into a fight with another horse, a big, powerful one. But I wasn't in The North Wind, and there weren't any other stallions among Arshenn's herd.

"It looks like someone attacked him." There was just enough truth in my words that Arshenn couldn't accuse me of lying.

119

"*That* is an excellent guess, girl from the stars," Arshenn said. "However, I don't think it was a *someone* so much as a *something*."

I didn't answer, but got the impression that Arshenn was able to glean just as much from my silence as he would have if I'd replied.

"You know what did this, don't you?" he accused.

Again, I didn't answer.

"Speak," Arshenn ordered.

He knew. He knew that I knew. It was pointless to keep pretending I was ignorant.

"Another stallion," I admitted.

Arshenn nodded. "Only there isn't another stallion here, at least, not anymore."

His words confused me, but I didn't have to wait long before he explained.

"This morning, when Husanil came out to do the feeding at dawn, he found the gate to the eastern pasture open and the horses grazing in it. That pasture has a downed fence.

"When the horses were counted, three mares were missing, and you can see what happened to their valiant protector."

"A rogue stallion," I breathed.

Theo, the stable master for the wild stable, had told me how rogue stallions steal mares from each other to add to their own bands.

"Yes," Arshenn snapped. "And when I find the unlucky person who left the gate open–" he trailed off suggestively.

Arshenn glowered at the stallion for a few moments, then turned on me once more. "Now, since you know *so* much about horses, get a halter on him."

I did as Arshenn asked and held Pride as still as possible while Arshenn inspected the deeper cuts. Standing so close to the animal, I observed numerous swelling lumps rising on his chest and sides, sure signs that he'd been kicked repeatedly.

Even as he worked, Arshenn was watching me. I could sense him trying to probe my thoughts. After every encounter we

120

had, I seemed to lose ground. Retreating was my only option; he must never know the truth of where I came from. If he ever found out, I was sure he would do something dreadful.

Finally, Arshenn finished his inspection. Since none of the injuries were life-threatening, I was sent back to the dwelling.

I didn't like leaving Pride in his stall without treating any of his wounds. However, it would have been foolish to express my thoughts. Arshenn already knew far too much about my abilities.

CHAPTER 15
RAGE

I had gone nearly a month without dreaming, but the next night I found myself in the council building. The round room was illuminated solely by moonbeams, which streamed through one of the overhead windows.

"How are you?" Myra asked. She stood with her back to me, a long maroon cloak flowing from her shoulders. The hood was pulled up, concealing her hair.

"I feel strange," I told her.

"Explain," she ordered without turning toward me.

"I- I just want it to end. I'm tired of all these secrets. It's like when I was with The Clan. I should have told everyone exactly what happened in the mountain. It might have been the wrong thing to do, but then I would have been free of it.

"It's the same now. Why not just tell them what they want to know? I'm tired of carrying everything alone. Does any of this really matter?

"Why are we born to live in this mess of a world? Everything we put our hands to fails, and everyone we love will eventually move on or pass away. Our sole consolation is that we are only here for a brief time. In the end, we are no different; we die like everything else."

My voice faltered. I hadn't really thought about what I was saying. The words had simply poured themselves out, like water from a broken vessel.

"That doesn't sound very much like you," Myra observed.

"Maybe, not," I admitted. "I used to think life was too short, but now I wish it didn't drag on for such an eternity."

"You have given up."

"No," I argued. "In the end, I'll do whatever I have to in order to survive and protect The Clan. I just wish it wasn't so hard and that- that I wasn't doing it alone. I've lost almost everything, but I can't stop or I'll lose what little I have left."

There was no answer from the hooded figure. Slowly, she turned toward me. The moon reflected full on her face and glinting, gray eyes.

It was not Myra.

The woman in the maroon cloak was far older.

"Myna," I breathed, panicking a little.

"Now you do understand me. You understand me exactly," she said.

I was mute. Her words shook me to the core, even as the dream faded and I woke into the predawn hours.

I wasn't gasping this time, nor did I cry, but my limbs wouldn't stop shaking. I felt cold, frozen almost, even though the room was as hot as ever.

I tried to wrap up in a blanket, but it made no difference. I was shivering from head to toe. One thought pressed itself desperately to the front of my mind.

Fire.

I needed a fire or I would freeze to death. It didn't make sense, but the dream had left that strong of an impression on me.

Rising, I staggered to the kitchen. The hearth was cold, but just the brief journey had gotten my blood flowing and cleared my head enough to shake the vision from my mind. Instead of fire, I found it was really a drink of water I wanted.

As I dipped a cup in the water bucket on the table, I glanced out one of the windows and saw a figure walking through the horse pasture. It was Todd, heading to his apprenticeship.

Every morning, he escaped into the dawn. How I wished I could.

Not that I minded working with Yetta and Jiyata, but the entire dwelling was oppressive. There was always this sense that something bad could happen at any moment without warning. It affected me less than the others because I wasn't used to being afraid, but they had spent their whole lives living like this. It was unimaginable to me.

The fears that I had known growing up were things to be overcome and defeated. The fear that lurked here was something that followed you everywhere and never relented.

The next day, we returned to the lake to wash the household's clothing. Even though it was early, the temperature already seemed unreasonably hot.

I waded out into the water, enjoying the cool feeling of the lake. Jiyata glanced at me nervously as I began scrubbing several pairs of pants. Worrying seemed to be a part of her personality.

As I finished with the garments and headed back to shore for another set, I turned toward the woods. I felt no pull in that direction now. Nothing was waiting for me there anymore.

Suddenly, I heard a cry of panic behind me. A little boy was floundering in the water fifteen yards from the shore.

I hurled the sodden pants I was holding into the reedy shallows and rushed toward the child. When the water was up to my waist, I stopped running and started swimming.

Several of the nearby men had spotted the boy, but I was closer and got to him first. I drew the panicking child to me. I couldn't feel the bottom beneath my feet, so I had to tread water.

"Be still," I told the boy sharply as he continued to thrash around. He froze, and I towed him back to shore.

His mother was waiting there for us with a terror-stricken face. I handed him off and was about to go collect the bundle of pants I'd thrown, when I realized that every eye was on me. Self-consciously, I headed back to Yetta and Jiyata.

"You know how to swim?" Jiyata asked, as the crowd of women slowly returned to their work.

I nodded.

"Wherever did you learn?"

The answer to that question was not simple. I had learned from a Keeper named Kit. She was the one who had shown me the secret cave in The Valley of The North Wind. Inside was a pool of water, where I learned to swim with Kit instructing me.

She was fifteen years older than I was and had known my mother, Aslin. She told me that many years earlier, Aslin had done the same for her, so it seemed right to pass the knowledge on to me. Eventually, I showed Gann the cave too, mostly because he resented being left out.

My friendship with Kit didn't last long. She took a life mate less than a year later and, to my knowledge, never visited the cave again.

So the secret passed to Gann and me, as I assumed it had been passed down for many generations. We went there together from time to time, but I enjoyed it more when I was alone.

"Someone taught me when I was younger," I finally responded to Jiyata's question.

I leaned down and began laying out the wet pants in the sun. When I was finished, I gathered up a few more unwashed articles of clothing.

The first was a shirt. Judging by the numerous holes where it appeared sparks had eaten through, I assumed it belonged to Todd. Recently, he'd started wearing shirts on a regular basis—flying embers in the forge where he was apprenticed probably had a great deal to do with it.

I took it to the nearest rock and started scrubbing mercilessly.

From time to time, I could still feel eyes boring into my back as the workers and the watchers stared at me. What bothered me most was that I was certain an account of today's events would get back to Arshenn through Husanil, who had witnessed the whole thing.

The next day was spent more peacefully. During the afternoon, I worked the spinning wheel again. Yetta was darning a pair of socks while Jiyata patched several holes in a large blanket.

After putting away the spinning wheel, I help Yetta make the evening meal. There was a brief interruption when Todd arrived home. As usual, I was forced to observe him unsuccessfully spar with Arkensallay for twenty minutes. The matches were shorter these days.

125

Once I was back inside, it was a simple matter to finish the meal and set the table. Husanil arrived and took the slaves' rations just as Yetta, Jiyata, and I were settling down for our dinner.

We didn't sit very long.

Apparently, something wasn't to Arkensallay's liking because he bellowed loudly for Yetta from the other room.

Yetta exchanged a fearful glance with Jiyata before hurrying to answer the call. Unconsciously, I rose to my feet and went toward the doorway after her.

"Don't," Jiyata instructed me, but I ignored her warning, curious to know what was going on.

Without entering the room, I peeked around the corner of the hallway. From my position, I could see nearly the entire room. Arkensallay was towering over a cowering Yetta.

"Are you trying to murder me?" he demanded angrily. "Did you do this on purpose? Do you want me dead?"

Yetta was far too shaken to answer. She remained silent, head bowed, a position of complete submission.

"Look at this!" Arkensallay held up several tiny bones that we must have missed when deboning the fish. "How dare you attempt something so low and underhanded? Is this your revenge on Jiyata for having the blessing of the gods? Do you try now to take away the gift they have given her?"

"My apologies, my lord," Yetta mumbled, eyes low, hands fidgeting nervously in front of her.

Arkensallay's face twisted into a sneer. "You'll be more careful next time. I will make certain of it," he snarled, raising his hand.

"Stop!" I commanded, striding into the room.

I didn't even think about what I was doing; I just did it. The whole situation reminded me of the day in Treescape when Myra and I had stood up to Rollan's brothers. However, Myra wasn't here, so there was no one to stand beside me now. Still, I found I did not care.

Arkensallay wheeled around, face red and distorted.

"I cleaned the fish," I told him. "The fault lies with me."

"Yetta is the oldest. Everything placed on this table is her responsibility," Arkensallay snapped. He turned back toward the older woman, poised to strike.

"You coward," I spat. My words had the desired effect. Arkensallay completely forgot Yetta.

"What did you say?" he hissed, turning on me. "How dare you? I am a strong and powerful warrior! How dare you call me a coward?"

I stared at him, unflinching as he approached. Jiyata had come into the room and was standing close beside Yetta. Both were trembling and wide-eyed.

"How much courage does it take to kill a mouse?" I asked. "None, for you know it cannot fight back. Yet you would treat it as if you had slain a mountain lion."

Arkensallay was purple and shaking with rage. Neither Arshenn nor Todd had stirred from their seats.

"Have you ever killed a mountain lion?" I threw at him. "Or are you content with hunting mice?"

I was surprised he hadn't hit me yet. It felt amazing to stand up to this pathetic excuse of a human being. I could feel the adrenaline coursing through my body and knew it was making me reckless.

Arkensallay raised his hand to strike, but at that moment, something clattered loudly to the floor. Both of us looked to see what had fallen. It was Todd's spoon. He leaned forward in his chair to retrieve it. As he placed the utensil back on the table, his eyes were on his brother.

Arkensallay turned back to me, his face conflicted.

Arshenn rose from his seat at the far end of the table.

"Answer the girl's question," he ordered coolly, looking on with an almost amused expression.

Arkensallay raised his lip in a snarl at his father, then swung his purple face toward me.

"No," he growled at last. "I have never killed a mountain lion."

There was a moment of utter silence.

"Sit down," Arshenn told his son.

Reluctantly, Arkensallay took his seat as Arshenn made his way around the table, approaching me with slow, measured steps. Todd remained where he was but closed his eyes as if in pain when Arshenn passed his chair.

"I have slain a mountain lion," Arshenn announced, stopping just in front of me. He was taller than either of his sons and towered a foot over my head.

"It gave me this." Arshenn ran a finger down a scar on the back of his hand. "It killed my brother, who hunted it with me, and nearly took my life as well. But, in the end, I triumphed and slew the creature."

I should have been afraid. Nonetheless, I looked straight into his cold, black eyes and said something I shouldn't have. "That makes two of us."

There was another moment of silence before Arkensallay surged to his feet once more.

"Liar!" he screeched, jabbing a finger at me. "The girl's a liar!"

Arshenn raised a hand to silence his son.

"No," he pronounced. "I always know when people are lying." He glanced over his shoulder at Todd, who was sitting hunched in his chair. The fresh bruises around his eye from today's sparring match adding an air of defeat to his look of discomfort.

"The girl from the stars is not lying." After making that statement, Arshenn returned to his seat.

With a gesture, he dismissed Jiyata, Yetta, and me. The two women rushed from the room, Jiyata with her arms circling Yetta. I followed more slowly.

CHAPTER 16
TRAGEDY

As soon as we entered the kitchen, Jiyata burst into tears.

"You should not have done that," she wailed, her face contorting in terror.

"It was instinct," I told her. "And it worked, didn't it?"

Yetta shook her head. "Do not think that. You have won no victory. We never win. You may not have been punished today, but Lord Arshenn will not forget what you have done. He is cruel above all things. He will bide his time until he knows exactly how to hurt you, then he will not hesitate."

"Probably," I admitted carelessly. "But what does it matter?"

Jiyata was taken aback by my answer. "You should not speak so," she gasped. "You have a chance to escape his hand."

I looked at her questioningly.

"If you are patient and submissive for a little while, you will be able to leave this place. Then neither Lord Arshenn nor Arkensallay will have any power over you."

"I don't understand," I replied.

"Todicmadaya is a second son. Once he establishes himself, he will have a house of his own. If you are pleasing to him, he will surely take you as well."

"I am *not* going anywhere with him," I answered coldly.

Confusion crossed Jiyata's face. "But I thought–" she stopped, pausing midsentence. "You should want to go."

"Why?"

"Todicmadaya is not like his father or brother. He will–"

"No," I cut her off. "He's not like his father or brother. He is worse than they are. He is the kind of person who gains your trust just so that he can turn on you. Arshenn may be malicious and coldhearted, but he lets you see it. Not like Todd- Todicmadaya.

"He is treacherous. If you don't see that, then you don't know your son as well as you think. He's a liar and a murderer!"

My torrent of words came to an end. I felt the heat of emotion burning in my cheeks. In an instant, all of my despair had turned to fury. Perhaps I hadn't been completely honest with Todd or myself when I told him that I wasn't angry, or maybe it had just taken this long for my wrath to surface.

Jiyata looked as shocked as if I'd struck her.

"No," she whispered. "My Todicmadaya is better than that."

Silence filled the kitchen for a long moment. The table was still covered with our uneaten dinner. I'm sure no one was feeling particularly hungry just then.

We heard the men finish their meal and leave the main room.

Yetta was the first to speak. "You look tired, Jiyata," she commented. "Why don't you go to bed? Astra and I will clean up."

Jiyata blinked at her, then, with a quick glance at me, she nodded. I watched her retreat down the hall with hasty steps.

Slowly, Yetta sank into one of the chairs. I remained standing. Neither of us made a move toward cleaning the kitchen.

"I am old, Astra," Yetta spoke without looking at me. Instead, her gaze traveled to the fire. It hadn't been fed in hours and was little more than embers.

"But I was young once, and understand Jiyata's feelings, even if I do not hold them any longer myself."

Finally, Yetta turned to me. Something about her face was different. The hard creases of her wrinkled skin were softened in the fire's glow.

"She still has hope," Yetta said.

"Hope in what?" I asked.

"Hope in a better life," was the simple answer.

"But you don't?" I wondered, dropping into the chair across from the old woman.

Yetta shook her head and turned back to the fire. "No, not anymore."

A weary sigh escaped her lips. "I was older than most when my father sold me to Lord Arshenn as his first wife," she told me.

I stirred uncomfortably at the mention of "being sold". Yetta didn't notice. She was looking toward the withering flames without seeing them, her mind wandering back all those years into a memory.

"Even then, I wasn't beautiful. My price was a mere two goats. Lord Arshenn, as he is now, would never have taken me, but at the time, he was a fifth son, and there was little enough of a future for him.

"Only first sons and sometimes second sons, if they have won their father's regard, are left anything at his death. Never has a fifth son been granted so much as a crust of bread.

"The day we were married, I believed my fate was to belong to a working man, but I did not mind. As long as I could bear sons and win his favor, I assumed I would be happy enough.

"You have seen a poor sampling of our people. Most women are not so treated. Indeed, many are very happy and well cared for. They love their husbands and raise their children in happy homes.

"But not here and not me. For you see, the sons never came, and Lord Arshenn has a wicked heart.

"I honestly can not say what happened to his brothers. However, in the ten years following our marriage, they began to disappear. The oldest drowned in the sea, the second perished in a sparring match, another fell down a flight of stairs and was dead before he hit the bottom, and the last, as he told you, was slain by a mountain lion while the two were hunting.

"The hunting incident happened a few moons before Lord Arshenn's father died. By that time, he was the only one left and named the sole heir to the family land. That is how he came to be master of this house instead of some lowly man working in the city."

"He murdered all of his brothers?" I asked, readily believing Arshenn capable of such a thing.

Yetta shrugged. "Maybe. I don't know for certain, but their deaths were most convenient for him. Each time, he had a perfect alibi. When his oldest brother drowned, he was working all day with his father in the forge. It was a total stranger who accidentally stabbed his next brother while the two were having a friendly competition. The man was very sorry afterward, and all the onlookers declared it a complete accident. Lord Arshenn wasn't even present at the fight.

"The one who fell and broke his neck was quite drunk, so it was deemed an unfortunate mishap. Even the last time, when Lord Arshenn brought back his brother's body and that of a huge mountain lion, it seemed pointless to accuse him. Men who hunt such beasts die all the time. Lord Arshenn even had the scar and the creature's carcass to show.

"If he killed them, it was remarkably well-concealed, and if he did not, then it must have been the gods' will that he become a first son. Before that time, my life had not been too miserable. We'd lived in a small house in the city. Lord Arshenn worked as a blacksmith, much as Todicmadaya is learning to do. I knew he was displeased with me for not bearing him any children, but he was preoccupied. Only once he became the sole heir to his father's house did things change."

Yetta paused and pursed her lips.

"What did he do to you?" I asked.

"I swore never to tell anyone of that time. All I need say is that he began to loathe me. I stopped leaving the house because I didn't want people to see what my life had become. My sisters and mother used to visit me and, sometimes, I would go to see them as well, but I put a stop to that. I couldn't let them know what I was suffering.

"After a few years, Lord Arshenn bought Jiyata. She was just a child when she came here, a terrified young girl. Most people think that I should have hated her, but I never could. In nearly every way, she was like my own little sister, who I have not seen in many years.

"I would see her again now if I could, but Lord Arshenn has forbidden it."

"Why?" I asked.

"Do you still not understand?" she wondered. "I am the lowest kind of creature on earth to him. A woman who cannot bear her husband a son."

"That isn't fair," I told her.

Yetta shrugged. "That is how life is. Jiyata had two sons, and Lord Arshenn was appeased. Even now, she has some influence over him. I don't believe he loves her, but sometimes, she can soften his will."

"Does she love him?" I asked.

"No," Yetta responded. "She fears him. Fears that one day she may lose his favor and end up like me. Fortunately for her, while Todicmadaya has never lived up to what Lord Arshenn expected in an heir, Arkensallay is exactly what he wants. Jiyata will, most likely, bear no more sons, and Lord Arshenn may marry a third wife to try and add to his line.

"He probably would have done it a long time ago, but again, there was something else which preoccupied him."

"What was that?" I wondered.

Yetta leaned forward and spoke softly. "It was the crown."

"The crown?" I echoed uncertainly.

"He wanted to be The Lord of the Brimming Lake, and he almost succeeded."

"What happened?"

"You know that when the lord dies, all the men of the land take part in a tournament. Then the winners of each house duel to the death. Lord Arshenn almost made it to that final battle. However, in the last match among The House of the King, he lost to the current Lord of the Brimming Lake, Lord Tohoshin.

"What was worse, he received the scar upon his face and other terrible injuries from that battle. Truth be told, he nearly died. While he is still a strong man, he cannot lift his right hand over his

133

head now, so the chances of him ever being able to claim the lordship are doubtful.

"He hates Lord Tohoshin, but can not show it. That hate has festered inside of him and seems to have made him even crueler than he was before. He is planning something, always planning something to hurt those around him.

"I pray to the gods for his life to come to an end. On that day, Arkensallay will become the master of this place. Jiyata may be allowed to stay, but Arkensallay treats Jiyata worse than Lord Arshenn does.

"What Jiyata wants is a refuge, and she has placed her hopes in Todicmadaya. He has always treated her with kindness. She envisions herself living with Todicmadaya when she is widowed. That is what she prays for.

"In her mind, when Lord Arshenn is dead, she will be free of the misery and fear that have engulfed her life. She has hope that she may one day be happy."

"She is wrong," I said. "Todicmadaya cares very little for anyone but himself. If Jiyata rests her hopes for the future on him, she will be as bitterly disappointed as I have been." My throat closed, and I could not continue.

On our return from the mountain and during the winter that followed, I'd thought I'd come to know Todd. Now that I had some perspective, I could see how cleverly he'd tricked us. We'd started to trust him. I'd trusted him. Trusted him enough to bring him among my people, like a fox in a hen house.

He'd repaid that trust by murdering two people who he claimed were like his own family. Looking back, I could see how every action had been skillfully designed to shield his true intentions.

Intrigue had drawn me to him. Everything about Todd had fascinated me, from the descriptions of his home to the stories he told of the gods. I'd been so blind to all of his faults.

Not anymore. Now I saw him for what he really was. A liar. A betrayer. A murderer.

He'd promised not to tell anyone about The Clan, but he was just biding his time, waiting until the talk of his exploits died down. Then he would probably come up with some story about how he'd seen a vision and could lead his people in a great conquest against a rich and prosperous land.

Like his father, he was always plotting. If he had spared me in hopes that I would tell him about my people, he was mistaken. I didn't care what they did to me. I was as good as dead anyway, but I would never betray my people.

You already did, a voice inside my head whispered.

"I do not disagree with you," Yetta broke into my thoughts. "But, even though you and I understand, Jiyata has nothing left besides this hope. I have never asked for much in my life, but please, for her sake, leave that hope alone. Let her believe it. Let it sustain her."

I nodded, and we were silent for a moment.

"What will happen to you?" I asked.

Yetta gave me a questioning look.

"When Arshenn dies, what will happen to you?"

A coarse laugh escaped Yetta's lips. "I will be turned out to starve to death," she answered.

I flinched.

"Don't look so grave," Yetta told me. "I don't think that will be your fate. You belong to Todicmadaya. He may sell you or keep you, but you are far more valuable than I. Each year, I grow less able to do the housework and am more and more useless. The only reason I have not been turned out yet is that Jiyata begs Lord Arshenn to let me stay."

"This is so wrong," I muttered. "In my land, the old are treated with respect. They are sometimes even asked to pass on what they have learned to the children of the community. They are *never* left to starve."

Yetta laughed again. "You speak of a strange way of life," she told me. "You must come from a perfect land."

I shrugged. "It's definitely not perfect," I answered. "There are still many problems, but it certainly seems like a better place to live than here." I stopped my words. I'd said too much. Not that I didn't trust Yetta, but I couldn't be careless.

Yetta rose slowly, and the two of us started cleaning the dishes.

I was in the main room, gathering the last of the plates from the table, when a thought occurred to me.

"Yetta," I started, walking back into the kitchen, arms laden.

"Yes?" she asked. Her sleeves were rolled up, and she was washing the dishes with soapy water.

"You said you had hope once. What were you hoping for?"

Yetta flushed. I'd never seen such a flood of emotion on her face before. Normally, all of her features were carefully composed and gave away nothing.

"There was- a man, Khankeyen," she began, eyes turning back to her work. "He was a slave, the head slave back then. He was gruff but kind."

I could tell that this story wasn't going to end well. I wouldn't have pushed her for more details, but she spoke of her own accord.

"I- he- well, we spoke of leaving together. He wanted to make a run for it, but I knew it would be foolishness. During market days, he would try to earn money, doing- doing whatever he had to."

"He was the man you mentioned who fought in the pits and won his freedom," I guessed.

Yetta nodded, not meeting my eyes. "He was able to free himself, and I told him to forget me, but he was determined that we should be together. He died trying to earn enough money to buy my freedom."

I didn't know what to say. Even as I opened my mouth, Yetta continued. "It wouldn't have mattered how much he won. Lord Arshenn would never have sold me. Much as he despised my presence, he wouldn't have wanted either of us to be happy. He also would have seen it as a blight upon himself if a former slave bought his first wife from him."

"Then why didn't you run away with him?" I wondered. "If you two could have been happy?"

Yetta hesitated. "I never told Khankeyen, but I was pregnant at the time with Lord Arshenn's child."

"What?" I gasped. "I thought you—" I cut off in confusion.

"I told you I never bore him a son," she replied. The dishes were all washed now, and she turned to face me. "The child was a girl."

"Then where is she?" I asked.

The hardness came back into Yetta's face. "It was impossible for me to be pregnant. I was far older than Jiyata. The odds were completely against it. I thought the gods had finally heard my pleas and were blessing me for a lifetime of loyal service.

"Todicmadaya had been born a few months earlier. Lord Arshenn was delighted to have a second son, in case the first did not survive the rite of manhood. He hoped that I would bear him a third to all but secure his bloodline. However, when the child was female, he flew into a rage."

Yetta paused and leaned close to me. "No one knows this," she whispered. "Not Arkensallay or Todicmadaya or any of the rest of the household. They all believe that my child was born dead. Only Jiyata and I know the truth."

Horror filled my mind as I began to understand.

"The child was born premature, but she was healthy. She would have lived. She would- she would have been about your age now. But Lord Arshenn said he'd supported me long enough, though I was useless, and he would not support a worthless girl child.

"Even Jiyata could not stop him. My baby had only taken a handful of breaths before he smothered her life. She was the most innocent, precious thing in the world and—" A soft sob escaped Yetta, she turned away from me. Her shoulders began to droop.

I regretted making her remember these nightmarish memories. Wordlessly, I stepped forward and put my hand on her shoulder. I couldn't imagine the pain she had been through.

A moment later, she continued speaking. "That is why, when Lord Arshenn dies, and I am abandoned, death will come as a relief.

"I would have found a way to end my life on my own long ago, save, I cannot leave Jiyata alone with that monster. I will remain here to protect her as best I can, but I do not fear death. There can be nothing worse than what I have lived through."

We were both still for a minute.

"What was her name?" I asked gently.

"What?" Yetta seemed confused by the question.

"Your daughter, what was her name?"

Yetta shook her head. "She has no name."

"You never gave her a name?" I asked in wonder.

"Fathers name their children after the gods so the child will be blessed, but her father rejected her. She will remain nameless in death. It is the worst fate imaginable."

Yetta's voice was full of misery. She kept it all concealed so well. I had never imagined the depth of the grief she carried inside. Tonight, she only meant to explain a few things to me, but the words had poured forth. Words she must have desired to speak for such a long time.

"Why is it so bad for her to be unnamed?" I asked.

Yetta sighed. "Those who are nameless at death do not belong to any god or any house. They are the slaves of all. And if you think man is the cruelest of creatures, then you know nothing of the gods. They give only despair.

"Once, I believed as others do, that the gods bless those who remain faithful. But no good ever came to me as a result of following their laws. Now I pray to them only for death, Lord Arshenn's or my own, it does not matter which, yet they still do not answer me."

She trailed off.

"Yetta," I said softly.

She blinked, and her eyes focused on me once more. "Just as you never got to be with your daughter, I never knew my mother. I know nothing can replace the void their deaths left in our lives, but, if you would like, why don't you be my mother, and I will be your daughter? I have little enough to offer, but I have been alone all my life. If I can find a mother now, I won't feel so alone anymore."

Yetta was frozen.

Perhaps I had spoken too hastily. Perhaps I had crossed some line. I hadn't wept when my mother died; I was too young to even perceive her absence. However, for Yetta, the grief was fresh every single day. Maybe what I had said only made the memory of her lost child more painful.

A tear rolled down one of Yetta's cheeks. Then another fell on the other cheek.

"Oh, Astra," she whispered. "I did not know your mother was dead. Yes, I will be your mother, and you shall be my child."

She reached forward and wrapped me in her arms. I found tears clouding my eyes too, because I had never before been embraced by my mother.

CHAPTER 17
HOPELESSNESS

In the morning, I apologized to Jiyata. What I had told her was true, but what right did I have to say it?

Both Jiyata and Yetta advised me to stay out of Arkensallay's sight for a while. Neither he nor Arshenn were early risers, so I helped get breakfast ready. Todd walked through on his way to the city, but didn't stop even to greet his mother.

Jiyata was slightly wounded, and I began to worry that I might have changed her interpretation of events such as this.

You didn't really do anything wrong, I told myself. *If her eyes have been opened to the truth, then so be it.*

However, I knew Yetta didn't share my private opinion. "He certainly seems preoccupied today," she observed as Todd vanished across the fields, taking a shortcut to the city.

Jiyata nodded. "Yes, he told me he's working on his first independent project. I wish I could see what it is."

Once the meal was prepared, I retreated to our sleeping room, where I spent the day quietly with nothing but handwork. Arkensallay might not forget what I had done, but in a day or two, the retribution wouldn't be as bad.

My greatest fear was that he would take vengeance on Yetta or even Jiyata. All day, I kept my ears pricked for the sound of raised voices. Thankfully, there were none.

Yetta brought me lunch and dinner. Once the men had left the main room in the evening, I offered to clean up so that the two women could get some rest.

They gratefully accepted, and I spent the next few hours washing dishes. It was late when I finished, but I didn't feel tired, not to mention that my dreams of late had been anything but comforting.

Earlier, I'd started working on stitching up a torn shirt belonging to one of the slaves. I quietly fetched it from the sleeping room where Jiyata and Yetta were enjoying their repose.

The fire in the main room still had some white-hot embers, which cast enough light to work by. Even though the summer heat was nearly unbearable, Arshenn had the fire lit every night before he came in for dinner, refusing to eat by candlelight alone.

I sank to my knees on the hearth and took up where I'd left off. The shirt was hardly worth saving, but Arshenn never bought his slaves new clothing. They had to find a way to afford it themselves or continue wearing the patched and re-patched garments.

I wondered how many of the men sleeping in the slave house were saving for their freedom and how many had given up and spent the little money they managed to earn on wine. More than once, I'd seen some of them stumbling back after a long day at market. Arshenn never cared how drunk they got, so long as they were ready to work the next morning.

In less than half an hour, I'd done all I could for the shirt. I was folding it and gathering my sewing supplies when someone entered the room. I hadn't heard or seen anything; however, I sensed his presence.

My shoulders stiffened slightly, but I did not turn. I already knew who was standing behind me. Todd was the only person able to move that silently. I waited in perfect stillness as he came and knelt beside me on the hearth.

My head was held high, eyes straight forward, folded shirt clutched tightly in my hands.

"Astra," he said in a quiet voice.

I slowly glanced to the right and looked at him. He studied my face for a moment, then relaxed a little.

Something was in his hand. Slowly, he held it up.

"I made this for you," he told me. "I hope you'll forgive me, but the center of the stone is unusually hard, and I couldn't cut through it, so the shape isn't exactly perfect."

141

The object to which he referred was a blue stone, one of those from the cave in The Valley of the North Wind. Across its surface now ran numerous strands of metal, silver in color, like the web of a spider. They were so thin as to be almost invisible. On opposite sides, two long, black cords were attached.

I wasn't sure what the object could possibly be, but I figured it was important, since it certainly would have taken a long time to set the stone in such an intricate network of silver metal.

"Astra, will you marry me?"

Of all the things I had expected to come out of his mouth, that was the very last one.

I physically recoiled. "What?"

"Be my life mate—or whatever. Isn't that what your people call it?" he asked.

"No," I told him.

"Well, you know what I mean anyway, don't yo–"

"No, I won't marry you," I interrupted him.

Todd hesitated, glancing down at his hands, which still held the blue stone entwined in silver.

"Think about it for just a minute," he began slowly, looking at me through his dark eyelashes. "Everything will be much simpler if you become my betrothed. We can have our own home and be happy."

"Yes," I muttered. "Everything would be just wonderful until I couldn't bear you enough sons or you found someone younger and prettier."

Todd's mouth dropped open slightly. "That would never happen," he spluttered. "I know that things haven't been right between us recently. But there was a time when we were friends. We've both made some mistakes, but I'm willing to forgive and forget if you are."

"My only mistake was not killing you when I had the chance," I spat.

Todd flinched at my venomous words.

It was difficult to keep my voice low as anger swelled within me. "I did consider you a friend," I told him. "I trusted you once, but all it led to was betrayal."

"What are you talking about?" Todd demanded.

"You turned on us. Attacked those who cared about you. How could you have—"

"You and Cole were trying to kill me!" Todd interrupted. "Besides, I never laid a finger on him. Plus, you were the ones hunting me. I'm sorry about your leg, but I was defending myself. I never planned to bring you here. I tried to find Cole and lead him back to you, so he could take you home. But you were dying, and I didn't know wh—"

"I'm not talking about me and Cole," I snarled. "I'm talking about Kisa and Rollan."

"Kisa and Rollan?" Todd spoke their names as if he'd never heard them before.

"You may not have been on the best terms with Rollan and considered him fair game, but how could you hurt Kisa?" I nearly sobbed.

"I didn't." Todd shook his head. "What happened to Rollan and Kisa?"

"You attacked them!" I hissed.

Todd's eyes widened. "I didn't- I- don't understand. Who told you that?"

"Cole," I answered firmly.

Todd clenched his jaw. "Cole lied to you."

I let out a little laugh. "Cole lied to me?" I echoed him. "No. Cole has never lied to me. Cole is the truest person I know."

"But I never—"

"Then why did you act so defensive in the cave?" I interrupted. "You sure looked like you'd been in a fight."

"I was the one who was attacked."

Raising one skeptical eyebrow, I waited for Todd to go on.

"I was minding my own business, bringing one of the stallions in from the field—like I was told—when four of your North Wind *friends* jumped me," Todd insisted. "I figured my cover was blown, so I ran for the cave. They followed as far as the valley entrance, and I figured someone might come along to finish the job.

"I wasn't sure who had given me away. So yes, I was a little cautious. I had only one thought on my mind, escape."

"Yet, you paused long enough to steal the stones," I pointed out bitterly.

"I couldn't come back empty-handed."

"Wasn't the information about how to attack my people enough?" I asked.

"I wasn't going to tell anyone about The Clan," he answered softly. "I just needed something to show. I didn't want to have to kill anyone."

"You mean anyone else," I retorted.

"What are you talking about?" he demanded.

"Neither Kisa nor Rollan survived your attack. They're dead now. You murdered them!" I snarled at him.

"No," he whispered. "Kisa can't be–" His voice rose until he was almost yelling. "I didn't attack her, or either of them. I never would have–"

The look on my face showed how little I believed him. His words faltered.

"I don't fully understand what happened the day I left," he started again. "But I don't think you do either. You don't have to believe me, but I promise you, in the name of the gods, I never even saw them."

"Todd, just stop," I ordered. "I'm done believing your lies."

I turned away from him and finished gathering up the supplies I had been using to mend the shirt.

On my right, Todd rose.

"Fine," he said bitterly. "Don't listen to me."

I expected him to walk away immediately, but he hesitated, then bent down.

My body went rigid as his hands reached over my head. His fingers barely brushed my skin as he placed the blue stone in the hollow of my neck, then secured it in place with the two black pieces of cord.

"Wear this," he ordered, voice full of defeat. "They'll think- well, they should leave you alone if you have it on."

I blinked, not understanding, then he was gone. In the dying firelight, I raised a hand to the new weight on my chest. My fingers traced the stone set in the twisted metal. Finally, I realized that it was a necklace.

Todd had made me a necklace once before. The first one had been far simpler, adorned only with a claw from the bear that had almost ended my life.

Part of me wanted to tear this token from my throat, especially after what he had said concerning it. However, the blue stone was a piece of home, the only piece I had at the moment, and I did not have the will to remove it.

Needless to say, my sleep was troubled that night. I saw no living person, but I was once again in the stable of The North Wind on that last, ghastly day. I refused to get up, refused to look in any of the stalls, no matter what I heard.

I sat down in the hall and put my hands over my ears. The noises were still audible. I heard screams, both from humans and animals. None of them were familiar, and none of them called my name, for which I was eternally grateful.

Just as I was starting to think I might make it through this dream without anything worse happening, the door to the stall across from me slid slowly open on its own. I could do nothing but stare in horror at the abomination that crept out.

The animal was completely covered in blood. It staggered toward me on wobbly legs. Not until it was quite close was I able to tell that it was a goat. The creature suddenly stumbled forward and fell across my lap.

My breath came in great gasps as I vainly tried to push the animal's carcass away. The instant my hands left my ears, the terrible cries that filled the air were intensified.

No matter how much I struggled, I was unable to get the goat off my legs. Blood was everywhere, so much blood, too much blood. My hands were completely saturated with it.

The screams grew louder and louder until I gave up trying to move the creature and clapped my bloody hands back over my ears.

It didn't help. Nothing helped. The shrieking was too loud. It filled every moment, every thought. Only in the instant when I was certain my eardrums would burst, did I realize that I was shrieking too.

CHAPTER 18
PUNISHMENT

Yetta shook me awake. The nightmare in the stable had been the most vivid of the night's dreams, but there were plenty of others. Each had driven out the last. I couldn't seem to shake the feeling of something warm and sticky on my hands. There had been so much blood.

"More nightmares?" Yetta asked sympathetically.

I nodded but didn't share the details. I chose to try and forget the horrors of the night rather than dwelling on them.

Settling into the routine of cooking breakfast helped calm me. However, I found I had no appetite when we sat down to our share of the warm bread, fresh milk, and greasy bits of ham.

Todd was not present for breakfast. I assumed he'd left even earlier than usual, probably trying to avoid me. Yetta had wordlessly eyed the blue stone necklace I still wore. Jiyata had given me a warm smile when she saw it but made no comment.

In the late afternoon, there was a commotion outside. Husanil stepped into the kitchen, where Jiyata and I were cleaning vegetables for dinner. Yetta was sitting at the hand mill, grinding wheat.

"Lord Arshenn requests your presence immediately," he reported.

"Todicmadaya must be back," Jiyata guessed as she and I approached the door.

"He would like all of you," Husanil said when Yetta made no move to join us.

Concern crossed the two women's faces as Husanil departed.

"What's going on?" I asked.

147

There was a long moment of silence. The fear in Jiyata's eyes turned to panic as she hurried past me.

"Nothing good," Yetta muttered, following her out of the kitchen.

Todd had returned, but he was not the center of attention at the moment. The slaves stood in a line, with Arshenn pacing up and down in front of them. Husanil flanked his master.

Todd and Arkensallay were a short distance away, their backs to us as we slowly approached.

Arshenn glanced our way. His eyes went instantly to the stone at my throat, but he gave no other acknowledgment of our presence. He quickly returned his attention to the assembled men.

We came to a halt when we neared Arkensallay and Todd. The only thing breaking the ghastly silence was the footsteps of the pacing men.

Finally, Arshenn stopped in front of one of the slaves, a short, dark-haired man with a long scar on his right arm, which ran from his elbow to the missing tip of his forefinger.

"Rounce," he said softly. "Who was it?"

"It is hard to know, my lord," the slave, Rounce, replied.

Arshenn almost snarled and stepped toward the next man. "Who was it?" he echoed. The slave just shook his head.

"Anyone?" Arshenn called.

He turned away in disgust when no answer came.

"If you are all in league together, then you will all be punished together," he pronounced with his back to the small cluster of men. There was an uneasy stirring at his words.

"Husanil, fetch the whip," Arshenn ordered.

Husanil dipped his head and hurried off.

"It was Cartner," one of the slaves blurted out. Instantly, every eye was on the speaker, a lanky young man with close-cropped, dirty blond hair.

"I woke up this morning before dawn, and his bed was empty. I didn't think much of it at the time, but it has to be him."

"He's been talking about some wench in town for the past two moons," another man added. He resembled the first speaker

148

almost exactly, except that his hair was about four inches longer and completely unruly. There were a few murmurs of agreement from the others.

The man, who I took for Cartner, looked around in bewilderment. He was older than most of the other slaves. It was hard to guess his true age from studying his face. He had wrinkles, but there was so much grime covering his skin, it was impossible to make them out very well. He was of average height and not well put together, with matted hair, a bland shade of brown, and pale blue eyes.

"I didn't go anywhere this morning," he protested, as accusing eyes fell on him from all sides.

"Yes, you did," the first speaker shot back. "You might as well go ahead and own it. I ain't taking a whipping for your sake."

Just at that moment, Husanil returned bearing a long, black whip. The kind I would never have used on a horse.

"I swear by the gods that I did not go anywhere." Cartner turned his eyes toward Arshenn. He stumbled forward a few steps and fell to his knees. "It wasn't me. They're lying," he gasped. "Please believe me."

There was a moment of stillness. It appeared that Arshenn was making up his mind.

I knew that wasn't the case. Arshenn's mind was made up; right or wrong, he didn't care. The reason for the delay was the painful suspense. He loved the mental torment he was inflicting as much as the physical punishment that was sure to follow.

"Well, Cartner," he began slowly. "If you've made enemies, that's your fault. It's every man for himself around here. They have no reason to protect you."

"But they're making it all up!" Cartner insisted.

"Take him to the post," Arshenn ordered over the man's pleading protests.

Two of the other slaves seized the kneeling man and hauled him toward the stable. Outside was a pair of tall, wooden poles. Normally, they were used to tie horses.

Not today.

Today, Cartner was tied to one of the posts, his arms stretched over his head. Much as I didn't want to witness this, I knew I had to. Arshenn wanted everyone to watch, not only as an added humiliation for the man he had deemed guilty but as a warning to others. I forced the emotion out of my face and looked on expressionlessly.

One of the two men who had spoken out most strongly ripped Cartner's shirt away from his back, exposing it to Arshenn and the black whip he carried.

I heard the parting of the fabric and, in the back of my mind, I knew I'd have to stitch it up later. Funny how something like that could pop into my head at a moment such as this. I focused on that thought to distract myself from the scene unfolding before me. My trick stopped working the moment the first blow fell.

The whipping was unlike anything I'd witnessed before. My people didn't believe in physical punishment once one reached a certain age. We'd all received a wrap on our knuckles from our teachers at one time or another for unruly behavior, but around the age of ten, even that ended.

Instead of our bodies, it was our honor that was damaged when we did something against the community.

But that wouldn't work here, I realized. *These people have no honor.*

Cartner cried out with each stroke of Arshenn's hand as the whip cut deep furrows in his skin. Blood ran down his back and began to pool in the dry dirt.

Jiyata turned her face away, unable to bear the sight of pain and misery. Yetta looked on, but without seeing anything.

Finally, it was over. Cartner was cut loose but was too weak to keep his feet. He slumped to the ground with a piteous cry.

"Get him out of here," Arshenn ordered, handing the whip back to Husanil and heading to the forge.

A few of the slaves came forward and dragged the wounded man into the stable. Even after they'd closed the door, I could still hear his muffled groans.

Yetta's hand fell on my arm, and she drew me back toward the dwelling. We finished making dinner in silence. Much as I tried to focus on my work, my mind kept drifting back to the events of the afternoon.

Once dinner had been eaten, and we were cleaning the dishes, I turned to Yetta. "Why did they take him into the stable?"

"So that he won't keep the rest of them awake tonight with his moaning," Yetta answered. She must have been thinking about this afternoon as well, because, even though my question had been rather vague, she hadn't required any context to answer it.

"Do you think he's all right?" I asked.

It was Jiyata who answered this time. "Slaves don't usually die from a simple whipping. Most of the time, it only takes a few days before they're ready to go back to work."

I nodded, but even the words, spoken in Jiyata's honest fashion, did little to reassure me.

When I lay down in bed, I couldn't seem to repress my feelings anymore. The instant I closed my eyes, I saw the man lying broken on the ground, bleeding out into the straw of the stable.

At first, I tried to push away the image; then, my eyes snapped open. What was I becoming if I could force myself to turn a blind eye to the pain of another? In that split second, my mind was made up. I lay still, but every inch of my body was tense.

It was a long time before the breathing of Yetta and Jiyata fell into the pattern of those in a deep sleep.

As soon as I deemed it safe, I rose and quietly changed into my clothes. I stole from the room as silently as a shadow. Just before I left the sleeping quarters, I paused. If it was this easy to escape, why didn't I just go?

How far would they actually pursue me? I wouldn't go straight back to The Clan, but that was all right; I knew how to survive. I could even take a few weapons and some supplies.

As quickly as the plan came to me, it fizzled out. If I left, Jiyata and Yetta were sure to be blamed for it. If only I could take them with me. The task of keeping all three of us alive in the wild

151

would be nothing compared with the challenge of trying to convince the pair to leave in the first place. Yetta would never go without Jiyata, and Jiyata would never leave Todd. And that was the other reason I couldn't go.

Todd.

He knew where The Land of the Clan lay and how to find it again.

He's going to tell anyway, I thought. *He's just biding his time.*

The longer I imagined running, the worse of an idea it seemed. I might not be allowed to rejoin The Clan, even if I did manage to reach the borders in safety. Then what would I do?

As I crept into the kitchen, I let all thoughts of escape pass out of my head.

Not tonight, I told myself. *Maybe someday, but not tonight.*

Bright moonlight fell through the windows, giving me enough light to see without a candle. I started searching the shelves for the items I would need—some cloth for bandages and a jug of water for cleansing.

I was just about to leave the dwelling when I heard a footstep behind me. "You'll want this too," a voice said in the darkness.

It was Yetta. I whipped around to find her holding out a small wooden bowl. She chuckled slightly at my astonishment.

"You couldn't leave a horse to die in that stable, much less a man. I figured you'd find your way over there before long."

I relaxed slightly.

"You're too kind," she warned me softly. "It's going to get you killed someday."

She took a few steps forward and gave me the bowl. The smell coming out of it was familiar and herbal.

"What is this?" I asked.

"It's a salve," she answered. "Like the one I used on your leg."

"Thank you. I'm sure Cartner will be grateful," I said.

I'd thought Yetta too callused by the cruelties of life to make a gesture such as this for someone she never spoke to.

"I'm not doing it for him," Yetta replied mildly. "For all I know, he got what he deserved. But his pain hurts you, so I thought I'd try to help, for your sake."

My throat tightened. "Thank you," I said again. This time it came out as a whisper.

She nodded gruffly. "Don't get caught."

With the salve and other supplies in hand, I headed for the stable. The door was slightly ajar, letting me see for the first few yards.

Before I even entered, I could hear the flies circling.

I paused just inside the door, allowing my eyes to adjust to the gloom. After a moment, I spotted the shape of a human body lying off to the left, far back in the shadows. Even when I pushed the door open a few more feet, the light didn't quite reach Cartner's still form.

As I made my way to his side, I half feared that the man was dead. When I was a few paces away, I heard the raspy sound of his shallow breathing.

Carefully, I arranged the articles I had brought from the dwelling so I could find them easily in the dark. I didn't dare light a candle for fear of discovery and because the stable was full of hay. It had been such a dry summer that the entire place could go up from nothing more than a spark.

Cartner was either unconscious or in a deep sleep. He was lying on his stomach, so I didn't have to move him to start treating his injuries.

I rested a hand gently on his flesh and found it burning. Wetting one of the rags with water, I started bathing the long cuts on his back. I tried to be as thorough as possible, but in the dark, it was hard to tell if I was missing spots.

After washing each abrasion, I applied a small amount of an herb called marigold, which I'd taken from the kitchen. It was one of the few I recognized. I knew the sharp-smelling plant would help the wounds close faster and keep them from getting infected.

When I was about halfway done, Cartner groaned. My hand froze, still extended over the man's back. I wasn't sure what the slave's reaction would be to finding me here.

A moment later, he was still again. I continued with my work at a faster pace. As I applied more marigold, his hand twitched. My vision was well adjusted now, and I saw his eyelids flutter and remain open, but he didn't move.

Consciousness seemed to be coming back to him slowly. Another groan escaped his lips, louder this time.

"Easy," I said soothingly, precisely as I would have to a wounded horse. "You're going to be all right."

There was a long moment of silence.

"Girl from the stars?" a haggard voice wheezed in the darkness.

"I'm here," I answered.

More silence. I continued working.

"Why are you helping me?" Cartner sounded more awake now.

"Why do humans ever help one another?" I asked.

"They don't," the man returned darkly. "Unless they want something from you."

"I don't want anything from you," I promised.

Ten minutes elapsed in which neither of us spoke. I changed out the cloth I'd been using for a fresh one. Cartner wasn't groaning anymore, and I thought he'd fallen asleep.

My assumption was proven wrong a moment later.

"I didn't do it, you know," he muttered. His voice carried a thick accent, and he was lazy about the pronunciation of the end of some words.

"That doesn't matter to me," I told him, shaking my head even though it was far too dark for him to see. "In fact, I don't even know what it was that Arshenn was so upset about."

"Lord Arshenn," Cartner corrected me quickly.

Normally, I would have been annoyed by this, but the way he said it was so natural, it broke my heart.

"*Lord* Arshenn," I pronounced for his benefit.

"It was his horse," Cartner continued a moment later.

"Pride?" I asked in surprise. This was the first I'd heard about the stallion's involvement.

"Yes," the slave groaned. "Someone left the gate open this morning, and the horses got out."

"It happened before," I remembered aloud. "Only, that time, another stallion came and stole some of the mares."

"Did quite a number on Pride, too," Cartner recalled.

"Yes," I agreed.

"This time, Lord Arshenn was twice as furious, even though Pride and the mares weren't far away. There were lots of footprints around the gate, as if someone's been going that way often in the early morning when the dirt is still wet from the dew."

The breath caught in my throat.

"Why did the others accuse you?" I choked out.

Cartner sighed. "I'm old and slow. The brothers, Hont and Gupen, dislike me. They're always getting me in trouble. They'd be just as happy if I died."

I was only half listening. I knew who had been creeping away every morning, cutting through the fields.

"I don't have no woman," Cartner went on wearily. "What one would even look at me? An old, broken-down slave without a penny to his name."

"How did you become a slave?" I asked, putting down the rag and picking up the wooden bowl full of salve.

"My father was a failed tradesman. Before me and my brothers were ten years old, he was so far in debt that we were all sold as slaves. I've had many masters and lived many places, but never seemed to fit in anywhere."

I carefully laid a scoop of the pulpy goo from the bowl on Cartner's back and began using it to seal his wounds. The skin beneath my hands felt cooler now, which I took for a good sign.

"Do you still get to see your brothers?" I inquired. "On market days?"

There was a pause before the answer came to me out of the darkness. "No, I haven't seen my brothers since they were sold and wouldn't recognize them now if we did run into each other. I don't know if they're alive or dead."

"I'm so sorry," I whispered.

Neither of us spoke again as I finished with the salve. I'd only used half of it and slid the wooden bowl under a loose board. I also concealed some of the clean cloths for future use.

"I've done all I can," I told Cartner, preparing to rise.

Somehow his hand found mine in the dark. He gripped me tightly for a moment. "Thank you, girl from the stars," he whispered. For the last few minutes, his words had been growing softer. A moment later, exhaustion finally claimed him, and he was asleep. Not unconscious, but truly sleeping.

My hand was still grasped in his. I gently tried to free myself, but the fear of waking him made me stop. Instead, I waited, doubting he could hold on very long while asleep.

I don't know what time it was when I woke up, but the early morning birds were singing. It was still dark in the stable, and I could hear Cartner's rhythmic breathing just in front of me.

My hand was free, so I scrambled to gather up the items I was taking back to the kitchen. Carefully, I pulled the stable door closed and approached the dwelling.

The sky was mostly black. Only slight traces of indigo could be seen in the east. The dwelling was quiet, and I thought the household was still asleep. However, I nearly ran into someone the moment I entered the kitchen.

I froze as my eyes met Todd's. He took in everything at a glance, from the blood-stained rags to the half-empty jug of water.

"What–" Todd started, then stopped. He wasn't stupid. He knew where I had been and why. Anger flared up suddenly deep in my chest. I pushed past him.

"Astra?" Todd asked in a wavering voice. "What's wrong?"

I ignored him. It was his fault that a man had been beaten nearly to death, his fault for being careless and not admitting it.

"Astra?" he tried again.

I bit my tongue to keep from screaming accusations at him and waking the entire dwelling. Instead, I slammed the water jug down on the wooden table with a thud and turned to face him. My gaze hardened as our eyes met for a second time.

I knew what he'd done, and he knew that I knew.

He closed his mouth and swallowed, then turned and fled without a backward glance. This time, he took the road instead of cutting across the fields. Somehow, I doubted he would ever take that shortcut again.

As soon as Todd left, my anger burned out, leaving me feeling weak and sick. What had I ever seen in him?

CHAPTER 19
PHANTOMS

The next night, I again stole from my bed. All day, my thoughts had been on the man in the stable. The treatment had certainly helped him, but he needed more care. His body was weak from years of being overworked and underfed.

It was a struggle not to fall asleep the instant my head hit the pillow. The minutes seemed to stretch on for hours. I dozed a little, then snapped awake, ashamed of my lack of discipline. At last, the dwelling was quiet.

I was more careful tonight. I'd left everything I would need sitting in the kitchen so that I wouldn't make any clatter. This time, I resolved to be so silent and swift that not even Yetta would realize I was gone.

Just as I gathered my supplies from the table, I saw a ray of light coming through the window from outside. Slowly, I set the items back down and crouched in the shadows.

I knew it couldn't be the dawn. The light appeared to be cast by flames fluttering softly in the wind. Cautiously, I crept to the window and pushed the curtains open a tiny bit, giving myself a clear view of the yard.

Figures.

At first, I only saw the three holding torches. A moment later, my eyes comprehended that there were at least a dozen. Each was wearing a long, black cloak. Their hoods were pulled up, masking their faces in complete shadow.

One I hadn't even noticed walked by quite close to the window. I held my breath until it was past. On the shoulder of its cloak and on the back, I could make out some sort of red mark. It was a vertical line, split by a second line close to the bottom. It wasn't very large, but the red coloring was brilliant and glinted in the firelight.

Even though what I was seeing could have easily qualified as the beginning of one of my nightmares, I knew I wasn't asleep.

One of the figures, flanked by two others, approached the stable. Fear stabbed through me, not for myself, but for Cartner. Who were these people, and what business did they have with him?

A few minutes later, the first figure reemerged into the firelight. Behind him, the other two were half-dragging, half-carrying Cartner. He'd been bound hand and foot. A rag was tied over his mouth to serve as a gag.

The horror of the situation froze me. This could not be real. My perception of reality must have become skewed, making me unable to realize that this was a dream. At least, that was what I tried to convince myself.

All the cloaked figures moved in as the wounded man was brought out. They converged around a lone figure. Cartner was brought before it.

The figure raised an arm and touched Cartner's face with a long, black claw. At an unseen signal, the dark figures formed ranks. Four of them lifted Cartner's struggling body between them and vanished into the trees beyond the stable.

One of the remaining figures suddenly turned toward the place where I crouched, peeking through the curtains. A sense of dread, unlike anything I'd ever known, filled me. This was something impossible, something out of one of Todd's stories. Slowly, I eased myself backward. Then rose and raced down the hall, back to my room.

The bed was still warm. What had felt to me like hours had indeed only been moments. I climbed under the blankets, despite the smothering heat of the room. As I lay there, quivering from head to foot, I longed for sleep, for nightmares. Anything, anything at all, would be better than reality.

This place, this horrible place, filled with evil I could not even explain, was worse than any nightmare I had ever endured, and I was going to be here for the rest of my life. There would be no waking, no morning light to chase away the darkness of my bad dreams. Now my nightmares would be my only refuge. At least I could take comfort in the fact that the pain and horror they caused me was not real.

I don't know if I slept at all the rest of the night, but dawn found me conscious and alert.

As I set a platter of bread on the table for breakfast, Husanil came in looking grave. He went directly to Arshenn and reported that Cartner had disappeared during the night.

"In his condition? How is that possible?" Arshenn bellowed.

"I am not certain, my lord," Husanil answered, bowing his head.

Arshenn's face turned sour. "Take Hont and Gupen," he ordered. "Find that worthless scum and bring him back to me alive. I will make an example out of him for all to see."

Husanil nodded his ascent and departed.

Not even for one moment did I consider confessing to Arshenn what I had seen last night. He wouldn't believe me. I wasn't even sure I believed it myself.

Three days later, no trace of Cartner had been found. I hoped that wherever he'd ended up, it was a better place than his home here had been.

On the next market day, Arshenn returned earlier than usual with a sullen-looking young man who was Cartner's replacement.

Part of my mind was convinced that I had been dreaming the night I'd seen the figures by torchlight and that Cartner really had just run off. However, I couldn't quite make myself believe it.

In the days following, I saw very little of Todd. When I did see him, I could not keep the accusation out of my eyes. The entire situation would have been avoided if he had just told the truth.

One afternoon, Yetta and I were polishing the table in the main room while Jiyata finished dinner. Only a frail breeze, trickling through the open windows, did anything to alleviate the relentless heat. Outside, the sounds of Todd and Arkensallay sparing reached us. Today, they were using wooden staves.

When we finished with the table, its surface was so glossy I could almost see my reflection. I collected the rags and the polish, which was some kind of waxy concoction. Yetta stooped and picked up a few stray bits of dried grass, which had escaped from one of the mats. She headed toward the fireplace, where a fire had been built not twenty minutes earlier.

I'm certain her intent was to discard the chaff into the flames. Just as she walked by the hallway to the kitchen, Todd came barreling through it. One of his hands was clutched tightly to his chest.

He and Yetta ran smack into each other. Even though Yetta was short and stout, the collision with Todd's larger frame sent her toppling to the ground with a cry.

Todd recoiled, letting out a sharp hiss. He glared down at Yetta. "Be more careful next time," he snapped furiously, drawing back his foot as if he was going to kick her.

I'd never seen such an ugly expression on Todd's face. Not when he'd attacked us the first time, not when he'd fallen and broken his arm, and not even in the cave when he'd run from me.

"Todd, don't!" I gasped before he could bring his foot forward.

My voice checked him. He must not have noticed me before, because he spun around in surprise.

His behavior had shocked me so much that I didn't know how to react. Wordlessly, he turned away and vanished down the hall leading to the men's rooms.

Go after him, a voice whispered.

Not going to happen, I told it.

Instead, I helped Yetta to her feet. She was slightly bruised but didn't seem to be broken anywhere.

When we served dinner, Todd was not at the table. Neither Arshenn nor Arkensallay made any mention of his absence.

I was scrubbing potatoes in the kitchen with Yetta several days later when I heard Arshenn calling for Jiyata and me. Jiyata was in the main room. I stuck my head in to make sure she'd heard. She had and was in the process of packing up her sewing.

Together, we stepped into the yard. It had been quite a while since we'd been called to view a duel, but neither of us were surprised to see Arkensallay and Todd facing each other, ringed by men.

As the match began, I could tell that something was different. Todd was usually lithe and quick on his feet, one of the reasons Arkensallay's greater strength didn't win each bout in a matter of minutes.

Today, Todd seemed slow.

"You shouldn't be at the drink before a fight," Arshenn snapped. "It's dulled your skills and your mind."

Todd was struggling hard to keep Arkensallay from landing a blow, but it didn't take long for one to get through his guard. The flat of Arkensallay's blade slammed into the side of Todd's head.

Jiyata let out a strangled cry as Todd toppled to the ground.

Arshenn approached the fallen Todd. He looked down on his son without a speck of compassion.

"Where is the wit that outsmarted the trickster?" Arshenn spat. Todd struggled to get up and managed to make it to his knees.

"Where is the mighty champion who slew a great brown bear?" Reaching out a hand, Arshenn seized the bear claw necklace Todd wore. With a swift jerk, he tore it away from Todd's neck, sending claws flying in all directions.

"Is this what you plan to become?" Arshenn demanded. "A drunken fool, unable to defend himself?

"If fighting does not tickle your fancy, there are other ways to gain honor." I took an unconscious step forward, straining to hear what was said as Arshenn leaned in closer to Todd. "Ways of war and conquest."

I thought I saw Todd's eyes flicker to me for just a moment, then away again.

Arshenn snarled at his silence. "On your feet!" he ordered, turning his back on Todd and marching to the edge of the circle of spectators.

"No," Jiyata breathed. Her hands were clasped tightly to her chest.

The duel began again. This time, Arkensallay was clearly playing with his brother. He'd get in close and give him a push or trip him. It seemed Todd was sent to the ground every half minute or so. Each time, he was slower to get back up.

The fight dragged on and on. There was no competition; it was painfully obvious who the better swordsman was. I kept expecting Arshenn to call a halt to the pointless match, but he didn't. From the look on his face, it seemed he was enjoying this duel more than any before it.

Finally, Todd stopped getting up. He crouched on the ground, gasping for breath. The last hit had been pretty hard, and I could see blood running down the side of Todd's face.

"Everyone back to work," Arshenn announced. The group departed to their various duties.

"Until tomorrow," Arshenn threw back over his shoulder.

I turned as well, knowing that dinner wasn't going to make itself. Jiyata rushed forward. I would have tried to stop her if I had anticipated her action. Instead, I left her to it.

"That took longer than usual," Yetta commented as I rejoined her in the kitchen. Quickly, I recounted today's duel to her. She didn't comment but instead pursed her lips until they were white.

A moment later, Jiyata entered. Her eyes were full of tears. A sickening feeling of dread filled me.

"What's happened?" I asked.

"It's Todicmadaya," she gasped.

"What's wrong with him?" Yetta inquired.

"He's bleeding badly." Jiyata's voice came out as a hoarse whisper. "He ran off to the barn and told me not to follow, but he's hurt. What if he keeps bleeding and dies?"

Her voice had risen to a heartbreaking sob.

"I'm sure he'll be fine," Yetta tried to comfort Jiyata. She gently took the younger woman's hand. "If he had strength enough to tell you to stay away, he can't be in that bad of shape."

Fresh tears filled Jiyata's eyes. "He's not well," she whispered. "His wounds need to be cared for." There was a desperation in her words that I couldn't help experiencing as if the emotion were my own. Her eyes turned on me.

"Please, Astra," she begged. "Please, will you go to him?"

"What?" I blinked in surprise.

"He'll let you help him; you're the only one."

I opened my mouth, not sure what to say. If Todd didn't want Jiyata, why would he want me?

"Please, please, please," Jiyata whispered. "Please help him. Save him."

I paused, conflicted. Even if I didn't owe it to Todd to try and help him, Jiyata had been nothing but kind to me since I arrived. How could I refuse her request, especially when she was so upset?

CHAPTER 20
THE END OF THE WORLD

Before I headed to the stable, Jiyata loaded me down with bandages and more of the salve Yetta had given me for Cartner.

I didn't care if Arshenn or anyone else knew what I was doing. However, if they saw me, they might interfere, so I checked that the coast was clear before walking across the open space between buildings.

Arkensallay's mare and her colt were the only horses currently in the stable. The mare glanced up but didn't even bother laying back her ears. I would have liked to think that after the struggle we'd been through together, she'd come to like me. Sadly, I believe it was more the fact that she was just too exhausted to make a fuss. Her foal was quite a handful, constantly galloping about and kicking at her nastily.

Todd wasn't anywhere to be seen on the first floor of the stable, so I resignedly climbed the wooden ladder to the hayloft. Not an easy feat to accomplish while carrying so many supplies.

At first glance, I thought the loft was empty too; then I spotted Todd. His eyes were closed, and he was sitting in the farthest, darkest corner, leaning against a large bale of hay.

I gritted my teeth as I approached him.

Todd spoke without opening his eyes. "Mother, you shouldn't be here. I told you to leave me alone."

The words didn't sound angry, but they were full of exhaustion and defeat.

"I'm not your mother," I answered, and his eyes snapped open.

"Astra?" My name came out as a hoarse whisper. "What are you doing here?"

"Somebody's got to patch you up," I told him, coming over to where he was resting.

Sitting down, I stretched my hand out toward him. I brushed some of the dark, shaggy hair away from his forehead to reveal a gash just above his left temple. My fingers came away wet with blood.

Reluctantly, I moved several inches forward and used a wet cloth to clean the wound.

Jiyata had been correct about the injury being serious. Half an inch lower and it could have been fatal. I wondered if Arkensallay realized what he'd almost done.

Todd's eyes were closed again, and he didn't stir as I worked.

Soon, the wound was clean, but it was still bleeding. Firmly, I held a cloth against it.

"Why are you doing this, Astra?" Todd murmured wearily, eyes still shut.

I pursed my lips. "Your mother asked me to," I replied at last.

Todd made no comment.

I got the feeling there was more he wanted to say. A few times, I saw words begin to form on his lips, but he didn't speak.

Even among the fragrant hay, I could still distinguish the sour smell I had first inhaled the night of the dinner party. I wondered if that was why he'd performed so poorly today and why he was having trouble forming coherent thoughts.

I might have tried to make conversation, but I didn't know him anymore. Instead, I worked in silence, focusing only on the task at hand.

It took fifteen minutes for the wound to finally stop bleeding. I heard them call dinner at the dwelling. Todd made no move to leave the stable, and I was committed to helping him for the time being.

Even though the sun was at least two hours from setting, the hayloft wasn't well lit. Golden sun rays touched a few bales on the far end of the room, but the mounds of hay surrounding us were no more than dim outlines.

Gently, I removed the cloth from the cut. Todd's breathing was shallow, and I wasn't sure he was even conscious.

I dipped my first two fingers in the salve Jiyata had given me. The herbal substance reminded me of when Kisa used to treat our team's injuries. I had to blink a few times to clear my eyes as I pushed the memory away.

Slowly, I applied the salve and let it sit for a moment before covering it with a bandage. The green goo was sticky enough to hold the small piece of linen in place. Another cloth should probably have been wrapped around Todd's head a few times to keep it in place, but I didn't want to wake him.

Instead, I left the long strip of cloth close by, hoping Todd would be able to do that part himself when he woke up. I gathered my supplies and was debating about whether or not to slip away when Todd spoke.

"Astra," he whispered, opening his eyes. "Are you leaving?"

"I've done all I can," I told him. "Unless you have another injury?" I tried to keep my voice even.

He hesitated, so I dropped back down beside him. "Where else are you hurt?" I asked.

"I'm fine."

It was a lie. I could both see it in his eyes and hear it in his voice.

"Show me," I ordered.

Slowly, Todd reached across his body and pulled his sleeve away to reveal another cut on his upper arm.

This second abrasion wasn't nearly as bad as the first. I would have been able to stop the bleeding, only a little oozing at this point, in a matter of minutes, except his sleeve kept getting in the way. I tried rolling it up, but it wouldn't stay, and the filthy hem kept touching the wound while I was trying to clean it.

"Take off your shirt," I told him.

Todd shook his head sharply, wincing as he did so.

I squinted at him and slowly reached forward to undo the buttons.

His hand fell on mine, stopping my fingers.

"No, don't," he pleaded.

It was my turn to hesitate. "Why?" I asked in confusion.

His jaw clenched, but not in anger. In the dim light, it was hard to tell, but it seemed to me he had tears in his eyes.

"Let me see," I said a moment later.

He didn't answer, and my hand slowly began undoing his buttons again. There was no will left in him to resist. I drew in a sharp breath as I saw the skin beneath the fabric. Every inch of it was bruised, scraped, or cut.

"Todd," I gasped softly, staring at his mangled flesh. "What happened?"

"The same thing that happened today," he told me quietly. "You've seen it. Every day it's the same."

As carefully as I could, I took the shirt from Todd's shoulders. I wetted another cloth and gently started to wash the wounds. Some were close to being nothing but scars; others looked like they'd been made yesterday.

"I'm- sorry," I whispered. "I didn't realize it was this bad."

"It's not your fault," Todd answered, flinching as the cloth touched a patch of raw flesh.

How had I not seen the amount of pain he was in? When we were with my people, he'd been the only one to realize how close to breaking I was. Here, I had overlooked his agony just because I was angry.

"Todd," I began slowly, loneliness crashing over me in a sweeping wave. He glanced up, and I licked my lips before going on. "Just for a few minutes, let's not be Todicmadaya of The House of the King or Astra, Second Clan Leader. Let's just be Astra and Todd."

"Okay," he agreed. "Why?"

My hand holding the cloth slowed as I answered. "Because I want to forget for a little while where we are and what's happened between us.

168

"Tell me one of your stories. Tell me how all of this ends. I want to hear about the end of the world."

"The end of the world," Todd mused. "It's just a legend. No one knows what will really happen. The future is nothing more than a shadow until it becomes a memory."

"Then, where did the story come from?" I wondered. He'd mentioned it a few times on our journey home from the trials, but it never felt like the right time for him to tell it.

Todd shrugged slightly. "As with most of our stories about the gods and their doings, no one remembers."

"I want to hear it anyway," I decided.

Todd nodded.

"As you know," he began, "here, at The Brimming Lake, we are a people divided. Both The House of the King and The House of the Warrior believe their own gods will triumph in the end. As a result, each house tells a slightly different story.

"Since I am from The House of the King, I will tell the legend of the king's ultimate victory, which my house hails as the truth."

His voice changed after he said those words. When Todd was telling a story, his entire countenance was different, and I could almost believe he had lived through all the events he described.

"The gods have waged many battles over the centuries, and they will have many more in the future. At last, the day will come when Arsh, the king, he who is the crown upon the head, will defeat Husam, the warrior, he who is the edge on the sword.

"That day will start just like every day before it. The sun will rise in the east, men will awaken and go about their business, but a great evil will be done, which will begin a chain of events leading to the end of the world.

"A wicked man, who has rejected the gods and serves only evil, will seize a person precious to the gods. In the darkest of hours, blood will be shed. Both god and man alike will watch but do nothing.

169

"When the deed is finished, judgment will come upon the people. Fire will rise from The Brimming Lake and consume all the surrounding lands. Unsatisfied, it will then turn its hunger on the city below. No matter how much water is poured out, the flames will not die.

"Those unable to flee will perish. The fire will rage until all that is left of the city is a patch of ground so black nothing will ever grow upon it again.

"Anyone who manages to escape will be forced to leave The Land of the Brimming Lake forever. All they will have are the staffs in their hands and the clothing on their backs. They will travel many miles, hoping to escape the wrath they have awoken.

"The Lord of the Brimming Lake will perish in a strange land, leaving his followers to fend for themselves. Without him, they will be scattered and divided, like lost sheep.

"Knowing that a new leader must be found, the houses will hold tournaments, as is our custom. A champion will be chosen from each, but before they can meet in battle, something miraculous will happen.

"The gods will send two champions of their own: the forgotten hero from The House of the King and the warrior, who is not of The House of the Warrior. These two will defeat the other champions and then strive against each other."

Todd trailed off as my hands fell still. I'd treated the worst of his injuries but found myself wishing there was more I could do.

"Who wins?" I asked.

Todd blinked as if coming back to himself.

"This is where the story splits," he told me. "My house believes that the forgotten hero of The House of the King will win. Once the blood of the warrior, who is not from The House of the Warrior, has been shed, there will be discord among the people and among the gods.

"Husam and Arsh will take up their swords, and a battle will begin. The final battle. The battle that will decide the fate of men.

"The king's wives, Jiya and Sur, will stand beside the king and face Tohopke and his wife, Zeruiah.

"The torturer, Zeruiah, will attack the fair one, Jiya, with the great whip she carries. Zeruiah will strike again and again, and Jiya will be pressed back as she blocks each stroke with her long knife and iron bracers. Finally, she will make an attack of her own, severing the whip of her opponent.

"All the while, Sur, the dagger in the soul, will strike against him who she hates most. With twin saber swords, she will battle her brother, Tohopke, the beast hidden in the forest. Their fight will be swift, but Sur will be too quick for the wild one's wooden staff.

"She will rake her swords across his back, opening two long slash marks. This will send Tohopke into a rage like that of a boar. He will charge his sister, the sharpened end of his staff thrust forward.

"Sur will dodge, but the blow meant for her will pierce Jiya, the heart in the chest. Her cry will be so loud and sharp that every rock and mountain will shatter, making the earth writhe beneath the feet of the watching humans and the warring gods.

"Though Jiya's wound will be grievous, she will not perish from it. Arsh will turn from the warrior and come to the aid of his favorite wife.

"With one swing of his mighty sword, he shall cleave the hand holding the whip from Zeruiah's wrist. Her black blood will flow across the ground, infecting the plants with a deadly sickness. It will eat away everything green from the earth in a matter of minutes.

"Having disabled Zeruiah, the king will turn back to his old foe, Husam. No matter how long they battle, neither will be able to obtain the upper hand.

"Sur will score another hit on her brother, this time on his right calf. The hater will begin to gain ground against the wild one."

Todd's voice took on a weary tone, as if the account of the battle saddened him.

"Just before Sur can strike the final blow, Zeruiah will sneak up behind her and stab Sur through the heart with a knife. As the life leaves her, great pieces of hail will fall from the sky, killing men, flattening trees, and crushing stone.

"Dezi, the weeper, watching from the shadow of the forest, will leap forward, sobbing in horror. He will fall to his knees before the dead goddess.

"Taking his love in his arms, Dezi will press her to his own heart and give his life force to her. Sur will open her eyes again. In his last moments, Dezi will reach out and caress the face of the girl he loved once more. However, even his act of sacrifice will not be enough to stir the hater's dead heart. She will rise to her feet without so much as a tender look.

"Even as Dezi lies on the ground in death, tears will continue to stream from his eyes. They will turn all the rivers and lakes of the earth salty like the ocean. Soon, there will be nothing left to drink.

"Sur will call Todkala, the fox creeping through the night, to aid her. Todkala will hesitate, for his strength lies in cunning, not direct assault, but in the end, he will go to her side and face Zeruiah.

"Finally, she who is the dagger in the soul will strike down her brother. It will not ease her hatred, but she will be glad to have done it with her own hand. When Tohopke is slain, his heart will burst, and all the animals of the world will die with him. Each will struggle and gasp for life, but it will not be granted them.

"All the while, the battle between the king and the warrior will grow fiercer and fiercer. Arsh will be cut across the chest. Husam will have a terrible wound on his thigh. Still, the two will fight on against the pain and each other.

"Even though she fights with only one hand, Zeruiah will push Todkala back. When the torturer sees that her husband has fallen, she will attack fearlessly, no longer caring if she dies.

"In fear, the trickster will flee from her. He will run to his brother for protection. As he reaches Arsh, the king will seize his younger brother and shove him directly at Husam's sword.

"Todkala will be impaled by the warrior's blade. This distraction will allow Arsh time to strike a mortal blow against his old friend.

"Both Husam and Todkala will fall together. The king will use his blade to put out the eyes of him who was the edge on the sword. When this is done, another great fire will rage. It will devour the earth and the oceans at once.

"The king will kneel beside his brother for just a moment. With his hand outstretched, Todkala will beg for life, but the king will not sacrifice himself as Dezi did. He will bid farewell to his brother and then watch him die.

"Sur will have finished off Zeruiah by this time. Arsh will gather Jiya, still wounded, in his arms and call Sur to his side. The three will stand together in the circle of dead gods, the earth around them destroyed.

"When the blood of the five dead gods meets, a red liquid will flow out of the ground. Hotter than fire, it will begin to purge everything, leaving in its wake nothing but black land and gray ash.

"From inside the circle of dead gods, a bright light will erupt, a golden light that will carry the king back to his heavenly home of old. Just before he steps forward, he will pause and look at the group of scattered humans who have witnessed the end of the world. He will feel generous toward them and call for those of The House of the King.

"Many will come, but he will reject all who were not born of the right house or any who are defective, slow in the mind, or cowardly. The king's generosity will be so great that he will call his faithful followers who have died. Thus, hundreds of generations of The House of the King will be raised to join him in victory.

"Once all of Arsh's true followers have assembled, they will step into the blood of the slain gods and be made pure. Together, they will stand with the king in the brilliant light. The rest of mankind will be abandoned to perish on the ruined earth.

"Arsh, his two wives, and their followers will be taken into the sky. A great feast will be held there. Everyone will have enough to eat, and the glorious king will give each man land of his own.

"And all things will be perfect forevermore."

CHAPTER 21
DOUBT

I felt strangely emotionless when the story came to an end.

"It's a tragedy," I breathed.

"What is?" Todd asked.

"All of it," I replied. "The entire story of the world is a tragedy."

"Why?"

I shook my head. "There's no hope. There's no hope in any of it."

"But the king will–"

"Will what?" I wondered. "Will take only those born a certain way? Only those who are good enough? I'm not of The House of the King. Doesn't that mean I will never be accepted?"

Todd reflected on my words. "I'm not sure," he answered at last. "I'm not sure about anything anymore."

The silence went on for quite a while as I pondered all I had heard. Slowly, my thoughts turned toward The Land of the Clan and The North Wind.

"Let's say that I believe you aren't lying about- about Kisa and Rollan," I started. The words came out almost unbidden.

Todd looked at me sharply.

"Why would Cole lie to me?" I put to him.

"I don't know," his voice was full of exhaustion as he answered me.

I nodded. One of them had to be lying, but which one?

The sun was setting now, casting deep shadows across the gloomy hayloft. Yet, I felt no need to stir, no need to leave. My instincts were telling me to lay down, to sleep here, among the hay, and let all the troubles of this world fade. Here I would find no nightmares. This was a familiar place, a safe place.

Beside me, Todd let out a long sigh. He hadn't bothered replacing his shirt. In the dusky light, the bruises on his body looked even more ghastly.

"Why don't you leave?" I asked him. "Why not get a dwelling of your own?"

"I can't," Todd whispered, eyes downcast.

"Why not?" I wondered.

"Because I'm not going to leave you here alone," he replied in a resolved tone. "Unless," pausing, he raised his dark eyes to my face. "Unless you would come with me?"

Two hours ago, I would have been incensed by his words, but now a part of me longed to say yes. Then I would be free of this place, beyond the grasp of Arshenn.

"What about your mother?" I asked.

And mine? I added mentally.

Todd's face fell. "I can't help her," he admitted.

I nodded, understanding his situation only too well.

A weary sigh escaped my lips. "What are you going to do then?" I asked.

"Pray for my father's death," Todd muttered readily.

I laughed a little, but without much humor.

"If you wish it, I will find a way to get you home," Todd promised suddenly. His tone, which a moment before had been sarcastic, was now completely serious.

"Won't that put you in a bad spot?" I asked.

Todd shrugged in defeat. "I don't really care anymore. It's not right for me to keep you if you don't want to stay."

Again, he offered escape, but the same obstacles barred my way, plus a few extras to boot.

We didn't talk much more but sat together until it was pitch black outside. By then, Todd seemed to be feeling better.

The dwelling was dark, and we parted ways wordlessly. Something had changed between us. I didn't think of him as the enemy anymore.

In the morning, Jiyata expressed her gratitude. She continued to thank me throughout the day. It was embarrassing enough, but to top things off, I caught Yetta grinning at me every time Jiyata brought it up. Apparently, she found my discomfort amusing.

A few days later, Todd asked me to go with him to market day the next morning. I agreed and found I was actually pleased to see his eyes light up.

Since the night in the loft, he'd been coming home earlier. In the sparring matches with Arkensallay, he was more alert and defended himself better. Still, he lost every time. However, the margin of skill between the two didn't seem quite so great as before.

Once we entered the city, it didn't take us long to break off from the others. Todd didn't ask permission, and Arshenn made no move to stop us. It appeared he wasn't paying attention, but I had the distinct impression that he was completely aware of our departure.

At first, we wandered among the booths, just looking to see what was being sold. There were quite a few items I had never seen before. Todd showed me something called a sash. It was a decorative piece of fabric that one wrapped around their body. If I looked at it from the eyes of a Clan member, the item was a pointless waste of time and fabric. However, Todd's people saw it as something of value, a piece of vivid color that could be worn.

"Come this way," Todd said, grabbing my hand suddenly and pulling me down one of the side streets. A strange sound was resonating from somewhere up ahead, and a crowd had gathered.

As we got closer, I saw that a rugged, wooden stage had been constructed at the end of the street. On it were three men holding the oddest contraptions I'd ever seen. The noise I'd heard was coming from them.

The first man held a long, thin tube. He placed it to his lips and moved his fingers along its length. The sound that came out was shrill but not unpleasant.

Another of the men had a semi-circle of wood, almost like a bow, but there were too many strings, I counted at least ten of them, all running in the same direction. When the man moved his fingers across these, it produced the sweetest sound imaginable.

The third man was singing, as I'd witnessed Todd do in the past. He was also holding a cylinder, the end of which he struck with his hand at regular intervals. It gave a dull thud with each blow.

"I should have brought you to see this last time," Todd said, his mouth close to my ear. "I forgot you've never heard music before."

I nodded, my eyes fixed on the trio of men.

This thing, music, was completely new to me. Todd had sung a few simple songs in my presence, but there had never been anything accompanying them. The best way to describe it would be to think of a deaf person suddenly hearing the chirping of the birds for the very first time.

I could have watched them all day, and Todd made no move to guide me away. Every so often, the music would stop, then start again with a completely different sound, strange, but no less intriguing than the last.

After forty-five minutes, the men on the stage were replaced by a group of five. Three of them held the contraptions that made the music. The last two, one a man and one a woman, used only their voices. The sound now was louder, more energetic.

The crowd around us grew excited. Before long, many were swaying in place. Suddenly, several people began making erratic movements as though they had lost their minds.

"What are they doing?" I called to Todd.

I didn't catch his answer the first time. The words were swept away with the noise from the stage and those watching.

"What?" I asked.

"They're dancing!" Todd yelled back. "Keep watching."

At first, everyone "danced" independently, but when the music changed, two lines formed, facing each other. Todd joined one of them. I moved back, trying to stay out of the way.

In fascination, I observed as Todd and the others made identical foot movements. It reminded me of some of the drills I'd seen done at The Barracks. However, it appeared that the participants here were enjoying themselves.

When the music faded and began again, the lines broke up. I expected that to be the end, but I was incorrect. The men and women who had been in the lines began to pair off. A young couple whirled past me, their rapturous expressions so intimate they seemed only to see each other.

I caught sight of Todd with a girl of about Kisa's age. Their feet moved in unison. When he stepped backward, she stepped forward. When he stepped left, she stepped right.

At one point, the girl made a misstep. A slightly mortified expression crossed her face. Todd laughed and said something which seemed to put her at ease. As I watched him, I felt guilty for thinking he could ever have raised his hand against Kisa, but Cole had told me that he had.

We didn't stay too much longer. I would have been content to remain forever, but Todd tempted me with something I could not resist. He said that at sun high, all the three-year-old colts and fillies that were for sale would be paraded.

To my surprise, we had to cross the river to the side of the city designated for The House of the Warrior.

"Don't tell my father," Todd said with a wink as we stepped onto one of the bridges. This half of the city was nearly identical to the other. From the buildings to the people, I could see little difference.

The place Todd took us was on the outskirts. There was already a huge crowd gathered for the event. Carefully, we threaded our way to the front until a wooden fence brought us to a halt. The space where the animals were to be shown was rectangular and quite large. The two long sides appeared to be a quarter of a mile in length. There was a set of steps leading up to a narrow stage in the center. Nine men stood at intervals along the platform, which nearly halved the arena.

"We're just in time," Todd announced gleefully.

A moment later, the horses began filing in. Most were led by a handler or two, but a few of the better-trained colts and fillies were ridden. A large number was displayed on each horse's halter.

As the first one approached the fence where Todd and I stood, along with hundreds of other observers, the colt rolled his eyes and reared slightly.

The handler turned on him, and the short whip he carried was applied to the beast's neck. The poor colt dropped back to the ground, still keeping his eyes fixed on the massive crowd.

It wasn't surprising that the foal was on edge. I'm sure he'd never seen so many people before in his life.

The men on the platform in the center of the arena began calling out the name of the colt's owner and any notable horses in his lineage. Almost without taking a breath, they moved on to the next one. I got a little lost, but everyone else seemed to have no trouble keeping up.

I was slightly floored when nearly thirty colts and fillies were paraded by, and the closest man announced that they had all been sired by the same stallion. In The North Wind, we were careful about which horses were bred, working hard to keep the animals from becoming inbred. Also, we tried to preserve as many bloodlines as possible. Here, that was not the case.

One filly, whose legs looked far too long and thin, had the same father and grandfather. I couldn't imagine the spindly little thing would be much good for riding or any form of work, but everyone around me exclaimed their admiration as if such a delicate build was desirable.

The horses and handlers made a loop around the arena, then left via a second gate close beside the first. Todd told me that the animals were being taken to a large field close by. People who were interested in having a closer look could examine them and try to barter a price.

"Barter?" I asked. "What does that mean?"

"I keep forgetting you don't know anything about money," Todd chuckled. "Imagine I had something for sale that you want."

"I have to give you pieces of metal for it," I replied.

180

"Coins," he corrected me. "But, let's say that I want ten coins and you only have seven. You could ask me to take less."

"Okay," I said uncertainly. "So, if you say you only have seven- coins, they'll give it to you anyway?"

"Not always," Todd shook his head, making his dark brown hair fall into his eyes. "And you shouldn't tell anyone you only have seven coins.

"Even if you did have ten coins, maybe you don't think what I'm selling is actually worth all ten. You could tell me why you think you should get it for less."

I shook my head. "But how can you determine whether something is worth ten pieces of metal or two?"

"Experience," Todd answered. "You can always—"

But I had stopped listening to him and turned away. One of the horses had caught my attention. It was the same filly I'd seen my last day at the market, the one who had been so wild when a man attempted to ride her. She was being led now, but her ears were laid flat on her skull. She eyed each human and horse with distrust and aggression.

"It's her," I whispered.

Todd turned to look and squinted. "Isn't she that crazy filly supposedly sired by the phantom stallion?" he asked.

I nodded as the filly aimed a kick at a man walking too close behind her. The large hoof struck the man on the shin. He let out a sharp cry and dropped the lead rope of the colt he'd been guiding. Startled by the noise, the freed colt and several other horses leapt forward. Two more managed to escape from their handlers.

The silver and red filly wasn't among them, although she strained at her halter for several minutes. There was a sudden rush as men poured into the arena from all sides.

They were very efficient, and soon the situation was under control. However, no one would walk anywhere close to the wild filly.

While the other animals were rounded up, the filly's handler had given her a series of hard blows to bring her back

181

under control. The result was a thin trail of blood, which ran down the side of her face, adding to her savage appearance.

I sighed softly as she was led out. I couldn't imagine what kind of person would buy her after the display she'd given here today. It would probably be someone who would kill her or get killed themself trying to break her spirit.

After the last horse had exited the arena, Todd asked me if I wanted to go to the field and look at the horses there. I shook my head, and we departed.

I was silent on our way back.

My mind was filled with the memories of other horses I had known. Hundreds of them, but only a few stood out.

Every once in a while, you meet a horse that is simply meant for you. It's impossible to describe the connection exactly, but you feel it when you're in the saddle. The horse's body seems to merge with yours until neither of you knows where one ends and the other begins. When you gallop through the field together, it's like growing four legs and learning to fly without wings.

Instead of heading back to the dwelling or trying to find his family, Todd took me to another part of the city. It was close to the palace and the temples, so we had quite a walk, but it was worth it.

"This is the art quarter," Todd announced.

Art was a strange concept to me. I'd seen some of Todd's drawings before. In The Land of the Clan, we considered such things a waste of time and paper.

Here, there were more than just drawings. The People of the Brimming Lake could turn almost anything into art. Cups and plates could be made in bright colors instead of boring brown.

I saw doors carved in the perfect likeness of trees and horses. Entire walls were painted into meadows like the sunrise paints the clouds pink in the morning. They even had plants with long vines, which they trimmed and guided to grow into complex patterns.

I was so busy trying to look at everything that it was a shock when the crowd began thinning out, and I realized it was nearly sunset. Guilt filled me when I thought of Yetta and Jiyata preparing the evening meal alone.

We didn't stay in the city much longer, and no one seemed disturbed by our long absence from the dwelling. If anything, everyone seemed to be in a good mood that evening, even Arshenn.

CHAPTER 22
FLECK

My second day spent in the city did much to change my opinion of the new land in which I lived. It had shown me another side of this mysterious place. At first, I had considered The People of the Brimming Lake uncivilized and savage, just as was told in our history. To be fair, many of their practices were monstrous and repulsive, but I had finally seen past the worst of their transgressions to find that there was something extraordinary inside.

The Clan was their exact opposite. We knew a great deal about growing food, building roads, and raising animals, but at our heart, we were empty. There was no art, no music, no beauty, no passion for anything. We were lists of rules, without any true life.

Once, I'd considered The Clan to be superior to The People of the Brimming Lake. For so long, I hadn't even thought to question it, but I was starting to wonder.

Not that I was condoning some of the actions I'd witnessed in the past months. Todd's people were far from perfect, but so were mine. My time training as a Clan Leader had clearly shown me that. Even the fact that I considered both in the same group stunned me. Two completely independent civilizations, who differed in nearly every way, yet each lacked something.

My people were stuck in time, never to move forward. Todd's people were moving forward, but only toward a future just as violent as the past, which had nearly destroyed our entire race, a past we all shared and could not escape.

I was in the main room of the dwelling a few days later, repairing a torn floor mat with Jiyata, when Todd came bustling down the hall. It was a peaceful afternoon, and my mind had been wandering for some time while my work lay idly forgotten.

Jiyata jumped at Todd's sudden appearance. He was out of breath and panting but wore an excited expression.

"Astra, come with me. I have something to show you. You too, Mother," he added as an afterthought.

Jiyata and I exchanged a hasty glance. Todd was far too pleased for anything to be wrong, but here the unexpected was rarely pleasant.

All my worries evaporated the moment I stepped from the kitchen door into the sunlight. Standing there was the silver filly. She was tied to one of the posts in front of the stable.

"Todd–" I started, but hadn't really planned what else I was going to say.

"It's a horse," Jiyata murmured in confusion.

Todd smirked at both of our reactions. I hastily shut my mouth, which had been hanging open.

Slowly, I approached the filly, pausing when I was only a few feet away. Her nostrils flared, and she backed away. I allowed her to retreat, watching the movement of her graceful neck and strong legs.

"She looks unusual," Jiyata observed from a safe distance.

"Her father is the phantom stallion," Todd informed his mother proudly.

"She's beautiful," I whispered.

"I got her for you," Todd said, coming to stand beside me. "Every time you laid eyes on her, I could tell how much you wanted her."

My throat was too tight to say anything, but when I looked at Todd, I knew I didn't have to. He understood.

"She's not really much of a present," Todd went on, turning back to the horse. "Untrained and wild as she is. Plus," he motioned for me to come to the other side of the filly. "There's that."

He pointed to a laceration running down the side of the horse's neck to the top of her front leg.

"I bet whoever did that to her got the worst of it," Todd remarked.

I reached out and, even though the filly flinched, she allowed me to run my hand down her side, parallel to the wound.

"What is that?" bellowed a deep voice, making the horse jerk away. When she came to the end of her short lead, she rose slightly on her hind legs.

"It's a horse," Todd explained sarcastically to Arkensallay, who had come from inside the dwelling.

"She's not put together quite right," he returned, eyeing her thick legs. "Does she ride well?" he asked.

"She hasn't been trained yet," Todd admitted.

Arkensallay chuckled. "You think you're going to break that horse? I'll enjoy watching you try."

Arkensallay shuffled off toward the dwelling, probably going to tell Arshenn about the filly.

Jiyata was still standing ten yards away. "You've never trained a horse before, Todicmadaya. Are you certain you know how?"

"It'll be all right, Mother," he assured her, then turned to me. "Do you think you can tame her?"

I nodded.

"What do you want to call her?" he asked.

"Fleck," I answered, finding my tongue at last. "I'll call her Fleck."

Arshenn refused to allow the filly to join the rest of the horses in the pasture, lest they learn her wild ways. So Fleck was kept in the stable. The stall we put her in had an adjoining paddock.

Her shyness of humans was obvious, but the morning after her arrival, I learned something interesting. Fleck wasn't nearly so uncomfortable with women as she was with men. Either because men were the ones who had always mistreated her or because some horses are simply more drawn to the softer scent of a female, Fleck seemed far less afraid when I approached her alone. She was still tense, showing the whites of her eyes and laying back her ears occasionally, but she didn't try to kick or bite me.

I slowly started to work on gaining her trust. The first couple of days, I brought her grain and remained while she ate it. Then I started coming at random times during the day, just to sit in the stall for twenty minutes or so. She watched me closely, always making sure I was within her line of sight. Not once did she approach me, nor did I approach her.

I'd trained quite a few horses, although none with such a harsh past. A few visits later, I brought a halter to the stall with me. I hung it over my shoulder instead of holding it in my hand, but that didn't stop Fleck from eyeing it carefully.

From a distance, we studied and learned about each other. My visits became more frequent, but still, she remained on her side and I on mine. I'd nearly lost hope, until one day, she lowered her head and started eating hay off the ground with her back toward me. It was a small gesture, but it was progress.

The next day, I approached her. She went rigid. Slowly, I started running my hands over her soft flanks. The silver fur was mixed with spots of dark gray and russet red, no larger than pebbles. With gentle movements, I eased my fingers up and down her shoulders and neck, then to her legs. Fleck twitched a few times, but for the most part, remained still, every muscle in her body taut.

Carefully, I examined the injury on her neck. It was scabbed over, and there was no sign of infection. Soon, my fingers found their way to her tangled mane. Most of the horses here had silky manes, which flowed down their necks like waterfalls. Fleck had not inherited this feature. Her mane was thick and so matted in some places that it stuck up in long spikes.

Fleck jumped if I moved too suddenly, so I was certain to keep my movements slow and steady. Starting at her withers, I began making my way forward, easing free the tangles of hair.

After nearly an hour, I'd gotten out the worst of the knots. There was a good-sized pile of horsehair in the stall at our feet.

Once her mane was free, I ran my hands through it a few times. She didn't seem to mind, even when I shifted closer to her head and started to work on her forelock.

I'd seen the horse attempt to bite a number of people, so I kept a careful eye on her mouth as I wrestled with the tangled hairs between her ears. Another half hour passed, and those were gone too. Fleck didn't look nearly so savage now that her mane wasn't such an unruly mess.

The next day, I went to work on her tail. I was more nervous about this task because it involved standing close to her powerful hind legs. The afternoon before, I'd left a halter hanging up next to her food dish, so she'd get used to seeing it.

Today, I had a bridle with me. The jingling seemed to make Fleck uncomfortable at first, but eventually, she grew accustomed to the sound. When I headed in for dinner, I left the bridle hanging next to the halter.

Before long, Fleck was willing to let me brush her, scratch her ears, and even pick up her feet. I took a saddle blanket into the stall with me a few times to try placing it on her back. She walked away and wouldn't allow me to approach her with it, so I decided to relent on that one for now. Instead, I focused on working with the halter. It took two days of coaxing before she'd let me walk up to her in the small paddock and secure it over her head.

The first couple of times, I had to corner her, then wait for her to drop her head so I could fasten the clasp behind her ears.

Once it was on, I led her around the small area for a few minutes before turning her loose and starting the process over. I was careful to keep my hands gentle, so she only felt the slightest pressure when I wanted her to start walking or turn and go in a new direction. After a while, she began following me naturally, even without the halter.

Todd came by to check our progress. Even though she'd warmed to me considerably, she shied from him. Two days later, I started working toward riding her. In one corner of the little paddock, I placed an extra piece of fencing to section the area off into a triangle. Fleck was uncomfortable entering the space, which was so small she could hardly turn around.

The only way for me to lure her inside was with food. A couple of days elapsed before she would enter, but soon the temptation proved too great for her.

In the beginning, I left the opening slightly ajar. On the fifth day, I drug the fence shut behind her. This caused a small fit of panic. Once she'd calmed down, I opened the fence immediately and let her out.

We proceeded in this manner until she grew accustomed to me shutting her in. Also, I began climbing the fence and reaching over to touch her back and sides while she was eating. My goal was to acclimate her to having someone above her and touching her.

At first, she would move away, and I knew that the contact made her uncomfortable. Slowly, she started to ignore me and focus only on the food in her bucket.

Finally, the day came when I slid from the fence top and sat fully on her back. I was talking to her soothingly the entire time, just as I had done ever since I'd introduced the new feeding arrangements.

Fleck was a little startled, but she had grown used to my strange behavior. She twitched, glanced up to make sure it was me, then turned back to her breakfast.

That was the moment I knew things were going to turn out all right. I still didn't try to introduce the saddle or even the bridle, but not a day went by that I didn't sit on her for at least a few minutes.

There were several hiccups. One day, she went into a bucking fit, and I had to jump off. However, for the most part, she accepted the training.

It felt so good to be on the back of a horse once more, doing the thing I had always loved most. A part of me, which I had put away during the trials and thereafter, seemed to have been found again.

With Fleck, everything else faded, leaving only the two of us, except on the rare occasions when Todd would come to see how we were getting on.

One day, I was sitting on Fleck's back with nothing but a halter and a lead rope knotted into reins. We were working on the transition between a trot and a canter. Fleck preferred the faster gaits, and getting her to slow down was nearly impossible once she got it in her head to run. I didn't mind so much but knew that obedience was an essential part of her training.

Todd stood just outside the fence and watched as I made several attempts before getting her into a controlled trot. As soon as Fleck turned in his direction, she froze. I let her look for a moment, then encouraged her to step forward. Her nostrils flared, but she did take half a dozen tentative steps, bringing her right up to the fence.

Slowly, Todd reached up to pet her. Fleck twitched nervously, but I held her still as Todd rubbed her nose.

His hand soon fell into a rhythm, and the tension in the horse's body dwindled. A moment later, Todd turned to me. "Looks like things are going well."

While Todd's words were optimistic, his face was pale. I feared that Arkensallay had hurt him in the morning's sparring match.

"She's wonderful," was my answer.

"I knew you could tame any horse," he replied with a smile.

I couldn't help smiling too, but sadly. He didn't know about my failure.

"Tomorrow night, there's going to be a festival in the city," Todd changed the subject. From his tone, I could tell he was excited and guessed that this was the real reason he had come to visit the paddock.

"What's a festival?" I asked.

"It's a time when everyone gathers and celebrates."

"Celebrates what?"

"This festival is specially dedicated to the warrior and the king. We remember that once they were good friends. It is one of the few days of the year that the two houses join together in honor of the gods."

I nodded, unconsciously stroking the soft fur of Fleck's neck. "The closest thing my people have to a celebration like that is The Telling. You got to experience one of those; is it much different?"

"Yes," Todd answered. "The Telling was interesting, but all we did was listen to one story, then it was over. Tomorrow, hundreds of stories will be told, songs will be sung, and then there's the sacrifice."

I wasn't sure I liked the sound of that, but Todd rushed on. "There will be lots to see, and everyone will have a good time."

"All right," I conceded.

Todd gave me a questioning look. "All right, I'll go with you," I told him. "That's what you were wanting me to say, wasn't it?"

Todd gave me a crooked smile. "You'll love it," he promised.

He was wrong.

I didn't love it, but it did give me much to think over.

CHAPTER 23
FESTIVAL

Arshenn detested festivals, so we were spared the presence of Todd's father during the evening of the celebration.

Feelings of pity filled me for Jiyata and Yetta. The two didn't get a choice and had to remain behind as well.

Arkensallay did walk to the city with us. Only two hours earlier, he'd given Todd a nasty cut across the knuckles when he'd won their sparring match. However, he was relatively subdued without Arshenn to back him up.

Before long, Arkensallay broke off from us, muttering about getting a drink.

"Let's see if we can find a good storyteller or some musicians," Todd suggested. Without waiting for an answer, he took my hand and pulled me into the crowd. We found a group of musicians, as Todd called the people who used the strange contraptions that made the beautiful sound called music.

Along with the music, there was dancing. I watched at first, and then Todd tried to teach me some of the simpler steps. It was pretty hopeless. I was absolutely terrible. While I could distinctly hear the patterns in the music, my feet and ears were completely disjointed. I never moved at quite the right time, and every missed step set me further and further off.

I couldn't help laughing at how awful I was. It was so rare that I straight up failed at anything, but this was one of those times.

"You're really bad," Todd told me with a teasing smile, after his tenth attempt to get me into the correct rhythm. After that, we gave up and moved away from the musicians, leaving far more talented dancers to take our place.

The sky was all but black. Huge torches had been erected along both sides of the river. The firelight glimmered on the dark water as if the sun had somehow been plunged beneath the surface and broken into a hundred different fragments.

In the eerie glow, we found a group of people, both young and old. They were gathered around an ancient man resting on a wooden bench. Even seated, he leaned heavily on a wooden crutch. His unblinking eyes were the clear blue of the summer sky and flashed brightly in the darkness. A hooded cloak of red fabric was drawn up over his head, even though the night was as warm and dry as every evening before it had been for many months.

A hush fell over those assembled when, a moment later, the man shifted the position of his wooden support. It was the first sign of life he'd given.

"Welcome," he greeted us. "It is brave of you to have ventured forth on a night such as this, for, as the sun sets, more than just humans wander these streets."

The man's voice had an enthralling effect upon his listeners. We were completely bound by his words. I had thought Todd a good storyteller, but this man was a master.

"Many years ago, when I was but a boy, I snuck from my family's home on a night just like this one. I wished to attend the festival, but my father was too weary to take me, so I went alone.

"When one is young and indulging in a forbidden activity, everything seems so wondrous. I pinched a few things to eat and ran along the riverbank as the torches were being lit. The river was much louder and more powerful in those days. Had I fallen in, the chances are I would not be sitting here with all of you.

"But the gods smiled down on the vigor of my youth. I frolicked among the crowds for many hours until it was time for the sacrifice.

"Most of the children my age had been tucked away in their beds. I, however, was far from sleepy. As I approached the palace, where the sacrifice was to take place, I saw someone, or I should say something, lurking in the shadows.

"I turned to get a better look, and now there were two of *them*: lonely creatures of the night, garbed in black. Even as a youth, I knew that they were evil. Quickly, I put some distance between myself and the foul spirits. When I dared look back, they had vanished, leaving no trace.

"It might have been that I was on edge from having seen them once, or perhaps the gods opened my eyes that night, for that was not the last time I saw them.

"It was just after the completion of the sacrifice that I perceived one of them lurking by the shrine of the unknown god. Even as I watched, a man walked a little too close without realizing what was concealed there.

"In a moment, the creature took hold of him and drew him back into the darkness of the shrine. A group of his friends came in search of the man. They looked everywhere, even inside the shrine itself, but they never found him.

"Curiosity overcame my fear, and I too stole up to the dark monument. You have all seen it. You know that the shrine is small; there is but one entrance and nowhere to hide. I promise you, in the name of the gods, the place was empty.

"The dark creature had vanished into nothingness, dragging the man with him. Rumors circulated the next day. Nine people had gone missing during the festivities. Not a single one of them was ever seen again.

"Every year, a handful of people vanish. Some say that it is merely the work of too much drink, that those who have overindulged fall into the river, which bears them away to the sea. Others say it is just another part of the rivalry between The House of the King and The House of the Warrior.

"But I have seen the truth with my own eyes. They may be old now, but once they were keen as that of any hawk, and I have seen the shadowed ones and know what they can do."

The man looked sternly at some of the younger members of his audience. "So be careful, little ones," he advised. "Hold tight to your mothers and don't leave the sight of your fathers, lest you meet a fate too horrible to describe. For what could be worse than to lose your soul?"

Silence hung over the listeners for several moments after the old man stopped speaking, then cheers and applause broke out.

Many people, including Todd, put coins into a small basket at the man's feet as the crowd broke up.

Todd and I wandered a little after that. There were other storytellers, but none so good as the first. People were everywhere, almost as many as on market day. Some wore strange coverings on their faces, which were called masks and loosely resembled a human face. Half of the masks had red eyes, as the warrior was supposed to have, and others had gold eyes, like the king. Todd explained all of this to me as we shared a loaf of sweet bread he'd bought from a street vendor.

Suddenly, the night air was rent with a deep booming.

"The drums," Todd announced. "It's time for the sacrifice."

He led us toward the palace at the seaward end of the river. It seemed the entire population of The Brimming Lake was traveling in the same direction.

I kept a tight hold on Todd's hand so that we wouldn't get separated. He was skilled at threading through the crowd, and we arrived at the palace in a matter of minutes.

The open platform, which spanned the river just in front of the palace, was packed with people. Todd and I managed to find our way to a place near the front. On the palace steps before us, two men stood with long, thick-bladed swords in their hands.

The man on the right wore a mask with gold eyes, while his counterpart's mask had eyes of blood red. Both figures were unusually tall and dressed in long, light-colored robes.

On either side of the masked pair were about a dozen oxen, each held by a priest. Indeed, the top of the stairs was nearly as crowded as the bottom.

"Those are the head priests of each house," Todd told me, gesturing to the two tall men wearing the masks.

They were utterly still, swords held up, as if on guard. The only movement from the top of the steps was the occasional swish of an ox's tail.

At some unseen signal, both of the masked men turned away from the other as an ox was brought to each of them. As one, the two priests raised their swords high. My eyes were fixated on the weapons. I knew what was about to happen, and I was both transfixed and repulsed at the same time. I wanted to turn my eyes away, but found that I could not. Then, as if a signal had passed between them, the priests simultaneously brought their blades down on the necks of the oxen.

Their robes were no longer pure. Now the light color was marred with spots of crimson blood. A great cheer went up from the people as the two animals staggered and fell to their knees. With a second blow, one of them was dispatched. The other continued fighting until the sword was brought down on its neck for a third time.

Blood poured from the animals' bodies. It ran down the steps toward us. The men, who had been holding the two deceased oxen, produced huge wooden bowls and began collecting the blood. They couldn't catch it all, and a torrent of the red liquid made its way to where the crowd was assembled below.

To my surprise, instead of backing away, the people moved forward to meet it, some even going so far as to kneel in the stream of crimson.

The head priests moved on to the second pair of oxen. These were more unruly. With the scent of blood in the air and the corpses of their predecessors before them, it took firm hands to hold the creatures in place as the tall men approached, swords held high.

It was the same as the last time. The head priests hacked until the animals stopped moving. Bowls were again brought to catch the blood.

This process was repeated until half the animals had been slain. Then the head priests returned to their original positions. They removed their masks, and each was given a bowl brimming with blood.

The head priest from The House of the King, who was closer to us, lowered his entire hand into the bowl, submerging it to the elbow. He withdrew it clenched into a fist and hurled the contents onto the waiting crowd. The people around me went wild as the blood splattered on them. They raised their hands, crying out in jubilance. The head priest, who had dark, curly hair, repeated the process until the bowl was empty.

My tan shirt was sticky with blood. When I looked over at Todd, I could see that his face and clothes carried a crimson hue. Still, he and the others screamed for more.

When the two men had each emptied their bowls, they handed them off and took up the swords again. As they continued slaughtering the animals, other priests, with full bowls, began throwing their contents on the cheering crowd. They did not remain at the top of the steps but came down and walked among the people, coating everyone they met in scarlet.

"Why are they doing this?" I asked loudly in Todd's ear so he could hear me over the roar of the crowd.

"The gods want to see us covered in blood," Todd answered.

"Why?" I wondered.

"This festival honors the time before there were two houses. When we are covered in blood, we all look the same. Then even the gods can't tell us apart," he yelled before turning back to continue calling for the priests' attention.

The red substance was everywhere. Every piece of clothing was stained, each raised hand was drenched, and every face was splattered.

I paused for a moment, distancing myself mentally from the chaos of the place so I could evaluate this new revelation. It was true. At the moment, those around me looked very much the same. However, beneath the thin layer of blood, they were still exactly the same people who they had been an hour ago. This moment of change, covered by the blood of an animal, was temporary, not even skin deep.

CHAPTER 24
AGONY

After the last ox had been slain, Todd, myself, and hundreds of others went to the ocean side, and my wish of seeing the great waves once more was granted.

On the seashore, we washed the blood from our bodies and clothes. My shirt and pants were stained with large, dark splotches. Todd insisted that I would have good luck whenever I wore them. Walking back in the warm night air helped dry my clothes somewhat. As we neared the dwelling, the family's two dogs approached us, letting out low growls. They stopped when they recognized Todd and let us pass.

So as not to disturb Jiyata and Yetta, I slept in my slightly damp garments. They smelt of salt and memories.

I didn't sleep well that night. My dreams were dark but not horrific. I awoke early, in the twilight before dawn, and wandered out to the stable. Fleck let me mount her without so much as a halter. Sitting on her back, I idly watched the sun rise.

At the sound of footsteps, Fleck turned, and I saw Todd approaching. He didn't look like he'd slept much either. With an adjustment of my legs, I guided Fleck over to the fence.

"Good morning," Todd greeted me.

"Morning," I returned gently.

Todd slowly reached out to touch Fleck's forehead. Her muscles tightened, but she didn't pull away.

"Want to get on her?" I asked. There was a calmness about the morning, and it seemed impossible that anything ill could happen so long as the feeling prevailed.

"Just like that?" Todd asked, taking in the lack of saddle and bridle.

"Why not?" I wondered.

Todd laughed uncomfortably. "I'm not sure what I'd hold onto."

"You can hold onto me. Just hop up behind."

"You make it sound so easy," muttered Todd.

He carefully climbed the fence, and I coaxed Fleck up next to it. Slowly, Todd lowered a leg over her back, then let his weight descend. Fleck tensed and hopped forward twice. Todd hastily wrapped his arms around my waist. I could feel his heart racing against my back.

"Easy girl," I whispered, giving Fleck a gentle touch on the neck. She lowered her head and turned to look at us.

"What's she doing?" Todd asked warily.

"She's never been ridden double before," I answered him. "It feels weird to horses the first couple of times."

"Oh," was Todd's only response as I guided Fleck into a walk. Todd's grip on my waist relaxed a bit but tightened any time Fleck's motion changed in the slightest.

"Are your mother and Yetta in the kitchen yet?" I asked after about five minutes.

"They were just starting breakfast when I came out," he told me.

"I'd better join them then," I sighed, directing Fleck back toward the fence where Todd had mounted.

Before we reached it, a figure caught my eye. It was a man standing about forty yards away by the forge. He was watching us with cruel eyes and a wicked smile. The instant I saw him, he turned and stepped into the building.

Fear cut through me. Fleck came to a sudden halt.

"What's wrong?" Todd wondered. I doubted he had seen what I had, or he wouldn't have asked.

The man had been Todd's father, and the expression of hateful, triumphant joy on his face could mean nothing but ill for those he had looked upon.

"I don't know," I muttered, sliding down from Fleck's back. Todd was quick to follow my lead as I headed for the gate.

My feeling of apprehension didn't abate as I helped serve breakfast. Todd left for his apprenticeship after eating, and the dwelling grew quiet, too quiet. Neither Arshenn nor Arkensallay were there for lunch. With Todd gone too, we didn't even set the table in the main room.

The day continued to grow hotter and hotter. I felt sticky even as I sat darning a pair of socks inside the dwelling. Buzzing flies had invaded, trying to escape the heat by seeking out whatever shade they could find.

The buzzing grew louder until I realized it wasn't just flies I was hearing, but voices. I put down the mending and moved to the window, which overlooked the yard where the well stood in the center of the half-circle of buildings.

At least fifty men were approaching the dwelling. Arshenn was in the lead, mounted on Pride. Beside him, on an equally impressive silver horse, was The Lord of the Brimming Lake, whose name I recalled was Tohoshin.

"Yetta, Jiyata," I breathed.

More words than those would not come, but the two women hastened to my side. Something in my tone alerted them that this was a serious situation.

There was a sharp gasp from Yetta as she took in the scene. Jiyata let out a strangled cry and covered her face with her hands.

"What's going on?" I asked, turning to Yetta.

"I do not know, but I doubt it will be good." She shook her head as the three of us peered through the window.

Arkensallay emerged from the crowd of men and strolled purposefully towards the dwelling's entrance. I went to meet him, impatient to know what was happening.

Jiyata and Yetta shadowed me as I entered the hall connecting the main room to the kitchen. Just as we emerged into the room, we came face to face with Arkensallay.

"Come with me," he growled, giving me a stern look.

My hesitation was momentary; anything other than compliance would have been sheer stupidity. I stepped forward. Yetta made a move to follow, and Arkensallay turned on her.

"Not you," he snapped. "Only her." His long finger jabbed at me.

Yetta stopped moving but wrapped her hands protectively around my arm. "Why do they want her?" she blurted out.

"None of your business," Arkensallay retorted. "Let her go or—"

Before he could make any threats, I placed my hand over Yetta's and slowly eased out of her grip.

"It'll be fine," I promised. "You stay here."

She didn't release me willingly, but I was able to free my arm and take a step toward the door. Yetta was undecided and might have tried to press forward, but Jiyata took hold of her as I followed Arkensallay outside.

I blinked a few times as my vision adjusted to the bright light of the mid-afternoon sun. The men grew silent at my appearance. Every eye was on me. I stood facing the crowd but not looking at them. I kept my head up and shoulders straight as I focused on a point beyond the group.

Arshenn had dismounted. He came forward and spoke harshly close to his son's ear. "When I said 'drag her out', I meant literally."

Arkensallay appeared slightly deflated as Arshenn replaced him at my side. His hand gripped my arm just above the elbow, as he had the day Todd completed the rite of manhood. Now his hold was just as firm, but I could feel his fingers tremble ever so slightly as he thrust me toward the group of men.

"This is the girl," he spat, letting go of my arm. He began to stalk up and down, addressing the crowd.

"She is not who she claims to be. She is not 'the girl from the stars'. She is from the land of our enemies."

I'm sure my face betrayed the horror I felt as my heart skipped a beat.

"What enemies?" asked Tohoshin. The Lord of the Brimming Lake's expression was skeptical.

Arshenn lowered his voice to a deep and serious pitch. "Those who worship neither the king nor the warrior, but are blasphemers."

A stir rippled through the crowd.

"They are the ones who drove our ancestors from their homes long ago," Arshenn continued. "They dwell there still, in a place that should be ours, Edden, The Untouchable Land, a domain rich in food and abundant in comforts. They took it all for themselves, leaving us to die in the wilderness, ravaged by the war of the gods."

The Lord of the Brimming Lake glanced between Arshenn and me. All the while, the assembled men were hanging on Arshenn's every word.

"Each year, our land yields less and less. We pour out our sweat and blood in vain. This year, many will go hungry during the winter. But in the land we came from, the ground is fertile and the labor easy."

Arshenn's voice had risen to a yell as he faced the mob. Faster than an adder strikes, he turned and seized me once more. I had stood, forgotten, until that moment.

"She can tell us how to find Edden!" Arshenn called loudly, pulling me right up to the front of the crowd.

"Just a moment," Tohoshin said, stepping forward and raising his hands in a vain attempt to calm the mass of men. It appeared to still be growing, and I could see more people in the distance coming to join the congregation.

Tohoshin looked me in the eyes. His were a mild blue, the color of the sky on a listless spring day. They weren't friendly, but they weren't hostile either.

"Are you really who you claim to be?" he asked. "Did you come from the stars as we have been told?"

I'm not sure how I would have answered him, but I was never given the opportunity.

"How can you ask a *woman* such a thing and trust her answer?" Arshenn bellowed. "I have watched her these past six moons, and I can assure you, she has deceived us."

202

He raised his hand and pointed to the paddock where Fleck was standing. She was as far away from the swarm of men as she could get, watching warily with her large, dark eyes.

"What god would ever allow a woman to ride a horse, but I swear to you, this girl trained the mongrel you see before you."

"That's the evil spawn of the phantom stallion!" a man in the crowd yelled.

"She can swim too. One of my slaves saw her! The gods would never teach a woman such things!"

More voices. More accusations. There were too many to even be heard over each other.

The Lord of the Brimming Lake raised his hand and attempted to gain silence. It took him several minutes. This time when he turned to me, there was anger in the lines of his face.

"Girl," he started. "Tell us where you are from."

I didn't answer. Arshenn's grip on my arm tightened.

"Tell him the truth," he growled. "Now," he added when I remained silent.

"No," I whispered.

"What?" Tohoshin almost gasped.

"No," I said louder.

The entire assembly of men grew still.

"How dare you?" Tohoshin hissed. "Don't you know who I am?"

"I don't care," I responded. "I'll die before I tell you a thing."

Tohoshin's face was livid with rage at my refusal. "Then you shall die!" he turned to one of the men next to him and put his hand out. Instantly, the man placed a sword in it.

A thrill of fear went through me, but I pushed it down. I had no intention of letting them win. They could kill me, but I would never tell them about The Clan. The Lord of the Brimming Lake raised his sword to strike.

Then, to my utmost astonishment, Arshenn released me and threw himself at Tohoshin, seizing his sword hand before it could fall.

"You fool!" he snapped. "What good is she to us dead?"

Tohoshin forgot me almost instantly as he turned in fury upon Arshenn, but Arshenn wasn't paying any attention to The Lord of the Brimming Lake.

"I have sent someone to fetch my son, Todicmadaya. He will tell us what this girl will not," Arshenn announced.

My heart sank. Arshenn knew exactly what path to take to get what he wanted.

Not even a minute later, Todd appeared, wearing a confused expression as he took in the scene before him. Rettrin, the man who had come to dinner trying to sell his daughter as a life mate, was with him.

All attention was briefly turned away from me as Todd stood staring. His eyes met mine. They were wide with fear. I shook my head ever so slightly, internally begging him to remember his promise and keep silent.

"What–" he started, but was interrupted at once by his father.

"You've been holding out on us, my son," Arshenn began. Slowly, the crowd parted before him as he approached Todd. "You've learned a great secret; one that could be the salvation of your people."

"I don't–" Todd tried again with the same result.

"A rich land, abundant in food. A place where everything needed is close at hand. You've been there."

"The Undying Garden? It can only be reached with the help of the gods," Todd replied. His words sounded weak.

"Don't fill our ears with those lies again!" Arshenn snarled. The crowd around him murmured angrily in agreement. "We do not want your garden, but Edden. It's a real place. The land we came from."

Todd's tan face went white as his father came to a stop just in front of him. However, this time, Arshenn's words were gentle, coaxing even. "It is all right. You might have thought we wouldn't believe you or wouldn't care. I understand your hesitation, but the

204

time has come to reveal your secret. Tell us the truth, and all will be well."

Silence followed Arshenn's words. A long silence. Todd was looking at the ground.

Keep quiet, Todd, I thought. *Just keep quiet.*

Finally, Todd raised his head and licked his lips. "There is no secret to tell," he announced.

"Are you sure?" Arshenn growled.

Todd's eyes flitted to mine for a second. I gave him a tiny nod of encouragement.

"Yes," he answered. Relief flooded through me, but it was short-lived.

Arshenn didn't speak. I could see the fury rolling off him like waves of the ocean as he whipped around and marched back toward me. There was a hideous light emanating from his eyes.

It was all I could do not to shrink from him. Todd tried to stop his father when he realized he was coming for me, but Rettrin moved to intercept. Arshenn loomed up in front of me, blocking the two from my sight.

Arshenn leaned toward me. I clenched my jaw and forced myself to remain still as he hissed in my ear. "I can see that you are ready to die to preserve this secret."

My heart was thundering in my chest. A cold sweat rose on my brow despite the heat of the day.

Slowly, Arshenn circled behind me. "But is he ready to watch you?" he wondered.

My breath stilled. The blood turned to ice water in my veins.

The crowd had continued to swell, as though someone was rallying people from the city and sending them here.

"With your approval, *my lord,*" Arshenn said, addressing Tohoshin with almost mock civility. "I will extract the information."

The Lord of the Brimming Lake hesitated.

"Do it!" a cry sounded from the mob. The words were taken up by a hundred voices.

205

Tohoshin gave Arshenn a deep nod, and the men grew silent once more. Arshenn smiled menacingly and grabbed my wrist. His swift gesture yanked me forward a few steps.

Todd was being restrained by Rettrin and a few other men. His brown eyes met mine helplessly. I shook my head again. It was a slight movement, but it drew Arshenn's attention.

He struck me across the face as hard as he could. The metallic taste of blood filled my mouth. A moment later, I spat out a mouthful of the crimson liquid.

"Don't–" Todd gasped, fighting to get loose from those who held him.

"You know how to make it stop," Arshenn told him.

Todd closed his mouth and looked at me once more. I didn't move, but with all the powers of my eyes, I conveyed to Todd that I didn't want him to speak. No matter what they did to me, I didn't want him to say one word.

Arshenn waited until it became clear that Todd wasn't going to answer him.

"Whip her," Arshenn ordered.

A moment later, I found my arms tied above my head, just as Cartner's had been.

When the whip struck me for the first time, it felt like hot embers had been raked across my back. A strangled cry broke from my lips. Both flesh and fabric were torn away, and I could feel blood running down my skin.

The blow took my breath away. I had just enough time to suck in another before I was hit again. I tried to fight down a cry, but didn't quite manage to keep it inside as the cruel thong of the whip connected with my back a second time.

My feet were bare, my toes stained red with my own blood.

It reminded me of last night, when the crimson liquid had flowed while the crowd screamed for more. Were the gods watching? Were they pleased with this too? Were agony and despair the only things they understood?

I was aware of Arshenn winding up for a third strike. I bit my tongue against the pain, but it didn't help. A sharp yell escaped as his blow opened another cut on my back.

Arshenn's hand was raised yet again. I tried to brace myself, but there wasn't much I could do.

"Stop!" Someone screamed, almost at the point of tears. It was Todd's voice.

No! I thought desperately.

"Don't–" I started to protest. Someone slapped me across the face, not as hard as Arshenn, but hard enough to make my head start spinning and my words stop. I couldn't even stand now, but that didn't keep me from trying. I gripped the ropes encasing my wrists and attempted to pull my battered body upright.

I gasped for breath. My mouth was filled with blood, from biting my tongue or from one of the two blows to the face, I did not know.

"I'll tell you what you want to know. Just stop!" I heard Todd shout.

You can't! You promised! I wanted to scream. I opened my mouth, but all that came out was a rush of blood.

I was still trying to speak when something blunt struck the back of my head. The last thing I remembered was someone loosing my arms and dragging me away as darkness came crashing in.

CHAPTER 25
DESOLATION

When I came to my senses again, it was by degrees. I noticed the smell of hay, then the feeling of something prickly pressing against my right cheek. Slowly, my eyes opened, letting in the late afternoon light.

I didn't move.

It was the despair just as much as the agony keeping me immobile. What was the point anymore? I'd failed everyone I'd ever known. Soon, even the memory of the place I'd once called home would be destroyed, and I lay bleeding out into the straw of the stable.

I wouldn't die. That was far too much to hope for. I would live, most likely to be the very last of my people.

A loneliness sharper than anything I'd ever known enveloped me, neutralizing even the brutal pain from my back.

That was when I heard soft footsteps at the entrance of the stable.

Go away, Todd, I thought bitterly.

It wasn't Todd.

I turned my head just enough to see Myra drop down into the hay beside me. She sat there, observing me but making no comment.

My mind wasn't working quite right due to- well, everything.

"I'm not asleep," I told her, knowing beyond a shadow of a doubt that I was right.

"No, you're not," she agreed freely.

"Then what are you doing here?" I asked.

"That's an interesting question," she began. "Let's talk about it for just a moment." Myra's voice was intense, and her gaze bored into me. The rest of my surroundings were fuzzy, but I could see her clear, gray eyes perfectly.

"When you were a child, you used to dream of your parents. That lasted a long time, but eventually, you moved on and started seeing your mentors who had passed away. You even dreamed of Rickie for a while. Now, it's me."

I couldn't say anything. Hundreds of dreams from the past crowded into my mind, each as vivid as a memory. I was sitting on my father's knee, walking through a pasture with my mother, learning how to repair a leather strap, riding Rickie through a field of green, and here, talking to Myra.

"There's something I must ask," she continued.

"What is it?" I muttered.

"You know that I'm dead, right?"

I tried to swallow the lump in my throat, but it didn't go away. Instead, it continued to swell, threatening to choke me. I couldn't answer or even look at her.

"I died in the mountain. It was my choice, but some part of you won't let me go. Why do you think that is?"

It was still impossible for me to get any words out. Myra leaned toward me so she could look straight into my eyes.

"You know it's not really me. You know I'm not actually here. Somewhere deep down, you've known it all along."

I closed my eyes.

"You understand, right?"

I didn't want to hear this.

"Who am I, Astra?" she pressed relentlessly, rising to her feet.

Slowly, I opened my eyes and whispered, "You're me."

A smile spread across Myra's beautiful face. Her eyes shifted from gray to green. Myra was gone, and I was left with nothing but a reflection of myself.

"You've been talking to yourself all this time," she mused in my voice. "Do you know why?"

She looked at me with my own green eyes, obviously expecting an answer.

"I don't know," I whispered. It hurt to think.

"There's an empty place inside of you, Astra. A piece of your soul is missing. It's not something you lost, but something you never had. Ever since you were little, you've been trying to fill that hole. First with your parents, then with your horses, next with your training, and now with yourself.

"You've worked so hard to be perfect and don't understand why you keep failing. You pour yourself into others and still don't feel complete. You've traveled across the world and haven't found what you are looking for."

"What am I looking for?" I whispered.

The other me smiled. "You will know it if you find it, but it's something so much bigger than you can even imagine."

We were both silent for a moment.

Slowly, she turned toward the door, but then looked over her shoulder at me. "Before I go, let me tell you one more thing.

"Get up.

"You can die here in this stable, or you can take up the search again. It's your choice, but somehow I already know what you're going to do."

I blinked, and she was gone.

I was alone.

I had been alone this whole time.

But the solitude didn't last. A moment after my apparition vanished, Todd took her place, and I was actually glad to see him. There was much to do.

Before we could start, I had to find out how bad the damage was. Carefully, I sat up, trying to keep my back from flexing as much as possible.

Todd sank down beside me in the exact spot my vision had occupied.

"I'm so sorry, Astra." Todd's head dropped into his hands. "This is all my fault."

"What's done is done," I told him.

"No," Todd shook his head while it was still in his hands. His words were muffled, and I was pretty sure he was crying.

"Everything is my fault. I'm the reason you're here. I should have found a way to help you escape. I should have–"

"That doesn't matter now," I interrupted. "We just need to decide what to do next."

Todd raised his head to give me an incredulous look.

"What did you tell them?" I asked.

Todd shook his head helplessly. "I told them how to find The Land of the Clan and what kind of weapons your people have," he whispered. I felt my spirits drop a little.

"I tried to send them to the north, to find the ruined city, but Arshenn knew I was lying. He always knows. He said he'd…" Todd hesitated and changed what he was going to say. "I had to tell them the truth."

"What are they going to do?" I wondered.

"I don't know," Todd admitted. "The Lord of the Brimming Lake and his advisors have retired to the palace to discuss the different options."

"Is your father with them?" I asked.

"No," Todd returned blackly. "He and a group of his friends are in the house. I have no idea what they're plotting."

"Do you think Tohoshin and his advisors will decide to attack my people?"

"They might," Todd answered. "The Lord of the Brimming Lake is fairly passive, but a lot of people are pretty riled up."

"When will we know?" I asked.

Todd shrugged. "Today. Tomorrow. The day after. What does it matter? We have no way to stop them."

"Then what can we do?" I wondered despondently.

Todd was silent for a moment. He had an idea, but for some reason he was hesitant to speak.

"We can run away," he suggested. "Just the two of us. We could leave all of it behind."

He'd proposed this before, but the situation hadn't been so grim.

Slowly, I shook my head.

211

"Think about it," Todd insisted. "No more troubles, no more worries. You don't have a place with The Clan, much less here with my people. This is our chance to be free."

I wanted to agree. I wanted to go with him.

"I can't, Todd," I whispered. "I have to try and do something, but I won't hold it against you if you go."

"Do you really think I'd leave you now?" he asked me fiercely.

Despite everything happening around us, a smile spread across my lips.

"So, what's your plan?" he asked.

"I don't have one," I admitted, my mind racing as it desperately searched for an answer.

"Maybe we could–" I started, but cut off as the stable door creaked open.

Todd leapt to his feet and whirled around to face the intruder. It was Jiyata. Todd relaxed when he saw her but remained standing.

She hurried to him. I could see tears in her eyes.

"What's wrong, Mother?" Todd asked.

"He's taken her!" Jiyata sobbed hysterically.

"Who's been taken?" Todd wondered in bewilderment.

"Lord Arshenn has taken Yetta! He sent me to get something from one of the storerooms. When I returned to the kitchen, he and Yetta were gone. The bowl of dough she had been kneading was on the floor. There were drag marks and blood!

"I ran to the window and saw Lord Arshenn and his companions heading across the eastern pasture."

"Are you sure Yetta was with them?" I questioned.

"I don't know," Jiyata admitted. "But I can't find her anywhere, and she would never leave on her own." Jiyata buried her head in her hands. Todd gently placed a hand on her shoulder.

"We have to go after them," I announced.

Todd gave me a questioning look.

"Even if Yetta isn't with them, we should at least try to find out what Arshenn is planning," I reasoned.

"You're right," Todd said. "But we'll need to hurry."

Jiyata returned to the dwelling to get me a change of clothes.

While she was gone, I retrieved the half-used bowl of green salve I'd left after treating Cartner's wounds. Todd cleaned and dressed my back as best he could.

When Jiyata returned, I quickly changed into the dark brown pants and black shirt.

"I'm ready," I announced, walking out of the stable to where Todd and Jiyata were waiting.

Todd turned to his mother. "You need to go back inside and pretend not to have seen anything."

"But–" Jiyata began to protest.

"Please, Mother," Todd begged.

"If Arshenn returns and Yetta is all right, there's no reason for you to get in trouble for leaving," I pointed out.

Todd nodded.

"All right," Jiyata agreed reluctantly, turning toward the dwelling.

Todd and I headed for the eastern pasture. It was slow going at first as I adjusted to the ache of my back. The salve had dulled the pain of my wounds, but they still stung. I was nowhere near as bad off as Cartner had been, and I probably had Todd to thank for that.

The pasture was full of long grass, almost ready to be cut for hay. We could easily see the path Arshenn and his companions had taken.

"Do you think they're close?" I asked after half an hour of traveling.

"I have no idea," Todd answered distractedly, eyes studying the ground to make sure we were still on the right trail.

Soon, we came to the edge of the pasture, where a wooden fence cut across the land. On the opposite side, the grass was short, and I could make out nothing to indicate where the men had gone.

"Are you sure we're in the right place?" I wondered.

"No," Todd shook his head.

213

We slipped through the fence and studied the ground beyond.

"I don't understand," Todd muttered. "The city is to the north. There's nothing out this way until you run into the sea."

"It looks like there were horses here," I said, pointing to the ground.

Todd moved to my side. "You're right," he breathed. "And not that long ago." He nodded to a fresh pile of manure.

"Do you think someone met them with horses?" I wondered.

"I don't know, but there were only three or four men at my house, and it looks like twice that many horses were here."

"Then maybe it's not them," I sighed. "Should we follow anyway?"

Todd shrugged. "I don't have any better ideas."

At first, the tracks weren't very clear, but before long, the hoofprints multiplied until there were at least thirty sets.

I began to worry as the sun headed toward the horizon. The path wasn't hard to follow by day, but I didn't know if the moon would be bright enough for us to continue.

"Look!" I pointed ahead after another forty minutes. In front of us rose a clump of bushes and tall trees. We had seen others like it, but standing around this thicket were more than two dozen horses.

Even though there were no humans in sight, Todd and I approached cautiously. We reached the herd of animals without seeing anyone.

The horses were tied on a picket line. Each wore a saddle and bridle.

"Where are their riders?" Todd wondered.

The clump of foliage wasn't large enough to conceal that many people. At the center was a boulder nearly twice my height. Todd and I circled the entire area but could find no trace of Arshenn and those with him.

Suddenly, Todd grabbed my arm and pulled me to the ground behind one of the largest bushes. I cried out as pain lanced across my back.

"Sorry," he whispered. "Someone's coming."

Todd nodded to the north. I peered through the leaves and saw a pair of horses heading straight for us at a gallop.

They reached the trees a minute later. The horses came to a stop, and their riders, two men in their thirties, dismounted. The animals were tied to the picket line with the others. Each man retrieved a folded piece of black cloth from his saddlebag. They headed straight toward the boulder. I scooted around the bush to watch them.

When they reached the large rock, one of the two placed his hand on its moss-covered surface. His fingers grasped something and pulled.

My jaw dropped as a concealed door swung open. The men stepped inside, letting the door close behind them. I looked at Todd, who was just as shocked as I was.

"You saw that, right?" I whispered. I'd already had one hallucination and wasn't sure I could trust my own senses at the moment.

Todd nodded. We waited several minutes, then crept toward the spot where the men had disappeared. Once we reached the boulder, Todd began searching beneath the moss. A moment later, his hand froze suddenly.

"There's a handle here," he told me.

He swallowed and then gave it a tug. The side of the stone opened before us.

Within was a small cavern the size of a horse stall. The walls were rough stone leading up to a domed ceiling. In the center of the floor was an open trapdoor. The two men were nowhere to be seen.

As the door behind us slowly swung shut, darkness closed in, but it was not absolute. A flickering light was coming up through the trapdoor.

"There's fire below us," Todd observed.

"What is this place?" I asked breathlessly.

"I do not know," Todd answered in a hushed voice.

"We shouldn't linger here," I said quietly. "There appears to be a gathering, and more might be coming."

Todd nodded. "The question is, do we go forward or backward?"

"Forward," I whispered. If Yetta was here somewhere, I had to find her and get her out.

"I'll go first," Todd offered. He approached the trapdoor and carefully lowered himself through. I followed and found it led to the top of a steep staircase.

The descent was long, at least sixty feet. The stairs didn't curve or turn in any way. They just went on and on, down at an angle so sharp I was reminded of a ladder. Our progress was slow. The steps were tall but not very wide. Each time I reached a foot forward, I had a small moment of panic when I expected to find a step, but it was farther down than anticipated.

The space around us wasn't open but enclosed in rock.

At last, when my thighs were burning and my back was agonizingly stiff from the repetitive motion of stepping down, we reached the bottom.

My feet sank slightly into the sandy floor. The tunnel widened considerably, leading straight ahead. The stone walls were twenty feet apart, and the ceiling was nearly lost to view in the shadows above.

About ten yards from the foot of the staircase was the source of the light. An iron brazier full of burning logs sat against the rock wall on the left. Beside it was a cluster of torches and a pile of firewood. Todd walked to the brazier and selected one of the torches before lighting it in the flames.

He was ready to head down the passage, but I needed to stop for a moment. I feared that some of the wounds on my back might have reopened, but Todd assured me that I wasn't bleeding.

A drink of water would have been the most amazing thing in the world at that moment, but we hadn't brought any with us.

Judging by how dry the air was, I doubted we would find any sort of underground rivers or streams.

I could have rested for another ten minutes but knew that we needed to get moving.

At first, there was only one way to go, straight ahead. The tunnel slanted down, taking us further underground. Everything was completely silent, save for the sound of our footsteps and the crackling of the torch. We spoke a few times, but the echo created by even so much as a whisper was unnerving.

"There's an opening," Todd pointed to a gaping hole in the wall. It was on our left and appeared as though a giant fist had punched straight through the stone, leaving jagged edges.

It wasn't a new passage, but more like a small room. Todd entered first and came to a sudden halt. A sharp gasp escaped his lips, and I hurriedly stepped around him to see what had caused his reaction.

For a few moments, I couldn't comprehend what I was seeing. Strewn across the uneven floor were various forms that mimicked human bodies. Only, they were the wrong color, and most of the features were horrific. Some of the figures wore tattered clothing. They weren't arranged in any particular order and appeared to have been brought here and dumped carelessly.

"Are they statues?" I whispered to Todd. I'd seen lots of statues in this land and once in the ancient city of Axella, but none like these.

"No," Todd answered softly. "They aren't statues."

"Then what are they?" I asked.

He tore his eyes from the forms and met my gaze. I took a step back. He looked horrified, but I didn't understand why.

"Todd?"

He licked his lips. "They're bodies, Astra," he told me.

"Bodies?" I gasped. "What do you mean?"

"These were once living people who died and were brought here."

I glanced around again, hardly able to believe he could be correct. "But this isn't what dead people look like," I argued weakly.

"Yes, it is," Todd assured me. "After they've been dead for a very long time."

I opened my mouth to speak, but no words came out. I tried to recall if I'd ever seen a dead body that was more than a few days old before. It occurred to me that once, back in The North Wind, we'd moved a water bucket and found the rotting remains of a rat under it.

"There's no smell," I whispered.

"It's too dry down here," Todd explained. "They dried out instead of rotting."

"But why are they here?" I asked. The room had piles and piles of bodies, at least two hundred. "Where did they come from?"

Todd just shrugged and headed out of the cavern.

The passage went on and on. There were other rooms, almost a dozen of them, all of which contained more bodies. As we stopped to look into each one, my sense of horror and confusion grew.

The further along the tunnel we traveled, the fresher and fresher the bodies became. Todd's bewilderment mirrored my own.

"This has been right under our feet all this time," he murmured.

The next side cavern held only a handful of bodies. I could tell that these people hadn't been dead for very long. There was some odor, but not the putrid stench I'd been expecting. Instead, I detected a sickly-sweet scent, closer to the smell of a dead plant than a dead animal or person.

"This is–" Todd started. "How did these people die? And how did they end up here?"

I had no answer.

The next cave was completely empty, as were the two after and all the rest that followed.

Without warning, Todd threw down the torch and snuffed out its light on the sandy floor.

"What–" I started.

"Shhh," Todd silenced me. "There are lights ahead."

CHAPTER 26
DARK SOULS

I looked down the passage to see many points of light ahead of us. They didn't appear to be coming or retreating. Slowly, we moved forward, careful not to make a sound.

The lights were farther away than they appeared. As we drew near, I saw that the tunnel opened into a vast, circular cavern. It was even larger than the council building of The Paramount.

Inside the chamber were figures dressed in black, hooded cloaks with red symbols displayed across the backs. They were identical to the beings I'd seen the night Cartner had been taken.

There were too many for me to count, probably close to a hundred. It was impossible to tell because of the billowing of their cloaks as they slipped in and out of the firelight.

Todd gestured to a small alcove in the rock close to the end of the hall. "We should get out of sight," he whispered close to my ear.

The two of us crept forward and hid as best we could. Looking through a crack, we were able to see most of what was going on in the chamber.

The figures were gathered in small groups, speaking in hushed voices. I could hear nothing of what was said. The room in which they stood had several other passages coming off of it.

We waited for what felt like an eternity. Several more cloaked figures joined the others, adding to the throng.

At a wordless signal, the hooded figures convened in some semblance of a circle. They were perfectly still. The silence that filled the place was deafening. Suddenly, one of the figures, I never knew which one, began to speak in the high language. The words were fairly simple, and I actually understood most of them.

The closest translation was: "We are in the darkness. We are in the shadows. The only power over us is blood. We are the evil in the world. Through evil comes strength. Through strength comes power. Through power we become the gods and write our own history."

Some of the words they used were in the wrong tense, and a few of the endings wer not what I had learned, limited as my schooling had been. I started wondering if maybe I was even worse at the high language than I thought.

"They're evil spirits," Todd whispered in terror.

In the ghastly half-light, I was inclined to agree with him. At least, until one of the figures stepped into the middle of the others and threw back his hood. Underneath was a man. He looked to be in his fifties, with shaggy blond hair that was streaked with silver and a thick brow ridge over pale eyes.

"We have been summoned," the man boomed, addressing the assembly in the common tongue.

Two other figures moved to the center of the circle and took up positions flanking the speaker. They did not remove their hoods but remained by his side.

"We have been summoned by a brother of our order. Let him now come forth," the blond man continued.

A tall figure stepped forward to stand before the three. Slowly, he raised his hand to his hood and let it fall back. I could have lived a thousand years without seeing that face again, and I never would have regretted it. Standing there, in the middle of the circle of men, was Arshenn.

Todd was completely frozen, his wide eyes locked onto his father.

"Before you speak, I trust you are prepared to pay in blood?" asked the blond man.

"Yes, I have made the arrangements, as our laws dictate," Arshenn told him. Excited murmurs spread through the assembly.

The blond man gave Arshenn a nod. "Then you have the right to address The Brotherhood."

221

Arshenn returned the man's nod. "My brothers," he began. "When last I spoke to you, it was to share with you an extraordinary opportunity. I told you I suspected that a new land, full of wealth and slaves, had been discovered.

"With your help, I was able to learn the truth, and it is even more incredible than I could have ever believed. That is why I come before you again, so that I might speak to you of the future.

"The new land is vast and abundant in resources. After hearing much about its location and defenses, I no longer desire to raid it, but to conquer it."

There was a stir among the cloaked figures and the slight murmur of hushed voices. Arshenn paid them no heed and continued, his voice growing in passion and volume.

"This is something our people need, for they have grown soft and complacent under the rule of weak leaders.

"The enmity between the houses, which we have fueled for so long, is fading. In order to continue the growth of our people, we must provide them with a fresh challenge.

"Just before coming here, I received word that The Lord of the Brimming Lake has decided not to act upon the information provided to him. He refuses to even send a scouting party to discover the exact location of this new land."

I couldn't help letting out a sigh of relief.

"Lord Tohoshin feels that with the harvest about to begin, it would be foolish to think of such an expedition. Instead, he wants to encourage his people to fill their barns with grain and enjoy a plentiful harvest, then perhaps revisit the idea of an attack in the spring.

"The fact that he would rather farm than fight shows him to be an unworthy leader. One who should have been dealt with long ago."

There were voices raised in agreement.

The blond man, who had listened intently to Arshenn's words, raised his hand for silence. Instantly, the chamber was quiet.

"What is your plan?" he asked Arshenn.

"That which is keeping Lord Tohoshin here must be removed," Arshenn declared. "Without anything left to cling to, maybe he will become the leader our people deserve. Personally, I doubt it and believe he should be removed as soon as he is no longer of use to us."

"Your words stir my heart, Brother Arshenn," the blond man said. "What counsel do my fellow masters of The Brotherhood have to offer?"

The man on his left reached for his hood. He was about Arshenn's age and had a long face, with a large mouth full of jagged teeth, which were very visible as he began speaking.

"Too long has peace reigned. Change is uncomfortable for all, but it can grant great strength and power. This is a chance that may never come again. We must not let it slip through our fingers. A new land could be the very thing needed to push our people forward into a bright, new future."

As the man fell silent, all eyes turned to the last figure in the center of the circle.

Very slowly, he stepped forward and removed his hood. He was elderly, with long white hair and a hooked nose. I recognized him as the man who had made Arkensallay's spear.

"My brothers, this appears to be an opportunity that we should embrace. However, something has been festering in my mind since Brother Arshenn began speaking. I feel that I must raise my concern. I hope you will not hold this against me."

Arshenn bowed his head to the ancient man and spoke in a tone of deep respect. "Master Tiylious, you are well known for your wisdom. Please speak your mind, and we will listen."

Tiylious nodded gratefully. "The Brotherhood of the Crimson Symbol was formed many, many generations ago. Since the time our people first came to The Brimming Lake, we have been here. Our order has watched over the land and guided the people down whatever path we have chosen for them.

"We have rejected the gods and instead serve something greater. We have devoted our lives to the most powerful thing in the world.

"Evil.

"This practice has served us well, and we have used it to make The People of the Brimming Lake great. Only conflict, strife, and hatred can bring about progress. We alone control the fate of the land above our heads. Nothing, neither god nor man nor beast, can stop us, save one thing."

The old man paused.

"That thing is ourselves.

"If we do conquer this faraway land, if we take hundreds of slaves, and the ground is fertile enough that we are able to increase our wealth and power, what will become of us? If we leave the place of our ceremonies and sacrifices, how will we hold onto our customs and traditions? What will we have to hand down to our grandsons?

"I am not afraid of the road ahead, save that I fear for our Brotherhood. Please, hear my words and understand that nothing, not my wives, my sons, or even my own life, means more to me than this order. The things we have done together, the way I have felt as one of you, are more precious to me than breath itself.

"How can I be assured that if we go, we will still be as we are?"

After posing his question, the old man stepped back to his place and drew up his hood once more.

It was then Arshenn's turn to address the crowd. "Well spoken." Arshenn's voice was sincere.

"I could not have said it better myself. Do not think that this has not weighed upon my mind as heavily as it does on yours. However, we have never before allowed anything to come between the members of our order. When The House of the King and The House of the Warrior are at odds, do I turn against my brothers because they are born of one house and I the other?

"Never.

"What we do on the surface is an act, a farce to cover what lies beneath. This is the only place we can be who we truly are. Here, we are joined together as one, and our power is magnified.

No matter where our feet take us, we will remain strong because we will always be brothers.

"However, we have begun to grow stale. Too long have we lingered in the footsteps of those who came before us, doing only as they have done. Too long have we allowed our people to grow fat and happy. It is time for us to forge a new future and create a new destiny for ourselves and those who will come after."

"But we do not know if there will be a place for us to meet," a voice called out from among the crowd.

"If we cannot find one, then we will have one built," Arshenn assured him. "There will be many slaves taken when we conquer this new land. I will procure the strongest and see to it that their last act on this earth will be to build us a new seat."

"How will this be done in secret?" another voice asked.

Arshenn's answer was carefully planned. "As I said earlier, once we reach the new land, I see no reason for Lord Tohoshin to remain alive. His dithering in this great hour has only made the necessity of his demise all the more clear to me. He has brought nothing but weakness to The People of the Brimming Lake, and he must face judgment."

"I do not see how that will aid us," the same voice called.

"I am getting to that," Arshenn retorted. "We will put our own man on the throne. Through him, we will form this new land as we see fit."

Many voices spoke up at once. It was several minutes before the din could be contained.

The blond man was the one who finally put a single voice to what the others were saying. "Brother Arshenn, none of our order can be Lord of the Brimming Lake. It goes against our code."

"You know this better than anyone," Tiylious murmured almost too softly for me to hear.

Absently, Arshenn ran his fingers over the scar upon the left side of his face. "Yes," he mused. "I am aware of our laws. However, there is no law against putting someone on the throne over whom we have a great deal of influence. Through him, we can gain control."

"Indeed, we have often changed the course of the future, but always from the shadows," Tiylious spoke up. "This is not our way."

"No," Arshenn agreed. "It has not been. But new times call for new measures. This is something we must do to ensure the survival of our Brotherhood."

There were murmurs of approval, and all heads turned to look at Tiylious.

He was slow to answer. "Nothing matters more than my brothers. If this is the only way to preserve our order, then so be it."

A few cheers broke forth.

"Who is this man strong enough to become lord, but who can be so freely influenced?" a voice called from the far side of the cavern.

"My son, Arkensallay, will be the champion for The House of the King," Arshenn answered. "He is a great fool and will be easy to manipulate.

"Malkious, your son, Husamhind, might do as the champion for The House of the Warrior. If we can get them both into the final battle, then we will be assured of victory, no matter who survives."

Men were nodding, agreeing with Arshenn's plan.

Someone laughed from the back of the group. "Your sons are powerful," he said. "But are they able to win the tournament?"

A man, almost as tall as Arshenn, stepped to the center of the circle. When he pulled back his hood, a mop of dark hair was revealed. "I have seen Arkensallay fight," he stated. "He is a strong warrior, but there are better."

Another figure stepped up beside Arshenn and removed his hood to speak. I recognized Rettrin as his voice filled the rocky space.

"All that can be easily dealt with," he began. "The arm of The Brotherhood reaches far. It will not be hard to arrange the tournament so as to produce the desired outcome. Changing fate is what our order has done since the time of its inception."

"We will have to work carefully," the dark-haired man put in.

Rettrin smiled at him. "Brother Todkalais, it will be so well done that even Arkensallay and Husamhind themselves will believe they are the most skilled champions among The People of the Brimming Lake."

The dark-haired man, Todkalais, dipped his head in assent before raising his hood and stepping back to his place in the circle.

"We are all in agreement?" the blond man asked, glancing at his two companions.

"Yes," both men answered.

"Then the decision is made," the blond man announced to a chorus of cheers. "Brother Arshenn, I am assuming you have a plan of action."

"That is correct," Arshenn nodded. "Brother Rettrin and several others know the details. We will give each brother his assignment in a moment. First, I would like to present my sacrifice and pay The Brotherhood in blood for the deeds they are about to perform."

Excitement rippled through the group as Arshenn gestured to his left. Rettrin vanished in that direction and returned carrying a black bundle with the help of two others.

I strained my eyes, trying to make out what it was.

"We are in the darkness," Arshenn began in the high language, and the others took up his words. "We are in the shadows. The only power over us is blood. We are the evil in the world. Through evil comes strength. Through strength comes power. Through power we become the gods and write our own history."

Once the echo of their words had died away, the men pulled back their hoods to reveal their faces. Most wore expressions of delight and exaltation. Their grinning mouths appeared strange and twisted in the torchlight, and I couldn't help but shudder.

Arshenn took a long knife from his belt, which he used to cut away the black fabric encircling the bundle.

The instant the covering had been removed, I cried out and started forward. I would have charged headlong into the group, but Todd seized me from behind and held me back.

"No Astra, no!" he hissed in my ear.

I ignored him and struggled to break free of his grip. The bundle was a person, and the person was Yetta.

A thin trail of blood ran from her forehead to her chin, her wrists were bound, and her eyes were wide with terror.

"Let me go!" I snapped at Todd, trying to free myself from his hold. "You have to let me go!" I practically yelled when he didn't obey.

"No," he said, tightening his grip on me.

"Please," I begged, tears coming into my eyes.

Todd's right hand clamped over my mouth. I hadn't realized how loudly I'd spoken. If the assembled men hadn't been making such a racket themselves, they probably would have heard me.

Todd's left arm encircled my stomach like a metal band, and he seized my right wrist. I was still fighting him, but he had effectively pinned both my arms. Even then, my desperate struggles didn't subside.

Arshenn was holding Yetta in front of the men by the back of her neck. They jeered and screeched at her. Her face contorted in fear. I could see her lips moving as she pleaded for mercy.

I have to save her, I thought, pushing away from Todd as hard as I could.

You can't, a voice whispered.

Then I'll die with her, I snarled internally. And I would have, except Todd held me as securely as metal chains. No matter how hard I fought, I couldn't free myself from him. Todd moved us away from the crevice and started hauling me backward along the passage.

In horror, I watched Arshenn raise his knife and run it slowly along Yetta's throat. Even though the pressure wasn't enough to draw blood, she froze and stood completely still.

The blade didn't stop with her throat but traveled to her face, tracing across her cheeks, around her eyes, and along her lips. I think Arshenn whispered something into her ear as he raised his left arm, dangling the blade over her head for just a moment.

I stopped struggling. Todd's grip loosened as he pulled me back several feet. In that instant, I surged forward, trying to escape him and make it to Yetta's side.

Maybe if my body hadn't been so weak, I would have been able to slip away, but pain and exhaustion made my attempt clumsy. Besides, Todd was ready. We both lurched forward a few inches, but he almost instantly dragged me back, holding my body tight to his. The pressure on my wounds hurt, but I ignored it. There were more important things happening.

Yetta closed her eyes. The knife plunged toward her and buried itself in the base of her neck. The assembled men roared with glee.

As Yetta's body convulsed, several of them rushed forward to stab her with knives of their own. Others ripped out handfuls of her hair or gave her body a swift blow with their fists.

I didn't realize I was screaming into Todd's hand until I stopped, too shocked and appalled to do anything but stare.

Yetta's lifeless body fell to the ground, blood flowing across the floor. The robed men were panting and frothing with excitement.

"Now," Arshenn bellowed. "To our future!"

Great cheers met his words.

My legs turned to water. Todd was the only thing holding me up. He practically carried me back the way we had come, his hand still covering my mouth. I didn't feel like yelling anymore. I didn't really feel anything except emptiness.

When we reached the nearest of the side caverns, Todd pulled me inside. It was dark, but some of the firelight still found its way in.

Slowly, Todd removed his hand from my mouth and his arm from around my body. Instantly, I dropped to my knees, hands by my sides in the dirt. Sorrow filled me. I blinked and saw the whole thing over again. Tears welled up in my eyes, and a sob rose to my throat.

Todd knelt at my side and put his arms around me again. Not in restraint this time, but in a protective and comforting way.

"I'm so sorry, Astra," he whispered.

I turned toward him, burying my face in his shoulder as the tears came in hot torrents from my eyes. His embrace tightened a little, and he held me as I wept.

We remained like that for a long time, even once I had grown quiet. Finally, I heaved a sigh and slowly straightened my body. He released me reluctantly.

"We need to get out of—" Todd started, but cut off when the light in the cavern began to grow. The sound of many feet marching along the passage was not far behind. They passed the entrance to the cavern and kept going, taking the light with them.

Wordlessly, I climbed to my feet and wiped my face with my sleeve, probably doing nothing but adding dark smudges to the tearstains. I glanced at Todd and could see that he'd cried too.

We stole into the passage and followed the crowd at a distance, staying out of the torchlight. Several of the men in the back of the procession stopped at one of the openings. It was where the most recent corpses rested. They flung something, which I could only imagine was Yetta's body, inside, then followed the rest of their companions.

Once the brazier and stairs were in view, we took cover in another of the side caverns, this one full of old corpses.

One by one, the cloaked men climbed the stairs. I was so busy watching them that I almost didn't see another small group of figures coming down the passage behind us. Thankfully, I was able to alert Todd, and we ducked down in time to escape being seen.

Arshenn was leading this group. His hood was up, but since he carried a torch, his face was visible.

A figure by the steps turned to greet him. "Is it done?" he asked. It sounded like Rettrin.

"Yes," Arshenn answered. "Soon, The Land of the Brimming Lake shall be no more."

CHAPTER 27
SACRED GROUND

We remained hidden until the last of the men had climbed the stairs and passed out of our sight. Cautiously, Todd stepped from the cavern, heading down the passage toward the end of the tunnel. I followed numbly.

The men had taken their torches with them, so the only light came from the brazier. Once he reached it, Todd picked up a fresh torch from the few that remained. He held it in the smoldering embers for a moment before the flames took, then it flared with sudden light.

"Think you can make it to the top?" Todd asked.

I nodded, and we started climbing. Going up was more demanding than coming down had been. I was gasping and out of breath long before I reached the halfway point. Finally, Todd came to a halt. I waited for him to climb through the trapdoor, but he didn't.

I heard him straining against something.

"Hold the torch for a second," he instructed. "The door's stuck."

He bent and gave me the torch, then returned to shoving at the trapdoor above his head.

"It's not moving," he said, panic seeping into his voice. "They must have locked it or something."

"There were other passages leading out of their meeting chamber," I recalled. "Maybe one of them goes to the surface."

"That's a good idea," Todd replied. I could tell he was trying to keep his voice steady.

Exhaustion pulled on my limbs as I began climbing back down. I had to stop once to rest. When at last I got to the bottom, my legs crumpled, and I ended up sitting in the dust.

There was concern in Todd's eyes, but he didn't say anything. Instead, he went to the brazier and gathered the remaining torches.

"Astra," he started gently as he approached me.

"I know," I gasped. "We need to get moving."

Todd nodded and helped me to my feet.

As we retraced our steps down the hallway, we came to the opening where Yetta's body had been thrown.

I faltered, and my feet took me to the entrance of the cavern.

"You don't have to go in there," Todd told me, walking to my side.

I shook my head, not trusting my voice, and entered.

The room was much as it had been before. The bodies were the same; there was just one more now. I walked carefully to the newcomer's side and crouched beside her. Yetta was lying face down, arms and legs splayed in an awkward position.

Gently, I turned her body until her face was visible. The eyes were closed.

"I should have died with you," I whispered.

You've felt that way many times before, a voice told me. I cringed, thinking of all the other people I wished I'd been able to die beside.

Todd came to stand just behind me. In the firelight, I could see that one of the bodies beside Yetta was a little girl, no more than six years old. I hadn't noticed her fragile frame before. A fresh wave of tragedy hit me as I pictured her murder in my head.

Slowly, I moved one of Yetta's arms around the corpse of the child. "She always wanted to take care of everyone," I whispered to Todd. "Even here, she can continue."

It was silly, of course. Both the little girl and the old woman were beyond needing anything from anyone, but I liked to think that the pair would be here together until the end of the world.

I staggered from the room, fighting tears. I leaned against one of the stone walls as a sob racked my body. Todd followed me from the cavern. He dropped the unlit torches and took my hand.

"I know you're not all right, but do you think you can keep going?" he asked after a long moment. I didn't much care what happened to me. However, looking into Todd's dark eyes, my mind began to wake up, because I did care what happened to him.

I took a deep breath and nodded. "I will grieve later. There are more important things happening right now."

Todd gave my hand a little squeeze before letting go and retrieving the torches.

Shortly after, we made it back to the large chamber where The Brotherhood's meeting had taken place.

The ceiling was so high above us that the light Todd held couldn't touch it. On the stone floor was an ornately carved symbol. The pattern was unfamiliar but had five points. Each apex ended in a passage, one of which we'd just come through.

Not only was the pattern carved onto the floor, but it was also painted over in white. However, a few of the sections had been stained red. I tried not to look at the crimson liquid.

Todd walked the perimeter of the chamber, looking down each tunnel in turn.

"This place- This place was built by those who built Axella," I realized suddenly.

"How can you be sure?" Todd asked.

"I'm not, but neither my people nor yours could ever build anything like this. It must have been made before- before the great war."

"I suppose," Todd agreed absently.

"Which passage should we try?" I asked him.

"They all look the same," he answered.

"I guess we just have to pick one then," I announced.

"Let's try this one." Todd pointed down the tunnel to the left of the one we'd come through.

"Okay," I agreed.

The new passage was nearly identical to the first. It had the same rocky walls and sandy floor. Before long, we even came to a jagged-edged opening in the wall.

I shuddered, but we looked anyway because if there was a way out, we needed to find it. As expected, the cavern was filled with bodies. They were older, nothing more than dried-up husks, really. We encountered several similar openings, all with corpses, none with a means of escape.

Finally, the tunnel came to a dead end. There were remnants of metal stairs, but the few pieces that were left were broken and twisted. The ceiling vanished into a long chute above our heads.

"This must have led up once," Todd commented.

"That's a good thing," I pointed out. "It means the other passages are likely to lead to exits as well."

There was one more cavern close to the end of the tunnel that we hadn't checked. Even though I was sure it was pointless, we dared not skip it.

Inside, we found the most deteriorated corpses yet.

"They're so old." Todd's voice sounded like it came from a long way off. "Very, very old." He'd turned his attention to something in the center of the room.

Hesitantly, he moved forward, careful not to step on anything but stone. It wasn't until the torchlight drew near that I realized what he was looking at was a figure resting on a great, carven seat.

All of the other corpses had been strewn carelessly upon the floor, but this one was sitting, very much as it would have done if it were alive.

"It's him," Todd exhaled, coming to a halt.

"Who?" I asked, giving him an incredulous look from my place by the door.

"He's wearing the crown of eleven points," Todd whispered. "It's the three-day lord."

Instantly, a story Todd had told me nearly a year ago popped into my head. It had been about a man who won the lordship of The Brimming Lake but only ruled for three days before mysteriously disappearing.

"How can it be him?" I asked, picking my way across the cavern to join Todd.

He made no answer but handed me the torch. Now that I was closer, I could see that the seat was carved from a single piece of stone.

Slowly, Todd reached out and placed one hand on either side of the circle of metal, which rested on the head of the corpse.

"Don't, Todd." My words came too late; he'd already lifted it free.

Using the bottom of his shirt, he cleaned away the filth to reveal the shiny, silver metal beneath. Even in the gloomy light, I could tell that the crown was beautiful. The thick, silver ring was flawless. I'd never seen metal of such a pale color before. The crown appeared to glow as it captured the light from Todd's torch and reflected it back even brighter.

The points were not made of the same metal as the rest. Only one of them had the same look and reflective properties as the crown itself. It was well-suited and appeared to be part of the original design. None of the other points matched. They seemed to have been grafted on by less-skilled hands. None had the smooth surface or seamless angles of the first. Even still, the piece was impressive.

"Why did you take it?" I asked.

"He's worn it long enough," Todd murmured. "Without its weight, he can slumber here, on his throne, entombed with his brothers and sisters until the end of time."

I nodded, studying the body before me. The skin, if it could even be called skin anymore, was nearly black. It had shrunken to the bones of the skull, leaving pits where the cheeks used to be. The nose had collapsed, and the lips were pulled back to reveal the absence of teeth.

Despite all of that, the eyes were closed and, somehow, that lent a peaceful air to the dead, withered face.

We had to light the second torch on our way back to the meeting chamber. I trembled at the idea of what would happen once the torches ran out. Normally, the dark didn't bother me. However, the idea of being trapped in the pitch black with hundreds of corpses was hard for me to stomach.

You won't be alone, I reminded myself. *Todd will be with you.*

The next tunnel we tried was the one on the other side of the original passage. We didn't make it very far before the path ended in a pile of boulders. Todd attempted to shift some of the rocks, but everything was firmly set in place.

After returning to the meeting chamber for a third time, we tried the next tunnel to the right. Almost instantly, I could tell that there was something different about this passage. The walls were smoother and the ceiling higher. It felt like we were going uphill, which I hoped was a good sign.

Fifteen minutes later, we came to a place where the path split. It appeared that the main tunnel continued much as it had before. The other option, which branched off to the right, was smaller and had half a dozen steps leading upward into a long hallway.

"What do you think?" I asked Todd, wiping the sweat from my face. I'd have thought it would be fairly cool down here, away from the sun, but it certainly was not.

"Let's see where this goes," Todd gestured to the turnoff. "Hopefully, it will lead us to the surface."

I nodded, and we turned to the right. After the steps, the tunnel began growing smaller. The walls were so narrow I could reach out both my hands and lay one palm flat on either side. The roof was still about three feet above my head, but it felt nearly claustrophobic after the topless expanse of the passage we'd come from.

There were more steps up, and then the floor turned to the same hard stone as the walls.

When the hall came to an end, there was a door with a metal plaque on it reading "Water Control". I opened the door eagerly on account of my parched throat, but was disappointed to see that there wasn't so much as a drop of water to be found. Instead, I saw a vacant room.

Just before we entered, Todd pointed to the floor. It was dark stone, and in the thick dust, we could see at least two sets of footprints. Goosebumps rose on my neck as I surveyed the small space, not wanting to step inside but unable to resist taking a closer look.

One of the walls was covered by a metal plate. Long shafts stuck out of it at intervals. Some pointed up and others down. I think there was writing around them, but it was too faded and chipped to make out. I would have liked to stay and investigate further, but Todd reminded me that we needed to keep moving.

We returned to the main passage, but it didn't take us long to reach a second hallway. This one ended in three doorways, all of which were open.

Curiously, Todd entered the one on the left and held up the torch. It was a room of sorts. There were enormous shelves in long rows filling the entire space. Besides a layer of dust, there wasn't so much as a cobweb on them.

We still walked down every row, just to make sure we weren't missing anything important, but we found nothing. The room on the right was identical, but the one in the center, which picked up exactly where the hall ended, was different.

This last room was about twice as large as the others and had what appeared to be shelves as well, only each was a separate entity. The units stood about seven feet long and had three shelves stacked on top of each other, leaving several feet of clearance between them.

Again, we searched the room in vain.

"What's that?" Todd wondered as we were leaving. He brought the light close to the open metal door, then ran his hand over the surface, wiping away the grime to reveal a word.

"Can you read it?" he asked.

"It says Dormitory," I told him.

"What does it mean?"

"It's a place where people sleep," I answered, glancing back at the room once more and realizing that what I was looking at were beds, not shelves.

"Why would people sleep down here?" Todd shuddered.

I shook my head.

We left the three rooms behind. Whatever mysteries they contained were beyond my ability to fathom. This side hallway hadn't been very long, and, minutes later, we were back in the central passage.

There were dozens of turnoffs leading to many rooms. These never held bodies but were much like the first few we had seen. They were all empty.

Now that we knew where to look, I could make out labels on all the doors. The ones with rows upon rows of barren shelves read "Supplies". There were also rooms labeled "Farming Equipment", "Seed Vault", and "Medical Station". This last room was quite different from the others. It had once been entirely white with large cabinets everywhere. The color was peeling from the walls in long strips, and several of the cabinets lay in disarray on the ground.

Even without counting the side halls, this passage felt longer than the others and sloped up at an exhausting rate. I was panting before long, both from heat and exhaustion. Todd fared far better than I but insisted on making us stop several times to rest.

Although I hadn't eaten in more than a dozen hours, it was thirst, not hunger, that consumed my thoughts. Everything was so dry; I'd even stopped sweating, and my skin felt feverishly hot.

The tunnel eventually began to grow narrower as the floor turned from sandy dirt to stone. Our progress slowed to a crawl. Each breath of parched air burned my lungs, my entire body ached, and my legs nearly gave out a couple of times. I hoped Todd wouldn't notice. I didn't want to stop again for fear that once I sat down, I'd never get back up. Todd had already lit a third torch, and I could sense the panic he was fighting.

Finally, the tunnel ended at a metal staircase. Glancing up at the steps rising into the ceiling, I felt all hope vanish. I wasn't sure I could go another ten feet, much less climb hundreds of stairs.

"You were right," I said softly to Todd, looking at the upward path in despair.

"About what?" he asked.

"We should have just run away."

Todd was silent for a moment. "No," he replied. "I don't think I was. That would have been the easy way out, but the wrong choice."

I glanced at him, unsure of where this new opinion had come from.

"There's so much darkness in this world," he began. "I used to just accept that. Now we know the faults of our forefathers. Can't we learn from them, so their mistakes won't be made again?

"Our peoples are very different, but neither yours nor mine are particularly good. It doesn't matter who is better. I don't care about that now. What I do care about is keeping them from destroying each other, because then we will be just like our ancestors. You and I are among the few who know the truth. I think it's time everyone else knew as well."

His words stirred something deep in my mind. The fog of doubt and indecision was swept away.

"Yes," I told him as he moved toward the steps. "And our people aren't so different as you believe."

In my mind, I saw the cloaked group assembled once more. This time, when they removed their hoods, it was the council members standing there, plotting and scheming on how to control those around them. Our peoples were nearly identical. Both were flawed and evil and broken.

Taking a deep breath, I put my foot on the first step. The climb was impossible when I thought about all of the steps together, but if I only focused on the next one and then the one after that, it didn't seem quite so difficult.

Thankfully, this staircase wasn't very tall. When Todd stopped, I tried to see around him, but all I could make out was the solid stone ceiling. He gave me the torch and the crown, then reached up and pushed. Nothing moved. Terror gripped me. What if this entrance was locked too? Would we escape this place or, like the three-day lord, would this be our tomb?

CHAPTER 28
MORNING LIGHT

Todd climbed up another step and pressed his shoulder against the ceiling. I could hear him straining as I waited with bated breath.

Something moved. There was a grating sound, and part of the roof swung open.

I had hoped to be met with blinding daylight, but there wasn't so much as a trace of sunshine from above. Disappointment washed over me until I felt a welcome sensation brush across my face.

Wind.

It came through the trapdoor in a gentle gust of coolness.

"We made it," Todd whispered.

A moment later, he disappeared through the opening. I dragged myself after him and found that we had emerged in some kind of building. After I was clear, Todd released the trapdoor. It closed on its own, sealing the tunnels once more.

"Where are we?" I panted as Todd took the torch from me.

"We're in the shrine of the unknown god," he answered. "Close to the palace of The Lord of the Brimming Lake."

Todd walked to the far end of the room, and I could see that the structure only had three solid walls. The fourth side had a large opening, which let in the night air.

The walls it did have, along with the roof, were all black. The only piece of furniture was a table set up in the very center of the small space. On it rested a box, which looked extraordinary.

It was about a foot and a half long, a foot wide, and a foot tall. The glossy black sides had gold letters carved right into them, which glittered brightly in the firelight.

Slowly, I reached out to touch the box. It felt warm beneath my hand. I had expected it to be stone, and maybe it was, but if so, then it was a kind of stone I'd never come across before. The surface was perfectly smooth and had almost a silky feel to it.

"This writing is in the high language," I realized out loud.

"You can read it?" Todd gasped.

I turned my attention to the words. The torchlight was flickering, making the letters seem to jump across the surface.

Carefully, I lifted the box from where it rested. It wasn't as heavy as I had expected.

Todd drew in a sharp breath. "You aren't supposed to move it," he informed me when I glanced in his direction.

"Why? What is it?" I wondered.

"No one knows," Todd replied. "It's been here for a very long time. Many people have tried to open it, but none ever could. Then, after what happened to the three-day lord when he came to this shrine to pray, it was considered an unlucky place. No one has wanted anything to do with it since. Now that we know what's hidden here, I understand why."

I nodded, then turned back to the box.

"Well?" Todd asked.

"I can't," I said, shaking my head. "I know what language it is, but I never learned it well enough to read more than a handful of words."

I felt so furious with myself. Even though I could usually understand the high language when spoken, reading it was a completely different matter.

If only Myra was here, I wished. *Or Cole.*

"I might be able to work it out if I had some time," I announced, finally seeing a few words I recognized. "Do you think it's worth taking with us?"

Todd considered for a moment. "Maybe," he said. "I th- do you smell that?"

I sniffed experimentally. After the tunnel, the air had seemed cool and fresh, but now that I was growing accustomed to it, I could detect an acrid edge.

"Yes," I said. "But I'm not sure what it is."

Slowly, I stood and followed Todd as he left the shrine.

Dawn was turning the sky from black to indigo. We couldn't see how close the sun was to rising, because the dark shape of the palace cut off the view to the east.

The smell was more pungent outside.

"It's smoke," I realized.

Todd shot me a hasty glance.

"There must have been a fire," I whispered. "And something's still burning."

"There should be guards here." Todd pointed at the palace.

He walked toward the steps leading up to the platform over top of the river. Suddenly, he stopped and let out a little cry.

"What's wrong?" I demanded, hurrying after him, a sense of dread filling me.

"The river," he spluttered. "It's gone."

He was right. The riverbed was nearly dry.

"How?" I asked.

Todd shook his head in bewilderment. "I don't know. It's impossible. The river has never been dry before. Even during our worst droughts, there was always water."

"Maybe something is blocking it upstream," I suggested.

"This is bad. We need to warn The Lord of the Brimming Lake and tell him what we've seen," Todd announced.

"Do you think he'll believe us?" I asked.

"We have the crown of eleven points. That should catch his attention. If he needs more proof, he can always go into the tunnels and see the rest for himself," Todd replied.

Without hesitation, he sprang up the steps and began banging on the great doors of the palace.

Nothing happened.

"I have news of a plot against The Lord of the Brimming Lake!" Todd shouted. "Open the doors! Lord Tohoshin's life is in danger!"

There was no answer.

"I don't think anyone is in there," I told Todd in a small voice.

"Where would they have gone?" Todd asked.

"I don't know," I replied. "But I think something bad happened here."

The sky was getting lighter by the minute, and I was able to make out what looked like a collapsed building about forty yards away, in the direction of the king's temple.

We agreed to rest for fifteen minutes and then start searching for someone who could tell us what was going on.

Just as the sun's first rays shot into the sky, we started moving again. Todd was looking around in anguish. In the morning light, we could see that the once great city had been reduced to rubble. The charred ruins were still smoking in the morning air.

"It's just like Axella," Todd whispered.

"It will be in a hundred years," I agreed.

"This is my father's doing," Todd hissed as he took in the destruction.

Flames had consumed all of the wooden buildings, the bridges were gone, and the streets were covered in ash. Even the stone structures hadn't escaped. They had fared better, but the mortar between the rocks had crumbled to bits, tearing chunks of rock and stone from the buildings until they toppled. The palace still stood, as did the temples, but their walls were blackened and ominous in appearance.

What made the entire scene even more ghastly was the absence of people. They were gone—all of them. Not a living soul remained, save Todd and me.

Despite the warm night air, the sunlight felt cold as it reached over the palace and bathed the razed city in the light of dawn.

"Let's go hom- to my father's house," Todd said, breaking the silence. "It's on the outskirts and might have escaped the flames. Maybe we'll find some clue as to where everyone is."

We didn't try going through the city; it was too dangerous. In a handful of places, the fires were still burning. Many of the fields and buildings were destroyed. Among the few that survived, we found a well and were able to quench our thirst. I'd never tasted anything sweeter in my life.

Getting to Todd's dwelling took more than an hour. I could sense that Todd was eager to rush ahead, but I was at the end of my strength.

When we at last reached the cluster of buildings belonging to Todd's family, he heaved a sigh of relief. The area was untouched by the flames. Beyond the dwelling, I could see that the fields hadn't escaped completely. Fire had destroyed most of the crops. However, the flames had stopped a good distance from the buildings.

The place was deserted, without any sign of life. Even Fleck's paddock was empty.

Todd left my side and raced forward. He threw the door open and leapt inside the dwelling.

"Mother!" I heard him cry. A moment later, he reemerged, disappointment plain to see on his face.

"Don't worry," I told him gently. "I'm sure she's fine. She must have gone with the others."

"With my father," Todd growled.

Yetta's brutal murder instantly sprang into my mind. I swallowed the lump in my throat. "I don't think he'll hurt her," I managed to get out.

The look in Todd's eyes told me that he did not share my belief.

"He may still want to use her against you," I tried to reason with Todd. "She's no good to him dead. Besides, if both she and–" I struggled to get the name out, "Yetta, vanished, it might draw suspicion."

Todd nodded, but I could see that he was far from convinced.

"We have to save her," he announced. "I can't stand the idea of her being with that- that monster."

"We should take what we need and go after them," I agreed.

Todd let out a hard laugh. "You're dead on your feet. How far do you think we'll make it before you collapse?"

"I–" Normally, I would have protested, but I didn't even have the strength for that.

"Neither of us has slept or eaten. We've been traipsing around in the dark for hours, and you were wounded yesterday."

Yesterday, I thought. *Surely it was longer ago than that.* So much had transpired that I had to count back the hours before I would accept that Todd was correct.

"You get some rest, and I'll gather supplies," Todd suggested.

The last thing I wanted to do was sleep, because, inevitably, with sleep came dreams. After the horrors of the past twenty-four hours and my grim outlook of the future, I couldn't imagine what would be waiting for me when I closed my eyes.

"I'm not taking 'no' for an answer. Just rest for a few hours," Todd begged.

"Okay," I agreed with a sigh.

We entered the dwelling, and I headed toward my bed. "It's kind of a mess," Todd warned, following me down the hall.

I came to a sudden halt as I entered the room where I usually slept. The place wasn't a mess; it was a disaster area. Everything had been overturned, and many items were missing. I wasn't even quite sure where to start looking for my bed.

"They must have left in quite a hurry," I murmured.

Todd nodded.

I carefully picked my way through to where my bed had once stood. Only one blanket was left. Beneath it, I found the wooden frame unevenly balanced on three legs. The fourth one was broken.

"My room's not as bad. You can sleep there," Todd suggested.

"Your room?" I echoed.

"It won't be as dark," he replied. "But it's in better shape."

There's always the hayloft, I thought wistfully, but didn't bother voicing my preference. Todd probably wouldn't think much of the suggestion.

I'd never been in the men's section of the dwelling. It was down a hall, which hooked around, and had six rooms coming off the second portion.

Todd's was more or less intact. The less part, I suspected, didn't have anything to do with the exodus of his family. I made no comment as I stepped over the piles of clothing on the floor and sat down on the edge of the bed.

"Wake me in two hours," I told Todd as he retreated to let me sleep.

His bed could have been made of rock, and I still would have found it comfortable. My dread of sleep, and the dreams that would accompany it, couldn't hold out long against the weariness that clung to my every limb.

I closed my eyes against the morning light and tried to clear my head. It was impossible with so many things all going on at once. I had plans to make and much to do. However, nothing could keep me awake long at that point. The fact that the bed was soft and cozy didn't hurt. It also smelled like Todd, which I found comforting.

CHAPTER 29
PREPARATIONS

Todd never came to wake me.

Opening my eyes, I found the room filled with late afternoon light. I surged to my feet, then had to sit back down almost instantly as blackness covered my vision and pain lashed across my back. I waited a few minutes and took a deep breath before trying again.

I was still in pain, but found that I could stand. As I pulled on my discarded boots, a feeling of apprehension filled me. The entire dwelling was silent. My footsteps echoed too loudly as I moved down the hall.

"Todd?" I called softly, not daring to raise my voice much above a whisper.

I made it as far as the kitchen before I found him. He was sitting with his back against a wall, head bent over slightly, eyes shut. I froze in horror, then noticed the slight rise and fall of his chest and realized he was only sleeping.

It looked like he'd been gathering what remnants of food were to be found in the kitchen. Silently, so as not to wake him, I finished what he'd started.

Even though we'd lost countless hours, I could not be angry with him. This morning, I hadn't even considered that he was just as worn out and exhausted as I was. I'd been so focused on my own needs that I hadn't considered his. I'd have to get better at that.

Once I'd checked every shelf, with little to show for it, I started hunting for other things we might need. I found some extra clothes and a few blankets.

Unsure of what else to do, I returned to the kitchen. Todd was still asleep, his shaggy hair covering most of his eyes. If he were awake, he would have smoothed it back, only for it to fall forward once more a moment later.

Close beside him were the box and the crown. Stealthily, I lifted the box and took it to the window.

This morning, I'd been under a lot of pressure. Most of that was gone now, and I wanted one more crack at reading the writing. I tried to focus on the few words I did know. One meant to open, which I hoped indicated that the writing contained instructions for revealing the box's contents.

I could make out little more, except the word seek. I puzzled over another word before coming to the conclusion that it meant children, or maybe it was grandchildren. Either way, I didn't see how it could relate to opening the lid, if the box even had a lid. Examining it in the light, the black surface appeared to be all one piece. The letters were indentations in the surface, with gold paint filling the small spaces. There was only one small hole, not even big enough for my finger.

I was still trying to make out one of the other words when something moved outside. Instantly, I forgot the box. Standing in the courtyard formed by the buildings was Fleck.

So they hadn't taken her after all. Or maybe they tried, and she resisted. Either way, she was here now, and she was not alone. A pair of other horses were standing with her.

They didn't look to be in good shape. The first was well into his twenties, and the other had a crooked leg.

I set the box down and hurried to the door. Fleck balked and turned to run, but stopped when I called her name. Her eyes were huge as she watched me slowly walk out of the dwelling.

There was no point in approaching her directly. She seemed ready to gallop off at a moment's notice. Instead, I went into the stable to get a scoop of grain. There wasn't much left, but the barrel hadn't been scraped completely dry. I calmly entered her paddock and poured the food into her bucket.

I could see the wheels in her head turning as I repeated the familiar routine I'd done dozens of times. Leaving her to make up her mind, I left the paddock by way of the stable and headed back toward the front, where I could watch from concealment.

Slowly, the mare took several steps forward. She paused before passing through the gate. The two horses with Fleck followed, staying behind her. Then the old one pricked up his ears and trotted forward, intent on the grain.

Fleck instantly surged forward, the last horse limping after. Quickly, I stepped from the stable and swung the gate shut behind the animals. None of them so much as glanced in my direction; they were all too busy trying to keep each other from getting a nose in the feed bucket.

I suppressed a smile as I walked back to the dwelling. It was time to wake Todd.

When I put my hand on his shoulder and gave him a gentle shake, he bolted awake, leaping to his feet. It took him a moment to realize who I was and where we were. I wondered what dark dreams had plagued his mind.

"I'm sorry," he told me. "I didn't mean to close my eyes for more than a minute or two."

"Don't be sorry," I replied. "We both needed the rest. It would have been ridiculous for us to try and do anything this morning, considering the state we were in."

Todd nodded. "I suppose. How's your back?"

"Sore and a little stiff, but I'll live," I answered ruefully. "What about you?" I asked.

Todd furrowed his brow. "Me? Nothing happened to me."

I sighed. "Come on, Todd. Not that long ago, I found you up in the hayloft bleeding to death."

He looked away awkwardly and muttered, "I'm fine." There was still a large bruise on his upper left arm and a cut across the back of his right hand.

"I got some things together," I announced, letting the subject drop.

Todd nodded as I showed him the preparations I had made. "I also got us some horses," I said, drawing him to the window that overlooked the stable.

He gave the animals a skeptical glance. "Two, maybe two and a half decent ones," he commented, but his mood improved drastically when he realized we wouldn't have to walk.

I was all for packing up and leaving at once, but the sun was only a few hours from setting.

"We wouldn't make it very far," Todd pointed out. "Plus, if we stay here tonight, we'll have time to look for more supplies."

I hated the idea of waiting, but there was a lot of merit in Todd's words. So we spent the next three hours poking around for anything useful. There wasn't much to find. The dwellings closest to Todd's had all been emptied.

We did manage to scavenge some saddlebags and a small sack of grain in one of the abandoned stables. We gave some of the grain to the horses that night and planned to give them the rest before leaving in the morning.

Arshenn hadn't taken many of his blacksmithing tools, and Todd claimed some of what was left. I wasn't pleased with the idea, since the extra weight would slow us down.

My hand slipped to my necklace for a moment. Cupping the blue stone in my palm, I understood why Todd wanted them. He was very gifted, and if his people had to start over and rebuild their society, he could help them immensely with his talent.

We found a few other things: some rope, a bag of dried apples, a wooden staff, three water jugs, and a leather satchel to hold it all. All the weapons had been taken, save the knife Todd always carried with him, the same one he'd had during his rite of manhood.

It was dark by the time we returned to Todd's dwelling with our loot. There was still a tinderbox on the hearth. We built a fire and began packing our stuff.

The box, the crown, and the blacksmithing tools were placed in the saddlebags with a few blankets to keep them from shifting around.

Todd still had the backpack I'd brought from The Land of the Clan. We filled it with food, the tinderbox, and a few articles of clothing. Todd would have to carry it until my wounds healed. The satchel I could wear with minimal discomfort. I stuffed it with all the odds and ends that would fit.

The moon was rising by the time we finished. Even though I'd slept most of the day, I was still exhausted. Judging by the dark circles under Todd's eyes, I'd say he felt the same.

We both ended up sleeping in Todd's room. I took the bed again, while Todd made himself a nest of blankets on the floor.

I had pointed out to him that there were several other beds in the place, and I was more than willing to sleep anywhere, but he told me quite pointedly that he wanted nothing to do with his father or brother or anything that belonged to them.

Part of me understood his sentiments, although I had been tempted to say that we should at least take a look at Arshenn's room to see if there was anything useful to be found. A dread of the man kept me from making the suggestion. Besides, what were the chances of Arshenn leaving behind anything that he thought he could make use of?

Just before lying down, Todd went to his chest of drawers. After pulling out a few ragged shirts, he found what he was looking for and tied it around his neck. It was his old necklace, the one with the carved fox that he used to wear.

I smiled when I saw the familiar piece of stone. Todd noticed my expression and blushed. "It felt strange not wearing anything around my neck," he admitted. "But I didn't want to risk my father breaking this one too."

During the day, my rest had been free of dreams, but not that night. At least it wasn't a nightmare.

I was riding a swift horse. The reins were loosely held in my hands as the animal practically flew across the grassy earth. Two other riders flanked me, but I didn't look back at them. I could barely see their horses out of the corner of my eye.

The ground beneath my beast's hooves turned stony as we began climbing an enormous mountain. Still, the animal I rode didn't slacken its pace even for a moment.

We climbed and climbed until we were among the clouds. My horse plunged fearlessly into one of the white walls. I couldn't see even a foot in front of my face, much less the horse on which I sat, but still, the animal careened on.

Finally, we left the clouds behind and started our descent. Rocks skittered under my horse's feet, but it didn't notice, continuing on even faster than before.

Looking down at the green pastures below, I spotted the stables of The North Wind. My heart leapt with joy. I'd missed my home so much. In the late summer, it was the most beautiful place in the world.

I do not know if my desire was to lead us to the main stable or if we would have ended up there anyway, but in a few minutes, my horse came sliding to a stop just outside the door. I got down and turned to see where the other horses were.

The sun was shining straight in my eyes, making me squint. At first, I thought I was mistaken, but then I realized that only one of the other riders was still with me. The second must have been lost somewhere along the way.

I opened my eyes. It was still mostly dark in Todd's room, but outside, the sky wasn't completely black. Dawn was coming, and with it, the start of a new journey.

CHAPTER 30
MEETING

Neither Todd nor Fleck were thrilled when I boosted him onto the mare's back. We had no saddles, so he was riding bareback. It was probably for the best since Fleck had never worn one before.

Todd had insisted that he'd ride either of the other two quite willingly, but that Fleck scared him to death. Nevertheless, I paired them together. Fleck was stronger than either of the others, and Todd weighed a fair bit more than I did.

He tried to be brave about the whole thing as I got up on the old gelding. I'd given the horse with the crooked leg the baggage.

We set out toward The Brimming Lake. I assumed we would be able to track Todd's people easily since it was impossible for that many people not to have left a trail.

I would have preferred heading straight back to The Land of the Clan and warning my people of the coming invasion. However, Todd wouldn't be able to rest as long as his mother was in Arshenn's clutches. After what we'd witnessed, how could I blame him?

When we reached the banks of The Brimming Lake, Todd let out an exclamation of shock. The water had vanished, leaving the lake almost completely dry.

"Even with the river gone, I still thought there might be water here," he said. "I've never seen it this low before. What could have happened to it?"

"I'm not sure," I shrugged. "But I can guess."

"What do you mean?"

"I'd imagine your father had something to do with it. He must have found some way to cut off the water supply to ensure the city would burn."

Todd nodded but didn't comment.

Soon we entered the shade of the trees. The horses were already sweating, although it wasn't as hot as it had been a few days ago. The first traces of autumn were beginning to appear.

Fleck had accepted Todd as her rider so long as he didn't hold the reins too tightly. She set a swift pace as we marched along. The older horse, which I rode, kept up pretty well, but the horse with the twisted leg hobbled along at a painful gait. I would have stopped and turned him loose, but he appeared eager to stay with the other horses.

As the hours wore on, our pace slowed. During the hottest part of the day, we stopped to give the animals a break. There wasn't much grass for them to eat in the forest, but they were able to reach their heads up and eat leaves off some of the lowest-hanging branches of the trees.

We'd only been stopped for ten minutes before Todd said, "Don't you think we should keep moving?"

I glanced at the horse with the crooked leg. He wasn't putting any weight on it and might turn up lame at any moment.

"A few more minutes would be good," I suggested.

"All right," Todd answered less than enthusiastically.

"I'm sorry," I said. "We can go now. I know you're worried about your mother."

"I'm not sure what we are going to do after we find her," Todd sighed. "Things haven't really changed. I don't know how to protect her."

I just shook my head helplessly.

A few minutes later, we mounted the horses once more. I tried to recall if this was the same path I'd used when I first came to The Brimming Lake. Nothing looked familiar, but that was the very beginning of spring, and now we were at the end of summer. The entire landscape, which had been barren six months ago, was clothed in lush foliage.

By late afternoon, the limping horse came to a stop and refused to go one step further. I dismounted and relieved the beast of his burden, dividing it among the other two. I hated to leave the lame animal, but we didn't have many options. We'd just passed through an overgrown meadow; hopefully, he'd find his way back there and recover his strength.

Without him, our pace increased. I was pleased to find the old gelding had a decent amount of stamina. As I had assumed, we had no trouble tracking The People of the Brimming Lake.

Just as the afternoon was fading to evening, we caught sight of a few stragglers. Several ancient women were shuffling slowly along the track before us, while a few small children followed weakly. An old man with a missing leg hobbled forward on a pair of crutches just ahead of them.

A moment later, we crested the hill and looked down on a hastily pitched camp. The trees were spread out in the glade below, allowing makeshift tents to be put up and fire pits to be built. There was little order, and herds of animals seemed free to roam.

Todd pulled Fleck to a halt and turned back to me. "We should leave the horses here," he suggested. "We'll be less noticeable on foot."

I nodded. "Sounds good. I was wondering if–" I'd spent the afternoon thinking about what we were going to do.

"Yes?" Todd asked when I stopped midsentence.

"Maybe we should find The Lord of the Brimming Lake," I answered.

Todd grimaced. "Are you sure that's a good idea?" he wondered. "What are we going to say?"

"We'll tell him the truth. If we explain how the fires started and what happened to The Brimming Lake—and that your father is planning to kill him—maybe he'll listen."

Todd blinked. "And you think he'll believe us?"

"Yes," I sounded more confident than I felt. "We're trying to save his life. Plus, we have the crown. I'm sure he'll want to know where it came from."

Todd still didn't look convinced.

"Do you have a better idea?" I asked, then waited, hoping he'd think of something.

"Even if we can get to Lord Tohoshin and convince him we are telling the truth, then what? He can't take everyone back," Todd replied.

I understood what he meant, even before he continued.

"There's nothing left for my people back there. The city is destroyed, the water has vanished, and their homes are gone. All they have is the hope of a new and prosperous land," Todd pointed out.

"I know it's a hard situation, but we have to try talking to Tohoshin," I said.

"Why?" Todd asked.

I thought for a minute before answering. "Because I don't know what else to do, and I can't just walk away. If Tohoshin dies, then there will be a war. Maybe this time, we'll succeed where our ancestors failed, and we'll completely destroy ourselves."

Todd gave me a defeated look. It mirrored the feelings I had been battling for a long time.

"Things may be dark now," I began. "And I may not have any hope for the future, but I'm not going to give up until I find some."

Todd nodded slowly. I don't know if he understood, but he accepted my words.

We left the horses in a little clearing. Fleck began hungrily cropping the grass, but the old gelding was too exhausted even for that.

Taking the saddlebags with us, we slipped into the camp. It was easier than I would have imagined. There didn't seem to be anyone on watch. A few slaves were tending the flocks of sheep and other animals, but they paid us no mind.

"Where is everyone?" I heard Todd mumble after about twenty minutes of walking through the camp unchallenged.

I shrugged, then nearly ran into Todd as he froze. I peeked over his shoulder and saw why he had stopped. Husanil was twenty feet ahead of us, building a fire.

A gasp escaped Todd. I stretched up even farther to see the figure of Jiyata nearby, preparing food.

After the flames had grown steady and there was little danger of them going out, Husanil walked away. Jiyata moved to the fire, where she began setting out strips of meat on a spit.

The instant Husanil was out of sight, Todd sprang forward.

"Mother," he said softly.

Startled, Jiyata rose to her feet, then she caught sight of Todd, and her face contorted.

"Todicmadaya?" she whispered. "But how?"

The two embraced for a long moment. As soon as Jiyata released Todd, she turned and hugged me as well.

"I thought you had both perished in the flames." She straightened, pulling back from me, a beaming smile on her face.

"Is Yetta–" she started suddenly, looking around as if the named woman might step from anywhere.

A feeling of coldness crept over me.

"No," Todd answered gently. "She is dead."

Jiyata's face fell. "I was afraid it was so. I feared it for all of you, but for her most of all. May the gods show kindness to her spirit." Tears were filling Jiyata's eyes as she spoke.

"How did she die?" she managed to ask.

I exchanged a quick glance with Todd.

"This isn't the time or place to tell you, Mother. We need to leave," Todd said.

Jiyata looked confused. "Leave? Why?"

"We are going to take you away from Arshenn," promised Todd.

"Lord Arshenn isn't here," Jiyata told us.

We both froze.

"Where is he?" Todd exclaimed at the exact same moment I asked, "Do you know where The Lord of the Brimming Lake is?"

Jiyata shook her head and gave us a flustered look.

"Gone," she answered.

I let out a sharp breath. "We're too late," I said.

258

Todd looked equally distressed. "Is the tournament about to begin then?" he asked.

"The tournament?" Jiyata echoed.

"To see who the new lord will be," Todd clarified.

"No, no," Jiyata responded quickly. "He's not dead; he has left."

"Left?" Todd and I both asked in disbelief.

Jiyata nodded. "Him and most of the warriors."

"Arshenn–" Todd started.

"Yes," Jiyata told him. "And Arkensallay. We're to follow their path as quickly as we can. They will conquer the new land for us so that by the time we arrive there will be food and shelter for everyone."

Jiyata seemed extremely optimistic.

"I don't think it's going to be quite that easy," I couldn't help putting in.

"What do you mean?" Jiyata asked. "The Lord of the Brimming Lake told everyone that there was a rich land, Edden, from which our people had once been exiled. He said that the fire and the lake drying up were signs from the gods that now is the time to return and claim what is ours."

"We have to stop them," I breathed.

"But why?" Jiyata asked.

"Because those are my people," I answered, not surprised to see a shocked look cross her face.

"B- but," Jiyata stuttered. "They've gone to attack–"

"And a lot of your people are going to die," I told her grimly, before turning to Todd. "Our journey isn't over yet."

He nodded.

"We have to go, Mother, but–" Todd was interrupted by the return of Husanil.

"You," he snapped when he caught sight of Todd.

Todd faced him. "Yes, me," he answered firmly.

"You shouldn't be here," Husanil growled. "You hid during the fire and didn't ride to battle with the warriors. You are a coward!"

Hadn't I thought the same of Todd not so long ago? And maybe I had been right, but he certainly wasn't a coward anymore. He squared his shoulders and looked Husanil straight in the face.

"I am going after my father and the other warriors. Bring me a horse worthy of the journey."

Husanil hesitated. He was used to taking orders, but not from Todd.

"You have brought enough shame on your father's house." Husanil narrowed his eyes. "Will you truly go after them? Or will you flee?"

"I swear it by the king of the gods," Todd responded. "Now get me a horse."

Still looking slightly uncertain, Husanil scurried off.

"Astra," Todd said in a low voice. "Go get Fleck and meet me on the far side of the camp."

I shot Todd a questioning look, but he had already turned to Jiyata. "We'll need some supplies," I heard him say as I hurried back to where we'd left the horses.

I mounted Fleck and led the gelding. We traveled in a wide circle, sticking to the forest as much as possible. There didn't seem to be anyone left to stop me, but I was taking no chances.

Todd and Jiyata were waiting when I reached the far edge of the camp. Todd held the reins of one of Arshenn's geldings, a dark bay with long legs and intelligent eyes. He had several bundles tied behind the saddle, which I assumed were filled with provisions.

Todd handed me the saddlebags we had been using. They were much lighter now. I glanced inside and saw that the blacksmithing tools had been removed, leaving only the box and the crown. I laid them in front of me, over Fleck's withers.

"Mother," Todd said, turning to Jiyata. "Please have Husanil look after this horse."

"Of course," Jiyata nodded.

"Are you okay?" I asked as we watched her walk away.

"With my father gone, she'll be safe here. I don't want to drag her into this mess," Todd answered.

260

I nodded. Much as I loved Jiyata, she wasn't used to traveling and would be more of a hindrance than a help.

"We'd better get going," Todd said, tearing his eyes away from his mother. "We have a lot of ground to make up."

We traveled for little more than an hour before the thick trees drowned out most of the sunlight. Fear that one of the horses might injure itself in the dark made us stop when the shadows lay thick on the land.

We didn't bother with a fire.

"Did Jiyata say anything after I left?" I wondered. The horses had been cared for, and we'd both eaten some supper. Now we were wrapping ourselves in our cloaks, preparing to sleep.

"I asked when the men left, to get an idea of how much of a lead they have," Todd answered.

I could tell from the grim sound in his voice that the answer was not good.

"And?" I pressed.

"They departed at dawn this morning, with most of the supplies. Each man had an extra horse."

"How long before we catch them?" I wondered.

Todd shook his head. "I'm not sure we can."

"If we don't, then many lives will be lost. The lives of your people and mine."

CHAPTER 31
SETBACK

We pressed on early in the morning. Both horses were fairly fresh and made good time. The trail was still easy for us to see. I couldn't imagine the men were that far ahead of us. There had to be at least five thousand of them. A group that large couldn't travel all that fast, could they?

However, we saw nothing besides hoof prints and trampled grass all day. We stopped about an hour before dark. Todd's gelding, whose name was Bendel, didn't appear tired when we called it quits. Fleck was a little worn but not exhausted.

The place we chose for the night was on the banks of a river. I didn't remember if it was the same one I had crossed with Cole or if we had veered too far from that path to find any familiar landmarks. Already, I had a feeling that we weren't heading in quite the right direction. I found that thought to be comforting. If the men never found The Land of the Clan, there would be no bloodshed.

Todd had told them the general direction, but I didn't know if even he or I would be able to find it again, much less those who had never come this way before.

As night fell, I scanned the dark horizon for firelight. I didn't see any. Todd built a fire with the tinderbox.

My sleep was deep and dreamless, but both Todd and I woke late. We packed everything up quickly and departed shortly thereafter. A dread of falling even further behind began hanging over me.

For two more days, we followed the same pattern of waking and riding until the sun left the sky. Todd was constantly sore from the many hours in the saddle. My muscles were a bit stiff as well. For all my years of experience, I was woefully out of shape.

The days had been cooler than usual, and, as we made camp on the fourth evening, I could feel a change of weather in the wind.

Come morning, a light rain began falling. It drizzled on and off until noon, then halted for a while. I hoped we'd seen the last of the wet weather, although the cloud cover kept the temperature down nicely. The only downside was it made the sky grow dark faster.

Sometime in the late afternoon, a storm hit. One moment, we were riding along, then, suddenly, a downpour was upon us. Fleck and Bendel both jumped but calmed down when they realized it was just rain.

Before we could decide whether to stop and make camp, lightning struck somewhere close at hand. The almost instantaneous clap of thunder caused both horses to rear. I managed to cling to a handful of Fleck's mane.

Todd stayed on too, until Bendel spun around and raced into the woods. Todd was flung from the saddle and landed hard on the ground.

"Todd!" I called over the storm but couldn't come to his aid as quickly as I would have liked.

Beneath me, Fleck was a ball of nerves. She had more than half a mind to follow Bendel back the way we had come. It took all of my strength to keep her under control as another flash of lightning and peal of thunder followed the first. Finally, she froze. I slid to the ground, careful to keep a firm hand on the reins.

With Fleck in tow, I hurried to Todd's side. The storm had brought the night down with it. I could barely make out where he was lying.

"Are you all right?" I asked as I reached him, relieved to see that he was sitting up.

"No," Todd growled. He leaned to his right and spat into the dirt.

"What hurts?" I asked.

263

"My side," Todd replied. "I think I cracked a rib." He spat again.

"Is that blood?" It was too dark for me to tell, but I couldn't think of what else it might be.

Todd nodded, which I barely made out in the gloom.

"That's really bad," I told him. "Try not to move."

I think he nodded again, but I'd turned away. Fleck was tense and jumpy. I carefully pulled the blanket, which had been wrapped around the crown, from the saddlebags. It was the only blanket we would have unless Bendel returned.

The fabric was mostly dry, and I draped it over Todd's shoulder, grateful that he hadn't attempted to stand. There was no food and no fire, so the three of us spent a miserable night huddled together.

Todd slept some, but I didn't. I was too terrified that I would wake in the morning to find him dead. My only relief was that he didn't spit up any more blood.

The gray dawn found us soaked and shivering. There was still a light drizzle coming down, but the storm had passed.

"How do you feel?" I asked Todd when he opened his eyes.

"Better," he replied, slowly getting to his feet.

My first inclination was to stop him, but I was too late.

"I'm just a little sore," he told me, stretching in different directions to test the injury. "I may have bruised a rib, but I don't think anything's broken."

I sighed in relief, glad that the gloomy morning had brought at least a little good news.

"I guess it's just the three of us now," Todd commented, glancing around.

"Indeed," I replied.

We didn't make it very far that day. The rain stopped, and the sun came out around noon, which lifted our spirits a little.

We made camp in the early afternoon. Todd's side seemed to be bothering him, and we were all exhausted. Our food supply had disappeared with Bendel, so I left Todd to look after Fleck and set off into the forest. I didn't have anything to hunt with, except Todd's knife, which he had loaned me.

I moved silently, hoping to come upon some animal unawares. After quite a while of finding nothing, I turned back, but paused when I caught sight of a brook.

It made a soft, gurgling sound as it flowed along its stony banks. The water was crystal clear. I hoped I might be able to see fish in it.

Approaching slowly, I knelt and bent forward to peer into the water. Two pairs of green eyes reflected back at me. The first was my own, but the second–

My head snapped up, and I saw a creature standing on the opposite side of the river, almost close enough to touch. Its body was that of a dog, but leaner, taller, and more pointed, with long legs and huge feet. The shaggy fur was a glossy black and the eyes a blazing green.

I stared at it in complete wonder. The animal met my gaze calmly. Slowly, it raised its head and let out a long, melancholy wail, which was both joyful and sorrowful at once. I had heard the noise before, but then it had been far away in the dead of night.

A moment later, the creature stopped, looked at me once more, then turned and vanished into the woods as if it had never existed.

I was awestruck and remained by the brook staring after the animal until I remembered that I needed to get back to Todd. I managed to find an apple tree on the way and collected as many of the fruits as I could carry.

"Good, you're back," Todd said in relief when he saw me. "I was worried."

"Have I been gone that long?" I asked.

Todd shook his head. "I heard a wolf in the woods."

Wolf.

That was the name Todd had given the green-eyed animal. He'd told us a story about them as well, only, in the story, they hadn't seemed half so majestic as the creature by the brook.

We ate the apples and settled in for another night.

The following day, we continued our journey. Both of us walked, and Fleck carried the saddlebags, newly stuffed with apples.

"We won't catch them on foot," Todd warned.

I nodded. "I've been thinking about that."

"Maybe one of us should ride ahead?" he suggested.

"I'd have to be the one to do it," I announced.

Instantly, Todd shook his head. "They'd never listen to you. I'll go."

My stomach turned cold. "I'm not sure Fleck would allow it," I said quickly.

Todd gave the mare a sideways glance. She'd only allowed him to ride her with a lot of coaxing and while I was present.

"What if," I started, looking at the trail ahead. "What if we stopped following them?"

"You mean, give up?" Todd wondered.

I shook my head. "They haven't been traveling the most direct route. We have a better idea of where we're going. What if we head straight for The Land of the Clan and try to make it there before them?"

"The idea was to stop them from getting there at all," Todd reminded me.

"That doesn't really appear to be a possibility anymore. I'd like to give my people some warning. That way, if there is a battle, at least it won't be a massacre. Plus, if they are stalled long enough by the mountains, we might still have a chance of reaching Tohoshin," I told him.

Todd nodded.

We turned away from the path the others had taken and headed northwest, toward where I believed The Land of the Clan lay.

Making our way through the trees and fields that hadn't been trampled flat was more of a challenge, not to mention that it was sometimes hard to know what direction we were going.

I couldn't help but think of the last time I had traveled through these trees. I had been going in the opposite direction, but then too, I had been in a desperate race against time.

The day was mellow, the air carrying the faint crispness of autumn. In less than a month, the trees would start to shed their leaves, but the weather was pleasant for now.

We found a small pond to sleep by that night. There were some mushrooms growing on the trunk of a fallen tree to go with the apples for dinner. It wasn't much, but at least it was something. I removed Fleck's pack, and she waded into the knee-deep pond. The water had a brackish taste. However, it was better than nothing.

Todd fell asleep early. I lay on my back, gazing up at the sky. Most of it was hidden by tree branches, but a few stars were visible.

In the morning, Todd looked like he'd hardly slept at all. "I'm getting too old to sleep on the ground," he joked.

I couldn't help but laugh. We loaded up Fleck and left. The mare seemed well adapted to our current mode of travel. She kept whatever pace I set, and only deviated when she caught the scent of water. A couple of times, she led us to streams or ponds we would have overlooked.

At one of these, we saw a few silver fish just below the surface. Todd tried to hook one out of the water, but he wasn't quick enough.

It was apples and mushrooms for dinner that night. However, for breakfast, there were only apples. Much as I hated to do it, we spent the morning looking for food.

Todd located a few berry bushes, which we stripped clean, but that was all we found. When we resumed our journey in the afternoon, Fleck was the only one with a full belly.

CHAPTER 32
RECOLLECTION

The next day, Todd's side seemed better, but I still kept a close eye on him to make sure he wasn't growing fatigued. We covered a lot of ground and enjoyed pleasant weather.

As dusk settled on the land, we came to a bramble patch. I was leading Fleck and guided her along the outskirts. She stumbled over an outlying branch, causing a stir in the brush to my right.

A rabbit darted out, then froze when it saw us. That moment was all the time Todd needed to get out his knife. The blade flashed through the air, clipping the rabbit neatly.

"Good job!" I exclaimed, looking at the slain creature.

Todd held a finger to his lips for silence.

I kept still as Todd retrieved the knife. He motioned toward the briar patch beside me. Reaching down, I grabbed the branch that had caused Fleck to trip with one hand and a rock in the other. With a heave, I pushed the branch forward then backward, shaking the foliage. Two more rabbits came darting out.

Todd threw his knife, and I threw my rock. I missed, but Todd connected with another of the furry creatures. He only injured this one and had to rush forward to keep it from escaping.

For the first time since our journey started, we were going to have a hot meal. Or so I thought until I remembered that Bendel had been carrying the tinderbox. I would have been at a loss for how to build a fire, but Todd pulled out a flint.

"Joss gave me this," he said, using it against his knife to create a spark. "I've never been without it since."

I smiled sadly at the memory as I started gathering wood for the fire. Todd set about cutting the meat from the rabbit carcasses.

"Joss was the best of us," I murmured several minutes later.

"Yes," Todd agreed. "If he'd made it back, I don't think things would have turned out the way they did."

I considered his words, then asked, "You mean with Cole?"

I think Todd nodded, but in the twilight, it was hard to tell. "I'm sure Joss would have been able to figure out what was going on, and you all might have listened to him."

"That day was so strange," I recalled. "I have no explanation for what happened."

I added a few more logs to finish the woodpile. Most of the rabbit meat was cooking on stones by the fire. I came to sit beside Todd as he tended it with a long stick.

"Maybe Cole wanted me to leave for some reason," Todd continued.

"No," I shook my head. "He knew you were going to be heading out soon. We all did."

"Someone could have made him do it. His father is one of The Clan Leaders," Todd pointed out.

"But no one else knew who you were or where you came from," I countered. Then paused. *Unless someone figured it out...*

"I still don't think Cole would have lied to me," I protested, more to myself than to Todd. "And he definitely would have told me once we left The Land of the Clan."

"Maybe not," Todd speculated. "Maybe he felt like he had a duty to perform and thought it would be easier for you if I was the bad guy."

"Even that didn't work," I nearly laughed at the memory. "I still couldn't bring myself to shoot you. I just wanted to run away."

Todd winced. "I'm sorry about what I did when you tried," he said so quietly I had to strain to catch the words. The scar he'd given me wasn't visible, but his eyes dropped to my leg for a moment.

"I'm sorry too," I told him. "For a lot of things that happened since."

Todd gave me a confused look. "How do you mean? All of it was my fault. I was the one who put you in such a terrible position."

"It's exactly the same position I put you in," I pointed out. "I wanted to force you to live according to the laws I knew. That was wrong of me. And I- I wanted you to stay with The Clan, even though it wasn't what was best for you.

"It was selfish of me, and I am so sorry for that, Todd."

He laughed. "After all you've been through because of me, you're the one apologizing? I won't have it, Astra. It's too ridiculous."

His voice was light, but in my mind, the subject was more serious. "Maybe one day, all the wounds we have given each other will mend, and everything will be as it should have been," I said wistfully.

"That will be the best day of my life," Todd told me, his fingers reaching out to touch my arm. Gently, they traced the scar caused by the bear's claws nearly a year ago.

Almost automatically, I pulled my sleeve down to cover the blemish.

"Why did you do that?" he asked wonderingly.

I gave him a hard smile. "Because it's ugly."

Todd frowned. "I don't think there's any part of you that could be considered ugly."

A lump rose in my throat, and I felt my eyes water slightly.

"Who told you something like that?" he demanded.

I just shook my head, not trusting my voice.

"I've got plenty of scars too," he admitted. "They're part of who I am. They tell the story of my past. I wouldn't trade them for anything."

I stared into the fire for a moment, then asked, "Do you mind that I call you Todd? Instead of Todicmadaya?"

Todd laughed gently. "Not really."

"But it is your name," I replied. "Part of who you are, and I can't help feeling like I took that from you. If you want, I can start calling you Todic–"

"Don't," Todd interrupted me.

"Why not?" I wondered.

Todd sighed and glanced at the ground. "I've always been Todicmadaya. It's kind of a joke. My father named Arkensallay, his firstborn, after the king of the gods and after himself. Then he named me after the king's younger brother, the most pathetic god. Todkala never really does anything right in any of the stories. He's good at causing trouble and destroying things, especially friendships.

"I don't want to be like that, but everyone's always associated me with him because of my name. You were the first person who didn't think of him when you looked at me. And ever since I met you, I've started to feel like a different person. A better person.

"When I returned to The Brimming Lake, I started changing back into Todicmadaya, and I didn't like it.

"I prefer to be Todd."

"Okay," I nodded. "Then that's what I'll call you."

I gave him a wry smile. "Plus, Todicmadaya is such an impossible mouthful."

Todd chuckled, but grew serious quickly. "I don't believe in the gods anymore. If they do exist, then they can't have any power, or they would have stopped Arshenn and his group a long time ago."

I shrugged, not knowing how to answer since I hadn't ever believed in them.

We ate some of the rabbit meat and packed the rest. The few apples that remained we saved for breakfast.

Cicadas and crickets sang me to sleep that night as I lay down beside the dying fire.

When I opened my eyes, I was looking at a bale of hay. Disoriented, I sat up. The hayloft was empty. Morning light was shining in through the window at the end of the room. I rose and found my legs a little shaky. Slowly, I descended the staircase to the main floor of the stable. It was just as devoid of life as the hayloft had been.

Dust floated lazily in the golden sunbeams, which penetrated the long hall. Everything was silent and peaceful.

271

Suddenly, a hand fell on my shoulder from behind and started pulling me down the hall backward. I couldn't turn around and see who it was, nor could I resist the iron grip. Just as we passed the last stall, we stopped, and I was shoved against the door.

A dead goat lay in the hay. Panic filled me as I realized this was about to become a nightmare. A sudden shriek went up from close by, not from one voice but from a thousand. Goosebumps broke out on my arms.

The hand on my shoulder constricted. This time, it pushed me forward. We came to the large, double doors at the entrance of the stable, which were slightly ajar. Night had fallen outside, and I could see a great assembly of people gathered. Around them, torches burned, casting twisted shadows across the scene. At first, I thought the firelight was why the men and women appeared to be red. It took me a moment to realize I was wrong.

As I was pushed across the threshold of the stable, I recognized the scene and found myself standing on the steps of the palace as the festival sacrifice was taking place. The priests were just in front of me, with their backs turned. They were hurling blood at the people gathered below.

The seething mass of humans was a single, living thing, crying out for blood. The priests were doing all they could to answer that cry.

Handful after handful of the crimson liquid was sent flying at the assembled horde. Too much, in fact. There hadn't been this much blood. Even those on the front row hadn't been as drenched as they were now.

The ones closest to me were completely saturated and looked like they were about to bleed to death.

"I thought you should know," Myra's voice whispered in my ear.

The pressure on my shoulder vanished. I spun around, but no one was there. Instead, a wall of blood fell on me, clouding my eyes and clogging my mouth and nose. I couldn't see. I couldn't breathe. I could barely move at all.

The warm liquid engulfed me. I thrashed around, trying to escape, but it was impossible.

I woke with a start, clawing at my face to free myself of what had never been there. The moon was shining down into the clearing. Even at only half full, it was bright enough to illuminate the surrounding foliage.

To my left, Todd jerked awake and stared at me in surprise. "What's wrong?" he asked, surging to his feet.

"Nothing," I told him. "Just a bad dream."

Instead of settling back down, he came to sit beside me. "I'm sorry," he whispered, putting an arm around my shoulders and pulling me against him.

"Happens all the time," I responded. The dream hadn't been nearly as bad as some. The racing of my heart was already beginning to quiet, but I didn't pull away from Todd.

My mind was wandering over what I had just experienced. Something was nagging at me, as if I was missing an incredibly easy answer.

Todd and I sat like that for a long while. Soon, I started growing drowsy again. Todd's body gradually shifted into a more relaxed position until he was flat on his back with my head resting on his chest.

The even rise and fall of his breathing told me that he was asleep once more. The warm night air was soothing, and I was close to joining him.

My eyes closed. I had started walking in a new dream when it hit me like a thunderbolt. My body stiffened as my eyes flew open.

I finally understood. I finally knew the truth. It was just possible. I didn't want to allow myself to believe it, but there was a small chance that they could be alive.

CHAPTER 33
THE POINTS ON THE CROWN

The days felt so much shorter now than when we had left The Brimming Lake, only ten days ago. No matter how early we rose, the sunlight seemed to vanish in the blink of an eye. It didn't help that the landscape never changed, trees, trees, and more trees, with the occasional river and meadow thrown in.

Fleck was very good at finding water, and we seldom ran short. Food was more problematic, but we managed. There was no meat after the two rabbits, but we continued finding a meager supply of edible plants.

I fervently hoped we were still on the right path. How large was the world? Would it be possible to walk forever in this direction and never find The Land of the Clan?

Part of me wished it were true. If we never reached our destination, we would be free. I longed to run away with Todd and turn my back on my people. However, I knew the feeling came from the same part of myself that had almost given up and died in the forest six months ago.

I pushed the impulse away. I would not give in to selfishness. I had a task to complete, albeit an impossible one. Still, I would see it through to the end if it lay within my power.

I didn't sleep very well. Anxiety gnawed a hole in my stomach when I lay down at night. I feared that we would never reach The Land of the Clan, I feared that we would, and, worst of all, I feared that we would arrive too late. The only good thing was that by the time I did drop off to sleep, I was too exhausted to dream.

Finally, we came to a clearing on the edge of a rise, and I could make out, far in the distance, the familiar mountains I had never thought to see again.

Instead of lessening my anxiety, it only grew worse as we drew near the end of our journey. That day, we had to take a massive detour around a particularly steep wall of rock. Todd could have climbed down, and I might have been able to as well, but not Fleck.

We stopped early for the night. The sun was still an hour from setting, but the land ahead of us looked treacherous. Tall trees cut off the sunlight, casting long shadows, which made Fleck balk.

I spent the remaining daylight poring over the box we had taken from the shrine, making one last attempt at figuring out what secret message was carved into its black sides. After half an hour, I was ready to give up for good. There didn't seem to be much point in trying anymore. I returned the box to the saddlebags in frustration.

"Not going so well?" Todd asked. He'd built a small fire and was cooking some wild potatoes and carrots we'd found.

I didn't answer aloud, but gave him a look, which successfully communicated my present feelings.

He chuckled. "Wish I could help, but I can't even read normal writing, not to mention that strange second language your people have. They only teach priests to read and write. The rest of us don't seem to need it."

"I could have learned," I admitted. "But I was always busy with other things."

"It'll be all right," Todd told me. "We've got the crown. That's more important anyway."

I nodded.

"Do you know why the crown has eleven points?" Todd asked.

I thought for a moment. "Doesn't it have to do with the lords who wore it?"

"That's right," Todd informed me. "But only the lords who did something extraordinary added a point.

"The crown was made by the two sons of Peter, the founders of The House of the Warrior and The House of the King. Neither was the sole Lord of the Brimming Lake."

"If there were two of them, why didn't they make two crowns?" I asked.

"They were probably going to," Todd replied. "But shortly after arriving at the haven from Perdita's map, the founder of The House of the King fell ill, as a great many did during their long journey. No one believed he would recover.

"However, on the thirteenth day, he mustered his strength and sought his brother. When he found him, he was sitting on the throne they were meant to share, wearing the crown they had forged together, holding court alone.

"The founder of The House of the Warrior was a large man, broad of shoulders and loud of voice. Even on the journey to The Brimming Lake, he had continuously tried to overrule his brother."

"What were their names?" I interrupted with a question.

"No one remembers," Todd replied, shaking his head slightly. "Much of our history from that time has been forgotten. None of it was written down, so the accounts were given only by word of mouth, leading to some ridiculous rumors."

"Like what?" I wondered.

Todd gave me a laughing smile. "Oh, things such as the sun was deadly, and they feared its light, or that all the food they ate came from metal.

"Anyway, when the founder of The House of the King entered, his brother rose and feigned innocence. He tried to embrace his brother, but the founder of The House of the King was not fooled. The treachery was plain for all to see. When his brother approached, he thrust a dagger into his side, killing him.

"Instantly, he claimed the crown and throne for himself and The House of the King.

"Those who had followed his brother were furious. They mounted an attack, trying to unseat the only remaining son of Peter.

"The plot failed, but so many were killed that the founder of The House of the King decreed that in order to find a worthy replacement, a great tournament was to take place whenever a ruler died.

"At first, even this did not appease those of The House of the Warrior, for they feared The House of the King would use the tournament to remain in power. But when the current Lord of the Brimming Lake promised that no eligible man would ever be excluded, they were content to lick their wounds and wait.

"Using the knife he had slain his brother with, The Lord of the Brimming Lake forged the first point of the crown.

"After his death, the crown passed into the hands of one from The House of the Warrior.

"He was not a great leader, but deemed himself as such. He led a great expedition out of the safety of the haven, trying to escape the night, they said." Todd shook his head, as though the words made little sense to him.

"Not all of his party survived. Many were lost, and the rest were nearly crazy when they returned.

"Because of his half-witted act, the gods sent dark spirits to plague the people. Every so often, they would carry off a victim, and that poor soul would never be seen again.

"The foolish Lord of the Brimming Lake claimed he managed to slay one of the spirits, but he could never prove it because the body vanished instantly. Still, he insisted he had and added a point of his own to the crown.

"The next day, he was found dead in his own bed. So the crown was passed on from leader to leader, never tarrying long. When it reached the sixth leader, a man from The House of the King, a new age began for The People of the Brimming Lake. This lord beseeched the gods so fervently that they chased away the terrors of the night and brought us back into the sun. The people were able to leave the haven and walk freely beneath the blue sky from that day on.

"The Lord's rule was a long and peaceful one. Only after his death did the people demand a third point be added to the crown in remembrance of the great man who had given them back the light.

"The fourth and fifth were for two brothers who ruled one after the other. The first, and elder of the pair, built the palace and the temples for the warrior and the king. He also laid out the plans for the great city of The Brimming Lake."

Todd's voice held a sad note as he spoke of the beginning of something incredible, something we had witnessed the end of.

"It was supposed to be the most beautiful place on earth," Todd continued.

"He died before the city was completed, but his brother saw his vision through to the end. Together, they raised the people from living in mud huts to possessing a city built of stone and shod in iron."

"The sixth point was added several generations later by a lord who built a mighty fleet and set out to sail across the sea. He returned two years later with only three vessels left. The wonders he and the others spoke of were extraordinary. They brought back strange plants and animals, the like of which had never been seen before or since.

"The next point, the seventh one, was added for the man who captured and tamed the first horse. He spent twenty days lying prostrate in each of the gods' temples, imploring them to show him favor and bless the people with great boons.

"The gods answered by sending horses to the land. Before that, no horse, either free or wild, had been seen before. The lord instantly realized the gift the gods had sent. He captured a handful of the creatures and tamed them.

"Whenever more came to the land, he would trap them and add to his herd. Life grew easier for The People of the Brimming Lake as they discovered more and more uses for the animals. It should have been the beginning of a golden age, but it was not.

"Since the houses did not need each other anymore, a time of war spread across the land. The discontent that had always been between them erupted into battles caused by the smallest of offenses.

"No lord was left long on the throne. There were few who even wanted the position, for it was a death sentence. Before long, the population of The Brimming Lake had been halved.

"The eighth point was for a lord who survived a mortal wound during the last round of the tournament. They said his spirit was too proud to perish after he'd won the lordship, and though he never fully recovered, his heart was unshakable.

"Many lords followed, but it wasn't until a hundred years later, when a sixteen-year-old, newly returned from his rite of manhood, took the lordship, that another point was added.

"His name was Cyrindo of The House of the King. He is considered the greatest ruler in all of our history, for it was he that rebuilt the city, which had been destroyed by decade after decade of war. More than that, he began appointing priests to serve the gods, who showed him much favor. Every harvest under his reign was more bountiful than the last.

"The friction between the two houses was far from erased, but Lord Cyrindo began holding market days, where the two factions could unite as one. At first, there was bloodshed, but the harsh punishment for any who caused problems soon rectified the situation. Eventually, the two houses began to learn to live in peace again.

"Cyrindo added his point to the crown when The People of the Brimming Lake had lived ten years without a battle taking place. He passed away in his sleep several moons later, an old man who had achieved much.

"The next point was added a few generations later, by an arrogant ruler from The House of the Warrior. After his lordship was established, he abandoned the people for a three and a half year journey to prove his valor to the gods.

"He returned with the body of a bear, not a great brown bear, but one even larger, whose fur was pure white. The lord claimed it had come from a land where winter never ended, and the sunlight was cold instead of warm.

"He went on many such journeys, caring little for the affairs of the people and only for his own glory. He never returned from the last venture, and the gods sent a vision to the head priests, telling them of the lord's death.

"Although it was unprecedented, not even his own house argued much when the tournament was announced to replace him.

"The last point's story is a tragedy. A boy named Gosimer returned from his rite to find that his father had been lost at sea during a fishing trip. The young man was the oldest of five children, the other four girls. His family was very poor, so he had to slave away on another man's fishing boat to earn enough to feed his mother and sisters. But times were lean, and he never seemed to bring home enough.

"His sisters perished of hunger. One by one, he buried them behind the shack where his family lived. Winter brought a lack of work, and Gosimer's last sister died.

"When spring came, he was able to work again and managed to bring home much food, but his mother refused to eat. She had fallen heartsick over the deaths of so many of her children.

"The woman cursed the gods and slept forever, leaving Gosimer alone. Shortly thereafter, The Lord of the Brimming Lake died as well. Gosimer competed in the tournament, but he was weak from exhaustion and sorrow. He only fought one duel and was defeated easily. His left hand was nearly severed by a late blow as he lay in the dirt.

"Maimed as he was, Gosimer could no longer work on the boats. He refused to be a beggar. Instead, he tried to become a priest. But when he spoke to the head priest of his house, the man told him that another, greater destiny awaited him.

"The head priest had a brother named Arnetsk, and he sent Gosimer to live with him and his family. There, Gosimer became friends with Arnetsk's oldest son. The two trained with weapons every day when their chores had been completed.

"After two years, Gosimer fell in love with Arnetsk's second daughter. However, she was pledged to be married and had given her heart to her betrothed. Gosimer was forced to watch the girl he loved marry another. He fled Arnetsk's house and found enough work to keep himself busy, all the while brooding on the wrongs done to him.

"Ten years later, the tournament was held once more, and Gosimer prevailed, claiming the crown. With his newfound power, he lashed out at those he perceived as having wronged him.

"The fisherman, who hadn't paid him enough to buy bread for his family, he had set adrift far from shore, in a small boat with a hole.

"He burned the houses of his neighbors who had watched his family starve to death, refusing to let them salvage anything except the clothes on their backs.

"He hunted down the warrior who had given him such a dishonorable blow and crippled him for life. Once found, he ordered that both the man's hands and feet be chopped off.

"Arnetsk, he had put to death along with his wife for refusing to give their daughter to him.

"He was even crueler to the girl herself. With his own hand, he killed her two sons. Then he put out the eyes of her husband.

"There were others, too numerous to mention, that he had punished. Despite all of that, he was far from the worst of our rulers. Gosimer's mind was never strong. Everyone feared his wrath. Laws were upheld religiously, and it was a time of order and great prosperity.

"Three times assassinations were attempted, and each time Gosimer fought his way out. Even with his mangled hand, he was a deadly opponent. The assassins never made it out alive.

"After reigning for seven years, he ordered the eleventh point be added to the crown, so that the world would always remember the injustice he had suffered at the hands of men, which the gods had given him the power to vindicate.

"A couple of months after it was added, Gosimer was found dead with his hand wrapped around a knife embedded in his gut.

"Many years later, Matthan, the three-day lord, defeated his opponent and was made Lord of the Brimming Lake. As you know, he was the very last lord to wear the crown of eleven points."

CHAPTER 34
SMOKE IN THE MOUNTAINS

The last light of the day was fading as Todd fell silent.

"Why didn't your people make a new crown?" I asked after reflecting for several moments on the history Todd had related.

"They did," Todd replied. "But much of the art of blacksmithing was lost by then. Peter's sons were both masters, and nothing our smiths can do now even comes close."

I nodded, thinking of the perfect circle of silver, which glowed in even the smallest amount of light.

"Plus," continued Todd, "the lords started being buried with their crowns. I suppose they thought that it somehow still made them lord, even in death."

"In death, we are all equals," I murmured. "Once we reach the end, nothing matters anymore."

"No," Todd shook his head. "It may not matter much how and where you die, but what you do in this life remains with your soul even after your body has decayed."

"You still believe this life isn't all there is?" I asked. "Even though you admitted you're not certain about the gods anymore?"

Todd shrugged. "I'm not sure what's true right now, but it's better to be safe than sorry."

"How do you mean?" I wondered.

"Well, if this life is the end, then what do I lose by seeking the truth about the next world? But if there are gods and I live like they don't exist, then I've lost everything."

I didn't know quite how to answer him. Todd gave me a wink. "I like to be two steps ahead."

I couldn't help but laugh at his cheekiness.

In the morning, mist rose from the forest around us. It didn't linger long as the day grew warm, not hot, but very pleasant.

Todd was leading Fleck. I walked ahead of them, keeping an eye on the treacherous ground for any holes that might cause the mare to stumble.

I was also watching the horizon. We'd seen the Mountains of The North Wind yesterday, and I was eager to ensure we were still on course. However, the forest kept the peaks well concealed all morning.

In the afternoon, we forded a stream and reached another just before nightfall. Todd managed to hook a couple of fish from the water, and I found a small melon patch. Compared to what we had been surviving on, the food looked like a feast.

With the first light of dawn, we crossed the river and pressed further on into the trees. Around noon, we came to a large clearing, which finally allowed me to see The Mountains of the North Wind.

At first, I thought they were shrouded in mist, but after staring for a few moments, I realized it was smoke. My heart jumped into my throat.

"We're too late," Todd groaned, following my gaze.

"No," I snapped, "They might be waiting until tomorrow."

"We'll never get there in time," Todd pointed out. "I can't imagine it'll take any less than two days to reach the mountain from where we are now."

I set my jaw and thought for a moment. Then turned to Fleck and opened the saddlebag. Pulling out the blankets and other small items, I let them fall to the ground.

"What are you doing?" Todd gasped.

"Lightening the load," I answered without stopping. In the end, the only things I left were the crown, the box, and what was left of the food. I debated about the box, but its weight wouldn't make that much difference.

As soon as I was done, I leapt onto the horse's back. Todd wore a pained expression as I gathered the reins.

"Are you coming?" I asked over my shoulder.

He blinked. "You mean, both of us are going?"

"Well, I wasn't going to leave you behind," I replied.

Todd's face brightened as he hurried forward. With my assistance, and that of a large rock, he managed to scramble up behind me. Both his arms wrapped around my waist as I turned Fleck toward the mountains and pushed her into a run.

The mare picked up an easy canter. Burdened as she was, I knew her legs wouldn't last forever, but we needed her to give us all she had.

The forest flew by in a blur of green and brown. Fleck wove effortlessly between the trees and around the larger patches of pricker bushes. Every time she turned, even slightly, Todd's grip on my waist would tighten.

The sky grew cloudy, giving me no way to tell how long we careened through the trees toward the mountains.

Soon Fleck began to sweat, then her breathing grew heavy, and the speed of her legs slowed. I didn't know how long she would be able to keep up the relentless pace. I felt horrible using her in such a way, but bigger things were at stake.

We took a short break to let her rest for half an hour beside a pool of water, and then we were on the move again. Fleck was struggling as the sun vanished into the trees. I'd lost sight of the mountains and didn't know how close we were, but I still pushed her forward, trusting the mare's better night vision to keep us from running into anything.

If there was even the slightest chance we might reach our destination before dawn, I would take it. The moon rose large and silver, but only a faint glow managed to make its way through the canopy of trees.

Suddenly, Fleck fell to the ground. Todd and I were thrown clear. Instantly, I rose and glanced at Todd. He was rubbing the arm that had broken his fall, but seemed to be in one piece.

After assuring myself that Todd was fine, I turned to Fleck. She was lying on the grass, gasping. Guilt welled up inside of me.

Todd's knife had fallen to the ground just in front of my feet. I stooped and picked it up, then went to the mare's side. Carefully, I used the blade to cut loose the saddlebags from the mare's body.

I placed a hand on Fleck's head and knelt beside her. "How bad is it, girl?" I asked.

Her dark eyes stared into mine, and in them was a wild light; the mare wasn't defeated yet. Gently, I touched her face and ran my fingers down the length of her nose.

"I'm so sorry," I whispered, stroking her over and over again.

Todd had come to stand behind me. "Is she dying?" he asked softly.

Almost in response, Fleck twitched and rolled onto her side. She wasn't standing, but she wasn't lying flat anymore either. She was making a terrible wheezing sound, and her body was soaked in sweat.

"I don't think so," I told him. "But she can't help us anymore."

Todd nodded and picked up the saddlebags from where I'd set them on the ground.

"Goodbye, Fleck," I whispered, removing her halter and hating myself for what I had done to this poor creature. She'd never known any kindness in her life. In the end, even I had done nothing but betray her.

"I am so sorry," I told her again with one final stroke before rising to my feet.

Abandoning anything went against my nature, but I had no choice. I was fighting tears as I turned away, leaving the beautiful silver horse to the forest and the moonlight.

Now it was our turn to run, and run we did. Trekking day in and day out had made us strong. The wounds on my back were mostly healed and didn't give me any trouble. The first hour was the hardest. After that, my legs were deadened, and I didn't feel much discomfort.

We did pause to walk from time to time, but the relentless nagging in the back of my mind propelled me forward. Exhaustion came. I caught my second wind. More exhaustion followed until I was stumbling along, hardly even noticing which direction. Part of me longed to fall to the ground as Fleck had. There would be rest in defeat, but I wasn't ready to give in yet.

When dawn broke across the land, I saw that the trees in front of us were thinning out. We emerged, blinking in the fresh light of day, The Mountains of the North Wind rising before us. For the last hour, we'd been walking at a slow but steady pace.

A small rise hid the base of the mountains from view. We crested it and looked down at an abandoned camp. The men of The Brimming Lake had been here, that was easy to see. Thousands of feet and hooves had trampled the earth. There were still a few tents and other supplies, which had been left behind.

"They've gone into the valley," I breathed.

Todd nodded, looking at the mountain path in despair.

At the entrance, I saw several bodies. Some of them were dressed in gold, showing that they were soldiers of The Barracks sent to guard the valley. The rest were the bodies of those from The Brimming Lake. There were an unexpectedly large number of these, considering how badly the soldiers had been outnumbered.

All of them appeared to have died at least a day ago. I tried not to look too closely at any of the corpses. I didn't want to see the faces of those who would never again hold their loved ones.

Todd gave me a helpless glance as we headed into The Valley of The North Wind. The trail led steeply up. Hundreds of hoof prints cut into the once smooth path.

The climb seemed pointless. We were already too late.

"Up ahead is the dangerous part," I panted.

Todd nodded. Sweat covered his face and soaked his hair. His mouth was hanging open as he gasped for air. I imagined I looked twice as worn out as he did.

Just before we came to the most treacherous part of the valley, I saw several dead horses lying on the side of the trail. They must have slipped and injured themselves or fallen victim to fatigue. A fresh pang of regret filled me as I recalled the horse I had left behind.

We moved as silently as possible. The path twisted sharply, and the wall fell away on our left, leaving nothing but open space.

The greatest of the mountains rose on the right, its icy peak glittering in the sun.

Before we had gone ten steps, we froze. A wall of fallen rocks blocked our way. Bodies were everywhere, the corpses of Todd's people and their horses. We both stood in shock for a few moments, taking in the destruction.

I didn't dare look over the perilous ledge on the left. I was certain many more bodies had fallen over the cliff.

The urge to press forward finally overcame my horror. I began searching for a way through. The hardest part would be scaling the rocks without making a sound. Although, it was possible that every loose stone on the mountainside had already come down.

As carefully as possible, I climbed the shortest part of the wall. Todd was right behind me. His added weight shifted a few rocks. The sound of their movement caused several bits of stone to come clattering down from overhead. Clearly, there were more rocks ready to fall at any moment.

We scaled the wall without any mishaps. More bodies were on the other side. Probably at least three hundred men had lost their lives here, and that might have been an optimistic number. There weren't nearly so many horses, but I could well imagine that their bodies had been carried into the chasm because of their greater bulk.

After we passed the last of the still forms, I furrowed my brow. The signs of the invaders had vanished from the trail ahead.

Todd put his mouth very close to my ear. And was about to whisper something, but I shook my head.

Only after we'd traveled for another half hour and I was certain the dangerous part of the passage was behind us, did I turn to him inquiringly.

"They must have turned around," he told me.

"Good," I said. "Hopefully, they've headed back the way they came."

"Maybe. I'm sure the mountains took some of the wind out of their sails, but they may try something else. It's not like my people to give up so easily."

"Too bad," I muttered.

"They don't have much choice," Todd pointed out. "If they don't find food before winter, everyone will starve."

I shrugged.

"They're not all bad," Todd announced. "A lot of those men have families that they love. They will do whatever is necessary to help them."

"So my people should allow themselves to be slaughtered and made into slaves?" I shot back.

"That's not what I meant," Todd sighed.

We had stopped walking and were facing each other. "Well, you need to decide whose side you're on."

"I'm on your side," Todd told me. "And I don't believe you want my people to starve to death any more than I do."

I hesitated, my frustrated retort dying on my lips.

"So what do we do?" I asked.

"I haven't got the faintest idea," Todd answered. "We don't know where the army of The Brimming Lake went, or if your people have even realized they are here. We don't really know much of anything."

I sighed, lost in thought. All my ideas had hinged on stopping the attack before lives were lost. Now that they had already paid in blood, it would be much harder to convince the men of The Brimming Lake to turn around and leave in peace.

At least we've still got the crown, I thought, glancing at the bag Todd carried over one shoulder.

And the box... A different voice whispered.

The box. I couldn't read it, but I knew someone who could.

"We need to find Cole," I announced suddenly.

Todd's eyes widened. "Hang on a second," he began, but I held up my hand.

"He'll be able to tell us what's going on," I pointed out. "Plus, after we explain the situation, he'll be the most likely person to help us, and he can read the words on the box."

Todd did not appear to be convinced.

"Maybe I should go alone," I suggested.

"Absolutely not," Todd responded immediately, then started walking forward once more. He turned to call over his shoulder. "Come on. If Cole's going to kill me, we might as well get it over with."

I repressed a smile as I hurried after him.

CHAPTER 35
HOMECOMING

Since we'd spent the night running instead of sleeping, our progress was slow. We paused in the meadow to drink water from the spring and refresh ourselves.

"We should spend the night in the valley," Todd said.

I hesitated, wanting very badly to know what was happening.

"It would be stupid to go marching into The Paramount at midnight," Todd replied to my silent objection. "Plus, we can hardly stand."

"Then we should sleep in the cave," I told him.

He nodded. "We can find Cole in the morning."

The cave was just as I remembered it—my favorite place on earth, with its domed ceiling letting in the sunlight. I compared several of the brightly colored stones on the bottom of the pool to the one in my necklace.

"Here," Todd said. "I think you may want these."

It took me a moment to realize he was handing me my black cloak and my bow. I had left them here on our return trip from the trials.

I smiled as I fastened the cloak around my shoulders. It was thicker and more familiar than the maroon one I had been wearing, which I gave to Todd so he could hide his foreign attire. The bow and matching quiver I could conceal under my cloak in the morning.

The night was warm, but the stone beneath us was cold, so we laid the cloaks on the ground and slept back to back.

"It's so strange being in this place again," I whispered into the absolute darkness. "I never thought I'd return."

Todd didn't reply at first, making me wonder if maybe he'd already fallen asleep. "That was how I felt when I first made it back home. Everything was so foreign and familiar all at once. It was completely overwhelming."

Neither of us spoke again. We were too exhausted to fight sleep any longer.

Sometime in the early morning hours, I jerked awake. I might have been dreaming, but none of it lingered in my mind. What did linger was the thought that we couldn't wait any longer.

Todd was awake the moment I moved.

"What's wrong?" he asked in the blackness. "Another nightmare?"

"We need to go," I told him. "We can slip by The North Wind in the dark and find Cole before he goes to the council building."

There was silence for a moment. "All right," Todd agreed.

Finding our way out of the cave by touch, we emerged into the night air. The moon had already set, leaving only a little starlight to guide us, but it was better than nothing.

I had traveled this path many times. I'd even come here at night once. Todd had been with me then too. Strange as it sounds, I felt tranquil. There weren't going to be any more secrets; everything would be out in the open soon.

As we neared the valley's exit, I heard someone coming and saw the flicker of a torch. Quickly, I pushed Todd back into a shadowy recess and tried to hide both of us with my black cloak.

The footsteps drew closer at a hurried gait. It was hard to tell in the dark, but I counted at least a dozen men and women from The Barracks passing our hiding place. If The Clan didn't know about the invaders, they soon would.

Once the torchlight died away, Todd and I made a break for the end of The Valley. Its narrow sides opened in a great yawn, revealing faint streaks of twilight in the black night sky.

I knew better than to try and pass through The North Wind. People would already be stirring in the stables, and if there was one place I was sure to be recognized, it was The North Wind.

Instead, we cut across the outlying fields. Even in the dark, I knew where all the fences were. A few of the pastures had already been cut, and the long grass lay on the ground, waiting to be gathered into bales of hay for the winter.

"What are you going to tell Cole?" Todd asked.

"Everything," I answered honestly.

Todd chewed his lip. "He's going to kill me for sure."

I laughed at the teasing tone in his voice.

"I'll ask him not to," I promised.

"Won't make a difference," Todd sighed.

I laughed again. "It'll be all right. Besides, he's got bigger problems than you to worry about."

Todd grew serious. "What if he doesn't believe us?"

"This is Cole we're talking about," I pointed out. "He's our friend."

"He *was* our friend," Todd announced.

"Let it go, Todd," I told him.

"When someone tries to kill you, it's kind of hard to just forget about it," Todd muttered.

"He was misinformed, just as I was."

"I guess you're right," Todd said. "But, he'd better see you before he sees me."

"Agreed."

With the sky growing lighter, I pulled up my hood. Todd did the same, and his face became lost in shadows. I could only make out his features because I knew his face so well. Even though our concealment would raise the suspicions of some, it would be much worse if we were recognized.

After giving The North Wind a wide berth, we met up with the road leading south. I doubted we would see anyone else at such an hour. It was not often that The Paramount required horses, and those from The Paramount rarely visited the small village in the north.

Still, I kept a close eye out for other travelers in the growing twilight. Long before we reached The Paramount, I saw some.

Todd and I hurried off the road and hunkered down in the long grass of a nearby field as at least two hundred people passed us. All of them were wearing gold and every twentieth person carried a torch.

So they do know, I thought.

There could be no other explanation for such a massive movement of soldiers. The Paramount was sure to be in an uproar.

Even though we were exhausted from the day before, Todd and I picked up a jog. We didn't encounter anyone else on the road.

Dawn was upon us as we finally arrived at The Paramount. Early as it was, The Paramount was not asleep. There seemed to be people everywhere. All was confusion in the normally well-ordered village.

Todd and I slipped in as unnoticed as a pair of shadows. The air was foggy and the sunlight thin, aiding us greatly in our concealment.

The first place we went was Cole's dwelling. It was completely dark, but I knocked anyway. There was no answer, so we moved on before we could draw anyone's attention.

I gritted my teeth in frustration, knowing where I would have to go if I hoped to find Cole.

The press of people became much denser as we neared the village center. Todd stayed close on my heels. Most of the people we passed wore maroon or golden clothing, but I saw plenty of men and women from each of the other villages as well.

There was only one other figure in black. I turned around and went in the opposite direction to keep from meeting them. Even with all that, The Paramount was so small that it didn't take us very long to reach the council building.

I hesitated before the door. Cole might be in there, but so might the rest of the council. I didn't know what Cole had told them about me. In fact, I didn't even know if Cole had made it back. It was always possible that Myna and Core had chosen new Clan Leaders to replace my team.

I was still dithering about what to do when a thickly built figure headed across the town center toward the door. I gasped. The last time I'd seen him, he'd been the same height as I was. Now he was at least two inches taller than me.

"Rollan," I breathed.

At the sound of my voice, he turned, jaw dropping open as recognition washed over him. I leapt forward, covering his mouth with my hand before he could blurt out my name.

I was able to drown out most of the sound. I shook my head desperately, then leaned in close, hoping no one was paying attention to our exchange.

"I'm so happy to see you," I whispered. "But I don't have a lot of time. Is Cole here?"

I waited for his answer with bated breath.

"Yes," Rollan answered, nodding toward the council building.

"I need to speak with him. Can you bring him to where we played the games that one time?"

Rollan hesitated.

"It is more important than you can imagine," I said.

"All right," Rollan agreed. His voice was deeper now, and the baby fat had evaporated from his face. It looked like he hadn't cut his hair since the trials, so it reached to his shoulders.

I turned to leave, but his hand came to rest on my arm, stopping me. "Does your presence have something to do with the Broken being here?" he whispered.

"Yes," I answered. "I came to stop them."

Rollan weighed my words for a moment, then nodded and headed for the council building.

Todd had been lurking by the entrance but moved away hastily as Rollan passed through the door. He joined me, and we headed to the location I had specified.

It was empty inside, and all of the windows were closed. We lit a few of the lamps so it wasn't so dark.

I half sat, half leaned on the edge of the table my team had used when we came here together.

294

"I thought you said Rollan was dead?" Todd asked. He didn't seem to be able to remain still. Instead, he paced back and forth. Every time there was a sound outside, he'd glance at the door sharply.

"They–" I began, but was interrupted as the door swung open and a familiar figure entered.

Joy overwhelmed me completely when I saw Cole.

"Astra," he whispered.

"Hello, Cole," I said softly.

Cole staggered a step toward me, then paused.

I saw Rollan over Cole's shoulder. A third figure was with them. It was a girl, willowy in build.

"Kisa," I gasped.

I was right, I thought.

For a few seconds, I knew what it was to be perfectly happy. It was hard to make myself believe what I was seeing. Had I slipped into a dream?

"You're alive!" Kisa beamed her beautiful smile.

I ran to her and held her against me. She was laughing and crying all at once.

"But how?" she asked.

I released Kisa and was ready to explain everything. However, Cole wasn't looking at me. His attention had turned to Todd, standing stock-still in the back of the room. Their eyes met.

"You–" Cole spat, then started forward.

I flung myself between them, facing Cole. "Wait! You don't understand," I started.

"No," Cole hissed. "This is all *his* doing!"

"No, it's not!" I all but yelled. "You've got to listen to me!" I had my hands on Cole's shoulders, trying to halt his steady approach. It was to little avail; Cole hardly seemed to notice me, so intent was he on Todd. Rollan flanked him, fury written all over his face.

"Please, wait," a voice beside me begged. It was Kisa. "We're supposed to be a team. Myra and Joss wouldn't have wanted this!"

When she spoke the two names, both Cole and Rollan froze.

"Let's at least hear Astra out. She wouldn't have brought Todd here if there wasn't a good reason for it."

Cole folded his arms and turned his eyes on me. They were burning with anger. "You have two minutes to convince me not to kill him," he announced. As our eyes met, his face changed, and some of the anger vanished from it.

"Astra," the way he whispered my name gave me more hope than anything else had that he might listen to me. "What are you doing with him?"

"Todd didn't betray us," I answered before turning to Rollan. "Did you actually see Todd attack you?" I asked.

"No," Rollan growled. "The coward hit me from behind."

I nodded and glanced at Kisa. "What about you?" I pressed. "Did you actually see Todd attack either you or Rollan?"

"No," she replied. "I don't remember it at all. One second, we were on the outskirts of The North Wind looking for Todd, then I woke up in one of the dwellings."

"Isn't it strange that Todd managed to hit both of you hard enough to knock you out at exactly the same moment?"

There was complete silence. "Rollan, when you woke up, what was the first thing someone said to you?"

Rollan's forehead wrinkled. "That Kisa and I had been attacked by Todd."

"Who told you that?" I asked.

"I don't know."

"Was it someone from The North Wind?"

Rollan shook his head. "The Barracks, I think."

"Why was someone from The Barracks there?"

There was another moment of silence.

"And how is Kisa still alive when you told me that she was dead?" I asked Cole.

"That's what Rollan said," Cole replied.

"Because that's what they told me," Rollan explained.

"Did you see her?" I inquired of Cole.

"No," he answered. "I just saw Rollan."

"I only saw her briefly," Rollan stated. "She was covered in blood, from head to toe. There was so much of it; I still don't know how she survived."

"It wasn't all her blood," I responded.

"What?" Cole demanded.

"There was a stallion at The North Wind who was too aggressive to be kept near the other horses. So that he wasn't always alone, we got a goat from The Farm to live in his stall with him. The day everything happened, I saw the goat dead, with its throat cut. I think its blood was used to make Kisa and Rollan look like they'd been hurt worse than they really were."

I turned to look at each of my teammates in turn. "Someone played us."

"Who?" Rollan wondered.

"Myna," Cole said.

I nodded. "She must have figured out what was going on. Maybe someone overheard us talking or followed me to The North Wind—it doesn't matter, but somehow she learned about Todd."

"Then why didn't she just tell everyone he was a Broken?" Kisa asked. "I mean, if all she wanted was to get rid of him."

"She couldn't expose him without exposing us. That would have led to questions about the trials and leadership of The Clan." I bit my lip. "Also, I don't think he was the only one she wanted to get rid of."

"Both of us?" Cole asked.

"Me for sure, but I'm not certain she would have minded if neither of us ever came back. That was why she couldn't really kill Kisa and Rollan. She still needed Clan Leaders if we died. What did they say when you came back alone?"

"Not much," Cole recalled. "She told The Clan that Todd was exiled for attempting to murder Kisa and Rollan, but that he'd stolen something important to The Clan and she had sent you and me to get it back.

"I- I said that you were- were both dead." He struggled to get the words out, then fell silent.

"Why?" I wondered suddenly. "Why didn't you come looking for me?"

Cole turned away. His answer was so soft that I had to strain to hear it. "I did. I looked for many days. Eventually, I found a patch of trampled ground and your bow laying beside a puddle of blood, then some drag marks, and I- I knew you were dead, so I- gave up. If you were gone, then I just didn't care anymore.

"I'm sorry," he whispered, shaking his head. "I didn't- didn't want to stumble across your- your body if he'd- for his rite–"

Cole broke off, but I knew what he was trying to say. Out of the corner of my eye, I saw Todd stiffen.

"Was it all your blood?" Cole asked softly.

Todd pushed back his hood and stepped forward. "Yes," he answered, meeting Cole's eyes. The two young men were the same height. Todd was still slighter in the shoulders and probably always would be, although his days working in the forge had helped him fill out.

"It was all her blood. Maybe one day you'll get to pay me out for it, but that day is not today." The two boys glared at each other.

Cole's hand fell suddenly on mine. He drew me off to the side. Rollan took Cole's place, scowling at Todd, while Todd watched Cole and me with keen interest.

"I told you before, you've always trusted him too much," Cole whispered. "Seen only who you wanted him to be, not who he is."

"I know," I answered quietly. "But the more I treat him like the person he could be, the more he becomes that person."

I took a deep breath, remembering Todd as he was the day we'd first met, over a year ago. Everything about him was different now.

"He's here to help us," I promised.

Cole turned back to Todd, still undecided.

"I'm sorry you don't trust me because of what you think I did. But there is something more urgent that we must attend to," Todd addressed Cole.

"Agreed," Cole's voice was wary but not openly hostile anymore. "Several days ago, at least a thousand men attempted to pass through The Valley of The North Wind. I assume you have both witnessed the result?"

Todd and I nodded.

"After they failed to cross through the mountains, they traveled around to the east and made camp across the river from us. As far as we know, they've just been sitting there ever since. We have no idea why.

"We've stationed the majority of our soldiers along the river there. Others have been assigned to guard The Valley of The North Wind."

"Any idea what they are up to?" I asked Todd.

He shook his head, mystified. "Maybe they sent out scouts to see if they could find another way in?"

"Who are they?" Kisa piped up.

"The Broken, of course," Rollan told her.

Kisa's eyes widened, and her mouth opened, forming a perfect circle. Rollan put an arm around her comfortingly.

"Sort of," I clarified. "They're The People of the Brimming Lake—Todd's people—the ones from all the stories. I've been living with them for the last six months."

Three pairs of eyes stared at me in horror.

"They aren't all that different from us. They have families and laws, they make mistakes and aren't perfect, but neither is The Clan."

Cole nodded. "I think we have all made a lot of mistakes ourselves." His clear, blue eyes turned from me to Todd.

"I'm sorry," he said and offered Todd his hand. "I believed the words of others and misjudged you." Todd grabbed Cole's arm warmly and nodded at him.

"Now, what's your plan?" Cole asked him.

CHAPTER 36
THE OPEN BOX

"There is a plot to murder the ruler of my people. If the assassination is carried out, a new lord will be put in place by evil men, my father among them," Todd informed the others.

He moved to the table I had been leaning on and opened the saddlebags. Slowly, he drew forth the silver crown. Kisa let out a tiny gasp while Cole and Rollan looked at the skillfully made piece of metal with amazement.

"This is an ancient relic of my people," he told them. "It has been lost for centuries. If I bring this to the lord as a sign from the gods, I believe he will pause long enough to hear what I have to say. I pray that by saving his life, we can quell a conflict between our peoples."

"Will this work?" Cole asked, glancing between Todd and me.

"I don't know," I admitted. "We can only hope that The Lord of the Brimming Lake will listen to reason and understand that his life is in peril."

"It doesn't seem like very much," Rollan muttered.

"There is something else," I told them, pulling out the box.

Cole drew in a sharp breath. "What is that?" he asked.

"I was hoping you could tell us," I answered, placing the box before him. "What does it say?"

Cole reached out and took the box from me.

"Veritas. Veritas. Veritas," he whispered.

"That's the high language. It means truth," Kisa piped up.

Cole nodded and continued in the common tongue. "Truth. Truth. Truth. Are you ready to know the truth? Have you sought it your whole life? Or simply stumbled across it blindly? No matter how you have found it, the truth you seek lies within."

Cole paused. "It just says the same thing over and over again," he told us, turning the box slowly. "Every side is the same, except–" His hands froze, and he began reading again.

"The key to opening this box is the same key that allows you to hear the words left by your ancestors. Use the key in the place of secrets, and you might have a chance at finding the truth."

"What does any of that mean?" Rollan asked.

"We need a key," Kisa tried to clarify.

"There's only one key I know of," Cole recalled.

"The one to the room under the council building," I finished his thought.

Cole nodded. "Which is probably 'the place of secrets'."

"What?" Todd asked, looking at each of us in turn.

"Under the council building is a hidden chamber with a second message from Jessica, our ancestor, like we saw in the- the mountain," I explained. "The door is supposed to be locked and the key used to open it."

"But the key was lost," Kisa murmured regretfully. "Does that mean we can't open the box?"

"Maybe you could make another key," I suggested to Todd, my hand tightly gripping the blue stone at my neck.

Todd shook his head. "It's been tried before," he announced. "Many blacksmiths have attempted to open the box with metal keys and iron hammers; none of them succeeded. It is as if the box was sealed by the gods. Even your key might not work."

"I bet it would," Kisa argued. "Things made by the ancestors are special. If only we could find it."

"How did the key get lost?" Todd wondered.

"Someone stole it," Rollan replied.

"It was Myra's father," I told them softly.

"What?" Cole gasped. I think he said something else too, but I was suddenly back in the mountain once more. The message from Jessica was playing, and Myra was whispering something. I could just barely make it out.

That was in my room. Her words floated across to me.

301

The others were all talking over each other. "I know where it is," I cried.

"Then take us there," Cole ordered.

Wordlessly, I raised the hood of my cloak to cover my face. Todd did the same, and the five of us slipped out into the morning.

There weren't as many people in the village as there had been half an hour earlier. Almost everyone we passed nodded respectfully to Cole, Rollan, and Kisa while ignoring Todd and me.

We made it to Myra's dwelling in a few minutes. I paused at the door. "Where's Myna?" I asked Cole.

"She went to The Barracks this morning," Cole replied. "She shouldn't be back until around noon."

I nodded but still felt my stomach clench as I opened the door. It was like stepping into the tunnels beneath The Land of the Brimming Lake.

Inside, it was dark. The windows that never seemed to be opened were nailed shut. Everything was covered in a layer of dirt so thick I couldn't imagine the years it must have taken to accumulate.

The stench was overpowering. Rotting food was stacked in crates nearly to the ceiling of the main room. Even with so much clutter, the dwelling felt empty.

Kisa raised a hand to cover her nose. Cole was looking around in shock as if trying to figure out the reason for all of this.

"Myra's room is over here," I whispered, leading them to the left.

When I opened the door, all was exactly as I had left it. The window was cracked open, allowing a few leaves to drift inside. It could not have felt more opposite than the dark room we had passed through.

"The key is in here somewhere," I told them. "We just need to find it."

Everyone started searching. Rollan and Kisa began going through the dresser. Todd examined the small, wooden nightstand, leaving Cole and myself with the bed.

He ripped the blankets off and shook them out. I lay on the floor and looked underneath, but it was too dark to see anything.

Once Cole finished checking the blankets and the others' searches turned up void, we moved the bed. The room wasn't large enough for us to do much more than shift it over about a foot and a half. Everyone crowded in to look at the exposed area, but there was nothing to see.

I noticed the others deflate slightly. Determinedly, I crouched down and reached my hand into the blackness underneath the bed, which we had not been able to uncover. After a moment, I adjusted my position and stretched my fingers as far as I could in every direction. It was like searching in dark water for a lifeline; then I touched something small and hard.

Slowly, so as not to lose my grip, I drew my hand out. Clenched in my palm was a key. The piece of metal was long with a circular handle on one end and a few strangely shaped prongs on the other.

Kisa let out a cheer of joy. She and Rollan exchanged triumphant smiles.

"Let's see if it works," Cole said.

"Not here," I told him, "We're supposed to open it somewhere specific."

"Right," Todd nodded. "In 'the place of secrets'."

"Under the council building," Cole affirmed.

"Why there?" Kisa wondered.

"I don't know," I admitted. "But I think we should follow the instructions." I turned to Cole. "Is the council in session?"

Cole nodded. "Some of them are. Others are in the villages, trying to maintain order."

I licked my lips. "How much authority do you three have?"

"We're not considered full Clan Leaders," Cole frowned. "It hasn't quite been a year yet, so we're still in training."

The answer to my next question would be vital. I cringed as I asked it. "Is your father there?"

"No," Cole shook his head.

"Order them to leave," I told him.

"What?" he gasped.

"If you walk in there with your head held high and tell them to leave, they will do it."

"Why do you think that?"

"It's what they were chosen for—to comply, to be obedient, to accept orders without question."

I swallowed. "But you were chosen to be a leader, to make others listen and bend them to your will."

Cole was speechless for a moment.

"You can do this," I promised him. "You need to do this."

He looked away, then nodded his assent.

Just as we had in the early morning, Todd and I waited outside the council building with our hoods concealing our faces. As the minutes ticked by, I grew more and more nervous. What if Myna had returned early and was questioning the rest of my team? What if the council refused to leave and were demanding an explanation for Cole's bizarre request? What if– But the sudden exodus of more than a dozen men and women put an end to my internal questions.

As soon as the last council member had departed, Todd and I entered. Cole and Rollan were already removing the wooden platform, which concealed the staircase leading down into the hidden chamber.

Kisa lit the small oil lamp we'd brought from Myra's room. Without hesitation, I walked down the steps to the door. It swung open easily, and I jumped lightly to the floor below, skipping the last couple of steps.

Todd was right behind me, carrying the bag containing both the crown and the box. Kisa was next with the light, the other two right behind her. Todd lowered the saddlebags to the ground and pulled out the box, which he handed to Cole.

I'd been holding the key so tightly in my hand that the outline of the prongs was left embedded in my skin. Nerves made my hand shake as I fitted the key into the small hole in the box. Suddenly, the key snapped forward, as if it had been pulled. There was a dull thud as the metal impacted the back of the lock.

Cole tugged gently on the top of the box. Nothing happened. I twisted the key to the right, then the left. A sharp click, followed by a faint hissing could be heard as the two halves of the box split asunder.

A pair of objects rested inside, one in either half, secured to prevent them from shifting. Todd took one of the halves from Cole.

"It's just a book," he reported in disappointment, not even bothering to undo the straps holding the manuscript in place.

All eyes turned eagerly toward Cole. "It's–" he trailed off. "I'm actually not sure," he finished a moment later.

Dropping to one knee, he carefully started undoing the restraints. Once it was free, Cole rose, holding the object in his hand. It was only a few inches thick, with a circular shape.

Dismay filled me. All of our efforts had been in vain. There was nothing here that could help us.

I sighed and glanced at Todd. His eyes mirrored my own disappointment. I turned to Cole, ready to suggest we leave and attempt to implement the original plan.

Cole wasn't paying attention. He slowly turned the object, and part of it came loose, unraveling into a thin tendril.

"It's film," Cole whispered. "The thing Jessica said she used to leave her messages."

Instantly, he walked to the large, metal box, which had played Jessica's second message for us on our first visit.

"Kisa," Cole called. "Bring me the light."

Kisa trotted over obediently as he swung the side of the metal box wide open. Inside, I saw an almost identical circular object mounted within. Long, impossibly thin strands of the film stuff were threaded around various knobs and pegs within the box.

"See? It's the same," announced Cole.

"What should we do?" Rollan asked.

"Switch them," Cole told him.

The feat was easier said than done. We carefully pulled Jessica's film free and inserted the new one, trying to remember exactly how the tendril had been looped through the maze of metal knobs. Finally, we thought we had it right.

"Build a fire," I told Rollan. Both times we'd used machines such as this, once here and once in the mountain, we'd needed a fire.

Rollan nodded and set to work. With Todd's help and using Joss's flint, a merry blaze was soon glowing in the fireplace.

Cole turned the handle, just as he had once before. After he finished, Kisa covered the light, and we all held our breath, waiting to see what would happen. Slowly, light filled the far wall, followed by a crackling noise, which turned into a voice.

The image of a man appeared on the lit wall—an old man, ancient in every definition of the word.

CHAPTER 37
OUR FATHER

The man before us wore a white tunic. I could see the top of a staff clutched in his hand. Despite his apparent frailty, his voice was strong and deep.

"Greetings, my sons and daughters.

"I do not know in what time and place you are viewing this message. I do not know if you will be able to understand the words that I speak. I do not know what the earth looks like now or if The Clan still exists or how many years have passed. Even with so much uncertainty, and the possibility that this recording may be lost forever, I knew I had to do something.

"There are those who are trying to blot out the past by rewriting history. My daughter, Adel, wanted to leave a message of hope, but she is gone now. So, I must do it in her stead. I pray I have chosen the right words so that I may leave behind a remnant of the truth.

"My name is Peter. Once, I was a great scientist, someone thought to be very learned. There is little I have not seen or studied. In my youth, I traveled the earth and visited even the most remote locations. My colleagues deemed me one of the best-educated men in the world. Jessica, my older daughter, followed in my footsteps. We were chosen to lead The Clan Project because we were the best.

"For all of that, I can now say with certainty that I know very little. Mankind, even at the height of its existence, knew very little. However, we believed ourselves wise. In arrogance, we proclaimed our own intelligence, but we were fools who built a stronghold on a weak foundation. It crumbled beneath us, and we could not salvage it.

307

"Our greatest failure was trusting in ourselves when we should have put our credence in something better.

"I am guilty of this. I believed that logic was the key to explaining all mysteries. However, the more I sought for the truth in science, the less of it I found.

"There are some questions that only faith can answer. There are too many coincidences, too many miracles for any rational explanation.

"The very fact that the world exists at all cannot be explained. For where did it begin? Where did it come from? The galaxy, the universe, matter itself, where did they come from? Mustn't they have had a beginning? Many scientists, including myself, have tried to explain this. Each time, I came to the point where I either had to believe the laws of physics allowed something to come from nothing, a scientific impossibility, or that something more existed.

"After nearly a century of life and decade upon decade of study, I have found only one thing I know to be true: there is a greater power working in this world."

The old man paused. He closed his eyes and shook his wrinkled head slowly. It continued to move back and forth as he spoke the next words.

"I wish I could explain to you all that I have since discovered, but my time is short. I know all of this may sound strange, especially if you have never considered any of these things before.

"Truth is so quickly brushed aside and forgotten in the rush of everyday life. How easily we overlook the important things to focus on the menial.

"It took me many years to finally accept all of this. The book placed with this message is an ancient document, written long before my time. In the manuscript, you will find history, poetry, and a true story of love and sacrifice. This story is about the one who is a guide to the lost. A healer to the broken. A parent to the orphan."

"The unknown god," I whispered in realization. Todd turned to look at me, but the old man continued speaking.

"I know this message has probably left you with many more questions than it has answered. If you still struggle to accept all that I have said, I do not blame you. I have included some notes to help you understand, but no human can simply give you all the answers. It is within the journey that we find truth.

"I wish I could walk beside you and guide you to the right path, but my words are all I have to give."

The man faded from the wall, and silence replaced his deep voice.

"Where did this come from?" Cole asked breathlessly.

"It has been in the shrine of the unknown god for centuries," Todd answered. There was bewilderment on his face.

No one spoke for a moment. My throat felt tight, and I made a choking gasp to get air.

Todd turned to look at me. "Astra, are you–" he trailed off, eyes widening. "What's wrong?" he asked.

Cole and the others gathered around a moment later. It was impossible for me to explain to them why I was too emotional to speak or why tears were running down my cheeks.

After watching both of Jessica's messages, I had felt hopeless and empty. She had demanded sacrifices of us. With her first message, we had lost Myra, and with the second, we had been forced to live a lie.

Peter's message was precisely the opposite. Everything he said filled me with hope for the future.

There was more to this world than what we could see. Something greater.

The missing piece, a voice whispered.

I started sobbing and suddenly found myself in Todd's arms.

"Why are you crying?" he wondered gently.

"Because," I began, and then had to clear my throat. "Because I'm so happy. I'm finally beginning to understand."

"Understand what?" I heard Cole ask from behind me.

"The stories are all true," I managed to say. "Peter really lived. Jessica and Adel really lived. Matthan really lived. The Unknown God really lived—lives. That's who Peter was talking about when he said there was a greater power."

I wish I could have said more, but I was again too choked to speak. It might have been for the better; I wasn't sure I was being at all coherent.

"What is the meaning of this?"

My feelings of warmth and happiness evaporated the instant I heard the icy voice.

Myna had returned.

I wiped the tears from my eyes and turned to face her. Falow was there too. In his hand, he carried a long knife.

"Astra," Myna hissed when she caught sight of me. In the time since I'd last seen her, the woman seemed to have aged at least twenty years. All my life, she had never appeared to be touched by the hands of time. The gray eyes had been strong and clear, just like her daughter's. Her short, brown hair had always been cut in the exact same way, and there was never so much as a wrinkle to mar her ageless face.

The gray eyes were still bright, but the rest of her had fallen victim to time at last. She appeared haggard, her hair streaked with white. Her head wobbled a little, held up as it was by her long, spindly neck.

"Myna," I acknowledged her. "I have returned to help."

Myna's usually expressionless face twisted into a sneer. "I seriously doubt that."

"We've found something," Cole told her. "Something that will change the future. It can–"

"We do not change. We can not change," Myna snapped. "We must remain as we are, as we have always been."

"No," I answered her coolly. "Not anymore. A new day has come, a time for growth. We will no longer be bound by the past, a past full of lies. It is time for truth, and with truth will come freedom."

Myna's eyes narrowed. "You always were naïve. If you think the Broken on our border are going to help you take control of this land, you are quite mistaken."

"I did not bring them here," I told her. "I came to stop them."

Myna laughed, and in that dark place it sounded truly ghastly. "You won't have to. They are all going to die. It won't be long now. The fools are building boats, hundreds of boats that will carry them to their doom."

"What do you mean?" Todd asked.

Myna's eyes snapped to him. "The Broken–" she snarled. "I should have known. How many other Broken have you led past our defenses?" she growled at me.

"There would be very little point in trying to take by force what is already mine," I told her, moving a step closer. Falow drew near to Myna as I approached.

"This land already belongs to me. I am Astra of The North Wind, Second Clan Leader, I have returned to take my rightful place and you, Myna, are relieved of your position." Something in my voice triggered her fury.

Myna seized the knife from Falow and charged. Her age did not seem to hinder her as she sprang down the steps and flew at me like a wild animal.

However, her rage made her uncontrolled. I easily dodged the first attack and had already turned for the second as she rushed me again.

"Myna, this is pointless," I told her, motioning for the others to stand back. This was my fight. I did not want them to interfere.

"Your time is over," I told her. "Your decisions have been made. Now it is us who will lead The Clan. We will not yield to your choices or those that have been made in the past. There is another way, and we will take it."

"You will never have control of The Clan!" she spat as she thrust the blade at my head. I ducked and struck out with my foot, catching her just below the knee. She hissed and tried to bring the knife down upon me. I rolled to the left, rose, and whipped around.

This time, when she charged me, I used a neat little trick I had picked up from training at The Barracks over a year ago.

At the same moment, I seized her wrist and hooked her ankle with my foot, unbalancing her. The old woman toppled to the ground in a heap, the knife falling from her hand.

"Let's go," I said to the others. "We have much to do."

The doorway was still blocked by Falow. Cole was the first to mount the steps. Falow fell back, unwilling to engage us. I was right behind Cole, when some instinct told me to turn around.

Myna had retrieved the knife and was rushing toward Kisa. Todd cried out and moved to intercept. I don't know if he would have made it in time or not, but I was faster than both of them.

I pulled the bow from beneath my cloak and fitted an arrow to the string in a single movement. The next second, the shaft had buried itself in Myna's chest.

Kisa let out a shriek as Myna fell back, gasping for air. A tremor of pain went through my heart as I saw the bright gray eyes close for the last time.

Falow fled from the doorway.

We silently emerged into the council building. Rollan carried both halves of the box with him. Todd held the crown.

"What now?" Kisa asked. Her voice trembled, but her stance was strong and ready.

"We need to get across the river," I announced.

Todd's brow furrowed. "What did she mean when she said my people were going to die?"

"Remember last summer when you met us, and we believed carrying anything metal in deep water would pull you to the bottom?" I asked.

He nodded.

"That's because, in the river here, it's true. There's something called a magnet, which will sink a whole boat if so much as a fishhook is in it."

312

"Then when my people finish their boats and try to cross the river–" Todd began.

"They'll all drown," I finished for him.

"Unless we stop them," Cole told us.

"We?" Todd asked.

Cole nodded. "I'm coming with you. Maybe we can work things out peacefully."

Todd and I exchanged a glance. We both knew the chances of this ending without more bloodshed were practically non-existent. Cole would have understood that if he'd spent even a tenth of the time I had with The People of the Brimming Lake. Violence was part of their way of life.

"I'm coming too," Kisa piped up.

"And me," Rollan announced.

I couldn't help but smile at their courage.

"That is not wise," Cole told them. "To them, you will look like children. They won't understand that even though you're young, you are leaders."

Kisa nodded reluctantly, but Rollan crossed his massive arms. He didn't look very much like a child to me.

"We can't all abandon The Clan," Cole went on, appealingly to Rollan. Especially with Myna- gone, there's going to be a lot of confusion. If none of us come back, it'll be up to you two."

"But I–" Rollan started. "I want to be there, by your side. That's where I belong."

Cole raised his head heavenward and closed his eyes for a moment, then walked to Rollan and put both his hands on the boy's shoulders. The emotions he was fighting to control showed in his eyes.

"There is nowhere I would rather have you than by my side, but that would mean leaving Kisa alone."

Rollan's gaze flashed from Cole to the blonde girl, then back.

"I need you here, and she needs you here."

313

Rollan nodded, his eyes watering slightly. "I will do as you ask," he promised.

"Thank you," Cole told him, taking the two halves of the box. There were tears in his eyes too. "We won't be far away. I want you to keep the soldiers stationed where they are on our side of the river. A show of force might be helpful, and that way, if they do make it through, we can protect our land."

Cole's eyes rested on Todd as he gave another order. "Tell the soldiers not to attack unless they have to. I don't desire bloodshed if it can be avoided."

Rollan nodded once more, then he and Cole embraced. I found Kisa throwing her arms around me a moment later. I struggled not to cry myself, but I had cried enough. This was the time for action.

I hugged Rollan goodbye too, as Kisa embraced Todd.

"You'd better come back," Kisa commanded us solemnly. "I'm not ready to be First Clan Leader yet."

I watched her thread her fingers through Rollan's as we left them in the council building. If Cole and I perished, I knew The Clan would be in good hands.

CHAPTER 38
FLIGHT

Cole, Todd, and I went to Cole's dwelling for supplies. Since neither Todd nor I had eaten much over the past several days, we downed nearly half the food ration, which had been left for Cole's family. The rest we put in Cole's backpack with the crown and the box while Cole changed into clothes suitable for traveling.

Todd strung the key to the box on a bit of extra cord and knotted the two ends together. He gave it to me to wear as a necklace. It was long enough not to interfere with the blue stone that still hung at my throat.

Cole emerged from his room a few minutes later, a sword hanging from his belt. "They gave it back to you?" I asked in surprise.

Cole laughed. "No, this is a different one," he told us. "My friend, Jase, was pretty messed up after the trials.

"He transferred to The Barracks a few months back, and I go there to train with him almost every evening," Cole went on. "It helps me unwind from the council meetings.

"Kullen, he's the one in charge there, said I could keep this one to practice with even when I can't make it to The Barracks. I'm getting pretty good too."

Now that my attention had been drawn to it, I could see that this sword was longer and probably a good deal heavier than the ones they had handed out for the trials. It looked to be in good repair, with a razor-sharp edge and not a speck of rust.

By the time we set off, it was early afternoon. We headed straight for the north road. Once we escaped the village, there were very few people, and, even though a few stared as we walked past, none of them attempted to stop us.

315

On our long trek north, I related to Cole all that had transpired during my time at The Brimming Lake. He listened with complete fascination as I talked about the massive city divided by river and gods.

For Todd's sake, I skimmed over some of the more appalling details of my treatment. However, Todd began filling in the blanks I left, making them sound worse than they had actually been. A few times, even I cringed.

When I got to the part where Todd told his father about The Clan to save my life, Cole clenched his fists. I could almost feel him grinding his teeth.

"I can stop," I offered.

"No," Cole told me sternly. "I want to hear this. Although, I'm kind of changing my mind about wanting to save these… people."

Todd was looking at the ground.

"They aren't all bad. You'll understand when you hear what happened next," I replied, and then began to tell him how we had followed Arshenn and found the hidden tunnels.

My voice faltered when I began talking about Yetta, and Todd took over the story for me. I let him finish, not that there was much left. Our journey here had been rather uneventful compared with the rest.

"So those we can see are just the first wave," Cole mused. "The rest of your people are coming after them?"

Todd nodded. "Mostly women and children, plus some slaves to tend the herds and flocks. If they can find their way here."

"The mountains are kind of hard to miss," I pointed out.

The boys nodded. We were growing closer and closer to these very mountains now. Already, we had passed the most outlying fields of The North Wind.

"How were things here when you got back?" I asked Cole. Now that I had told him our story, I was eager to hear his.

"Coming back alone was- harder than I would have expected," Cole began.

I gave him a sympathetic glance.

"Not because of the wilderness," Cole went on. "But I felt like I'd failed The Clan, the council, my father, and you. Especially you.

"More than once, I thought about just crawling into a hole and waiting to die, but I still had hope that part of my team yet lived.

"When I got back, I found that not only Rollan, but Kisa was alive and had recovered. Together, we started our training again.

"Honestly, things were much the same as they had been, except–" Cole paused to think about his next words very carefully. "Everything went back to the way it was before we confronted my father and Myna. It was like that part of my life was a dream.

"Aside from Rollan, Kisa, and me, no one ever mentioned your name or seemed to remember you at all. It was- it was just like after Myra died, only you weren't there to go through it with me."

Cole glanced between the two of us. "Either of you. I've never felt so alone in all my life," he admitted.

Cole suddenly turned off to the right and started heading across one of the fields, away from the distant buildings of The North Wind.

"Where are you going?" I asked him.

He paused and looked back at me in confusion. "To The Valley of The North Wind," he answered. "Did you have a different plan for getting to the far side of the river?"

"Well, no," I replied. "But I thought we could take horses. Depending on our reception by The Lord of the Brimming Lake, we might need to make a quick getaway."

"And how do you plan on getting the horses through the valley without the sound of their hooves bringing down the entire mountain?" Cole laughed.

"We had to do a lot of climbing when we reached the part where my people stopped," Todd recalled. "The horses would never be able to make it through."

317

"I mean, we might be able to use them to get to the meadow," Cole suggested, considering for a moment. "But beyond that–"

"There's a second path," I interrupted him.

"What?" they gasped in unison.

"Why have you never spoken of this before?" Cole asked.

I hesitated. This secret I had kept longer than all the others because it had been mine alone. A handful of others knew about the cave and the Keepers and even the secrets in the mountain, but the knowledge of a second passage through The Valley of the North Wind was mine alone.

Once, an old woman, who had lived all her life in The North Wind, wandered into the valley. I had been the one to find her, and when I did, I also found a path. It was hidden even better than the cave.

After I returned the woman to The North Wind, I went back and investigated further. I found that the path ended in a narrow ledge along the largest of the mountains. The second path was smaller but led straight to the forest beyond our land.

"Because it's just as dangerous as the normal path," I told Cole.

"Then how do you think we're going to get horses across it?" Todd asked.

I swallowed. This was my last secret, infinitely more precious than all the others. I had never considered telling anyone, not even Gann, back when he'd been my friend. But these two, they were more than my friends.

I licked my lips. "I've done it before," I finally admitted. "I wrapped the horse's hooves in cloth to muffle the noise."

Cole's eyes widened. "You left The Land of the Clan before the trials?" he asked.

I nodded.

"When? Why?" His voice was breathless. I could hear how much I'd shocked him.

"The first horse I was given to train was- well, I failed. He had a strong spirit and- and a wild heart. He was never meant to be tamed by humans. However, The Clan has no place for such a creature, feral but beautiful all at once. Even the wild herds of horses we keep are friendly and safe to walk among.

"Not my stallion; he was a terror. No hand but mine could even touch him. That was why it fell to me to put him down when he proved unwilling to be broken.

"But I couldn't. I took him to the valley and led him through the secret passage. Once we were on the far side, I turned him loose. I didn't know if he would make it. I still don't know for sure if he's alive, but I like to imagine that he's out there somewhere, running free under the sun by day and the stars by night."

I came to the end of my narrative; both boys were still staring at me.

"Leave it to you to willingly risk your life trying to save some mangy, ungrateful horse," Todd muttered.

"Well, if you think it can be done, then let's do it," Cole said. He glanced up. "And quickly, if we plan to make it before nightfall."

I nodded; the sun was more than halfway through its daily journey.

Todd and I put our hoods up as we reached the outskirts of The North Wind. I did not think anyone would dare try to stop us, but if we were recognized, it was certain to cause a delay.

It appeared that only a handful of horses had gone out that day. With all the excitement on the border, I imagined not much work was being accomplished in any of the villages.

Cole and Todd stood out like sore thumbs in their maroon cloaks. Even though we drew plenty of attention, no one approached us as we entered the eastern stable.

I headed for Rykis's and Rysa's stalls. The two stallions were exactly what we needed. They were strong enough to each bear one of the boys through the mountains and still be fresh if we needed to make a run for it.

The horses greeted me with their velvety noses and soft whinnies. I had them both haltered and out of their stalls in a moment.

"Todd, saddles," I directed. "You can help him, Cole," I added. "I'm going to get some cloth for their hooves and find another horse."

As I went to the shed and retrieved a bundle of extra shirts from the stock we always kept on hand, I regretted the loss of Rickie even more than usual. He would have been the perfect third horse to join our party. Now I would have to choose another.

I considered Grandalo for a moment. He was one of my favorites, but he was also quite large. The thought of his heavy footfalls in the mountains made me shudder.

My next choice was Keith, a chestnut gelding who had always been a willing partner on long workdays.

He would be at the main stable, but I was certain to have a few minutes to spare before the boys had the two stallions saddled. I darted through The North Wind as quickly as I could.

Thankfully, Keith was in his stall. Without even bothering to find a saddle or bridle, I leapt on his back and rode him to the eastern stable, the bundle of clothing gripped tightly in one hand and the lead rope attached to Keith's halter in the other.

Just before entering, I slipped to the ground.

"Astra!"

I froze as someone called my name.

Swallowing, I turned slowly toward the voice. Gann had rounded the corner and was standing ten feet away.

"Someone told me they'd seen you," he said cooly. "But I didn't believe them. I never thought you'd come back here, not after the way you left." Gann's voice was hard, but there was a touch of regret in it.

I didn't know quite how to respond. In the many months since we'd parted, I hadn't once thought about what I would say to Gann if I ever saw him again.

Neither of us spoke as he slowly advanced toward me. Conflicting emotions played across his face, making me wary.

"Yet, I did hope I would see you again," he murmured when he was only a few feet from me. Something tightened in my stomach at his words. "I don't think I was ever able to make you understand how much I care about you, Astra."

He paused for a moment, but when I didn't respond, he continued.

"I missed you. I told myself that I wouldn't, but I did.

"Before you left, I thought you were the one that I would spend my life with. I waited for you. Waited for you to finish the preparations. Waited for you to come back from the trials. I would have waited a hundred years."

Gann pursed his lips in anger. "And you just threw all of that away for a Broken."

I flinched at his words. I hadn't thought anyone except The Clan Leaders knew the truth about Todd. Clearly, a few other select people had been clued in.

"How could you do that? You betrayed your people, Astra, and you betrayed me." His words were sharp and cutting, but his voice was filled with sorrow.

"Gann," I began as calmly as I could. "I am truly sorry that I hurt you. After the trials, things were very complicated. Everything that happened between you and me didn't help either. We were both under a lot of pressure and very emotional the last time I was here. I know now what happened that day. Todd didn't poison the horses, someone from The Clan did, and I know who was behind it."

"Wait, what?" Gann gasped in surprise, the hard mask slipping from his face. "You know?"

"Yes," I replied cautiously, suspicion suddenly prickling at the back of my mind. "It was done as a way to get rid of Todd."

Gann was silent.

"And me," I finished softly, meeting his gaze with accusation.

"No," Gann said quickly. "I didn't want you to leave." My mind was racing. I had figured out the set-up long ago, but clearly, I'd underestimated just how far the conspiracy had spread. A cold feeling gripped my chest, making it hard to breathe. I hadn't wanted to believe Gann was actually involved.

"I just- it was for the best. She said that he was corrupting you, and if he was gone, then you and I–" Gann's broken thoughts poured forth from him in an earnest plea.

"Who said?" I interrupted sharply. "Myna?" I demanded, already knowing the answer.

Gann's gaze was focused on the ground.

"Gann, what did Myna tell you to do?" I felt like I was going to be ill. "Was it you who poisoned the horses?"

"I- I didn't want to," Gann whispered desperately, shaking his head. I could tell that our conversation was not going in the direction he'd intended. "She told me it was the only way to get rid of Todd and show you that he didn't belong here."

"So you killed all of those horses and then attacked Todd as a way to convince me that I should be with you?" I asked incredulously.

"I didn't attack him," Gann insisted. "It was some of the others."

"All under the direction of Myna, I assume." Gann didn't deny it. "I can't believe you would agree to do something that horrible, that evil," I said, tears filling my eyes.

"I did it for you," Gann replied, his voice sounding angry once more. "Everything I ever did was for you—no, for us."

"*Everything* you did?" I whispered. "There's more?" I thought hard for a moment. "Did- did you poison Rickie too?" I asked.

Panic flashed across Gann's face.

"I–" he began weakly. Looking into his eyes, I knew the truth, and he knew that I knew.

"I- I had to," Gann confessed, true sorrow in his words. "She insisted it was necessary. She told me she had big plans for you and removing all distractions was important. She promised if I helped, I could be part of those big plans too. She said we would be together."

My jaw clenched.

"Myna lied to you," I spat. "I was never intended to return from the trials. I was supposed to die. That was her 'big plan'. She wanted Rickie gone so I wouldn't have any reason to come back. You should be thankful she didn't decide to have you removed as well."

I shook my head and curled my lip in disgust. "How could you ever think we would be together after killing Rickie? You knew how much he meant to me. You couldn't have kept it hidden forever. I would have discovered the truth eventually. What was your plan then?"

"I would have made it up to you," Gann told me desperately. "I know what that loss feels like. I lost Corbit too, remember? Besides, I would have made you happy, and you would have forgotten."

I felt my face grow hot with anger at his words. It was so sick and twisted it almost made me want to laugh.

"You have no idea how I feel or how to make me happy," I told him.

"No, I guess I don't. But at least I tried. Unlike you. Once that Broken got into your head, you abandoned me, along with everyone else in The Clan."

I nodded, a sudden feeling of calmness overtaking me.

"I'm sorry," I whispered, looking him full in the face. "I'm sorry I seem to have disappointed you so much. I'm sorry I was never the person you wanted me to be. I'm sorry I didn't live my life to suit your whims. I'm sorry I had hopes and dreams that were just too big for you to understand."

Gann's face twisted in anger. I knew the pain he was feeling, but I no longer cared.

"Things are going to be very different now. Myna's not in charge anymore; my team and I are. And you will never get another opportunity to hurt the ones I love, because you will never again be close enough to me to try."

Both Rykis and Rysa were fully saddled. Todd was standing between the pair, holding them. An extra saddle and bridle were on the ground at his feet.

"Everything all right?" Todd asked, handing the reins of both horses to Cole and scooping the extra saddle off the ground.

"Everything's fine," I told him. "I just ran into an old friend."

I laid a blanket over Keith's back, and Todd lowered the saddle into place.

"Who?" he asked.

"Gann," I answered.

Todd stiffened. "Wish I'd been there," he muttered. "I'd have given him a special greeting."

"It's better that you weren't," I replied, slipping the halter off Keith's face so I could put on the bridle. "We're trying to make peace, remember?"

Todd nodded reluctantly.

We left the stable a minute later, with the three horses in tow. I thought our escape was complete, but I was wrong.

CHAPTER 39
THE VALLEY OF VOICES

"There they are," Falow said, pointing at us as soon as we emerged from the stable.

With him was a crowd of about thirty. The First Clan Leader, Core, stood at the front, several other council members with him. They were flanked by at least a dozen soldiers.

"Cole? What is going on?" Core asked his son. In contrast to Myna, who had seemed to age more than a dozen years in the time since my departure, I could see little difference in Core's appearance. However, he had always appeared ancient to me, even when I was young.

"Hello, Father," Cole dipped his head respectfully. "We are going to stop a war."

"There isn't going to be any war," Kullen of The Barracks announced, coming to stand beside Core. "The river will protect us, as it always has."

"I'm not going to let those people die. I don't care who they are. It would be wrong," Cole announced in a firm voice.

"Son," Core's words took on a gentle but authoritative tone. "You are not a full Clan Leader yet. You have no right to–"

Before he could finish, Cole cut him off. "Let me ask you something. Where do these 'rights' you speak of come from? Who gave them to you? For the last fifty years, you've manipulated every situation, told everyone how to live, and what to think, just because you went to some mountain and thought you learned the truth."

Core glanced around nervously.

"I refuse to become what you are," Cole told him.

Core's mouth hung open. I was certain no one had ever spoken to him like that before.

325

"You- you are confused," he stuttered. "We must remember the words of our ancestors and the message they left. Someone's fooled you and made you believe things that are not true."

Core's eyes turned to Todd.

"Do you want to know what I believe?" Cole asked, taking a purposeful step forward to put himself between Todd and his father.

"I believe we have kept too many things hidden for too long. It is time to stop passing off lies as truth. Go back to The Paramount, Father. Go to the council building and see the new message that has been given to our people. You'll find it in the same place where you saw the old one. Maybe then you will understand what I believe."

Falow's eyes narrowed as he glared at Cole. He leaned over and whispered something to Core, but Core shook his head.

I took the momentary distraction to mount my horse. A moment later, Cole and Todd did the same. Core turned his attention back to us.

"I will do what you have asked," he said. "But, Cole, I want you to come back with me. Those people out there, the Broken, they'll kill you. Is it worth dying to try and save them?"

Cole seemed disgusted by the question. "Of course it is. They are humans, just like us. They have lives and families. How can you *not* want to save them?"

Without waiting for a response, Cole turned his horse to the east. Todd and I followed his lead, pushing the horses into a canter. I was surprised no one tried to stop us. They seemed to be waiting for an order that Core never gave.

We reached the valley a short time later. All three horses were well-muscled and used to long days of work. If Todd and I had each been riding one of these animals, we could have caught the men easily.

Even still, there was little more than three hours before the sun would sink beyond the horizon. We needed to make it through the valley before nightfall, or the chances of an accident would go up drastically.

I took the lead on Keith. Todd, on Rysa, was just behind me, and Cole brought up the rear with Rykis.

Our pace slowed to a walk as we entered the valley. "For someone who hasn't ridden much, you're doing very well," I told Cole.

He grinned. "I've had more practice than you think," he admitted.

I gave him a questioning glance.

"About a score of times, they've had horses brought to The Barracks so the soldiers could practice riding."

"Well, you seemed to have learned a lot," I complimented him.

"Thanks," Cole said. "I'm still much better with a sword when I'm on the ground, but riding doesn't terrify me the way it used to."

I suppressed a smile.

"Even Jase is finally comfortable on a horse," Cole mused, more to himself than to me. "Who would have ever thought it?"

We were able to pick up a brisk trot for the next part of the journey. I made sure to carefully count the turn-offs on the left. I knew the valley almost perfectly, but today was not the day to make a mistake. Every second, the sun descended lower into the west.

Soon, the turn-off leading to the cave was behind us, and we'd taken the left fork at the next split. I was still numbering the paths in my head as we rode along. *Nine. Ten. Eleven. Twelve. This is it!*

I slowed Keith to a walk and guided him down the narrow trail to the left. I could hear the boys behind me. After only five minutes, the path appeared to end in a tall mound of gravel. High stone walls pressed in on all sides.

Cole looked perplexed but turned to me. His eyes were full of confidence and trust. "Now what?" he asked.

In answer, I jumped to the ground. The boys imitated my example. Trying to choose the best side, I led Keith up the gravel mound. There was a bit of sliding, but he managed to make it to the top.

I was forced to move on so the others could follow me. On the far side was a place where two of the canyon walls overlapped, leaving a split just large enough to weave a horse through.

The boys joined me a moment later. We'd raised quite a cloud from scrambling over the rocks, and our clothes were covered in dust.

Once we'd passed through the opening and remounted, we were in another maze of stone walls. This one was not nearly so large as the rest of the valley, but it still had taken me nearly a year to memorize. The going was all uphill, and I felt sweat running down my back.

Finally, the walls around us seemed to close in almost to the point of completely choking out the trail we followed. Still, I led on as the path twisted and turned, then, finally, opened wide before us. We stood on a broad ridge with a clear view to the west, where the sun was preparing to meet the land.

A single ledge went on ahead of us, wrapping around the mountain.

The wind here came whistling up from the gulf before us. It sounded like voices were speaking. When I'd found Viot here, she had sworn she could hear her dead husband talking to her.

I'd listened for a time, but knew all she was hearing was the strange echo of the wind among the rocks.

"This is the place," I whispered. The clothing I'd taken from The North Wind was tied to the back of my saddle. Using Todd's knife, we cut the various shirts and other garments into pieces and started wrapping the horses' hooves.

Keith was a little uncertain about the process and the wailing wind, but Rysa and Rykis weren't phased in the least.

As I looked ahead at the long, winding trail we would be taking, memories washed over me like a wave from the ocean. The last time I'd stood here, I was even more desperate than I was now. I had been alone and afraid that someone would catch me and take my horse from me.

Once the boys finished with their horses' feet, we set out very slowly and carefully. It was dreadful to only be able to creep along at a snail's pace while the sun glided effortlessly toward the horizon.

Thankfully, the wind died down, and the occasional breezes didn't seem to do much more than ruffle my hair.

At one point, Rykis tripped, and the noise brought down a few stones. My heart thundered in my chest. All it would take to bring the mountain down on top of us was for just one of these horses to spook and take off.

Maybe this hadn't been the best idea. A single horse and person might be able to find their way across, but the three of us together had a far greater chance of causing noise and vibrations.

Another incident occurred at a spot where a small stream of water flowed down the mountainside. Over the years, the water had filed down the path until part of the ledge was missing.

Keith was shorter than the other two horses. His legs were just barely long enough to reach across the gap. Trying not to think about how far down the drop would be, I sprang across lightly, and he followed after.

I wasn't worried so much for Rykis and Rysa, but for Cole and Todd. Walking close to Keith made the path seem narrow to me; I could only imagine how much less space there would be beside one of the broad-chested stallions.

It was agonizing to watch the four of them cross the narrow gap. Todd was bringing up the rear now. As his stallion's hind legs stepped over the gap, one of them slipped.

Todd turned and grabbed at Rysa's saddle, trying to steady the stallion. He wouldn't have been successful had the horse's other legs not already been on solid ground. Rysa stumbled a little before regaining his footing. The cloth on his hoof came off and drifted down into the abyss below.

As he took a few steps forward, the sound of his metal horseshoe hitting the rock began to bring stones down upon us.

Todd instantly halted Rysa. Cole and I instinctively pushed in closer to the cliff face. A stone struck Keith on the leg, and he began to panic. I held his head as tightly as possible, and he froze instead of bolting.

Once the debris stopped, we cut another piece of cloth and fitted it to Rysa's exposed hoof.

"How much further?" Cole mouthed to me as we finished.

I glanced ahead. I couldn't recall exactly. The ledge seemed to continue on forever. I shrugged, and Cole glanced at the sun. It was halfway down.

Since I was in the lead, I picked up the pace, moving as quickly as I could. Keith felt taut, like he might explode at any moment. Trying to keep my movements rhythmic, I stroked him as we marched along, hoping it would have a calming effect.

The darker the sky grew, the harder it was to distinguish the path ahead. All of us were stumbling now, but no more rocks fell.

Finally, in the last shadows of twilight, I spotted the forest ahead of us. Quickening my pace almost to a run, I towed Keith forward and off of the ledge.

My heart didn't stop racing until Cole and Todd had joined me.

"We should wait until morning," Cole decided, his voice foreign after so many hours of silence. "I don't want them to think we're trying to ambush them."

Todd agreed rather reluctantly.

We unsaddled the horses and tethered them so they could graze. Todd built a small fire as Cole, and I finished sorting out the tack and the horses.

"Can I see the box again?" Cole asked Todd once the camp was set up. With a nod, Todd retrieved it from the backpack. I brought the key over and used it to unlock the box.

The book was the only item inside since we'd left the message in the room beneath the council building. A sudden fear struck me that someone might try to destroy it like Myra's father had tried to destroy Jessica's message. There was no help for it now. The message was beyond my protection. I hoped Core had watched it, and the others too. It wasn't meant to be kept a secret.

None of us had paid much attention to the book when we'd first opened the box. It didn't appear to be anything special; the binding was either dark brown or black. Now, Cole carefully undid the straps holding it in place and removed it. I recoiled. On the side which had been concealed, I saw a red mark identical to the one The Brotherhood had worn.

Todd's jaw tightened as his gaze fell on the symbol. We exchanged a long glance.

"Is this for evil too?" Todd asked hopelessly.

Cole gave both of us a questioning look, then turned back to the book in his hands.

"You're holding it upside down," Todd told him, reaching out and rotating the book so the symbol was the right way up.

Cole shook his head. "No, I wasn't."

"But–" I started, ready to back up Todd.

"Look at the words," Cole said, opening the book. "This is the right way." He turned the book again, so the symbol stood on its head. The mark didn't look so sinister now. It only appeared to be a red t.

Todd and I watched in silence as he began to study the pages. "What does it say?" Todd couldn't help asking.

"A lot of things," Cole answered with a furrowed brow. "It's long, very long. Longer than any book our people have. The writing is small and- perfect."

"Like in the mountain," I whispered.

Cole nodded. "I think it's a story," he told us.

"I love stories," Todd grinned.

A moment later, Cole put the book back in the box. "We'll have plenty more time to look at it later. Now we should sleep."

Todd and I couldn't have agreed more with his suggestion.

"Let's put the crown in the box," Todd suggested. "I don't think my people will be very impressed with a book."

Cole nodded. It took some maneuvering, but the two boys managed to wedge the crown inside the box alongside the book and seal it once more.

We didn't talk much as we prepared to sleep.

The night vanished in the blink of an eye. One moment, it was dark, and the sound of crickets filled the air. The next, I was blinking awake to see the first fingers of dawn spreading across the sky.

I rose and roused the boys. We didn't talk much as we packed up our few items and saddled the horses. We rode eastward, toward the sun and toward whatever the day would bring us.

CHAPTER 40
THE DUEL

As the first rays of light touched the morning dew, it turned them to gems every bit as beautiful as the one around my neck. The sweet smell of pine and cedar filled the air as we raced across the land, each of us with four extra legs.

We rounded the mountains before the sun had cleared the trees. From there, we followed the riverbank.

Todd, who was in the lead, suddenly pulled Rysa to a sliding halt. I brought Keith up short before he could crash into the stallion.

We'd reached the edge of the camp. Cole and I raised the hoods of our cloaks to conceal our faces.

Makeshift tents had been pitched with no semblance of order. It was quite similar to the camp where we had found Jiyata, save all the inhabitants of this camp were men. At least, they were supposed to be. In actuality, I couldn't see a single human being anywhere, although there were plenty of horses tethered close by.

"Are we too late?" Cole asked.

A sinking feeling entered the pit of my stomach. Had they already tried to cross the river? Were they all dead? Or had they succeeded and made it into The Land of the Clan?

I tried to keep my panic down as I pushed Keith forward. Todd guided Rysa beside him while Cole took up a position on his far side. As we skirted the camp, I saw signs that the men had been here not long ago, but now the entire place was deserted.

The silence was broken by the unexpected sound of cheering from the forest ahead of us.

Todd gave Rysa a nudge to get him into a trot; Cole and I followed in his wake. As we emerged from the trees, with the river on our right, we saw thousands of men assembled in a semicircle around two figures.

The pair had their backs to the river as they addressed the others. I couldn't hear the words, but every so often, another cheer would go up from the men.

"They must be getting ready to attack," Todd observed. Our horses had slowed to a walk.

Adrenaline began pumping through my body. Across the river, I could make out a group of gold-clad men and women from The Barracks. They were camped about fifty feet from the water, but a few sentries were stationed close to the water's edge, keeping watch over the men of The Brimming Lake.

"It's now or never," I told Todd as Rysa came to a full halt.

Todd nodded and swallowed but didn't speak.

He closed his eyes for a moment, then put heels to his horse and shot forward. Cole and I flanked him as he raced toward the assembled men.

They didn't seem to notice us at first. Todd stopped his horse about twenty yards from them. A few of the closest men gave us a questioning glance.

"I need to see Lord Tohoshin!" shouted Todd.

More of the men turned to look.

"I must see The Lord of the Brimming Lake at once," Todd cried. Beneath him, Rysa stirred uneasily with agitation.

Cole and I kept our horses still as Rysa hopped a few steps forward.

Most of the attention had turned to Todd now.

"You'll have to wait at least half an hour," someone in the crowd yelled.

"Why?" Todd called back as laughter passed through the assembly.

"The Lord of the Brimming Lake died three days ago," another voice bellowed.

My heart dropped. We were too late. Arshenn had already begun carrying out his plot.

"Then I need to talk to whoever is in charge. It is very important. All of your lives depend upon it."

"What is the commotion?" a deep voice asked. It belonged to one of the two men who had been addressing the assembly. He turned toward us, and I recognized him as the head priest of The House of the King, who had slaughtered the oxen on the steps of the palace. He wasn't young, but he wasn't old either. His build was solid as an oak tree, and he had a calm composure. His hair was dark and close-cropped, while his eyes were a bright blue.

"A new lord will be chosen this morning," he told Todd. "Whatever you have to say must wait until then."

"No," Todd protested. "The Lord Tohoshin was murdered, and everyone here is in danger—"

The second man, shorter and older, with long, silver-streaked hair, joined the first, scowling heavily at Todd.

"You will have to save your words for the next Lord of the Brimming Lake." His unyielding tone left no room for argument. He had a large, hooked nose, and I recalled that he was the other head priest, the one from The House of the Warrior.

"If we ever get done with the talking and start the final duel," a cheeky voice hollered.

Just then, Arshenn came pushing through the assembly, Arkensallay at his heels. Arshenn's lip curled with distaste when he saw us.

"We are ready to begin now," Arshenn announced. "The champion for The House of the King is prepared to meet his enemy in battle." Arshenn gestured to Arkensallay with pride.

The first priest who had addressed us, the priest of The House of the King, nodded. "Very well," he began. "Since we have narrowed the competition down to the very best of each house, the final—"

"Hold on," Todd interrupted. He moved Rysa closer to the priests. "I am a man belonging to The House of the King, and I was not given the opportunity to participate in the tournament."

There was a moment of silence. "Are you saying you wish to challenge the current champion of The House of the King?" the old priest asked.

"Yes," Todd called loudly for all to hear. "I wish to challenge."

Arshenn narrowed his eyes. "Surely, it is too late," he insisted. "The time for that has come and passed."

The dark-haired priest glanced uncertainly at his counterpart.

"It is not so," the old priest answered. "Any man who has been absent and not taken place in the tournament can challenge upon his arrival as long as the final combat has not begun. This is our law."

There was a murmur in the crowd. Some seemed in favor, others strongly opposed. I could easily guess who the opposition was.

"Silence," cried the old priest. "The gods have given us the laws. It is for us to obey them."

The men grew quiet once more.

"You have five minutes to ready yourself to meet this challenge," the dark-haired priest told Arkensallay. "After that, the duel will take place."

I don't remember telling Keith to move, but a moment later, he was beside Rysa. Todd had dismounted and was preparing himself for combat.

Slipping from my horse, I went to his side.

"What are you doing?" I hissed. "This isn't going to solve anything. You know you can't beat Arkensallay!"

"Yes, I can," Todd answered without looking at me. He'd shed the maroon cloak and was removing his shirt as well.

"You dueled him all summer," I reminded Todd. "I watched you lose to him every day!"

In a panic, I grabbed his shoulder, desperately trying to stop him. Calmly, he turned to look me in the eyes.

"He's going to hurt you!" I pleaded. "Maybe even kill you this time!"

"I let him win," Todd admitted softly, so no one would overhear us.

My hand slipped from his shoulder. I was too shocked to utter more than one word.

"What?"

He laughed softly at my stunned expression.

"But why?" I asked.

Todd glanced down, and then his dark eyes met mine once more. "Because Arkensallay promised if I let him win, he wouldn't lay a hand on you."

My mouth fell open as Todd walked away. Cole had joined us. He gestured to his sword, offering to let Todd use it. Todd shook his head.

With nothing but his knife, he stepped forward to face his brother. Arkensallay was waiting to meet him, a sword, even larger than Cole's, grasped in his hand.

The words Todd had said to me were still sinking in. Everything he had endured, all the pain and humiliation, it had all been for me. Even when I'd turned away and rejected him, Todd had never stopped trying to protect me.

The men formed a loose semicircle around the two brothers. Cole and I were on the open side. Several of those in the back pushed forward, filling in the empty space until the circle was almost complete.

I would have preferred the men of The Brimming Lake keep their distance. Although, they were far more intent on Todd and Arkensallay than Cole or me.

The priest of The House of the King announced the combatants, and the duel began. Arkensallay seemed uncertain as he faced his younger brother. Arshenn was looking on with a wicked grin, obviously impervious to his sons' secret arrangement.

Arkensallay began the duel very strongly. He struck hard and often, but no matter how much he swung, Todd was always able to dodge out of the way. Soon the blows grew wild and uncontrolled.

Todd fought back, but only half-heartedly. He was perfectly content to allow Arkensallay to wear himself out with exaggerated attacks.

"Get on with it!" Arshenn bellowed from the opposite side of the circle.

The men around him murmured their agreement.

Todd took the momentary distraction to dart in and make a slash at his brother's exposed side. I honestly think he could have done a lot more damage, but he checked himself and only landed a glancing blow before darting out.

A trickle of red ran down Arkensallay's side. At the sight of blood, a cheer went up from the crowd.

I couldn't hear the words Arshenn was screeching, but I considered that a good thing. The two boys circled each other for another minute, then Arkensallay rushed forward. Todd raised his knife but didn't back down this time. Just as Arkensallay was upon Todd, he stumbled and tripped forward, his neck moving right toward Todd's blade.

Instantly, Todd pulled away so that his brother collided with him and not the knife. Both boys fell to the ground, Arkensallay on top of Todd.

I wanted to close my eyes, but couldn't move, not even to draw breath.

Todd pushed away and tried to get up, but Arkensallay struck out at him while still lying on the ground. The sword sliced into Todd's left arm.

His cry of pain brought tears into my eyes. My whole body was shaking as Todd climbed to his feet. The hand that clutched his knife was covered in his own blood.

Just give up! I wanted to scream. *Let him win! Let him become Lord of the Brimming Lake. We tried to warn these people. They didn't want to listen to us. Whatever happens to them is on their own heads!*

I held my tongue as Todd transferred his knife to his right hand.

Arkensallay smiled. "Ready, little brother?" he asked, then charged.

It was the same attack I'd often seen him use to end duels with Todd. Rarely had Todd come away unscathed. I'd only seen him block it once. Panic filled me, but the sight of Todd's face held it at bay. The corners of Todd's mouth were upturned.

In a flash, Todd had ducked to the left, rotated fully, and kicked Arkensallay's legs out from under him. With a great crash, Arkensallay hit the ground. Todd wasted no time flinging his brother's sword away and pressing his own blade to his throat.

"Yield," he said, in the sudden hush.

Arkensallay must have given some sign of submission because, a moment later, Todd rose and raised his knife high. Cheers emanated from the crowd.

Arshenn was glaring at both of his sons, a terrifying expression on his face. However, as another man joined them on the field, his face cleared somewhat.

The newcomer was enormous, bigger than almost any other man present. He didn't have a sword; instead, he carried a long stick with a giant, spiked ball of metal on the end. From the numerous matches I had watched Todd and Arkensallay take part in, I knew the strange weapon was called a mace.

"The two champions are chosen," the priest of The House of the Warrior announced. "These are your champions." He gestured toward the enormous man with the mace. "Husamhind of The House of the Warrior and–" he glanced at Todd, who mouthed his name.

"And Todicmadaya of The House of the King."

Cheers sounded. The champion of The House of the Warrior raised his terrible weapon over his head and pumped it up and down. Todd barely managed to lift his small knife. His chest was heaving with the effort.

New terror seized me. "Todd will never be able to win," I couldn't help whispering to Cole.

"I know," Cole answered.

"You have five minutes to prepare yourselves," the same priest called. "Then the final battle will begin and continue until only one champion is left alive."

Todd stumbled unevenly over to us, his face pale and eyes dull. Instantly, I pulled out what remained of the cloth from The North Wind and started binding his wound. The blood seeped through the first layer almost instantly.

"You two should leave," Todd told us. "Once they have a new Lord of the Brimming Lake, they will attack immediately. Go now. I don't think they'll follow you."

"Not a chance," Cole told him.

Then he strode purposely forward into the center of the circle of men.

"I wish to make a challenge," he called, throwing back his hood.

CHAPTER 41
THE FINAL BATTLE

Every eye turned upon Cole.

"No, don't do this," Todd tried to say, but it came out as a gasp, only a little louder than a whisper.

The priest of The House of the Warrior squinted at Cole for a long moment before speaking. "You do not look familiar to my eyes," he said at last. "Are you from The House of the Warrior?"

"No," Cole answered.

"The House of the King?"

"No."

"Then what possible challenge could you make?"

"I am a champion of a house," Cole called.

The crowd broke into a chorus of laughter.

"What house do you represent?" a mocking voice called.

"The House of the Unknown God," Cole announced firmly. Slowly, the laughter faded.

Cole looked at me as the next words left his mouth. "I will fight any other champion in his name."

Hundreds of voices were suddenly talking over each other at once.

The two priests had to call for silence at least twenty times before the noise level dropped enough for their words to again be audible.

"Your challenge is heard," the dark-haired priest said with an air of uncertainty.

"This cannot be!" Arshenn cried, striding forward. Cole turned to face him without fear.

The priest of the king hesitated and glanced at the old priest.

"There is no evidence that this *boy* is telling the truth. Let him prove he is of The House of The Unknown God–" Arshenn spat upon the ground. "If he cannot, then how can we heed his challenge? I say we kill this blasphemer where he stands!"

Strong murmurs of agreement rose from the crowd, supporting Arshenn's demand.

"Very well, I will prove it," Cole answered, turning to me. "Astra, bring me the box," he instructed calmly.

I nodded and opened the bag, producing the black and gold box. Silence reigned as I carried it to the center of the circle and placed it in Cole's hands.

"This proves nothing!" Arshenn cried. "Anyone could have stolen it when we left The Brimming Lake!" His eyes turned to me. My hood had fallen back, revealing my face.

Cole raised his hand for silence, but it wasn't necessary. Every eye was already on us. I took the key from my neck and fitted it smoothly into the lock. With a click, the box popped open.

No one and nothing moved as Cole held up the open box. He removed the crown and showed it to all who were gathered there. The look of recognition and shock that crossed their faces might have been humorous in a different situation.

An awed hush fell as Cole turned it in every direction to make certain the silver piece of metal had been seen by all. He handed it to me a moment later.

"Recognize my challenge," Cole commanded.

The authority in his voice silenced even Arshenn.

"We have seen the sign from your god and recognize your challenge," the dark-haired priest told him in a hushed tone. "Prepare yourself for battle. Since The House of the King has already fought once today, you will begin with The House of the Warrior."

The large man, Husamhind, stepped toward Cole, grinning wickedly.

Cole nodded deeply before handing the box back to me. "Do what you can for Todd," Cole whispered. "I'll take care of this." He drew the sword from the place where it hung at his side.

I cringed. There was nothing I could really do to help either of them. For a moment, I considered my bow. It was still concealed under my cloak. I could end this battle before it even began. However, I had a feeling that would cause more problems than it solved.

I returned to the horses and sealed the book back into the box, but didn't bother trying to make the crown fit again. The key I placed around my neck once more.

Todd was sitting on the ground. The blood had soaked through the cloth bandage but seemed to have stopped there.

His breathing was steady, and his eyes were alert. I went to his side and offered him some water, which he accepted gratefully. There was a tortured expression on his face as he watched the two combatants in front of us.

"It shouldn't be this way," I heard him whisper. "Cole doesn't know what he's doing."

In the center of the circle, Cole crossed his blade with the weapon of Husamhind. Unlike the duel between Todd and Arkensallay, this battle started very slowly. Since the combatants didn't know each other, they were slow to rush in.

For nearly a full five minutes, they circled passively, with only a few strikes actually made. Each blow was easily parried by the other.

Finally, Cole darted forward and got inside Husamhind's guard long enough to slash at his side. The blow opened a cut across Husamhind's ribs. The other champion didn't make so much as a grunt of pain.

Cole managed to move back before Husamhind could react. After that, there was more circling, and then Husamhind suddenly planted his feet and brought his mace down with all his might toward Cole's body. Cole caught the blow on his sword.

The sound of the two metal weapons hitting each other was deafening. For ten terrifying seconds, Cole struggled, barely keeping Husamhind's mace from raking across his face. At last, he twisted away and retreated several steps. Husamhind took a hasty swipe at Cole's exposed back, but didn't manage to connect.

A moment later, the champion from The House of the Warrior charged Cole, swinging his mace in a great arc, aimed for Cole's head.

Cole dodged, but it was a clumsy effort, and he didn't escape entirely as Husamhind followed up with a second strike. This blow wasn't nearly so powerful as the first, but it was enough to throw Cole to the ground. He rolled away from his opponent, then struggled to his feet, clutching at his side with one hand.

Gasping for breath, Cole raised his sword to guard against further attack. It was a good thing too, because Husamhind was on top of him. Cole only narrowly avoided taking a direct blow to the head by spinning away and falling backward.

As the other champion passed, Cole lashed out with his sword. The tip of the blade managed to catch the other man just below the knee. Again, Husamhind gave no audible sign of his pain, but I could see him trying to keep his weight off the injured leg.

Cole struggled hastily to his feet. Both combatants were panting and took a few minutes to catch their breath. Then Cole stepped forward confidently to attack. He feinted a strike to the left. Husamhind instantly compensated, only to find Cole change his stance at the last moment and bring his sword down heavily on the other fighter's left shoulder.

Cole's blade buried itself deep in Husamhind's body. Still, the champion of The House of the Warrior didn't cry out. He staggered, then toppled backward. The sword remained lodged in his body as red blood poured out onto the ground.

Swiftly, Cole knelt beside the fallen man. Bending low over the other combatant, I think he might have spoken a few words. When they had remained like that for a full ten seconds, the priests came forward. One touched Husamhind's neck, checking for a pulse.

A moment later, the priest rose. "The champion for The House of the Warrior is dead!" he called.

Instead of cheers, his words evoked nothing but silence.

Cole pulled his sword free. He looked down once more at the body of his foe and closed his eyes. When he opened them, they were bright and unclouded.

A few men from The House of the Warrior came forward and removed the body of the fallen champion.

Cole remained in the center of the circle.

"I would like to speak now," he said. "There is something I must tell you–"

"We will not hear you," Arshenn's voice snarled. "You are no lord yet."

"For your own good–" Cole started again in exasperation, but didn't get a chance to finish.

"He is correct," the dark-haired priest pronounced.

"There is still one more battle to take place. The final battle," the old priest added with a hard look at Cole.

All eyes turned toward Todd, who had risen. His face was pale, but he was able to hold his knife in his left hand once more.

Arshenn was watching his son as well. I flinched, not liking the look of pleasure I saw in his eyes. We had spoiled his plan. One of his champions was dead and the other defeated, yet there was an almost triumphant expression on his face. It gave me a chill, despite the fact that the sun was shining down warmly.

"The duel will soon commence," the priest of the warrior announced. "At its conclusion, we will have a new Lord of the Brimming Lake!"

I hurried to Cole. "Are you injured?" I asked, glancing at his side.

"It's fine," he told me.

Todd stumbled over to us. "You're going to have to kill me," he whispered hastily.

"No." Cole recoiled.

"We don't have a choice," Todd answered. "You have to do it. You must be the next Lord of the Brimming Lake. My father has already turned the people against me, but you, you could win their respect. You must–"

345

"I don't want to be Lord of the Brimming Lake," Cole answered. "First Clan Leader is enough for me, thanks."

Todd shook his head. "They'll never believe I could defeat you," he whispered. "It has to be you."

"Time for the duel!" one of the priests called. A cheer rose from the assembled men.

Cole and Todd exchanged a long look. While an air of calmness emanated from Cole, Todd seemed on the verge of sheer panic. His eyes were wide, like those of a frightened animal.

Cole reached out slowly and placed a hand on Todd's good shoulder. "You can trust me," he promised.

Turning, Cole walked away from us and took his place in the center of the circle. Todd followed him.

I felt sick as I watched the two cross their blades. My heart was racing faster now than during either of the previous battles.

Cole took advantage of his sword's greater length. Each of his blows was just barely caught by Todd's knife. It was a good show, but I could tell Cole was holding back. I cringed, imagining the carnage he could have caused.

If it had been anyone, save Cole, I wouldn't have been able to watch. I trusted Cole implicitly, but seeing anyone come against Todd when he was in such a state was agonizing.

It soon became obvious to everyone that there was no competition. Injured and with an inferior weapon, Todd didn't have many chances to attack. After less than three minutes, Cole's sword connected with Todd's small blade. The blow wasn't very powerful, but Todd went down on one knee, and Cole knocked Todd's blade from his grasp.

The knife landed on the ground a few feet away. Cole darted to his right and retrieved it, then turned on Todd, who was struggling to rise. He froze when the edge of Cole's blade pressed against his neck.

"Yield." Cole pronounced the same word Todd had spoken to his brother.

Todd nodded, chest heaving too hard to speak.

Slowly, Cole lowered his sword and turned to the priests.

"I am the new lord," Cole announced. "There is something I must tell you. If you try to cross the river, you will all die—"

Before Cole could finish, Arshenn interrupted. "You are no more Lord of the Brimming Lake now than you were ten minutes ago. Don't try to scare us. The gods will favor us since this land is ours by right. We do not fear the coming battle!"

"I have defeated the other champions," Cole answered him coolly. "I am The Lord of the Brimming Lake, now hear me!"

"Two champions yet live!" I recognized Rettrin's voice from the crowd. There was murmuring among the people.

"You must slay your opponent!" Arshenn bellowed.

"Kill him!" someone screamed.

"We will be punished if two champions live!" another man yelled.

"The gods will be angry!" called a third voice.

Cole licked his lips and addressed the assembled men. "My God is not like your gods. He is not bloodthirsty. He will not be displeased with my actions."

"There can only be one," Arshenn hissed, stepping forward. "If you two will not fight to the death, then we will kill you both."

I saw Rettrin and several others of The Brotherhood beginning to advance. Rettrin drew his sword, eyes intent on Cole.

My hand went to my bow, but the men stopped at a gesture from the two priests.

"There can only be one," the dark-haired priest echoed, looking at Cole and shaking his head. "Finish him off now, with no more words, or you both will be slain."

Cole turned from the assembly to Todd.

My heart leapt into my throat. I was completely paralyzed; this was the worst thing I could have ever imagined. It was the mountain all over again. We were trapped. There was no way out unless we paid a price too great to fathom.

Todd was still on his knees, breathing heavily. He looked up at Cole through his sweat-soaked hair.

"Just do it," I heard him gasp, then he lowered his head.

The blood drained from my face. Cole couldn't. Wouldn't. Would he?

I tried to swallow, but it was impossible. My feet carried me forward, slowly, too slowly. Before me, I could see a closing door. A door I never managed to reach in time. A door where I was meant to die, but was granted life instead. Someone else's life.

Cole looked down at Todd's bowed head.

"What I do now," Cole called loudly, "I do because it has been done for me."

He dropped the sword in his right hand and turned his head to look at me. I was still a few yards away but froze when his blue eyes met mine.

"It should have been me, you know," he whispered.

"Wh- what?" I didn't comprehend his meaning.

"I was the leader. I was supposed to protect the rest of you, no matter the cost." He smiled sadly. "Can you imagine what you two would have done together? With me out of the way?"

Cole raised his head and looked up. "It should have been me. I was afraid then, but I'm not anymore. I'm not afraid at all."

He blinked, then looked once more at the boy kneeling before him.

"And maybe, just maybe, I'll find her waiting for me." Cole almost laughed. "Wouldn't that be nice? Then we could be together."

"Cole–" I started, but it was too late.

With only a brief second of hesitation, Cole held Todd's knife out before him, then buried the blade in his own abdomen.

My mouth dropped open. It felt like I should have been screaming, but no air or sound could escape my throat.

Slowly, Cole's body started to fall forward. Todd managed to catch him, but only enough to ease him to the ground. I don't know how I got there, but I was by his side a moment later, taking his hand and checking for a pulse.

It was too late. He had left us.

I rose and stepped backward, fighting the panic in my chest. The pain was too great. I couldn't endure this fresh tragedy.

I felt the urge to flee and try to escape the horrible sight before me, but I was surrounded on all sides.

"Unacceptable!" Arshenn screeched, bringing me back to the present. "The gods have rejected both champions! Now is the time for action, brothers! We have delayed long enough."

Arshenn drew his own blade and charged. I spun and groped for the sword Cole had dropped, then turned, ready to meet him and all others. Todd was the only thing I had left to protect, and I would die defending him.

I wouldn't have stood much of a chance, but no one paid any attention to me. The men who had followed Arshenn, about two hundred or so, raced past us. Most of the faces were a blur, but I recalled several of them from that horrible night in the cavern.

As they reached the boats, the remainder of the men came to life suddenly and sprang forward to follow, thousands of them.

On the far banks, I could see the soldiers of The Barracks leap to their feet, ready to meet anyone who made it across. They charged toward the shore, weapons raised high.

Todd staggered to his feet. "Stop!" he called. "You'll all die!" But they didn't pay any attention to him.

He staggered after them. Suddenly, he launched himself forward to tackle one of the figures. It was Arkensallay. The two wrestled on the ground for a moment before Arkensallay escaped his grasp and continued forward with the surge of men. Todd rose slowly, the wound on his left arm reopened and bleeding again.

The first boat was launched with Arshenn in the stern. He raised his sword and gave a great battle cry.

It was echoed by all as a second boat was pushed into the river. More followed as the first group took to the water.

The main mass of men reached the riverbank a moment later. They filled a hundred more boats and were preparing to launch when a different kind of cry went up.

In horror, Todd, myself, and the thousands of people on both sides of the river watched as the dozen boats in midstream suddenly vanished from sight. It was as if a giant hand had reached up and grabbed them from under the water, yanking them down into darkness.

A small amount of wooden wreckage was all that ever reappeared. Even those few remnants were swiftly borne away by the racing current, leaving no trace of the men who had disappeared.

CHAPTER 42
THE LAST STORY

Every eye was wide. Every hand stilled. Not a soul moved.

"The gods are angry," someone whispered finally.

"They're going to kill us all," a second voice whined.

Looking around quickly, I saw a half-finished boat, which was lying on the ground upside down. Several logs were beneath it, keeping the vessel level.

Without hesitation, I leapt atop it.

"Listen," I screamed, my voice far louder than the hushed murmuring around me. "Listen to me, and I will tell you a story. A true story. A history of a people who were divided.

"Listen, and I will tell you the history of *our* people as far back as I know." The last phrase I said was something like what I had heard twice a year at The Tellings. I used it now to be certain that those across the river would know I was speaking to them as well.

There were things I needed to say. Todd was looking up at me from beside the boat. He didn't have a clue what I was going to do, but his presence gave me strength.

"The world was once home to more humans than we can imagine. They built great cities and understood the stars. Their reach extended all across the earth. There was no place they had not been, from the depths of the sea to the peaks of the mountains.

"I have walked among the ruins of their great city, and I tell you that for all their knowledge and greatness, they were lacking. They lacked perfection, for they were every bit as flawed as we are today."

My voice faltered, but I forced it to grow louder. I wanted everyone to hear the truth.

351

"They made a war so great that nearly all the world was destroyed. Only a handful of humans survived, and this was where they came to seek shelter." I gestured to the land across the river.

"It is not some place that the war left untouched or that the gods created, but a place built by human hands to protect the last remnant of mankind from a dying world."

I shook my head. "Even then, when there were so few left, our imperfection followed us.

"Peter, the father of us all, had four children. They may not have all been his descendants by blood, but they were the ones he left to carry on when he passed away. He had two daughters and two sons.

"One of his daughters vanished.

"His other three children turned on each other and divided the people. One group remained here, while the other two were forced to leave. They found a place with a brimming lake, where life was possible. They dwelt there for many years, contending with their kin.

"Today, those divided by the children of Peter have come back together, and it is our choice to decide how the story ends. Will we continue to strive against each other? Will we murder our own brothers and sisters? Or will we be able to find peace?"

I swallowed. There was more to say and nothing left to be said at the same time. I could have poured out so much truth to them, but they weren't ready to hear it. I might have already spoken too much.

Instead, I waited.

"It's her," a whisper reached my ear.

"Perdita," someone gasped.

"She came back," a voice said.

All eyes were on me. They had heard my words.

With my head held high, I jumped down from the upturned boat. The crowd of men from The Brimming Lake parted before me like water. I marched boldly to where our horses had been. The creatures had fled when the crowd descended on their position, but the backpack was still there.

I drew out the eleven-pointed crown and held it high. The men were still watching me, Todd with them.

Holding the crown in both hands, I walked to Todd and placed it on his head. He stooped a little, so I could reach more easily.

"You are The Lord of the Brimming Lake," I announced.

"Hail, Lord of the Brimming Lake!" a few men nearby called. Their cry was taken up by all those assembled on our side of the river.

Todd looked down, slightly uncomfortably, then he raised his eyes to look into mine.

"And you're The First Leader of the Clan," he told me.

A lump rose in my throat, and I wished like anything his words weren't true. I nodded, too choked to speak. My eyes fell on Cole's still body. He lay, undisturbed, on the ground where he had fallen. Slowly, my footsteps took me in his direction until I was by his side.

I glanced over my shoulder at Todd and the rest of his people. They didn't frighten me anymore. I ignored their presence and knelt by the still body of my friend.

Cole's blue eyes had closed for the last time. His jaw was set, giving his face a noble look. Gently, I smoothed down the rumpled hair on his forehead. Tears filled my eyes. I licked my lips, tasting the salt of those tears.

I fervently hoped that this was the last friend I would have to lose. But was he really lost? Was Todd right? Was there something more after death? Perhaps the book would have answers for me.

There are times when we need to speak, when we need to say certain things, but this was not one of those times. As I reached out and touched the cold face one more time, my lips remained still. Sometimes, there are no words.

I saw Todd come to my side and sensed that many men shadowed him.

"Goodbye, my brother," Todd murmured gently. A tiny tremor was in his voice, but he controlled it well.

353

We remained in silence for a moment. "We'll put him in one of the boats," Todd told me suddenly. "So he can be borne out to the sea where- where he left her. Then they'll-" his voice broke.

"That sounds perfect," I agreed.

"And then you need to leave," he told me.

"But-" I started, the thought of walking away from Todd was too much.

"You must," he urged.

I shook my head helplessly.

"You have to go back to your people," Todd reminded me. "They need you."

"No," I argued. "I won't leave you."

His dark eyes met mine. "I won't be far," he promised, gently embracing me. "We both need some time to sort things out. Come back to me. In three days, at dawn, I'll meet you outside The Valley of The North Wind."

The rest of that day was a blur. With the help of several men, we put Cole into a boat and released it into the river. We'd freed him of all metal, so instead of being dragged down, the boat was carried swiftly away to the east, toward the place of the rising sun and the sea.

Before long, I found myself back inside The Land of the Clan. Rollan and Kisa greeted me warmly when I returned to The Paramount late in the day.

Cole's death was a hard blow for them. I fumbled through the account of what happened and wouldn't have managed to finish without Kisa's hand holding tight to mine.

When I finally made it to the end, Kisa buried her face in Rollan's chest and wept. There were tears on Rollan's cheeks, but he met my gaze steadily.

In the evening, the three of us called the council together. Addressing them seemed like a breeze after speaking to the congregation by the river.

I said many of the same things I had earlier, but not half so well. Whatever passion had taken hold of me in that moment had faded. I still made my thoughts clear and insisted that everyone be taken to the hidden room and shown the recording left by Peter. Falow objected, but not Core. He was much subdued by the news of his son's death.

"Cole gave his life because of this message," Core announced to Falow and the others. "He wouldn't have wanted it kept hidden and neither do I." He spoke very little the rest of the day.

Thankfully, someone had removed Myna's body from the room beneath us. After the message had been viewed, they all wanted to see the book, which I was more than happy to produce.

We talked long into the night. It wasn't until dawn's first appearance that everyone dispersed. I hesitated, not sure where to go myself. I almost ended up sleeping in the council building, but didn't.

Instead, I returned to Myra's room, choosing to enter by the window, so I wouldn't have to pass through the rest of the dwelling.

Tired as I was, I had trouble finding sleep. There was much to do. Also, I hadn't been this far from Todd in a very long time. His strong, protective presence was sorely missed. I fervently hoped whoever had been tasked with guarding the new Lord of the Brimming Lake would be extra vigilant.

Most of The Brotherhood had been in the first boats launched into the river as they led the way for the others. However, if only one had escaped, Todd's life could be in danger. Regret for not remaining to watch over him clouded my mind, making sleep almost impossible.

I rolled over, trying to find a comfortable position. The bed seemed too soft, just as it had after I returned from the trials. I was about to move to the floor when I heard someone call my name.

"Astra."

Instantly, I rose from the bed and glanced out the cracked window. Dawn was breaking upon the land. Outside, someone in a maroon cloak was waving for me to come.

I was through the window in a moment, racing after the figure. They headed north and didn't stop until we'd reached the wide field that opened where The Paramount ended.

The last of the summer flowers were in bloom beneath the golden morning light. The figure stopped, facing away from me. I came to stand beside the person, slightly out of breath from the chase.

"What–" I started to ask, but the figure lifted a hand and pointed straight ahead. People were walking toward us from several directions.

The first pair was a man and a woman. The woman had long, reddish-brown hair, the same shade as my own. The man, whose hand she held, had my green eyes. I had seen these two in my dreams before, and I would have run to them if my entire body hadn't been frozen in place.

Another man met them halfway across the field. He had the same look and eyes as the first but was a few inches taller and several years older. The pair embraced as brothers, and then all three headed to the west together.

After they departed, an older woman came into view.

Yetta! I wanted to cry, but all I could do was watch. Beside her, guiding her by the hand, was a girl, about my age. Never before had I seen such a look of joy from anyone as I saw on the face of my second mother. The pair didn't linger, but turned their back to me and followed after the other group.

As they walked west, a bull of a man came to greet them. He and Yetta paused to contemplate each other for a long moment, then a look of delight crossed his face, and they walked on together.

I eagerly waited for more. This time, I felt tears of joy fill my eyes as a boy came racing through the field barefoot. He wasn't particularly tall, but his smile was the brightest in the world.

It was Joss, my teammate lost on the road home during the trials. He turned and glanced east, then laughed suddenly. Cole was there, striding through the long grass, looking just as he had when I'd seen him last, peaceful and determined.

A smile lit his face as he reached Joss. Cole placed his hand on Joss's shoulder and, for a moment, pressed his forehead to the younger boy's. Then they embraced. I could hear Joss chattering excitedly but couldn't make out the words.

Cole turned to look at me, his blue eyes warm. He held out his hand, as if inviting me to come. Even if I could have gone to his side, I wouldn't have. There was somewhere else I belonged now.

The forgotten figure beside me stirred suddenly and stepped forward, then turned back to look at me. The hood fell, and I was facing Myra.

My face grew serious as we contemplated each other. "I found what I was looking for," I whispered.

She didn't answer, but gave me a knowing smile.

"You were right. It was far bigger than I ever imagined."

Myra didn't say anything, but closed her eyes and dipped her head to me. Slowly, she turned away and walked to Cole, accepting his outstretched hand.

They hesitated for a moment, looking into each other's eyes. Slowly, Cole leaned forward and kissed her forehead. Then they too started out for the west. Joss sprinted to catch up and passed them.

Once they had all vanished, I headed back to The Paramount, but I don't recall if I made it.

A short time later, I found myself waking up in Myra's room. The joy my dream had given me carried over into the waking world.

I knew that soon I would see the rest of my team and, hopefully, Todd as well. There were a lot of plans to be made before the rest of The People of the Brimming Lake arrived.

CHAPTER 43
DAWN

The three days seemed to stretch on forever, all the while passing in the blink of an eye. Kisa, Rollan, and I were constantly busy.

Core did not attend any more council meetings, and no one challenged me as I took up the position of First Clan Leader.

Early in the morning on the third day, several hours before the sun was even close to rising, I headed for The North Wind.

Kisa and Rollan were with me, along with Joel, Kullen, half the council, and a large escort from The Barracks. I had wanted to go alone and strongly considered slipping off by myself. However, now that I was a leader, I had more to consider than just my own wants.

The main path of The Valley of The North Wind had been cleared, but it was still a treacherous road, so our progress was slow. The sun was free of the horizon by the time we emerged from the valley. I felt the tension of those behind me as I led them into the unknown.

The men of The Brimming Lake had moved their camp back to the open plain north of The Mountains of the North Wind. They were assembled and waiting for us.

I blinked. Women were standing with the men. The rest of The People of the Brimming Lake had arrived.

Kullen tensed. Out of the corner of my eye, I saw his hand fall on his sword. They outnumbered us more than a hundred to one. I would be lying if I didn't admit that I was a little uneasy myself, at least until I saw Todd.

He was the first of his people to move. Swiftly, he came striding forward, the eleven-pointed crown on his head. In that instant, all of my uncertainty vanished. I motioned for the others to halt as I continued alone.

The two of us met in the gap between our peoples. He looked better. The wound on his left arm was covered with a bandage and didn't seem to bother him.

"Hello, Todd," I breathed softly.

He nodded to me, then began speaking loudly. "Greetings, Astra of The North Wind, First Leader of The Clan." Todd's voice was formal, making me hesitate.

"We come to you as a people without a land," Todd continued, voice strong enough for all to hear. "We are a people who have very little to offer but must still ask for your help. Will you aid us?"

He knew what the answer would be. I could see it in his eyes. Still, I paused. He'd had three days to plan his words, but I took less than thirty seconds to formulate my answer.

In the quiet morning, it wasn't hard to raise my voice enough to fill the open plain. "We will. Because we are a people who have forgotten how to believe in something bigger than ourselves. Will you help us find our faith?"

"I think we can manage that," Todd replied. "Still, there is one more thing I would ask of you. Our peoples can live in peace, no matter what your answer is. Astra of The–" His voice dropped to a quieter tone. "Astra, will you marry me and bind our two peoples together?"

The question was almost as unexpected this time as it had been the first time he'd asked. It felt as if the air had been sucked from my lungs, and for a moment, all I could do was stare. To everyone else, it might look as if Todd were making a political move. However, I knew that his request had been made solely for himself. I was free to decline and need not fear any damage to The Clan's relationship with The People of the Brimming Lake.

This time, Todd had no idea what my answer would be. The tortured look on his face made me hasten to reply.

"I will help you unite our two peoples," I began. "And I will be glad to do it as your life mate."

359

Todd smiled, and I couldn't think of anything more than how much I loved him.

"I have something for you," he told me, motioning to a man standing off to his left. "Although, I've already given it to you once, and the rest isn't really mine to give."

The man, and several others, came forward, leading Rysa, Rykis, Keith, and another horse. A silver horse.

"Fleck," I gasped.

"You found her," I whispered to Todd.

I don't know if he moved or if I moved, but a moment later, I was in his arms. Even with thousands of onlookers, it was a private moment for just the two of us as I buried my face in his shoulder. Strong arms wrapped around me, and I felt completely safe.

Tears of joy welled up from deep inside my soul, but didn't fall. I had lost so much, but I felt perfectly happy.

I always thought the trials and what followed after would be the greatest adventure and challenge of my life.

I was wrong.

A little more than three years after peace was made between The People of the Brimming Lake and The Clan, a bigger adventure arrived.

The two peoples had established a good trade relationship. The Clan still lived on the peninsula, but the borders were now open. It had been Todd's idea to build a dam upstream in the north and divert some of the river's water into a large gorge to create a new lake. It supplied those living on its banks with an endless supply of water.

The river was quieter now, and bridges had been erected. We still couldn't take any metal across, which had probably helped to keep the peace as much as anything.

The Clan was very guarded when the bridges were first built, but soon their curiosity got the better of them. They became as enamored with those of The Brimming Lake as I had been.

Their music, their dancing, their storytelling were all novelties to The Clan.

Looking back, life before seemed so dull. I wondered how so many generations had endured it.

Todd, Rollan, Kisa, and I worked together with a council comprised of members from both factions to make sure that life ran smoothly for all.

Even though Rollan and Kisa are not yet officially engaged, since they still consider themselves too young, I know they are planning to make the announcement soon.

Todd and I have been life mates for more than two years. He is so different from the skinny, frightened boy I met long ago. All the potential I saw in him has taken root, and he's grown wise and courageous.

The four of us spend a lot of time in council meetings but always make sure to spend more time among the people. Our transition from two cultures to one hasn't been perfect, but it is going as smoothly as can be expected.

Both peoples have redeeming qualities, something we've endeavored to preserve. But there are also parts of each that needed to be cut away. It is hard for the older members of The Clan to allow certain traditions to be removed, like the trials.

Everything is a balancing act, and at the center of it is the book we found in the box. I have read it all the way through. Some parts don't make sense to me, but I am trying to understand them and feel that someday I will.

Those in The Paramount have set about making copies of the book at my instruction. It is one of the few things which survived the end of the world and, in my opinion, is the most important. There is truth in it.

It was a day in early spring when the greatest adventure of my life began. The morning started just like many others. Todd was across the river, visiting his- no, our people.

I was preparing for a morning ride on Fleck, who had found a new home in The North Wind. Todd and I, and the rest of the council, had moved there as well, since it was the closest of the villages to where Todd's people had settled. Not all of the members were pleased about having to relocate, but I couldn't have been happier.

That morning, I brushed Fleck until her silver coat glimmered in the sunlight. Just as I was lifting the saddle onto her back, I felt something strange. The saddle fell to the ground. My hand went instantly to my stomach. I couldn't believe it; a new life was growing inside of me. I actually sat down and started crying right there in the stable.

Five months later, I gave birth to a beautiful little girl. She had dark brown hair, streaked with just a little red, and eyes as gray as a storm cloud.

My first impulse was to name her Myra, but I just couldn't.

Myra was someone else. I didn't want her name to become something casual, something I said every day. I didn't want the name to have any other meaning than what it already did.

Todd and I named her Twelfth.

Instead of a twelfth trials or a twelfth point on the crown, we had her. She was the future, our legacy.

EPILOGUE
SEEDS

"These are the last ones, father," a beautiful woman told the old man standing behind her. The pair were in a stone cave with a domed roof. A hole in the ceiling let in the bright light of the midday sun.

The woman straightened from where she'd been kneeling beside a pool of water. The gemstones she'd just deposited slowly drifted down to join a bed of others.

"Very good, Adel," the old man wheezed as he held one of the stones up to the light. He nodded in approval as he noted that the memory chip hidden within was invisible to his eyes.

Leaning heavily on his wooden staff, he bent and placed the stone in the water. "We must never speak of this place to your sister."

"Of course not," Adel agreed with a smile. Her green eyes twinkled as she took in her father's serious expression.

"She would never understand," the old man said.

The bright smile vanished from Adel's face momentarily. "She'll come around one day, I hope."

"I am not so certain."

"No matter. We have made the right decision. Hundreds of years may pass before what we have hidden here is discovered. But someday, it will be found."

"I pray that you are right. However, I fear our secret will never be uncovered, and the knowledge of the past will die with us," fretted the old man.

Adel laughed. "That's why we did it this way. Remember, Father?"

The old man nodded.

"Even when humanity was at its most primitive, people always found beauty in precious stones. One day, our children's children will find this place. They will take the stones and use them. They will make jewelry and ornaments.

"And then, someday, so far in the future that even I cannot foresee it, they will discover the true gift we have left them here. When they have once again built a society nearly as advanced as ours, they will find the message we have left behind hidden within each of these stones. If even one of them survives and is found, our past will not have been lost.

"All the history, all the art, all the music, every scrap of knowledge from our people, locked away since the beginning of their time, contained within something small enough to fit in the palm of a hand. With that information, I believe they will be able to build a better, wiser society than ours has been.

"They will learn about us and the choices we made. All the knowledge gathered in our time will be theirs, and maybe, just maybe, it will keep them from making our mistakes.

"All that, they will find in one stone," Adel promised before turning to her father with a kind smile.

"Let's go home," she told him.

He nodded, and the two began walking toward the entrance of the cave, leaving behind a pool of sparkling rocks, the seeds of knowledge that had taken many millennia to gather.

"This place is hard to find," the old man worried. "How will they even know where to look?"

"I've thought of that too," Adel promised. "I have already started telling my daughter stories about the special place in the valley. A place where the dead still speak of our legacy."

GLOSSARY
THE GODS

HOUSE OF THE KING

ARSH – The king – He that is the crown upon the head
Arsh was the ruler of the gods until his best friend, Husam, betrayed him and tried to usurp his throne.

JIYA – The fair one – She that is the heart in the chest
Jiya is the most beautiful creature in the entire world. She is the first wife of Arsh.

SUR – The hater – She that is the dagger in the soul
Sur is the younger sister of Tohopke. She was in love with Dezi once, but, after being forced to become Arsh's second wife, she erased all emotion from her heart save hatred.

TODKALA – The trickster – He that is the fox creeping through the night
Todkala is the younger brother of Arsh. He prefers manipulations and deception to direct confrontation.

HOUSE OF THE WARRIOR

HUSAM – The warrior – He that is the edge on the sword
Husam and Arsh were once good friends, but Husam grew jealous and tried to steal Arsh's throne.

DEZI – The weeper – He that is the sorrow in the tears
Dezi was in love with Sur. After she was forced to wed Arsh, his sorrow overtook him and he now mourns day and night, preferring his dreams to the waking world.

TOHOPKE – The wild one – He that is the beast in the forest
Tohopke cared very little about the conflict between Arsh and Husam until Todkala tricked him into giving his sister, Sur, to Arsh in marriage. Now he longs for revenge against Todkala.

ZERUIAH – The torturer – She that is the pain in the wound
Zeruiah is the wife of Tohopke. She is cruel and has a special distain for Jiya.

OTHER

THE UNKNOWN GOD
The unknown god is the ninth god. The one who did not descend to earth with the others. Very little is known about him. He has no temple, only a small shrine. Inside is a black box, engraved with golden writing.

ABOUT THE AUTHOR

*Photo by Brian Prewitt and Prewitt Studios

Danielle N. McDonough spent her childhood exploring the world through books. These stories, paired with her imagination, took her on hundreds of adventures to different times and places. Her favorites were about heroes, dragons, mysteries, and magic.

As a young adult, Danielle continued in her love of art and fantasy. She graduated from Full Sail University with a degree in film. After spending several years working on television and movie sets, she decided to step away from the film industry and pursue her passion for storytelling by writing her debut novel, *The Preparations*.

It was in Colorado, on a mission trip with her church, that Danielle had a dream about one of the members of The Clan. This dream was the inspiration behind *The Legacy* series. It took her four years to finish writing the series, but the journey was the greatest adventure she's ever been on, and she welcomes you to share it with her.

WWW.THELEGACYBOOKSERIES.COM